WHEN YOU DECIDE TO LIVE OUT A FANTASY, YOU MAY BE PLAYING WITH FIRE!

KELLY NELSON—Sheltered by a stable marriage, threatened by her own sexual curiosity, she embraced a handsome stranger, expecting to enjoy a brief affair.

KIRSTIN POLLOCK—She knew how to manage her men—and conceal her past . . . until she played cupid with Kelly's life, then had to pick up the pieces of her own.

ERICKA WALLACE—Her marriage was a compromise, her movie career a high-powered escape, until Kelly's fantasies drove her back to the man she thought she'd left behind.

LEONARD POLLOCK—He had everything other men envied, until Kirstin's "surprise" ignited his jealousy and rage.

JAMIE STERLING—Ericka's first love, now a celebrated playwright, he forced her to choose between marriage and a dream.

BRANDON MICHAELS—A brilliant architect, an eligible bachelor, he was the perfect candidate. The affair was meant to be quick, casual, and romantic. It became a passion raging wildly out of control.

FLING

_____FLING

**Pamela Beck
and
Patti Massman**

A DELL BOOK

Published by
Dell Publishing Co., Inc.
1 Dag Hammarskjold Plaza
New York, New York 10017

Cover photograph © 1985 by Anthony Loew

Dell ® TM 681510, Dell Publishing Co., Inc.

ISBN: 0-440-12615-0

Reprinted by arrangement with M. Evans and Company, Inc.

Printed in the United States of America

First Dell printing—May 1985

With the deepest love to the men in our lives—
in alphabetical order, Brandon, Brent, Dennis,
Michael, Stephen

Acknowledgments

WE OFFER OUR THANKS WITH THE GREATEST OF GRATITUDE to Marjorie Miller, who was there from the beginning—believing in us as writers and urging us to make this fantasy emerge as a reality; to Myrtle L., who if she didn't know the answer to something, knew somebody who did; to Al and Trudy Kallis, who've been a hotline for us to creative inspiration; to our literary agent, Elaine Markson, for helping us to beat the odds against getting a first novel published; to M. Evans's hardworking Linda Cabasin, whose timely responses and sensitivity to writers' concerns allowed us never to have to break our writers' stride; to Carol Aminoff, a dear friend, for generously reading our manuscript, draft after draft—and for liking it better each time; to Peter Arends, whose Scandinavian descent and marvelous imagination made him a valuable source; to Stephen Massman and Morrie Pynoos, for contributing to us a sanctuary in which to write—and to Daphne and Mary Pat, for all their assistance there; to Dennis Beck, a fount of knowledge, for his sound counsel and strong support.

And finally—a special kind of thanks to our publisher, Herb Katz, whose firm editorial guidance and remarkable insight helped us beyond measure.

Chapter One

HE WAS *DAVID*. MICHELANGELO'S BRILLIANT MASTERPIECE. HIS sculptured form was breathtaking—a geometrically perfect network of muscle. And then he moved. And she matched his motion. He was clearly not a stone-cold image of masculine perfection fixed upon a pedestal of immortality.

Faster.

Harder.

Use control.

Ahhh . . . good. Now tighten.

Squeeze.

Tighter.

Release.

Now tighter again.

Kelly Nelson heard his words. Short sharp orders.

Then gentle and pleased. She closed her eyes and tried even harder to satisfy him. Pelvis in. Pelvis out. She held it for that extra beat, and then smiled slightly at her control. Their hips moved in exacting pursuit. Her stomach was nearly concave and beads of perspiration ran down her back from the violent exercise.

She wanted to feel his weight above her. She wanted to feel him move in passion, cry out, insatiable. Kelly drew her thighs together into a tight squeeze; he would be far and away the greatest lay ever conjured by her wayward imagination. The fact that her marriage was so good felt like a mixed blessing—she had a maddening conscience, or maybe it was just a yellow streak, the final twist of the wedding knot. It was *always* fantasy and no action.

Kelly hummed along with the song that was vibrating through the chic Beverly Hills health club's extravagant stereo system as she maneuvered her hips around in furious succession. Her knees were bent slightly, her stomach sucked in, her pelvis locked into position, and her eyes fixed on the glorious three-way reflection of the man leading her exercise class. She lowered her line of vision to the instructor's red short shorts, which stopped precisely at the critical level, probably where his jockstrap began. Kelly looked longingly at the point where the delicious mound of bronzed thigh muscle began to curve in; it was whiter there, she decided, watching him move into a knee bend.

Kelly matched his bend evenly, her legs spread wide, her knees perfectly paralleling her waffle-soled

10

running shoes. This man was the last word in carnal creation, and Kelly wanted his classroom demonstrations to narrow into a more intimate performance. She wanted a private demonstration of the ultimate exercise—prizewinning pelvic thrusts, all under hotel cotton sheets.

Continuing her knee bends without a hint of strain, Kelly was three steps into mental foreplay when she was jarred by the sound of "Hey—you in the purple shorts, with the green leotard and brick hair! Good morning!" Kelly, feeling a hot blush coloring her cheeks, wondered whether her fantasy had been as obviously seen as felt. The rest of the class was already on the floor, busy working on flabby buttocks and outer thighs as they strained from what was referred to as the all-fours position.

The class was looking at Kelly, but nobody laughed. Apparently nobody had the energy.

"On the floor," the instructor called out.

He winked at her and she fell quickly onto the carpeted ground. She thought his thigh looked even more enticing as he swung it back and forth with such agility. Kelly wanted to bite it.

Ericka Wallace watched Kelly Nelson fall gracefully to the floor, envying the redhead's unyielding stamina. Ericka gasped for breath, tasting a mouthful of hair. Just ten more minutes and then she would quit. Her leg was killing her. From her awkward angle, Ericka could see nothing other than her thick dark hair, the newly installed racing-green carpet that tickled her nose, and her aqua leg warmers, which were stretched high over black tights.

Oh . . . this was miserable. Couldn't there be an easier means to beauty? Or couldn't she just be appreciated for her marvelous wit? No, the greedy little fuckers demanded beauty *and* wit!

. . . Nine, ten . . . she had met her quota. She collapsed nose down onto the floor. Maybe she could eat less, give up pizza, and have more sex. Anything but this torture. Ericka fell into a silken repose and listened lethargically to the music of Lionel Richie.

When the class began on the other leg, Ericka got back onto all fours again and repeated her performance, thankful and surprised that she had not been singled out for lagging behind. She joined the rest of the class, standing happily, shaking out the burning sensation from her legs, while the instructor moved over to the phonograph to change albums. He moved his rear end around flirtatiously and put on a record that he was certain would suit everybody. "Oldies but Goodies" was a sure bet, and Ericka was aware of the extra pep the music seemed to elicit. The class was bouncing around with snappy nostalgic energy.

Quite sure of himself, the instructor jumped back onto the little raised platform from which he led the class.

"And a one two three . . ." he called out, bending effortlessly to the ground. Ericka watched him for a moment before launching off into movement. His California blond hair, his Muscle Beach build, his gigolo smile—how could so many of the women in the class adore him so? Ericka thought he looked like a mindless stud, puffed-up muscles without a brain.

Ericka wiped a handful of sweat off her forehead onto her leotard, grimaced, and—while a beat behind—managed to keep up the pace. She had always considered herself to be in miraculous shape. Did the rest of these free-flying limbs and torsos belong to superhumans? *How do they do it? Do they exercise all day every day? Don't they have homes? Jobs? Families? Don't they get bored?*

Just a few more minutes, Ericka thought, looking at the clock. Almost over.

She caught her reflection in the mirror, hardly recognizing herself. In fact, she looked around, hoping someone else had shoulder-length dark hair and was wearing a black leotard and tights, with a pair of crazy aqua leg warmers. No, she was patently distinguished by the aqua.

Rising up onto her tiptoes, she stretched her petite frame to measure higher than her five feet two inches. Damn. She still looked shorter . . . and heavier. But I couldn't have gained weight, she thought, patting the imaginary excess of her outer thigh. I passed up chocolate mousse last night.

Just this morning, climbing into her leotard, she had thought that her figure looked terrific. Her waist looked especially tiny, her stomach flat, and the scale had registered an even one hundred. But now she sighed heavily, realizing how it was all an illusion, dependent upon, or relative to, the person next to whom she happened to be standing. Kirstin Pollock, the tall, blond woman on Ericka's right, was perhaps the most beautiful woman she had ever seen. Ericka felt dwarfed and self-conscious next to that graceful yet seductive shape.

The disarming accent, the precise bone structure, broad shoulders, voluptuous bust, curved but narrow waist and hips, and long thin legs marked Kirstin Pollock as decidedly Swedish. Ericka thought the Swedes held an obvious and unfair advantage over the rest of the women in the world, crediting them with the ability to outnegotiate the most powerful heads of state with the careful finesse of a dazzling dimple. Kirstin Pollock's soft blond hair was always swept up or braided into stunning styles that, Ericka decided, only a foreign woman could get away with. It was the difference between elegance and rigidity. An American would look like a tight-ass, Ericka thought, as she noticed Kirstin glance at the clock, then hurry across the room toward the phones.

Kirstin Pollock cradled the telephone receiver against her shoulder, twisting up a thick blond braid that had fallen loose from the exercising, and securing it with a hairpin. She deposited her dime in the locker room pay phone and waited for the dial tone. Tapping impatiently on the wall with a second dime, Kirstin amused herself by reading the raunchy graffiti scrawled along the wall. She especially liked the bits of scratchy dialogue when they included a retort or two. There was one that said: "Marriage sucks"—then, in a different color of ink just underneath: "So does divorce"—then, in still another ink: "So knock the bugger off and be a merry widow." That

14

was punctuated by a skull and crossbones design. Three independent inscribers, etching their uncensored violence on a dull wall ... graffiti, anonymously expressed and exposed. Kirstin started to write something on the wall, and then stopped short. Which abrupt and telling philosophy would she impart? And what if someone saw her? She, Kirstin Lindstrom Pollock, the flawless Swedish beauty of her husband's manor, scribbling raunchy graffiti onto a locker room wall. It was delightful.

"Pollock's Planned Communities," chirped the voice through the telephone receiver.

"Mr. Pollock, please."

"One minute please."

"Executive offices."

"Mr. Pollock, please."

"One moment please."

Kirstin held the phone away from her ear and grinned, mimicking the nasal, redundant greeting.

"Mr. Pollock's office."

"Hi, Doris. Is he in?"

"He's in a meeting. Hold just a minute."

Doris clicked off, and a moment later, Leonard Pollock's voice boomed through.

"Hi, baby doll!" Leonard always sounded so happy to be hearing from his wife. It was more as if he were addressing a lover, not a wife, but then again, Kirstin acted more like a lover than a wife.

"I know you're busy, but . . ."

"Never too busy for you."

Kirstin smiled and cuddled up closer to the phone.

"Listen, sexy, *Beverly Hills People* wants to do a spread on us. What do I say?"

"It's up to you, boss."

"Good. I said yes. It was a young kid, a writer, and I felt like if I said yes, he'd get a promotion. He sounded so eager."

"You're such a pushover—the perennial sponsor."

Kirstin flexed the pink heel of her new ballet slipper into the palm of her hand, carrying her extended leg toward the ceiling. There was a distinct advantage in being a sponsor—a studied science of creating a contact. Markers.

"Whose meeting am I interrupting?"

"A committee from the bank."

Kirstin stretched her leg up even higher, pleased.

"When you get home from the office," she said, "I'll have a surprise for you."

"What's that?"

"Well, you'll just have to come home early to find out, won't you. . . ."

Kirstin hung up the phone and thought for a moment. Now she would have to come up with something clever to surprise Leonard with.

Ericka Wallace helped herself from the huge stack of warm white towels, inhaling their fresh fragrance. Her leotard was pulled down to her waist, so that her shoulders could enjoy the cool breeze that brushed through the controlled air.

On her way back to her locker, she passed a young blonde stretched out, topless, along the locker room bench.

"If my jeans could talk, I'd be in big trouble," the

16

blonde drawled, imitating Brooke Shields in a sexy Calvin Klein blue-jeans commercial.

"I'll bet!" said the girl for whom she appeared to be clowning. She had a T-shirt with TANYA printed in big block letters across it and tiny red bikini underwear.

Ericka thought the panties were flattering and wondered where she had gotten them.

"So finish your story, darling," Tanya said impatiently. "Did he really come three times, or do you think he faked one of them? I've seen guys fake it. They give these quick grunts and . . ." Tanya demonstrated the movement, thrusting her crotch forward. "Who can tell if he really came or not? It's already wet from the first time."

"You're gross."

"No. Just skeptical. I think the guy's a liar."

"You're just jealous."

Ericka saw the blonde give Tanya a friendly slug on the arm. Then the girl pulled a sexy low-cut sweater over her head and shook out her hair. She grabbed her purse and duffel bag and sprinted merrily down the aisle.

"See ya, Tanya. Got a date with my liar lawyer lover!"

Ericka stepped out of her leotard, amused.

"Can I borrow your bra, Jennifer?" someone shouted across the room. "I forgot mine . . . and . . . look . . ."

Even from a distance, Ericka could see the girl looked ridiculous. Her flat chest and pointed nipples

17

were a sad sight under a clinging silk shirt. She needed something to lift her and give her shape.

"Funny that you should need one and I don't!" shouted the girl next to Ericka. "It used to be the other way around. See if you can use this!" Laughing, the girl showed off a very full bust as she tossed the bra across the room.

Dropping her damp leotard and tights onto the floor of her locker, Ericka Wallace wrapped herself in a small white towel. Now she was watching two older women exchanging tips and making luncheon plans. She thought they were cute, and admired their effort. They came three times a week as prescribed by the instructors, pulled out their exercise cards from the files, weighed in, got measured, and then went about the routines specified on their cards. Only the young ones like herself seemed to complain.

"What a body!" one of the ladies exclaimed, tucking her hair into a pink shower cap.

"I'll never look like that," said her friend.

Ericka realized they were talking about her and smiled a thank-you. "Takes work," she said, patting a sore thigh.

"So? Doesn't everything?"

"And would you look at that face?" the other woman remarked.

Ericka pinned her key to her towel, reached into her tote for her copy of *Variety* to read in the Jacuzzi, then pushed her metal locker door shut. "Keep up the hard work, ladies." She gave them a wink and walked over to the scale, wondering whether she should wait. After the Jacuzzi and steam she would probably drop a couple of extra pounds and the scale would read more favorably. However, Ericka was typically tough on herself, and she stepped up to measure her luck. Aha. Happy day. She had dropped a pound without the steam. The exercise had been worth it after all.

In a large Jacuzzi turquoise water bubbled and swirled, sending up a misty steam. Slowly entering the scalding water, Ericka touched her toes to the foam in pampered stages of temperature adjustment. Finally she was able to relax her shoulders down beneath the surface, just as Kelly Nelson plunged bravely in beside her, spraying water onto the copy of *Variety* Ericka was holding.

"Gotta toughen up, kid," Kelly was saying, creating a splash. "I saw you lagging behind in exercise class." Then, looking at the water-spotted newspaper, she apologized.

"God," Ericka said, massaging her strained muscles beneath the water. "Is this class getting harder, or am I just getting older? I hate to think I'm falling apart at age twenty-nine."

"I don't think they should admit any members under the age of twenty-one," Kirstin Pollock commented, sliding carefully into the Jacuzzi, her eyes fixed on the perfectly formed body of a young girl parading nude across the room. She looked to be about nineteen, at the oldest, and Ericka's gaze followed Kirstin's as the young girl stood swinging her towel back and forth, reading a notice that had been posted on the bulletin board.

"If I had a body like that, I guess I wouldn't

19

bother being modest, either," Ericka said, observing the girl's long chiseled legs, concave stomach, and rock-hard ass. "But I agree, she shouldn't have been allowed in. It's too depressing for those of us who have already met up with our first dimples of cellulite, as well as the other muscle-slackening evils of age."

"My stomach hasn't been that flat since my last trip to Mexico, when I got the *turista*." Kelly draped her arms out over the pool for support and began making quick sharp scissor kicks with her legs.

"Seeing a body like that so close up is maddening. I don't care how many hours I devote to exercising. I'll still never look like that again," Kirstin concluded, searching around the Jacuzzi for a strong jet and placing the small of her back against its powerful force. "Now, that feels wonderful. I'm going to close my eyes and forget I ever even saw that flawless form."

Ericka watched as Kelly rolled over onto her side and began whipping the water with a stringent bicycle kick. "Your energy level is obscene," Ericka said, beginning to leaf through *Variety*.

"I remember that you work in the film business, but exactly what do you do? I forgot," Kelly said.

"Mostly I work with writers and directors. My 'title' is Vice-President of Creative Affairs—"

"Ahhh," Kirstin said. "You weave dreams and crystallize statements for the masses. Which studio?"

"One that's got ludicrous judgment. Damn!" Ericka answered angrily, spotting the name of a writer she had been working with. "Goddammit."

"What's wrong?"

"Spineless executives," Ericka responded, absorbing the article. "For three months I've been arguing with the studio kingpins to buy this script that I see Fox has just picked up, out from under us. Our studio was too timid to get involved with it. Fox will probably make a bundle on it. If an idea has any kind of freshness to it, World Wide Pictures decides it's risky. Meanwhile, Fox makes landmark movies like *Star Wars,* and all we ever dare to do are lousy knockoffs of other people's hits. It infuriates me." Ericka began to close the paper.

"He's rather cute," Kelly said, pointing to the back page of the newspaper. "And obviously talented."

Ericka turned the paper over to see what Kelly was talking about. She gasped when she saw the picture, her breath taken away. A glossy portrait of Jamie Sterling, the only man she had ever loved, was smiling at her from its centered position on the oversized page. A million indistinguishable thoughts darted through Ericka's mind as Kelly read the headline aloud.

"NEW YORK PLAYWRIGHT JAMIE STERLING BREAKS OUT WITH *RESTLESS FIRES*—LONG SHOT LEAPS TO BIGGEST BOX OFFICE HIT ON BROADWAY."

With her heart beating unevenly, Ericka impatiently scanned the rest of the article.

"Do you know him?" Kelly asked, leaning in closer to Ericka to get a good look at the article.

Ericka turned toward Kelly and Kirstin, dazed. "Jamie Sterling was the one big love of my life. Do you know what it's like, to suddenly be confronted with his picture and success plastered all over *Variety*?

I haven't run into him or heard from him in about thirteen years. And then this. Well, Jamie was never ordinary. I suppose it wouldn't have been appropriate for me to have just run into him at the supermarket, or the car wash."

"Why did you stop seeing him?" Kelly asked.

"Because of a goddamn wedding invitation. *His* wedding invitation. Accompanied by a personalized, handwritten note: Dear Erickish, Hard to say . . . harder to say on the telephone . . . hard enough to say at all. Always stay as sweet as you are. Love, Jamie."

"Jesus Christ," Kelly said. "I wouldn't have known what to do first—slit my wrists or his throat."

"I didn't do anything much, except cry a lot. He had been one of my father's students at UCLA. My father always thought he was brilliant. Until that day, of course.

"After that I decided to dazzle him through the pens and cameras of the press. I wanted big block headlines of my success to haunt him. *See what you missed, Jamie Sterling? See what I've become!* But he screwed it all up. He beat me to the punch," Ericka said, out of breath and slapping his picture. "Look at this! He wasn't supposed to become a superstar and make headlines and hits." Ericka stared at Jamie. It was as if his ghost were haunting her from some untouchable memory; and he remained untouchable.

"It's not fair," Ericka finished weakly. "*I* was supposed to do that. *He* was supposed to end up unfulfilled and miserable with his miserable wife."

22

Ericka had tears in her eyes, and she fought them back, agonizing over the effect he still had on her.

For a moment Kelly stopped exercising. "Time has a way of touching up our pictures of the past," she said. "The Jamie Sterling you've been imagining all these years is probably worlds away from Jamie Sterling—the man."

"It's really true, Ericka," Kirstin added. "Time is distance. And distance can make something or someone look far better than they ever were. I'm sure I've romanticized Sweden that way. I'd probably sneeze to death from the hay, the cows, the horses, and choke on all the clean air. Not to mention how out of place I'd look running onto our old farm in my pencil-straight skirt and Charles Jourdan spiked heels. You absolutely can't visit a memory without the risk of destroying it."

Ericka forced herself to smile. "There's an old expression, something to the effect that every woman waits for the right man to come along, but in the meantime she gets married. Well, he came and went in my case, and *then* I got married," Ericka said, regretfully.

"First love is infatuation," Kelly said. "Ron and I got lucky, but we had no business getting married when we did. We were kids. I wasn't old enough to order a drink, but I was old enough to get married. That's nuts."

"Why? You're happy," Ericka argued. "I'm angry."

"Look what I gave up: experience—sex—youth—sex—the independent experience of growing up . . . sex. And self-sufficiency. And sex."

23

"You wanna get laid, Kelly? Is that what this is really all about?" Ericka asked, grinning.

"I'm still wild about Ron. I just wish I'd had a couple of other first loves and experimented like mad in the midst of all that curious passion."

Ericka turned toward Kirstin. "She wants to get laid."

Kirstin nodded knowingly, a glint of humor in her lovely lavender eyes.

"I read all these titillating pulp novels, and I'm amazed at the techniques I've apparently missed out on."

"The techniques," Kirstin reiterated, winking at Ericka.

"A couple of years ago I made a resolution to have an affair by the time I turned thirty."

"And?"

"Thirty came and went uneventfully. As did thirty-one. So now this year's resolution is to live out last year's resolution . . ."

"When are you going to be thirty-two?"

"In a week," Kelly sighed.

"You make it sound so dire," Kirstin said, still amused. "Why the deadline?"

"I don't want to wait around for my mid-life crisis! That may be easy for a man to do, but my desirability is infinitely more perishable. I'd like to get laid in my prime. I want to have an affair while I can still give a guy a hard-on just by appearing in my fabulously flimsy french lingerie. I want to play *Love in the Afternoon* without having to duck under satin sheets to hide a less than fiery form."

24

"A week's not much time. Do you have anyone specific in mind?" Ericka inquired. "Perhaps the blond Don Juan exercise instructor? I saw you checking out his bronzed biceps and the rest of his multiple muscles."

Kelly thought about the instructor for a moment, his geometrically perfect network of muscles. But did she want to have an affair with him? Just the fantasy. Not the man. She stood up woozily, then sank back down into the Jacuzzi. "I forgot," she said. "You're only supposed to stay in here three to four minutes. This has been closer to thirty."

Kelly took the *Variety* newspaper from Ericka and was starting to say something when she accidentally dropped it into the Jacuzzi. "I'm sorry," she said, bending down to pick it up. But Ericka stopped her, scooping the waterlogged paper out herself, rolling it into a soggy wad, and tossing it into the trash.

"It couldn't have happened to a better fantasy," she said of the discarded paper. "I say we forget about men altogether and we'd be better off. Why is it men are always the center of a woman's universe? Look at all the valuable brain power we waste on strategies, conniving, all in the hopes of becoming the center of their universe when that's not even what they're looking for. They're looking for an attractive axis to make their universe spin. We're supposed to smile and be their support systems. Their batteries. At least, that's what my husband says."

"Your husband's a liberated psychiatrist. Why would he say that?" Kirstin asked.

"Because liberated psychiatrists tell it like it is."

"How sad," Kirstin responded, frowning. "We should protect one another by not *always* 'telling it like it is.' "

At that moment Ericka's alarm clock wristwatch buzzed. She snapped down the button and checked the time. She realized that she had thirty minutes to be dressed and out at the studio.

"I've got to run," she said, drying herself off. "We keep saying that we're going to make a lunch date. Let's do it already. We can talk over some good food, instead of wilting in this steamy tub."

Securing a towel around her torso, Ericka walked over to the scale again, to take a final count. Down another half pound. Kirstin stepped up to weigh herself—the same. Then Kelly—up a half pound. She shouldn't have stopped for a doughnut on the way in to the club.

Chapter Two

"TORN BETWEEN TWO LOVERS"— KELLY NELSON HEARD THE song playing softly in the background, while she and her husband, Ron, made love in the darkness of their bedroom. She imagined her exercise instructor playing the part of her illicit lover . . . sweaty, tough, dripping masculinity as he took control of her. She imagined justifying a love affair to her husband, as the singer did in the song, and it would all be so understandable, as in the song.

Then the song ended.

But her fantasy forged wildly over the next melodic tale, blurring her husband into the background, as Kelly imagined herself back at the health club, lingering in the shower, with the locker room all to herself. She could almost feel the sensual vision she was creating, wet Sassoon-conditioned hair slapping against her back as the water picked up its fragrance, running the perfumed scent over her shoulders and down the rest of her body. Her passion climbed as she envisioned the exercise instructor stepping into the shower behind her. He was folding her long wet hair forward onto her breast, freeing the back of her neck and commanding it with his mouth. At the same moment his hands took an authoritative hold on her hips. The water would be pounding hard upon them when he lifted her away from its force, brushing her body against his. He would turn her firmly toward him, giving her no choice but to be governed beneath the spray, onto the warm slick floor.

Kelly climaxed to the fantasy-infused lovemaking session. A moment later she guiltily hugged Ron, wishing she could bury her pornographic dreams of gym instructors, sea captains, and runners with great legs and flat stomachs. . . .

Rolling onto her side and adjusting her position on the bed, Kelly looked over at Ron, thoughtfully observing him. His profile was like a shadow in the room dimly lit by moonlight.

"Do you ever close your eyes when we're making love and pretend I'm someone else?" she asked, stunning Ron out of sexual bliss.

He turned to her quickly. "Why?" Then he hesitated. "Do you?"

"I asked you first. Do you ever get into an elevator with some great-looking chick and think to yourself"—Kelly lowered her voice a lecherous octave—" 'Hey,

I wonder what she would be like instead of Kelly for a change'?"

"No. But you must, or you wouldn't have asked me."

"I was just thinking that after going to bed with the same woman for the past fourteen years, you might be getting tired of me. You can tell me the truth. Have you ever met someone else that really turned you on?"

"Why? Have you?" Ron asked her, sitting up surprised. He leaned over to turn on the light on his night table.

"Have I what?" Kelly looked down to avoid meeting him square in the eyes.

"Do you ever have fantasies about making love to another man?"

"We're not talking about me. We're talking about you."

"You do, don't you?"

"No," she lied.

"You sure do. I can tell."

Kelly shook her head in denial.

"You're lying," Ron accused.

"This is ridiculous. Everybody has some kind of sexual fantasies. Maybe you just block yours out. Maybe yours are repressed. I think you should see a shrink," she teased, trying to humor him.

"Well then, why don't you tell me about yours, as long as yours are so *obviously* on the surface. I can't believe it. All the time we're making love, you're running a friggin' porno flick in your head."

"Well, I never got to fool around before we were

married, and you did. That absurd double standard. Girls weren't supposed to be wild and sexual. We weren't supposed to crave a good lay. And then, presto! After marriage suddenly we were supposed to change. No hang-ups, and dying to have you stick it to us twice a day!"

"Kelly, that's really crass."

"Well, it's true. It's not.consistent. If I were to do it all over, I'd have fooled around like mad and gotten all this sexual curiosity out of my system before I married you. You know what it's like with another woman. I have no idea what it's like with another man. Does that make sense?"

Ron was getting uncomfortable.

"Well, does it? You're a lawyer. You believe in logic. Is that logical?"

"What do you want me to do about it, Kelly?"

"My fantasy would be to—freeze time! To be wild and free for just six months. I'd want tall men, short men, Italian, French, black, two at a time . . . a healthy and wild growing up condensed into six crazy months. God, a lover on the beach. I've never made love on the beach."

"Shut up, Kelly!" Ron had never spoken to her that way, and she watched him as he stormed out of the bedroom, pulling on his terry robe.

"Shhh," Kelly whispered, following him down the stairs and tying her own bathrobe into place. "You'll wake up the kids."

Ron was in the kitchen clanging pots and pans around and looking crazed. Kelly climbed up to the counter on a tall stool and watched him. He really did look ridiculous, moving things around without finding or even knowing what it was he was looking for. Kelly sighed heavily.

Ron glared at her.

"You didn't have to take it personally, Ron."

"Just how *am* I supposed to take it?" he asked pointedly. "How would you feel if *I* were dying to be free for six months to screw around?"

"I wouldn't like it," she said, examining the counter. "On the other hand," she went on, "if I were sure that the girls you were screwing were only for sex, it wouldn't be so bad. But your ego is just too big. You'd get flattered and get involved and it would all get out of control. You go bananas when one of your secretaries tells you she thinks you look sexy. It takes you a week to get over it. With me, they would be hard, cold sexual liaisons, a sprinkling of romance, but nothing serious. A while back I promised myself I'd have an affair by the time I turned thirty. Well, I guess I blew that one. I'll be thirty-two in another week."

Ron slammed a pot down on the counter and Kelly jumped up, grabbing him by the waist from behind. "I'm just teasing. If I really wanted to have an affair, do you think I'd tell you?" She felt his body stiffen with vexation, and she tried to counter it, kissing his temple lovingly. "Besides, I'd go crazy with jealousy if you were ever really with another woman."

"Would you?" Ron asked.

Kelly loved Ron even more for the hopeful look in his eyes.

"Honestly. It makes me furious just thinking about it. I can't even stand to think of you with one of your old girl friends."

Kelly felt warm nestled in Ron's embrace. His body heat relaxed her as he steered her toward the living room, over to a down-stuffed sofa, and they sank into it together.

"Look, honey. It's not good unless it means something. What we have is great. Believe me," Ron said.

Kelly's thoughts floated right over his assurances.

Not good unless it means something, Kelly thought. Ha! So it was peer pressure that had you labeled Campus Casanova. You must have hated having to live up to your reputation and suffered so through all those beautiful one-night stands. Those meaningless bits of ecstasy must have been sheer torture. Bullshit!

Kelly leaned back into Ron's arms, thinking it was pointless to argue any further. It occurred to her that it might not be in her best interest to take this subject too far, as she continued mulling over all the great chances she had passed up before Ron. She remembered going all the way with Danny Larson, and how it didn't count because she had all her clothes on. They used to call it "dry fucking." The image was still so clear. Flowers on a red-and-white-print skirt. Danny had his zipper open and was pumping hard against her. His breathing was so fierce; Kelly had to stop breathing altogether. Then it all spilled out and she could feel the warm liquid as roses and tulips ran together on the white cotton background. She had had to throw the skirt away.

32

Kelly's mind skipped, amused at all the old excitement of making out on the couch. Her date's hand would explore sensuously over her fluffy sweater, then her stomach muscles would jump in relief to that cool touch on her hot and hungry skin. What frustration when she had to push his hands away.

And then—God bless whoever invented the pill—99 percent safe. A NOBLE SABOTAGE OF THE MALE DOUBLE STANDARD. But by then she had already met Ron.

Kelly tucked her hand inside the front opening of Ron's robe, rubbing gently against his smooth, familiar chest. She circled the inside of his ear with the tip of her tongue, and whispered in a warm breath, "You're so sexy-looking in your new Polo robe. Like an ad for *Esquire*."

Kelly felt Ron squirm under her touch, and she backed away, surprised.

"Can't you take a compliment?" she asked.

"Yeah, well, it was hardly a compliment hearing about your sexual frustrations!"

"I didn't say I was sexually frustrated! I adore making love with you."

But by now Ron had had it, and he responded by folding his arms protectively over his chest, forcing a distance between them.

"It just burns me up," he said, moving Kelly aside and standing up angrily. "You know, it's not my fault that you didn't screw around before you met me. I don't see why *I* should bear the brunt of it."

What could Kelly possibly say? He was right. Of course it wasn't his fault. Ron Nelson had nothing specifically to do with her missing out on any kind of sexual odyssey. It was the fault of society for changing its standards right smack in the middle of her late teens. She was stuck, waiting for the moral scale of judgment to level out and clarify the hazy difference between gaining one's rightful experience and being a tramp. It was during that time that she had met Ron.

Kelly pulled Ron's bathrobe, drawing him toward her. Gently she kissed his waist.

"You're right, babes," she said. "It's not your fault, and I shouldn't do this to you." Kelly rested her head on Ron's hip, waiting for a response. She felt his hand fondling her hair, lifting up layers, and then holding her head lovingly.

"I understand," he said, in a way that made Kelly think that he really did. She pulled him back down to a sitting position on the couch and kissed his lips in a soft suggestion of a retreat to the privacy of their master bedroom.

─────────────────Chapter Three

SHOULD SHE WEAR HER STRAPLESS BLACK JERSEY OR THE NEW emerald-green silk? Ericka Wallace was not at all in a party mood. She might have fooled Kirstin and Kelly by so boldly dumping Jamie Sterling's picture into the trash at the health club this morning, but when, on her way to work, she had stopped at the studio magazine stand to buy another copy, she had realized that unfortunately she couldn't fool herself.

Her distraction from the damn article had been provided almost immediately by a terrible battle with Ellis Hart. That bastard, Ericka thought. Some writer-director he had turned out to be. If only she had gone to London to supervise the shooting, she could have made sure that the script had remained intact. It was the first film for World Wide Pictures for which she was completely responsible, and she had wanted it to work—to be, in spite of its blood and gore genre, heralded by the studio as a financial grand slam.

Instead, Hart, alone in London, had shot a different ending from the one they had so carefully plotted out. In the approved studio draft, the mangled creature was supposed to die, not the heroine. The ending had read nice and clean, happy ever after, with the beautiful leading lady emerging the victor.

Ericka hiked up the steep stone steps leading to her and David's Hollywood Hills home, thinking once again about the party she was expected to attend with him that evening, and dreading the formal event that celebrated the kickoff of her husband's Universal Pro-Am Tennis Tournament. Why couldn't she instead just cuddle up with a stack of screenplays and read?

Not a chance, she told herself, mellowing in spite of the day's madness with the surrounding vista of trees and flowers and tawny sunset. The tournament was far too important to David for Ericka to miss it.

She clicked off their house security system and opened the front door.

From the entrance hall she could see their large-screen television set, with the same tennis tournament David had been studying all week. She could hear him cheering and coaching aloud. He was still the college jock at heart, and she was amused at his ardent preparation for what had become the most important event in his life. Dr. David Kane had become the *Rocky* character, right down to the downing of those god-awful raw eggs.

Her footsteps resonated on the terra-cotta floor as she walked toward the family room. Opening the guest closet to hang up her coat, she was nearly hit on the head by a hockey stick, and she pushed it back, aggravated, into the clutter of hockey skates, fishing poles, skis, and every kind of racket imaginable. Ericka made a mental note to tell the cleaning woman to straighten out the closet and walked briskly into the family room.

David was pumping away on the Exercycle in front of the enormous television screen. Every so often he would flail his arms in a swing as if he were blasting the ball down the sideline. Ericka stood quietly at the doorway watching him. He hadn't even heard her come in, she observed, noticing that a smaller television set projected a tense overtime battle between the Lakers and Celtics, and Vin Scully's baseball commentary blasted out of the radio.

"Hey, champ," Ericka called out.

"Oh, hiya, Ericka. I want to watch this play. Oh shit. I have to play it back. Oh shit, Ericka, wait a sec."

She watched him get off the Exercycle and jog over to the Betamax tape system, where he put the tennis match on rewind. David continued to run in place, stopping his exercising only at the most crucial moments of play.

"Aren't we going to be late for your party?" Ericka asked, pouring herself a glass of sherry. She swirled it in the modern Baccarat goblet and took a healthy whiff. "Hmmm," she purred, her nose still buried in the satiny fragrance of Harvey's Bristol Cream. She used her finger as a swizzle stick and sucked it thoughtfully. Then she frowned at the sound of the phone ringing. She was too tired to speak.

"Are you still mad at me?" It was Hart.

"What the hell do you think you were doing on this film? What's the big idea of switching the ending on me?"

"What is this—direct by number? Scene by scene—as approved by you, Ms. Ericka Wallace!"

Ericka was struggling out of her jacket. Her temperature was suddenly smoldering again. "Look, Hart, why did you even bother to call?"

"No, you look, Ericka. Harry loved it. He thinks I'm brilliant. You, my love, are replaceable. I'm not. I am now what you call *hot*."

"You ingrate. If it hadn't been for me, you'd still be driving that run-down milk truck. I had to go and be generous and read your fucking screenplay." Ericka plopped down on the chair. She was exhausted. She picked her hair up, twisting it into a knot above her head, and glanced over at David, who was still jogging in place in front of the big screen.

"Hart. What am I going to do with you?" She knew the big guns at the studio would demand an explanation. It didn't matter that Harry liked it. Harry was just one of the V.P.'s. She was going to have to lie and pretend that she knew all along, or they would think she had lost control. She would say that she thought it provided them with the perfect chance to throw in a sequel, to get the full squeeze out of their money. That was the only solution, although they would still be furious that she hadn't cleared the changes with them. Oh hell. Ericka put her head down toward her lap, letting her hair fall forward.

"Don't you like the film?" Hart blurted, his previous show of aplomb fizzling into insecurity.

"Good God, leave me alone, Hart." Ericka brought her head back up. "It doesn't matter whether I like it or not, don't you understand that? There are politics, red tape, procedures, my job—"

"But didn't you like it?" prodded Hart.

"Christ, Hart!"

"Well?"

"Well, to be perfectly honest, I didn't like it to begin with. It's a stupid exploitation story." Ericka mused over the silence at the other end of the line. Perhaps she was being too tough on Hart.

"Hart, it doesn't matter what I think. I make movies for box office receipts. It's all big business, and anyone who tells you different is lying. Are the crowds going out to see the movie? And are they going a second and third time? That's all I care about. That is my art. Box office art." Ericka listened for a moment to more silence. "I still haven't figured out exactly how I'm going to cover this one up. Just for the record, why did you do it?"

"I didn't like that cunt, Jenny, getting off the hook."

"Oh, c'mon, Hart."

"You didn't like it."

What did you expect, roses and a standing ovation after you crapped out on me, Ericka thought. But

39

instead she said, "No, Hart, I liked it. I was just upset."

"You really liked it, Ericka?"

"Hart, I loved it. The crowds will love it."

"You don't mind that it doesn't have a happy ending?"

"Jesus Christ, Hart. You're the one who threw out the happy ending."

"But you thought the happy ending was better?"

"No, Hart. I like the stay-tuned-for-part-two ending."

"Don't you think it's more realistic?"

"Realistic?" Ericka's voice climbed. "Yes, monsters would usually win out."

"Ericka!" David shouted at her. "Would you use the phone in the other room or turn up the TV set!"

"Hart," Ericka said, winding up the conversation, "I gotta go. Take a Valium, or pour yourself some of that expensive brandy I gave you for Christmas, and go to sleep. I'll talk to you tomorrow."

"All right!" David shouted as he jogged in place. "Ericka, did you see that shot?"

She shook her head no, as he jogged over to the Betamax and played back the point for her. She didn't feel like looking over, but she did, to pacify him.

"Ready?" David demanded, looking at her. Then his finger touched the play button, and the machine started spinning. "Now watch . . . right here . . . see the way he runs up?" David coached.

Ericka nodded her head, trying to appear enthusiastic.

"You're not paying attention," David said angrily, and his finger snapped down on rewind.

"Yes I was," she said unconvincingly.

"Okay, now watch, this time." He pushed play.

Once again, from his frozen position, after having been through rewind, fast forward, and then pause, until David had gotten the action to exactly where he wanted it, John McEnroe cocked his wrist and sliced a perfect shot.

David turned to her.

"Now that was a great shot," Ericka said, taking a deep drag of her sherry. "Truly inspired."

The thick white carpet hugged Ericka's bare and tired feet as she climbed the stairs to get ready for the awards banquet. The small amount of exercise felt wonderfully painful, straining her thighs, which were still sore from the workout at the health club. She needed to rejuvenate herself in a hot bubble bath in order to face the evening. She felt irritable as hell, and the last thing she wanted to do was spoil this evening that meant so much to David. He should have been a professional athlete, not a shrink, Ericka thought. But how many nice Jewish boys chose sports over medicine?

Pulling off her shirt, Ericka walked over to the stereo and clicked on some kind of mind-tricking jazz. The Crusaders in their early days were marvelous, she thought, absently picking up a pair of David's dirty underwear off the floor. With her hand poised above the dirty-clothes hamper, she suddenly spotted deep red lipstick jeering at her from the white cotton Jockeys. Deep red, in what looked like freshly emblazoned Dior, definitely spelled "guilty again." Judging from the shade of red, Ericka surmised that David had found a new *inamorata*. His last mistress had worn a purplish color that Ericka thought seemed kind of ghoulish.

Funny how it used to be that you would find lipstick on a man's shirt collar, "kiss around the collar." Was "ring around the collar" really a covert reference to those little reddish, heart-shaped, textured rings? She imagined updating the detergent commercial to sing "ring around the jockstrap." They could air it between "Dallas" and "Falcon Crest."

Ericka didn't need a Ph.D. in psychology to know that her flippant attitude toward David's infidelity probably warranted closer examination than the lipstick itself. It had begun with Cleo. Cleo had been the only girl who Ericka had ever confronted David with, more than likely because she had been the first, or so David claimed, and Ericka had felt a need to go on record with her.

One day Ericka had found red hair in her hairbrush. The girl designing David's office had bright red hair, and it didn't take Ericka long to make the obvious connection. Cleo. Ericka had been upset that David had brought the girl into her bedroom, and that the girl had used *her* things, but there had been no serious pain in discovering David's infidelity. The real pain came from not caring what David did. That was what hurt the most.

The Cleo incident had blurred and faded with Ericka's quiet acceptance of her marriage. After all, she had married on the rebound, young and anxious to heal her romantic wounds. David Kane, the young psychiatrist, had been just what she had needed at just the right time. He was a good listener, and she had needed to talk. He had been good in bed, and she had needed to be made love to. Together they had discredited the merits of romantic love—it couldn't last, not through the duration of a marriage. David knew. He had read studies. He had heard it told over and over again through his patients, his frustrated patients who could never quite accept the fact. David wanted an open relationship. Ericka agreed, relieved. Jamie Sterling had made her nervous. She had always felt she had to pretend with him, to put on an act so he would think she was wonderful. David was so different. He didn't judge her. He told her how bright she was, how capable. He had encouraged her with just the right push as she worked her way up through the ranks of the film community, where only a couple of months ago she had finally established herself as an elite member of its exciting network.

Most husbands would have made demands, domestic and otherwise, but David had been supportive— all the way through his insistence that she retain her maiden name, thus, he claimed, retaining her identity. He wanted her to be in touch with her feelings. That was the shrink side of his character. Open up. Relax. Understand and accept your needs and priorities. Ambitions. Never mind that her drive was usually fueled by the unfulfilled void of Jamie Sterling. How in the world could she communicate that? *Ericka Wallace—VP, Creative Affairs.* She mouthed the newly bestowed title to herself for the thousandth time, testing the ring, trying to be thrilled by it, and failing.

Then she heard David bounding up the stairs and wished impulsively that she could love him the way she had loved Jamie Sterling. That, of course, she could never communicate. Openness in a relationship was one thing, but that sort of revealing would be exceeding levels of any human tolerance, even David's. She would just have to live with her private deceptions. There's so much deception in honesty, Ericka thought bitterly, because you find yourself on the spot so often and, trapped, are forced to lie. After eight years of marriage, she was still fantasizing the perfect scenario of running into Jamie, who would probably remain her first and only love.

"How long will you be?" David had appeared in the doorway.

"Fifteen minutes," Ericka answered, pulling off her panty hose.

"You've got great legs."

"Hmmm."

"Do you want to do it before we go?"

"We haven't got time."

"A quickie?"

"David. I'm exhausted. And we've got to get going."

"You're always exhausted. You work too hard."

"I've got a hard job."

"You work too hard at everything. Except at pleasing me. That's the only area in which you allow yourself to slack off."

"David."

"A quickie."

"When we get home."

"You'll be exhausted. You should try relaxing, Ericka. Then you'd be sexually insatiable just like me." He grinned.

"I should get you together with a friend of mine from the health club," Ericka joked, exasperated. "She's dying to make it with someone other than her husband."

"Bring her on," he joked back.

"Do you see that with many of your patients?"

David looked at Ericka. "Sexual frustrations? C'mon. All."

"It must be a horrible problem for someone whose only sexual experience has been with one man."

"Does this mean that you were *not* a virgin when I married you?" David responded, feigning disillusionment.

"David, I hope you don't *joke* with your patients."

"Or are you the one that is sexually curious?"

"Never mind."

"Is your friend obsessed?"

"Borderline obsessed."

"Textbook case."

"What do you tell your patients to do about an obsession?" At first Ericka was inquiring on Kelly's behalf, but now perhaps also on her own.

"It depends on the depth and subject of the obsession. As well as the consequences which could result from having acted it out." David swatted Ericka lightly on the rear. "Are we going to do it?"

"Tonight. I promise."

Chapter Four

WHY DO I ALWAYS HAVE TO FEEL LIKE HE IS DOING ME A favor by letting me work, Kelly thought angrily, standing in line at the laundry and depositing a load of Ron's shirts on the counter. She and Ron always seemed to be negotiating with each other, bartering with responsibility. For five months she had been working as an assistant to one of the top commercial photographers in the city, Bob Kaufman, and Ron did nothing but make her feel guilty about it. By his actions one would think that he was extending some great privilege to her by allowing her to work. Before this, the children had been completely in her charge. She had done everything. Now that she was asking him to give her a hand with *their* children, a car pool or two, or asking that he take his own shirts to the laundry, he was up in arms. The mechanics of running a house and moving children through the maze of growing up fell, by some unwritten law, into Kelly's territory. If she could squeeze a career into that, Ron had no objections.

"Hello, Mrs. Nelson." The woman behind the counter was addressing Kelly, her pen already scribbling Kelly's name on her pad, along with "light starch and hangers."

Kelly tried to smile, handed the woman the shirts, and took off to make her 9:00 A.M. appointment with Kirstin Pollock.

No. 409 . . . 411 . . . 413 . . . Kelly checked the addresses, looking for the Pollocks' residence. She had never been to Kirstin's house before, but she imagined that it would be magnificent. Holmby Hills was one of the most exclusive areas in Los Angeles, and this particular street, shaded with lush elm trees, was especially awesome.

Spotting an estate situated on at least two acres, and set back a considerable distance from the street, Kelly looked about for an address, fairly certain that she had located the Pollocks' mansion. Three brass numbers designed in heavy script confirmed her hunch, and she drove up the long stretch of driveway.

How nice of Kirstin to think of Kelly for the job. Kirstin and her husband, Leonard, were featured regularly throughout the social publications of Los Angeles and Beverly Hills, and Kirstin was giving Kelly the opportunity to do all the photography work on this particular photographic interview, covering a party the Pollocks were having. Kirstin's parties were legendary, and the focus of this spread was on how high-society hostess Kirstin Pollock set the scene. If Kelly could get enough assignments on her own, she would be able to quit her apprenticeship job with the demanding Bob Kaufman and free-lance.

Kelly stepped out of her car and, lugging a heavy case of camera gear, walked up the grand entrance steps. She rang the doorbell and waited, listening to the clear resonant chimes that seemed so appropriate for such a powerful structure.

Someone peeked through a little hole in the door and inquired who was calling. Kelly was ushered into the foyer by a housekeeper dressed formally in a black uniform with a crisp white collar and apron, then left alone for a moment to take in the palatial surroundings. It was difficult for her to imagine that she was actually friends with someone who resided in such opulence.

She bent down slightly to get a closer look at a sculpture displayed on a beveled glass pedestal. It was a Lipchitz, and she admired the lines, pleased she had recognized the artist. Then she looked up at a large Miró canvas that splashed color against an otherwise ordinary wall. She recognized the priceless painting from books she had seen and was surprised to discover that Kirstin and Leonard Pollock owned it. Just a few feet away was an even more impressive Picasso.

Out on the patio, Kirstin Pollock unfolded the crisp linen napkin onto her lap, inhaling the sweet scent of freesia and hyacinth wafting in from the garden. She reached for a piece of dry wheat toast, gently sliding it from the antique silver caddy.

The servants were well aware that in the Pollock household, when the temperature registered above sixty-eight degrees on the thermometer fixed just outside the kitchen door, breakfast was to be served on the patio.

"What a glorious morning," Kirstin said to Leonard, looking out at her favorite view of the tiered grounds expanding beyond their Holmby Hills estate. Multicolored tulips, daffodils, iris, and other spring flowers had begun to break through their buds. "Remember how reluctant we were when Milton insisted we have the party outdoors? He promised we wouldn't have to worry about rain." Kirstin glanced toward the cloudless sky. "I always say, when Milton Williams caters a party, he takes care of everything— apparently even the weather. I hope it stays this way for tomorrow."

"Mrs. Pollock. Kelly Nelson is here to see you," the housekeeper announced.

"Marvelous, Matty. Kelly's going to be photographing our party preparations. It's her first assignment as photographer and not photographer's assistant. Let's treat her royally."

Matty regarded her employer, wondering what sort of plans she had for Kelly Nelson. Whatever it was, the attractive redhead would surely benefit greatly with Kirstin Pollock as her mentor. Kirstin Pollock was a lucky charm for the chosen few she took under her wing. It was too bad that her careful cultivating talents had had a reverse effect on her children, now grown and struggling through their respective re-bellions, angry and resentful of their mother, whose acts and intentions they had totally misunderstood.

Kirstin Pollock had miraculously managed to turn the Pollock household around when, nearly twenty years before, Leonard Pollock took her as his bride. Before their marriage he had been an impossible man to work for. He drank heavily and he had a beastly temper. But those incidents were now few and far between. This young Swedish woman had tamed the lion, not with a whip, but with charm. At first Matty had been leery of her new mistress, an-other fortune hunter, only a smart one, and that, Matty fathomed, would be worse—especially since she was bringing her two children along with her. But a few weeks after the wedding, when Matty was ill with an incapacitating virus, Kirstin Pollock herself had pampered Matty, bringing her breakfast in bed. Well, she had *never* been served breakfast in bed, and it was something that she would never forget.

In a moment, Kelly was being escorted onto the patio and being offered coffee and hot rolls.

"Kelly, meet Leonard . . . Leonard, Kelly."

"It's a pleasure," Leonard said, rising.

Matty appeared on cue, helping Leonard into his suit jacket and handing him his briefcase.

"He's such an elegant-looking man," Kelly com-mented after Leonard had departed. "Tall. Strong build. Thick silver hair. Kind eyes."

"He's taken," Kirstin teased.

"But I'm running out of time, Kirstin. You'd better find me somebody quick. I'm counting on you."

The two women laughed, and Kirstin began the tour. She had to hurry. There were so many last-minute details, and she liked to attend to them personally whenever she and her husband were entertaining. Extra little touches, like picking up a few pounds of freshly roasted almonds that had been hand dipped in bright silver candy coating. They tasted as rich as one had to be to afford them. The glaze was so thick that the candy looked like the fine silver jewelry that Elsa Peretti had designed for Tiffany's. Kirstin thought nothing of driving forty-five minutes on the freeway to buy crunchy sheets of dribbled chocolate lace, then forty-five minutes in a different direction for an assortment of the most exquisite jumbo dried fruits.

The rental people were busy setting up, and Kelly watched, amazed. She looked out over the tremendous grounds, which were being converted into a Spanish landscape replete with Córdoba gardens. Kirstin explained that there would be flamenco dancers and small teams of passionate lovers dressed in black and wooing romance with musical verse, the artful endearments of Latin song. Adding to the splendor were intimate dance floors scattered strategically throughout the terraced grounds, where tango aficionados could tango, cha-cha dancers could cha-cha, and intoxicated bear huggers could caress to a steamy Latin ballad. After Kirstin and Milton had pored over volumes of Spanish material, noting the food, music, and customs and cheating with favorite Mexican and Latin American inserts—which Kirstin hoped no one would be sober enough to notice—Kirstin felt jubilant and sure that she had created a masterpiece. She was delighted to share her triumph with Kelly.

Inside the house, Kelly photographed Milton and his skillful crew of decoration artists temporarily transforming the Tudor-style interior into a Spanish villa. Milton wasn't just a caterer; he was ingenious in the way he created a total atmosphere. He was in the process of turning the entire Pollock estate into "Una Noche de Esplendor."

"Shall we store the liquor in the garage, or do you think it would be safer in the pool house? It's only until we get the bars set up around the garden," one of the men was asking. In front of him were six three-foot stacks of liquor cases.

"Matty, be a love and show this gentleman where to stack these cases," Kirstin answered, stepping over a mess of wires and cardboard.

Kelly followed, clicking pictures nonstop. She didn't want to miss a thing.

The kitchen was in no less of a bustle than the rest of the house. The countertop of an enormous white-tile island, centered in the middle of the room, was covered with bottles of imported burgundy that would be chilled and made into sangria. Kirstin picked up a bottle, examining the label, then looked over at the tall thin man who was preparing big bowlfuls of the sangria.

"Any samples, Jimmy?" Kirstin asked, taking two

wine-drenched orange slices and handing one to Kelly.

"You bet," Jimmy said, pouring Kirstin a glass.

Kelly declined, reluctantly. It looked delicious, but she had to go back to the photography studio. There was still more work to be done.

Kelly rushed into the studio, pulling her bulky V-neck sweater over her head and throwing it onto a chair. Quickly she deposited the rolls of film she had just taken at Kirstin's in her desk drawer, rolled up her sleeves, and began setting up props for the next shooting.

She could hear Bob Kaufman clicking away in the next room, photographing an exotic East Indian model with a tiger; both were dripping in four million dollars' worth of rubies for a Van Cleef and Arpels jewelry ad. Bob Kaufman was the current West Coast star of commercial photography.

Dipping her finger into a jar of Vaseline, she smeared the glob all over the inside of an ice cream scooper. Later Kelly would use this to form glistening mounds of mashed potatoes into what would have the exact appearance of smooth, cool ice cream balls. Bob Kaufman had taught her that mashed potatoes were the best substance to use in place of ice cream when photographing under long hours of hot lights because they wouldn't melt. Once topped with real fudge syrup and photographed, mashed potatoes would look even better than the real thing.

While hurrying with the props, Kelly also tried to straighten up the studio as she went along. Once both shooting sessions were over, she would then have to help Bob reorganize the studio for the bash he was throwing that night. The party was to welcome Kevin Clark, who was arriving in just a few hours from New York. Kevin Clark was Bob Kaufman's East Coast counterpart, best friend, and greatest rival.

Ron had reluctantly agreed to go, and she hoped he wouldn't spoil the evening for her as he had done on other similar occasions. Tonight she would ignore the exaggerated looks of boredom he would toss her way, hoping to get her to leave early. Ron thought creative people were flaky, and his patience for their trendy banter had a short fuse.

With the party in full swing, cigarette smoke hung in the air of Bob Kaufman's studio like a thin gray gauze. Kelly could barely hear over all the music and noise as Kevin Clark addressed her.

"Are you one of Bob's models?" he asked.

She smiled at him, flattered. She was glad that she had worn her new apricot suede pants and matching taffeta blouse, which Kevin now appeared to be admiring. "I work for him," she explained, "but as his assistant, not as his model."

"Well, you're certainly pretty enough to be a model," he responded, passing her the barely smoldering butt of a joint.

Kelly held the joint carefully with two fingernails, but it was just too short for her to be able to smoke it.

"Here, I've got a fresh one," Kevin offered. He

took out some grass, expertly rolled in cinnamon-flavored paper, and leaned in close to Kelly as he lit it.

Stretching her vision to check whether or not Ron was still standing with his back toward her, and thrilled that he was, Kelly inhaled deeply. Ron was not into smoking grass, except in the privacy of their bedroom, and Kelly was afraid that if he saw her doing so, he would use it as an excuse to make her leave, and why should she? She had to sit through his business parties, and he should have to do the same for her. But Ron refused to take anything that had to do with Kelly's photography career seriously, since it had begun only as a hobby. This was the first time she was actually making some money at it, and Ron was infuriatingly patronizing about the whole affair. Especially when it interfered with his life.

Kelly, however, was in ecstasy. Not only was it a real treat to meet someone as talented as Kevin Clark, whom she found herself liking almost as much as he liked himself, but she loved this new environment of photographers, writers, artists, anthropologists, and psychologists. Ron thought it was all bullshit.

Now she could see that Ron was talking to a tall blond girl, Darlene Woods, whom Kelly knew he couldn't stand. Kelly pretended not to notice him trying to gain her attention. She knew he was trying to give her the "let's go" signal. Turning all her attention toward Kevin Clark, Kelly made animated listening motions, intent on not having to leave. *You can't make me feel guilty, Ron*, she said to herself as she laughed at something Kevin was saying.

Then Kevin handed her a water pipe, demonstrating how to operate the steaming toy. Kelly could see Ron coming up to her angrily, and she quickly followed Kevin's instructions. The grass felt great. Ron began to look as if he were floating toward her, glazed and slow.

"Wanna hit, honey?" She offered him the pipe. "I guess not." Kelly giggled and gave it back to Kevin.

She was waiting for Ron to tell her he wanted to leave, when some fellow came in ringing a bell and inviting them all over to his house for a private screening of the latest Woody Allen film. Kelly jumped expectantly.

"Can't we go, Ron?" she asked.

"What d'ya say? Do I throw good parties or do I throw good parties?" Bob Kaufman had walked up and put his arms around the two of them.

"Progressive parties," Kelly heard herself saying. She felt pleasantly stoned and her voice was just an echo. She felt Bob kneading her shoulders.

"Very progressive," he said, offering her a drag from another joint. This time she decided to pass. Bob offered it to Ron, and Kelly was annoyed when he turned it down with a disapproving look that made him seem twenty years older and really dull.

"I guess we should all pile into just a few cars. Larry's house is only a couple of blocks away," Bob said, including the people standing around them.

All the arrangements were tossed back and forth across the room. Ron shifted his weight uncomfortably and held Kelly's waist with a firm hand.

"Forget it," he whispered in her ear.

Everybody filed out of the house, teaming up in different cars.

With an insistent grip, Ron steered Kelly toward his Porsche.

"Forget it," he said again, closing the door as final punctuation.

Kelly left her door open indecisively, tempted to go along with the others. Then Ron reached over briskly and pulled her door shut.

"It's not fair, Ron. I want to go to the screening."

"I don't." Ron started up the engine.

"We *always* do what you want to do."

"I said I don't want to go, Kelly."

"And I said I do. *I* was having a good time."

"Yeah, with all those flakes?"

"Then I'm a flake."

"Then you are."

Kelly closed her arms tightly around herself, outraged. Ron threw his brakes on abruptly, nearly going through a red light. Kelly jerked forward and wished a policeman would pull up from behind and give Ron a ticket. That would serve him right for being such a righteous bore.

Storming into the bedroom ahead of Ron, Kelly hurled her fox coat onto the bed and glared at him. "And you can stop blaming our having to leave early on your fucking golf game tomorrow morning. I'm playing too, you know, which means that I *also* have to get up at six o'clock for a seven-thirty starting time. Big fucking deal! Even if we weren't playing golf in the very early morning," she continued, watching Ron neatly put his sport coat into the closet, "you'd have come up with some other *cockamamy* excuse for leaving the party." Kelly heaved her outfit on top of her fur coat.

"If you'll remember, party number one was over. It was party number two that I could live without." Ron carefully snapped his slacks into a wooden pants hanger, then smoothed his shirt across the bedspread, examining it to decide whether it needed to be laundered or just to be pressed.

"You hated the whole evening," Kelly said. "Admit it. You couldn't stand it that all night long nobody, not once, ever mentioned law or football!"

"Now wait just a minute, Kelly. You like football just as much as I do, so don't give me that business."

"But there's so damned much more to life. You should have heard this one couple talking about their trip to New Guinea. It sounded fabulous! God, they stayed with tribes whose ancestors only one generation ago were cannibals! Some of the really old people in one of the villages they were at had actually tasted human flesh. The woman was telling me about this disease they get, called kuru. They get it from eating human brains. What happens is that you die laughing. It takes about twenty years for the disease to manifest itself. There's no warning, no symptoms. It would be like, let's say all of a sudden you were sitting with a client, and they were telling you something awful, maybe they'd just gone bankrupt, and all of a sudden you burst out laughing. Only, you laugh until you die! The whole thing sounded just wild."

"Oh yeah, just great, Kelly." Ron looked disgusted. "And if the kuru and the cannibals don't get you, it's also the number one malaria capital of the world. That sounds like anything but fun to me. I don't need thrills like nearly getting killed to have a good time. I don't have to try so hard."

"You missed the whole point."

"No, that is the point."

"Don't you have any curiosity in you?"

"Not that kind of curiosity. Christ, Kelly, a few hits of grass and you want to go off looking for cannibals."

"Well, you never want to try anything new anymore. Maybe if you'd had a little grass yourself, you wouldn't be so damn uptight all the time."

"Oh, so now I'm boring. Well, forgive me for not wanting to be the prize trophy of a crazy headhunt!"

Kelly engulfed her pile of clothes in one big armful and dropped them onto a chair. She flung back the bedspread and accidentally sent Ron's expertly smoothed shirt onto the floor.

"Shit—that shirt's still clean," Ron said, picking it up and examining it as if Kelly's carelessness might have ruined it forever.

"Well, I didn't exactly knock it off on purpose," she said, climbing into bed in her X-rated baby doll that had Raggedy Ann and Raggedy Andy appliquéd across the front—getting it on.

"Let's see how you would like it," Ron challenged, stomping over to Kelly's closet and pulling a dozen sweaters from the shelf.

"I don't believe this!" Kelly cried as she saw her sweaters hit the floor. She ran over to Ron's tie rack and in one clean sweep unfurled an entire row of dotted and striped silk high into the air.

With an even more furious flourish, Ron blasted two rows of Kelly's blouses into a horrible heap on the hardwood floor.

In traumatized silence, Kelly stepped angrily back into her silver evening shoes, grabbed her fox coat, threw it over her nearly naked body, and headed out the door. Although it was one in the morning, she had to get out of the house.

Finding the dining area of the Bel-Air Hotel closed, Kelly moved wearily into the hotel's adjacent cocktail lounge. The room was plush but intimate, occupied by only one couple and a bartender. She ordered a pot of chamomile tea and sat impatiently dunking the tea bag into her plain ceramic cup. Herb teas are so damn slow, she thought, insistent on her infusion efforts and badly in need of the tea's supposed soothing effects.

Damn tea. Damn Ron. She was so angry, so upset, that her hands were shaking. Why was he always trying to crush her spirit? In one breath he would rave about her enthusiasm. In the next breath he would berate her for her enthusiasm. It wasn't just tonight; it happened all the time and it seemed lately with an increased frequency. Was it her or was it him that had become so mercurial? Kelly honestly didn't know. At times Ron seemed so staid and narrow. Actually, that she could have managed, but the fact that he tried to impose that dullness on her had become just too much. So what that he was well rounded, well read, and well preserved? It was all without passion.

Was this the way it was going to be for the rest of her life? Get up in the morning—awakened by the jarring click of the alarm clock radio, followed by the irritating repartee of Ken and Bob on the seven o'clock morning news, to move about, drowsily, in the bathroom. No talking. More news. A quick breakfast with the kids. A little talking; kids will be kids. More news, only this time in print. A mad, busy day. Work. Kids. Car pools. Lessons. Marketing. Details. Then home again for dinner in front of the television set for the seven o'clock evening news. Obligatory and stilted exchanges with the kids. An assortment of fights, the twins, their daughter, each other. And sex, once or twice a week, squeezed in between the evening news and Johnny Carson. How was it that, with all that, Kelly still managed to be cheerful most of the time? No romance. Basic love. Or maybe things seemed worse than they actually were. And with that, Kelly burst into tears.

"Looks like you could use something stiffer than tea." A tall, handsomely built man took a sip from his drink, then sat down at the table next to Kelly's and smiled disarmingly at her.

Embarrassed, Kelly dabbed at her eyes with the cocktail napkin and managed a slight smile.

"You're too pretty to cry," he said simply. He had wonderful eyes.

Kelly gave him a look. What a corny line.

"It's true."

Kelly regarded him again. He looked great in his

worn-looking blue jeans and casual sweater, she thought. Unlike Ron, who always looked somehow awkward in jeans. Ron was more suited to slacks.

"Do you want to talk about it?" he asked. "Sometimes it helps to talk to strangers."

"Are you a shrink?" Kelly asked.

"Why, do you need one?"

"I might."

"I'm better than a shrink. I'm a stranger, and I'm free. Free as in I don't charge sixty bucks for forty-five minutes or whatever the hell the going rate is today—and I'm available. Brandon Michaels. Forty. Successful architect. Sexy. And single."

"You shouldn't have told me all that. You're no longer a stranger and I'll have to find someone else to talk to."

Brandon Michaels looked dubiously around the bar. His glance lingered momentarily on the couple sitting alone in the corner, clearly enraptured with one another, then moved on to settle on the unfriendly-looking bartender. "Looks like it's him or me. You don't appear to have much of a selection here and my guess is you definitely need to talk."

"Let's begin with you talking. We'll ease into me. I could still break into tears at any moment."

"Right. Let's see. I already told you my . . . vital statisics." He let his long lean legs stretch out under the table. "Aren't you warm in that heavy coat?"

Kelly had been so absorbed that temperature hadn't occurred to her. Now, as she started to slip out of her bulky fox, she remembered that she was practically naked underneath the loose fur. She felt herself blush self-consciously.

"What's the matter?"

"Nothing."

"Why don't you take off your coat?"

"Actually I'm still chilly," Kelly lied, reminding herself that Brandon Michaels had no way of knowing what she did or did not have on underneath the shield of her coat. "Are you in L.A. for business or pleasure?" she asked to change the subject. "Or both?"

"I live here," Brandon said, explaining in an easy, natural fashion how his Malibu home had been ravaged by the latest Malibu disaster, gale-force winds that had sent two catamarans crashing into his living room.

"The catamarans are still there, sticking out like some kind of strange sculpture."

Kelly was trying hard to focus on what Brandon was saying. She shifted about, now uncomfortably aware of her sexy state of undress. She felt flushed and her imagination was stirred.

"I've finally decided to give up on disaster-prone Malibu. I'm building a new house for myself up in Coldwater Canyon. Although it's still not a practical habitat, I've resigned myself to the liability that I can't live without creative surroundings."

Brandon's sleeves were pushed up and his arms, below them, looked strong and well defined. Kelly found herself wondering what they would feel like around her.

"The canyon has to be less treacherous than Malibu!" Brandon concluded.

Kelly crossed her bare legs and smiled, thinking of her own, very flat, very uncreative cul-de-sac. Well, it was great for her kids. And it was *near* the creative canyon. But she didn't say any of this out loud—the last thing she wanted to do was talk about domestic details.

Brandon shifted their conversation to contemporary art, and Kelly dived in, using the few buzz words she had at her command to sound knowledgeable. She was pleased to find that her technique worked. Brandon appeared to love to talk, so her buzz words were only needed to punctuate his dialogue.

"Have you been collecting contemporary art for long?"

"For years. Since I was in college. I took a lot of art classes."

"Do you paint? Or sculpt?"

"I paint and sculpt."

"Really?"

"Since I was eight."

"Let me guess—your artistic genius began with Play-Doh."

"Play-Doh. Dime store watercolors. They've got half a dozen of my best finger paintings hanging in the Whitney." He was regarding her in a piquant perusal. "By the way," he added, "there's a terrific show that'll be opening next Sunday at the Susan Gersh Gallery."

"On Melrose?"

"You familiar with Sam Francis's work?"

"No."

"You shouldn't miss it. His work is really exceptional. Now let's talk about you."

I'm sitting here in my skimpy little baby doll imagining what it would be like to make love to you, she thought, but instead just smiled and asked, "What would you like to know?"

"Where are you from? Are *you* out here on business?"

Kelly would have loved to play out a fantasy. To respond to his question by saying that she was a New York fashion photographer out in Los Angeles to meet with her extremely famous client, but she lacked the nerve and told him the truth—all about her marital spat.

"Well," Brandon said, amused. "My bungalow does have a fireplace, it's private, romantic, we could order champagne—wouldn't you feel better after a quick but torrid affair before you return to your dull but loving husband?" Brandon asked, fixing blazing blue eyes flirtatiously on her. "Your secret would be your revenge."

Cocky, but cute, Kelly thought, returning his gaze. She felt as though both her thoughts and her fox coat had suddenly become transparent. She briefly imagined herself taking him up on his offer. She could almost feel his hand moving downward deep inside her fur coat, resting temptingly on her bare shoulder. Then his hands would venture in every direction, his mouth would move along her shoulder down toward her breast, the soft fur of the coat falling away. She loved the sensuous shape of his mouth, the fullness of his lower lip, and the way it puckered irresistibly into an invitation. She could almost feel him tasting her lips, and a tortured thrill shot through her. Maybe she shouldn't have told him how little she had on underneath, she decided, trying to break her flood of thoughts.

"It would be great therapy," he assured her.

"I'd be lying to you if I said I wasn't tempted," Kelly admitted, standing, and regretting her cowardice. She pictured a crazy scene straight out of an old Cary Grant movie with Brandon chasing her around the room as she playfully used stuffed chairs as barricades. She loved the physical frenzy, the out-of-breath racing heart, the disheveled hair and clothing. They would order caviar and champagne, and *she* would be dessert. Kelly couldn't help feeling a little scared, a little tempted, and also a little chicken. "It's late," she said. "I'd better get going. Thanks, Dr. Stranger. I do feel better."

"I could make you feel better still," Brandon said, teasing and signing both their checks. Kelly tried to grab for hers, but Brandon was faster. And stronger.

They walked quietly through the moonlit grounds toward Kelly's car.

"Thanks again," Kelly said as Brandon opened her car door for her, blocking her way. He caught her in a close embrace. His breath felt hot on her neck and she wished that she could stay. His hands supported her around the waist and she figured his lips were only an inch or so from hers. She was tempted to kiss him; the setting was so right. Instead she backed away, awkwardly moving around him and into the car. He kissed her anyway—it was brief but memorable. Then he took out his business card and put it in her hand.

"Just in case you change your mind, or decide to change your house," he said, grinning.

Kelly stared after him as he disappeared into the darkness, then looked up frustrated at the big black sky above her that was made electric by so many brilliant dots. How insignificant she really was when pitted against the universe. She was just another dot. So if she had committed adultery, had had a little love affair, what harm would that have done when viewed against the overwhelming backdrop of space?

"Cocky," she said, aloud this time. "But definitely cute." She looked down at his business card: *Brandon Michaels—Architect.*

Ron's neck hurt like hell as he rolled over from his miserable sleeping position on the too narrow couch. Where the hell was Kelly? Damn her for leaving like that.

When he tried to stand up, every muscle reminded him that he hated sleeping on the couch. He limped over to pull the den drapes open. Darkness. Could something have happened to Kelly? A wave of worry spread through him. No. Kelly could take care of herself. The anger returned. The anger of running out of gas and not being able to find a service station open. The anger of having a wife he couldn't control. His friends' wives were compliant. They realized that they owed their comfortable lives to their husbands, that it was basically a man's world, and if they were clever they massaged and rejuvenated their husbands' weary male egos. But Kelly had become so damned independent.

He went into the kitchen to make himself a cup of coffee. It was already 3:00 A.M. and he wondered angrily where the hell his wife had gone. Looking in the refrigerator for some cream for his coffee, Ron saw that he would have to settle for nonfat milk. Along with the watered-down milk, he pulled out the ragged remainders of a chocolate cake and sat himself down at the kitchen table to watch the clock and stew.

Kelly kept her hand in a tight grip around Brandon Michaels' card as she stepped out of her car and got ready to go into the house. The card was buried deep in her coat pocket and its very touch unnerved her. Would she actually call him? Perhaps one evening when Ron was working late. Or a Thursday night poker game. Or maybe even for a matinee, a luxurious afternoon of lovemaking in broad daylight. Kelly pushed the electric garage door device and watched the shaky wooden affair moan downward. Then she put her key into the door. Damn, she just didn't have the nerve, she decided, taking the dreamy architect's card out of her pocket and tearing it up regretfully. She immediately stashed the pieces back in her pocket when Ron suddenly whipped open the door.

"Where the hell have you been?" he asked angrily.

"I was upset. I needed to get out."

"I drove all over looking for you."

"I needed to cool off."

Ron sucked in some air, frustrated. "You should have called."

"Let's just forget about it," Kelly said. She *had* cooled off. Her secret *was* her revenge. Not much of a secret, but for her it was something. An ego-soothng flirtation. Exactly what she had needed. A kiss. A kiss and an embrace with which to fuel at least six months' worth of sexual fantasies.

"Kelly, you can't have it all," Ron said finally, turning around and walking through the door.

"Not this again." Kelly followed. "If you start quoting that pop radio psychologist again—"

"Quit calling her a *pop* psychologist."

"She's just great at sweeping summations that sound terrific, but that's it. You can't approach the complexities of people's problems with some quick catchwords and category remedies. You like what she says and *therefore* she's correct, astute, and perfect. She makes you feel better because—"

"—she's realistic. You *can't* have it all. The kind of man that would fit your romantic notion would also be rotten husband material."

Kelly looked at her husband pleading a case he needed to believe in—that she also needed to believe in, in order to make their marriage work. She listened to the argument she had heard so many times before, the hollow harmony of truth . . . *that kind of man would not be stable, responsible, and would not provide Kelly with the security she needed.* It was a speech that even her parents had thrown at her. Well, she thought, then Brandon Michaels must be the flip side of Ron Nelson that this radio psychologist must

70

have had in mind in her discussions of rotten husband material. Enthusiastic. Impulsive. Artistic. And passionate about everything he did.

"I'm sorry that I'm not more romantic. Or more adventurous. Or more impulsive." Ron had sat down at the kitchen table and was spinning around the empty cake plate.

Kelly felt a huge wave of guilt and went immediately over to put her arms around him. She did love him. That wasn't the problem. And the point of this was not to hurt him or make him feel he wasn't enough for her. So what was she doing? Why was she demanding something from him that he could not be?

"No. *I'm* sorry. I love you."

Ron responded urgently, holding her tight and kissing her hard. It was an insecure kiss, and she felt even more guilty. This was not an insecure man. Ron was successful and sure of himself with the rest of the world.

"I think we'd better cancel our golf time," Kelly said, staccato, in between kisses.

Ron nodded his agreement, sliding his hand beneath her fox coat, then reacting with surprise at what she did not have on underneath.

"You went out like this?" His hands continued to explore.

"If you'll remember, I didn't exactly have time to get dressed," Kelly answered, massaging Ron's erection.

He pushed her away from him gently, stood up, and led her out into the backyard.

"What are we doing?" Kelly asked.

"You want impulsive. You're going to get impulsive."

They were outside, beside the pool, and Ron was undressing them.

"It's too cold."

"The water's warm."

"I'm too cold." Kelly was shivering.

Ron carried her into the surprisingly warm water, holding her close and sweeping her sensuously through the pool. He was pressing tight against her stomach, matching his hips to hers as he pinned her against the cool metal ladder. As he entered her, Kelly's fantasy about Brandon Michaels began.

There would be hot rays of sunshine touching her bare skin as she imagined herself lying sprawled out on an inflated raft, dragging her hand through the refreshing cool of the blue water.

"Even better without the fur coat," she would hear a man's voice say. She would lift her gaze to see the handsome form of that stranger from the Bel-Air Hotel.

Brandon Michaels would then pull his soft blue cashmere sweater over his head and toss it onto the patio. He would step out of his faded jeans, and she would see that his legs were as she had imagined: rockhard, hairy, and perfect.

"You'd better get out of here, Brandon. I'm married," she would protest.

". . . Ah yes, Ron Nelson. A fine man, I'm sure. Lucky devil." Brandon Michaels would slither into the pool and sprinkle water across Kelly's breasts, down her thighs, then flick a few drops toward her toes. Afterward he would pick her up in his arms and carry her out of the pool over to a cool spot on the cement. He wouldn't say a word. Just kiss her. Everywhere. She would want to touch him, to kiss him back, but she would be too overwhelmed by her own pleasure. He would be a master craftsman awakening her every sensation. His tongue would draw a ravishing design across her belly, down the side of her waist, the curve of her hip, then up again to press tenderly around her breasts.

"I see you like it impulsive!" It was Ron's familiar voice lifting her back out of her fantasy.

Kelly kissed him hard, trying to quiet his words. She didn't want him to break the spell.

In an instant she was back by the pool with her architect. Hmmm . . . that felt just right.

Chapter Five

ROCKS SIZZLED IN THE CORNER OF THE HEALTH CLUB STEAM room, and Kelly listened to water dropping and frying in a predictable pattern. Her neck ached with tension from the weekend, and she adjusted her head on the terry towel that she had folded and propped up as a pillow.

Throughout the entire weekend, Brandon Michaels had been with her, floating in and out of her thoughts. She would find herself trying hard to concentrate on the memory of that evening, wanting to recall with vivid recollection every line and aspect of his being. Sometimes it would all come through so clear, and at other times she could scarcely remember what he looked like. She was left with a patchwork gallery of elusive recollections.

She pushed the small of her back against the tile bench; the flatter she pressed, the flatter her stomach became. It was an excellent stomach exercise, and with it she employed the most precise and calming breathing exercises. She felt her chest rise and fall. Breathing in. Breathing out. It was so peaceful, and the moisture rolling across her stomach and down her neck—the wet relief of sweat—made the relaxation even greater. She hadn't had the energy to face this morning's early-bird exercise class. She just wanted to treat herself to the spa.

Kelly let herself sink into a faraway consciousness. She was only blithely aware of people coming into the steam, chatting and then walking out again. Their words floated up like an echo with the steam. Gold chain necklaces that they had forgotten to remove scorched their skin. The door was hot. The tile bench was hot. Some worried that their hair would frizz, and that all the sweat would make their faces break out.

Then a loud laugh pierced Kelly's meditations. Only Ericka laughed that way. Kelly looked up through the mist toward Ericka's voice. Ericka was wrapped in two towels, one around her body, the other a turban around her head. Next to her stood Kirstin, grinning like a sly but sexy cat.

"You ought to give lessons, Kirstin. You'd make a fortune. A sort of farfetched finishing school."

"You'd enroll?" Kirstin laughed this time.

"What are you teaching?" Kelly asked.

"How to get your man. And keep him," Ericka joked. "That's what this Swedish seductress is teaching."

"Gloria Steinem would have you hanged for treason."

"Gloria Steinem's methods are only mucking things up. If you think you don't have to play games to gain and maintain a relationship, you're badly mistaken." Kirstin's eyes were flickering. "It takes hard work."

"If I suddenly started putting *effort* into my relationship with David, wearing sexy lingerie, creating atmosphere, *playing* with him," Ericka said, setting up a place for herself on the bench, "David would laugh at me."

Kirstin shrugged. "You think he'd laugh. But I'm not so sure. Men *love* to be pampered. They love for you to make a fuss over them."

"David is a shrink, Kirstin. He'd be suspicious. Then he'd laugh his head off."

"Ron would love it. But who's got time?"

"I certainly don't. Besides, that's all I'd need. David wouldn't react like Leonard, by lavishing me with jewels and admiration, he'd just want to lavish me with his body—more sex. When David gets relaxed, he immediately gets a hard-on. And he's almost *always* relaxed anyway."

"I'd love it if Ron craved me all the time. It would make me feel lusciously cravable."

"It's not *me* he wants—he's just horny all the time. It gets annoying."

"You girls have to learn how to manage your men. You really do," Kirstin interjected, frowning.

"I manage my life, my career. I haven't got the time to *also* manage my man," Ericka said.

"It's because you don't care. If you had a lover, I guarantee you'd find the time."

Kelly smiled. Touché. She certainly would find the time to pamper one Brandon Michaels.

Ericka looked at Kirstin and wondered how she managed to dedicate herself so supremely to getting exactly what she wanted. Then she realized it was obvious. Kirstin's mind was like a computer—clever, organized, and quickly to the point.

"I almost got that fling out of my system," Kelly said wearily, noting Ericka's and Kirstin's surprise and then amusement as she launched into an elaborate retelling of her encounter with Brandon Michaels—how she had been titillatingly wrapped in the fox coat Ron had given her last Christmas, wearing nearly nothing underneath.

"Sounds like it would make a great ad for Bonwit Teller's fur department." Kirstin mused. "... *And all she needed was her fox. . . .*"

"Well, somebody certainly could write good copy for the concept," Ericka added.

"It would have been the ultimate tryst," Kelly revealed. "I was so close. The criminal aspects had even been diluted from so much fantasy wear and tear. If only I could have just gone ahead and done it, then, to erase my guilt, simply rearranged the order—pretending it happened before I was married; sort of a credit line. But I *couldn't* do it. I was so aggravated afterward. Who would have known? Who would have cared? It would have been fast and fantastic." Kelly stood up laboriously, slinging her towel over her shoulder. "Well, there's always next year," she sighed, pushing open the heavy steam room door.

78

*   *   *

"I have an idea," Ericka said, teasing, and making herself as comfortable as she could get on the locker room's cold metal bench. "Let's give Kelly Brandon Michaels as a birthday gift."

"That's a great idea!" Kirstin said, with her head upside down and the blow dryer spraying her golden hair in every direction. "Kelly would absolutely love it!"

"It was a joke!"

"But it would be perfect. What else can we give her that she can't go out and get herself?"

"You're insane. You can't give someone a fling for a birthday present, Kirstin."

"Oh, but she wants one so badly. Fate is asking us to do this for her. We've got the man. It's just a few days before her thirty-second birthday. How can we disappoint her by not taking advantage of all that?"

"Kirstin, you're dangerous."

"But it *would* make one hell of a birthday present. You have to admit that." Kirstin threw her hair back over her shoulders, stood upright, and shook her head. She reached for some bobby pins to put her hair up with, holding them between her teeth.

"The ultimate gift," Ericka chuckled, starting to come around. "It could be advertised in that catalog— isn't it Harrods in London that claims they can get hold of anything? I can just see it . . . the catalog listing would read: 'The Fabulous Fling.' They'd be writing up orders like mad. I may have to get one for myself while we're at it."

"We'll arrange it like we're taking her out for

lunch for her birthday," Kirstin continued demurely. "We set the stage. If she wants to act it out, it'll be up to her, and if she doesn't, it will have been a marvelous joke." Kirstin bent down, wiggling her overflowing bust into a lacy lilac bra. Afterward she stepped into a matching slip and a pair of sleek suede pumps.

Ericka took all this in with a heavy sigh.

"What she wants to do with the guy is up to her."

"Shall we have him gift-wrapped?" Ericka asked. "I'm picturing this tall, rustic-looking hunk with a frilly pink bow around his neck and a small white card inserted between his teeth." She laughed, finally won over. "This is going to be wild. But you have to make the call."

Kirstin smiled graciously, still in her slip, then led the way over to the pay phone. She leafed swiftly through the phone book, paused briefly, deposited a dime, and finally in a silky voice asked to speak with Brandon Michaels. In no time at all she was exclaiming, "Bingo!" and the two outrageous women burst into laughter, followed by a long, careful string of arrangements.

Leaning thoughtfully over his drafting table in the temporary office he had created for himself in his two-bedroom suite at the Bel-Air Hotel, Brandon Michaels placed the telephone back in its cradle.

What a bizarre proposition he had just received.

He picked up one of his mechanical drafting pencils and began doodling with it, distracted from the blueprint in front of him, and trying to recall what Kelly Nelson looked like. He smiled, remembering.

She was Pippi Longstocking, grown up and trans-formed into a radiant redhaired beauty. He remem-bered her eyes flirting a duet of Irish green country-side—fresh and longing for play. So this was the "play" she had in mind. She wanted a matinee. A lover for the day. According to her friends, she wanted romance. A seduction.

"She's never made love with anyone but her husband," the woman with the honeyed Swedish ac-cent had explained, trying to elicit Brandon's sympa-thy and to make him understand the gravity of what she was asking him to do.

What a pity, he had thought. All that woman for only one man. That was the problem with marriage. It was an absurd demand. Partnership, friendship—that was different, but *marriage* implied waste as far as Brandon Michaels was concerned, which was pre-cisely why he had avoided it. He was a forty-year-old bachelor with absolutely no inclination to tie the knot, or noose, as he saw it. Marriage was a convention that no longer had any meaning in contemporary society. Sure, it worked great in an agricultural soci-ety where the man went out and hunted for food while the woman stayed home to prepare it and raise a family to help in their survival. But to Brandon's way of thinking, the necessities of that partnership were dissolved with industrialization. If one wanted to have children, then perhaps marriage made sense, but only perhaps. With the divorce rate the way it was, a child often grew up with only one original parent anyway.

Everything about marriage seemed ridiculous to

81

Brandon. The concept of being with only one woman made no sense at all to him. What people were willing to give up for the illusion of security! Their sexuality would have to be forfeited. If Brandon were to be with only one woman, he would get used to that one woman and naturally she would cease to be exciting to him, no matter how exciting she had originally been. For the rest of his married life he would have to pretend. Pretend to be aroused by the sight of the same woman. The same woman whom he had just seen tweezing worrisome gray hairs out of her head. The same woman who had been scrubbing the calluses from the bottom of her feet. Or flossing her teeth . . .

Was that sacrifice for love, or for "security"?

What a dreadful waste, Brandon thought. For both him and the woman. No wonder Kelly Nelson wanted to have an affair.

Brandon picked up the telephone again and canceled the lunch date he had already scheduled for the day that they had chosen for the birthday fling. After all, this luscious married redhead, whom he now recalled vividly, desirably naked underneath the loose sheath of fur, was for him virgin territory. He was definitely looking forward to their tryst.

Chapter Six

KELLY GLANCED OUT THE WINDOW JUST IN TIME TO SEE THE sleek black limousine crawl smoothly up to the curb in front of the photography studio, where she was waiting to be picked up for her birthday lunch. She felt a thrill of anticipation as she looked out at the luxury vehicle hired to complete the perfect birthday lunch date, then darted back into the darkroom. Ericka and Kirstin were putting on a class act, and Kelly couldn't wait to see where they were taking her. They said it would be a surprise she would never forget, and that she should discard all notions of willpower. It's your birthday—indulge. Well, indulge was exactly what Kelly would do, and she was starved just thinking about it. Maybe she would even order a rich appetizer and two decadent desserts.

Hurriedly Kelly soaked the last glossy eight-by-ten in the appropriate solutions, then shook it out impatiently, watching the liquid droplets plunk off into the plastic tub. Finally she clipped it onto a string to let it dry. It was a picture of a nude woman draped in exotic flowers. Sex to sell flowers? Well, why not? They used sex to sell everything else.

The doorbell to the studio rang and Kelly stole a last look at the photograph, trying to imagine what she herself would look like draped in exotic flowers, her naked skin glistening slick. What a titillating ad she would make in *Playboy*. Or on a billboard; would she stop cars or cause accidents?

"Coming!" she shouted, squirting a sting of cinnamon Binaca into her mouth. The strong burning sensation attested to the breath freshener's potency.

It was the first time that Kelly had ever ridden in a limo, and she took a deep breath as she climbed into the plush backseat. I could get used to this, she observed, sinking back into the enormous space and savoring the exaggerated distance between her and the driver. The clear glass window that separated the driver from the rest of the car was carefully shut and Kelly laughed, wanting to test its security. She wanted to say something shocking or obscene to see if the driver was actually sealed off.

Kelly crossed her legs and affected elegance, enjoying the remainder of the ride while wondering where she was being taken in such elevated style.

When the limo rolled up the driveway in front of the Bel-Air Hotel, Kelly had to laugh, recalling the image of her last visit. Ericka and Kirstin had some sense of humor selecting the Bel-Air Hotel—in all probability as a playful dig at lost opportunity. That had to be Kirstin's idea. Well, at least this time she was arriving in a dignified fashion: fully clothed.

As she took the driver's outstretched hand and stepped out of the car, a ghostlike vision of Brandon Michaels, leaning lazily against a pink planter, appeared fleetingly, then dissolved. As it was, the episode with him had been haunting her all week, and now, back where it had all begun, with daylight casting shadows and illuminating details, Kelly had Brandon on the brain.

What if she *were* to run into him here? Would he think that it was intentional? Would he be happy to see her? What clever greeting would she give him? Would he even remember her? Suddenly Kelly's heartbeat was rushed, and she felt all nervous and excited, as though she were definitely going to see him.

She and Kirstin and Ericka would all be seated in the hotel's dining room sipping champagne and laughing merrily, girlishly. Then the waiter would come over to their table and hand Kelly a pack of matches or a cocktail napkin with an inscribed message. "I've missed you terribly," the passionately written words would read. Kelly would turn around and see Brandon Michaels, dining alone. He would put his own glass of champagne to his lips. (The only beverage that existed within Kelly's imagination was champagne.) Then he would toast her from afar, beckoning her to come join him. Ericka and Kirstin would naturally grant her permission, and, looking positively chic in her new jade-green silk suit, she would walk with a slow sultry swing over to his table.

"Excuse me. Are you Mrs. Nelson?"

Kelly looked up at the hotel doorman, surprised. She wasn't accustomed to driving in limos or to having doormen at posh hotels address her by name. "Yes," she said.

"This is for you." The doorman handed Kelly a note from his gloved hand.

Kelly reread the simply put but nevertheless puzzling message: "Go to Bungalow 6l." She looked over at the doorman, but he was busy opening the door to a bright blue Rolls-Royce.

Then it occurred to her what was going on. All this mysteriousness. It was more than lunch. It was a surprise party. A surprise thirty-second birthday. Of course, that's what it had to be.

Kelly rehearsed her reaction as she began her hike toward the bungalow, walking along the lovely garden path that overlooked elegant little ponds with ducks and swans swimming leisurely about. What a beautiful day. What a beautiful setting, Kelly thought, lingering purposefully on the wooden bridge to look out over the muddy green water and spy on the two ducks engaging in play. She was in no real hurry to enter the bungalow that would be jammed with friends. She wasn't in the mood for airy small talk. It would be like a cocktail party—where you get to see everyone but talk to no one.

How terrible of me, Kelly thought. I should be excited. They went to all this trouble and expense to plan a party for me, and I'm out here hiding like a small child longing to be alone. Longing to be kissed. It was this place. The Bel-Air Hotel. The souvenir of Brandon's kiss was still so vivid, and it was making her recall, in sensuous detail, a week's worth of marvelous fantasies. She could almost feel his breath again, warm and tempting across her neck, as she whirled around unnerved—mad at herself.

What in the world had gotten into her? Maybe she should see a psychiatrist. She was truly becoming obsessed. Meeting Brandon Michaels that night had been a disaster for her. Her fantasy now had a face. A name. A person. It was no longer an interchangeable sex object to fuel a mounting orgasm.

Why wasn't this just lunch with Kirstin and Ericka? That was all Kelly had wanted. She could tell them how she was feeling. About her craziness. They could laugh about it together, and their laughter would lighten her guilt. They would tell her how normal she was.

But she didn't feel the least bit normal at this moment. She felt miserably mean. She would make it up to Ron. She would walk over to Bungalow 61, knock on the door, and act surprised as hell to see fifty or so friends waving and shouting a chorus of "Surprise!" Then she'd mingle gratefully, "working the party," laughing tearfully, and telling everyone how she had had no idea.

Kelly stopped in front of a small white cottage that had bougainvillea growing thickly across one wall with purple flowers in full bloom. The roof was a glazed terra-cotta tile, and on the door were two brass numbers: 61.

Kelly listened quietly for noise. There was none. She put her hand to the door. A quick nervous knock. Three raps. Nobody answered. How strange. She put her hand on the doorknob and twisted it open.

The room was empty: an amazingly beautiful suite, furnished as Kelly had never seen a hotel suite furnished. As though somebody lived there. Somebody very rich.

Do I go in? Or do I close the door and go over to the dining room? All at once Kelly felt very foolish. Nelson was such a common name. An American staple in identities, like Brown or Jones or Smith. The note had been intended for a different Mrs. Nelson. Had the doorman said Kelly Nelson, or Mrs. Nelson? Kelly tried to recall.

Ericka and Kirstin would roar with laughter when Kelly told them what had happened. Now, feeling somehow more relaxed, she decided to take a quick look around before the real Mrs. Nelson showed up. If anyone were to discover her, she would simply hand them the note.

Very Park Avenue, Kelly thought, touring the elegant room. Everywhere there were expensive-looking objets d'art. Not what one would expect in a hotel room. Interesting canvases covered the bare white walls. There were ancient-looking masks, probably from Africa or New Guinea, and a large colorful tapestry encased in a Lucite box. Atop the irregularly shaped stone coffee table was a miniature model of a medieval castle formed entirely from glass. Next to that was an ultra-contemporary sculpture and a book on ethnic art.

Curious, Kelly looked about for photographs—for something that would identify the occupant. Was it a man? A woman? Or a family? Kelly quickly eliminated the latter. The place looked too orderly to be housing a family. The bar, she noticed, was heavily stocked with glasses that looked as though they had been chosen by a man. They were too large for a dainty hand to hold comfortably. The wineglasses were without gender, sparkling crystal, simply designed. This was probably a VIP suite, taken over by an Arab sheik or Texas oilman.

The bungalow appeared to be very large. In addition to the spacious living room, there was a dinette, a kitchen, and then two doorways off to the right. One of the doors was closed, and Kelly walked past it to the one that was open. She glanced inside, shocked at the sight of a king-size bed that was wrapped like an enormous birthday present.

Kelly just stood speechless.

White satin sheets enveloped the bed where yards of pale pink ribbon celebrated, crowning the passionate package with chaste and graceful tones that belied the wild and wanton sybaritism of the gift. Embroidered significantly across one of the pillows as elegant trim was the hot pink message FLING. Just above that was a plain white envelope that appeared small against the message. Kelly tore it open.

Our dearest Kelly,

We know there is only one thing
that you want for your birthday. . .
Love and Kisses,

There was no signature. It wasn't necessary.

Was this a joke? Whose place was this? A wealthy friend of Kirstin's? Or . . . Brandon Michaels'? Good God, would they have done such a thing? Kelly had told them his name and that he was staying at the Bel-Air Hotel. All they had to do was call.

Brandon Michaels watched Kelly from his surveillance post behind the door. He was amused at how long it had taken her to make her way into the bedroom.

"Happy birthday, Kelly," Brandon said, making his presence known.

She jumped. "You scared me. Oh, my God. I don't believe this." She laughed nervously.

Brandon smiled at her—the same easy smile that she remembered—and she laughed again, still in shock.

"I don't believe this," she repeated. "You're my birthday present?" Kelly looked into Brandon's eyes, trying to read his response to all this. What in the world was he thinking? "How was this arranged?" Kelly asked, feeling ridiculous. "Is this your place? Do you live here?"

"For about six months. Until my house is finished. I think I told you I was building."

"Yes, in the 'creative' canyon," she said awkwardly.

"Right."

Kelly laughed again. "You must think my friends and I are crazy."

Brandon nodded that he did. His eyes were sparkling and it was obvious that that sort of crazy appealed to him.

"I thought maybe it was a surprise party. When the doorman gave me the note . . ."

"We thought that would be what you'd think. Well, it is, sort of . . . although a bit more intimate."

"A bit." Kelly looked hard again at her fantasy man, standing so casually at her service. "They just called you?" she wanted to know. She wanted to know everything. What Kirstin and Ericka had said. What on earth had they told him? How very embarrassing.

"They said that you had never been to bed with anyone other than your husband and that you were dying to have an affair before you turned thirty-two."

"And what did you think about that?" Kelly asked, blushing intensely.

"That I would enjoy seducing you." Brandon tucked a wisp of red hair behind Kelly's ear, his finger lingering. Just his touch charged her with sensation, making her feel excited, nervous, guilty, and desirous all at once. Her heartbeat was rapid again. Now what? Would she actually go to bed with him? This was insanity.

He removed his hand and walked away from her into the living room. She followed, watching him make his way over to the bar.

"Who called you, Ericka or Kirstin?"

"Kirstin."

That was what Kelly would have guessed. "Did you remember who I was?"

"How many nearly naked redheads do you think I run into?"

What Kelly had wanted to hear was that of course he remembered her. That he hadn't been able to get her off his mind. That when Kirstin and Ericka had called him, he had jumped at the chance of seeing her again.

"What would you like to drink?" he asked, taking one of the too-large-for-small-hands glasses off the shelf and dropping a few ice cubes into it.

"What are you having?" she asked, relieved to be out of the bedroom, glad to be getting a drink. Perhaps she'd be able to think more clearly drunk. She certainly was not thinking clearly now. How could she . . . the chemistry between the two of them was driving her crazy.

"Rum and Coke."

"No champagne?" What was an affair without champagne?

"Would you like some?" Brandon asked sincerely, turning to look at her. "I do have some chilled. I was afraid that would make you uncomfortable. You know, the proverbial beverage of a seduction."

It was obvious from the expression on Brandon's face that he was trying to put Kelly at ease, and she appreciated his openness. She liked him a lot.

"Actually, I love champagne," Kelly said, a small smile forming on her lips.

Brandon twisted the top back onto the bottle of

rum he hadn't yet poured for himself and dumped out his ice cubes. "So do I," he said, opening the refrigerator and pulling out a bottle of Dom Perignon.

They were both silent as Brandon uncorked the bottle, loosening the cork upward with deft fingers so that it gave just the slightest jump when pulled soundlessly free. Kelly could see that the champagne was still very much alive as Brandon poured her a shimmering glassful.

"Well!" he exclaimed, his glass suspended in the air, positioned for a toast. "Happy birthday." He touched his glass to hers meaningfully, letting it linger for a long moment. Everything he did seemed to demonstrate absolute control. He had a sureness about himself that Kelly found alluring. Sexy. Masculine. He released his glass from hers and tasted the celebrated beverage. Kelly shyly followed suit.

"It's delicious," she said, savoring the luxurious liquid. Champagne at its costly finest. Dry but not too dry. Smooth. "Hmm . . . delicious," she reiterated, going for a second sip.

"As are you." Brandon regarded her openly.

"This is crazy, you know," Kelly said.

"What is?"

"My being here."

"Why?" Brandon walked over to his stereo set, selected an album, then turned it on. "I love this," he said, swaying his glass to accompany the music. "Chopin." Then he went over to the wheat-colored sofa and sat down, patting the cushion beside him for Kelly to join him. "Just pretend you're on a date," he advised.

93

"I don't date," Kelly said, moving closer to him, looking into his deep blue eyes, which registered fun and challenge. "I haven't been on a date since I was a teenager."

"It's like riding a bike. Sit down. The skills will all come back to you." Brandon took her hand and drew her gently down beside him. Their shoulders were touching, cashmere to silk. The night they had met he had also been wearing a cashmere sweater, a blue one that went with his eyes. In the fantasies that Kelly had entertained, the ones in which he was at least partially dressed, he had had on that blue cashmere sweater. Now, instead of blue, he was wearing a dusty pink one that somehow went well with his rugged tan complexion and broad shoulders. He probably had a whole drawer full of cashmere—all colors.

Kelly let her head rest on the pillow near Brandon's. His eyes were closed. He was listening to the Chopin. He smelled wonderful, she thought, astonished that she was actually sitting next to him, in his hotel room, all alone. She inhaled his clean musky scent. Her face was so close to his, she was dying to rub her cheek against his smoothly shaven one. To kiss him, tangled in passion for hours. His lips were full and seemed agile. Kelly realized that if she were to reach out and run her fingers through his soft and slightly wavy hair, which was graying at his temples and at the nape of his marvelous neck, as she was longing to do, she would be committing herself to what she was not yet committed to. *Oh, dear God, give me restraint.* I should get up now and leave. I must be crazy. I

94

can't go to bed with him. I should tell him that if I ever got up enough nerve to cheat on my husband, he would be the man I'd want. Kelly took a long, sorrowful gulp of champagne. Brandon would think she was an ass if she told him that. He was absolutely gorgeous, successful, probably brilliant. He could have any woman he wanted. What could Kelly say that wouldn't make her sound like an idiot? That wouldn't make him laugh out loud? As it was, what did he think of her? A silly, provincial housewife? No, if she were to leave, and of course she had no choice but to leave, she had to make her exit an attractive and memorable one. She had to leave him captivated by her somehow, intrigued.

Another taste of champagne for confidence. If he hadn't found her attractive, she reminded herself, he wouldn't have agreed to be her birthday present. *Courage, Kelly.*

"Relax," Brandon said, running his hand smoothly down her spine. He drained his glass, then poured them both another round.

Perhaps they could sit around and talk for a while, Kelly thought to herself, not wanting to leave. They could have a platonic affair. Champagne, romantic dialogue.

"Brandon . . . " Kelly began, not really sure what she was going to say. When Brandon opened his eyes and looked at her expectantly, her great ability for dialogue dissolved. *You're a whiz at small talk, dammit. Ask him about his art collection. Ask him about his work. You have loads of questions for him. Oh hell, ask him how he got so rich.* But every time Kelly devised a question, running it first through her head in silent rehearsal, she discarded it. Too out of the blue. Silly. Forced. Artificial sounding. Finally she settled on a question. "Have you always lived in L.A.?"

He looked amused. It was obvious that Kelly was groping for conversation. She tried to ignore his crooked smile as she pushed on. "Well?"

"No. A little Philly and a little Boston. Some New York. Paris. Rome. A lot of Switzerland."

Brandon tilted her chin up toward him.

"How did you happen to move around so much?" Kelly asked.

"Doesn't your husband tell you what a knockout you are? How fucking sexy you are? You're driving me crazy. Just shut up and close your beautiful eyes," he said, kissing her sweetly.

With that, Kelly finally shut up and let him kiss her. Closed into his tight embrace, she felt her willpower, soft as butter, melt away.

His touch was so different from Ron's. As were his kisses. His lips were fuller and more active. They demanded, they tasted, they played wildly, and she responded. She had forgotten how just a kiss could send chills through her this way—like electrical currents, charging her. There wasn't a single part of her anatomy that wasn't affected. It didn't matter that he had hardly any direct contact with her skin; just the roughness of his jeans through her thin silk suit had her ablaze. There were no safety zones, she decided, moving his hand instinctively away when it approached her breast, crushing the cool silk fabric against the heat of her skin. But wherever she moved those large wandering hands of his, they seemed to drive her still more crazy. She should have been marked "flammable"—ready to burst into flames of unquenchable fire. She could feel Brandon responding to her frustrated frenzy. When she finally pulled forcefully away from him, he stared at her surprised, both of them out of breath.

Kelly tensed, upset at how carried away she had gotten. She felt her chest, heavy, pumping up and down with agitated strain. What about all those countless hours she had spent years ago on couches, in cars, even half undressed on top of beds, kissing? Making out, as they had always called it. But it had never been like this before. Then Kelly had been young. Her sexuality had been something she could contain, if not always easily. But now it was different. She wanted to make love with Brandon at least as much as he wanted to make love with her. She didn't even quite know how it was that she was *able* to push him away.

In truth, Kelly had been wishing that Brandon would tear off her clothes, his own, and then make love to her. Fast, slow, hard, soft—she would have wanted to make love for hours because that was at least how long it would have taken for her to be satisfied. But something had made her pull away. The turbulent battle of Kelly's desire had lost out to the steel moral trap of her conscience. Was it fear that imprisoned her desires? Or was it guilt? This would have been perfect—a brief affair isolated from the reality of Kelly's actual life. Would she ever have

the chance again? No strings attached. No dangerous threatening emotions. Just lust. Lovely lust.

With great embarrassment, Kelly realized that her
hands were trembling as she picked up her empty
glass of champagne.

"I'm a virgin adulteress," she explained with a low,
restless laugh. "You'll have to go easy on me."

Brandon looked closely at the rumpled but still
beautiful redhead in front of him, pouring herself
another glass of champagne. Her hands were shaking so badly that he was sure she was going to spill
the champagne all over the place. He watched as an
unsteady stream sloshed into her glass. When she
was through pouring, he took the bottle from her,
his larger hand closing over her smaller one. What
was going on inside that lovely troubled head of
hers? He knew that he was attractive and aroused
women easily, but not like this. Kelly had so much
fire inside her that she could barely contain it. Fortunately lunch was on its way. He could hear the wheels
of the room service cart rolling noisily up to his
door. Now Kelly would be given a respite in which to
think. They'd have a calm, leisurely lunch. He had
ordered caviar, Irish smoked salmon, a cheese soufflé,
and a raspberry tart. Perfect foodstuffs, he thought,
for a married woman engaging in her first extramarital affair.

"I believe that's lunch," Brandon said, helping Kelly
to her feet. She rose awkwardly, fluffing out her hair
and adjusting her clothes. She wasn't the least bit
hungry, but she was grateful for the distraction of
food.

*   *   *

All this food, and Kelly could barely touch it. Caviar. Scrumptious caviar. Why couldn't she work up an appetite? Pale, thinly sliced Irish smoked salmon, delicately flavored. A golden crusted swell of cheese soufflé. It all looked and smelled so heavenly that Kelly longed to be hungry for something other than the handsome man who sat opposite her amusing her with dazzling tales of his past.

Even his birth had been novel. He had plunged precociously from his mother's womb without much notice, on his parents' private plane soaring high above the sea somewhere between Paris and London. It had been a beautiful day, and apparently Brandon had been eager to get out and play. Place of birth? The sky. A citizen of the wild blue yonder. Luckily it had been an easy delivery—a quick and surprising one. Brandon had emerged a couple of weeks early, hungry, and anxious to get on with it.

Brandon's grandfather had been a junk peddler. He had a cart with a horse and sold tin cups, old clothes, and just about whatever else anybody didn't want. Doing rather well, he decided to get rid of his old battered-looking cart and upgrade to a new one. He put his cart up for sale and found that the best offer he got was not from another junk peddler but instead from a sharp guy who owned a junkyard. That was how Brandon's grandfather entered the world of big business. He got himself into scrap metal, and it didn't take long before he became one of the largest scrap metal dealers in the world.

Then, one glorious day, his grandfather went out

to a shipwreck to buy a boat that he intended to scrap and sell. But when they took the boat out into dry dock, they discovered that the hole in its side wasn't that bad. It was possible that they could repair it and then ship their scrap metal to Europe instead of paying someone else to do it. After that they bought another boat. And then another. From big business to high finance. Before long, Brandon's grandfather owned one of the largest shipping lines in the world.

There were six heirs, Brandon's father and his five brothers. When the six sons joined the family business, Brandon's grandfather split the company into shares. Half the shares he kept for himself, and the other half he divided equally among his sons. When he died, he left his own remaining half to be divided equally among his male grandsons—none of whom had been born yet. His reason was that he did not want any sons-in-law coming into the family business and screwing things up. This provided great rivalry among the six sons as their wives tried desperately to produce male heirs for them. They all failed miserably, with the exception of Brandon's mother and father. Brandon, in turn, ended up with twenty-three female cousins.

Brandon's grandfather's zeal for work and high ambition skipped a generation. Brandon had inherited it, but his father had not. Not easily bound, Brandon's father departed from the family business at an early age. His brothers were only too happy to see him go, one less chef meddling with the broth. His parents then moved to Kentucky to breed horses, lost a small fortune, moved on to France to start a vineyard, and, after a couple of bad summers with failed crops, finally decided that working was costing them more money than playing. Happily they abandoned work and dedicated themselves to play.

Brandon was their firstborn, and since they had their heir, they didn't bother with any more children. Because they traveled so much, living mostly out of hotels across their global playground, Brandon was deposited in a Swiss boarding school as soon as he was old enough to be admitted.

"Poor baby," Kelly said, envisioning a miniature Brandon dressed in a navy-blue uniform and looking dejected.

"I didn't mind." Brandon paused to pour them more champagne.

They had been drinking heartily and Kelly felt delightfully high. "You sound like a chromosome blend of your father and your grandfather—you work hard *and* you play hard."

Brandon smiled sardonically. "I like to think I'm more like my grandfather," he said dryly. "My parents were crazy. Are still crazy. They were always either plastered or hung over. In love or in hate. You could hear them in their bedroom, one moment fucking their brains out, the next moment threatening to kill one another, or themselves. I was glad to get out."

"Why didn't you go into your grandfather's business?" Kelly asked.

"I was planning on it. Architecture was actually a hobby, an indulgence before I settled down into the business. And as you can imagine, *I* also did quite a bit of jetting about. As was, I suppose, my birthright." Brandon chuckled.

"Yes, air-born," Kelly teased back tipsily, enthralled by the image of Brandon's birth. "So you jetted about, finding yourself unstoppably inspired by the architectural masterpieces you visited."

"Correct. Paris. Germany . . ." Brandon got up and went over to the irregularly shaped stone coffee table, indicating the glass castle Kelly had noticed earlier. "I made this my first year at Harvard," he said. "I was fascinated with the construction of ancient castles. I did it in glass so that you could see through everything."

"It's wonderful." Kelly joined him to look at his creation. He showed her the secret passageways, the multitude of staircases, the dungeons. It looked like an ice castle, formed from sparkling glass tinted a pale blue. The glass he had sent for from Italy. It was hard to come by.

"I decided that by the time I turned twenty-four, I wanted to design and build a skyscraper. All concrete and glass and floating. I was intent on fulfilling my great fantasy before settling into the family business."

It seemed somehow incongruous to her. This great figure of a man, talking about his fantasies, phrasing it almost as she had phrased her own "by the time I turn . . . ," only on what a grand plane he fantasized. And at twenty-four . . . good lord. When Kelly was twenty-four, most of her energy had been focused on the noble goal of toilet-training the twins. "And did you?" she asked. "Design and build your sky-scraper?" She guessed he had.

"Of course." Brandon laughed. "What good are fantasies unfulfilled?" He gave her a wicked smile and kissed her lightly on the lips. "My contribution to the marvelous skyline of Manhattan," he continued.

"So what happened to all those boats?"

"We sold the company."

"That's kind of sad," Kelly said, disappointed. "Why couldn't your cousins take over?"

"Girls," he said disdainfully.

"Oh, c'mon."

"Don't get angry with *me*. It was my grandfather, remember?"

"So what's your hobby now? Besides women and wine?" Kelly sat down on the floor. "Where does play come in?" she wanted to know.

"With women and wine," he teased.

"And what about this art? Don't tell me it's furnished by the hotel."

"You like my collection? Part of my collection, actually. Most of it's in storage."

"Did you do any of these?"

Kelly's attention was drawn to the colorful embroidery that hung over the sofa. The whimsical design central in the lively hanging was a figure. Half man—half skyscraper. "Is that supposed to be you?" she asked.

Brandon explained how the embroidery had been made for him in the San Blas islands, by the Cuna Indians, a tribe of tiny people, all under five feet tall.

It was called a mola. One of his greatest hobbies, all kidding aside, was going on exotic adventures.

The masks he had, formed from wood, shells, and human hair, were souvenirs from Africa. The intricately carved Fushun figures—from the Fushun region of China. The long stick with what looked like a straw basket attached to it was a blowgun he had retrieved from New Guinea. There was a sterling silver and crystal vodka set he had smuggled in from Russia on a hunting expedition that he had made in the Verkhoyansk Mountains of Siberia. In his office hung the trophy head of the Asiatic bighorn that he had overwhelmed. It was an enormous sheep's head with thick curled horns.

The Cuna Indians, Africa, China, New Guinea, Siberia—Kelly wanted to climb into Brandon's pocket and go on all these exotic adventures with him.

With each exciting souvenir and the unusual stories behind it, Brandon filled Kelly with a complicated flood of responses, part sexual, part intellectual, all compelling. *She* wanted to be doing these things, making these discoveries. And she wanted to be doing them now. Not home rushing through car pools, squeezing in her work with Bob Kaufman, baking brownies, and falling asleep to Johnny Carson while Brandon was out traveling through ten different time zones on his way to Siberia. God, as she listened, how she wanted to go too. It had taken three suspenseful years of exhaustive Russian red tape before Brandon had managed to gain permission from the Russian government to go there. The pole of cold they call it, where temperatures drop as low as minus ninety degrees. She could see Brandon, wrapped in a thick fur-hooded parka, trudging through crusty snow, and warming himself with lusty shots of Stolichnaya from a silver flask to do battle against the biting cold. How heroic.

The images whizzed by. A reel of temptation playing in her mind—the sound track, Brandon's voice.

Kelly could see herself as well, wearing baggy khaki-colored pants, a loose-fitting shirt, and a hat. The photographer-adventurer.

Now they were about a hundred miles south of Panama, on the Caribbean side, in the San Blas Islands. The temperature was warm. The scene was paradise. Shimmering turquoise waters. Powdery white sand beaches. Brandon was back with the Cuna Indians. The brightly colored embroidery that they had made for him. And in her mind Kelly went along with him. Snapping photographs from his descriptions that were vivid enough for her to do so. His voice seemed to caress her. The Cuna Indians Brandon described were so unusual that Kelly wanted to shoot a thousand pictures, to submit to *Life* magazine. Or *National Geographic*.

Brandon stood up to put on a new record, this time choosing a Cole Porter selection. Then he went over to the bar and opened up another bottle of Dom Pérignon, pouring out two foaming glasses full.

Kelly was stretched out on the carpet, lying on her side watching him. Her shoes were kicked off and the fine silky fabric of her skirt was hiked up, revealing a fair amount of leg.

His work was building skyscrapers. His hobby was

105

exotic adventures. How could she not be completely swept off her feet by this man who seemed to be exactly the man she had spent years trying to convince herself didn't exist? Her desire was building to such a crescendo that all she could think of now was abandoning reason and diving into his outstretched passion.

Brandon handed Kelly a glass of champagne, then, without spilling a drop, scooped her up into his arms. His warm breath on her chest made her quiver as he carried her in his arms across the suite and into the bedroom.

"Happy birthday," he reminded her devilishly.

"Brandon, I can't." Her protest, she knew, was soft. As he kissed her sympathetically on the lips, she realized she was being abducted straight into the den of iniquity. Kelly started again to tell him that she really couldn't go through with this, but he didn't give her the chance. Instead he put her down, his strong body squeezing her up against the wall.

"To your re-deflowering," he teased, interlocking his glass with hers in a toast. He drank. Kelly did not. The hardest hard-on she had ever felt was pressing against her thigh. His kisses were thrilling her neck, her shoulder—and his tenacious grasp was definitely intent on wrecking her resolve.

No, no, no, she protested voicelessly as he undid her camisole top with his teeth. She moved away from him, over to the bed, then sat down carefully on the edge of the illicit nest, not wanting to chance crushing a wrinkle into it—not ready to submit. She felt the cool white satin beneath her. It was white ice, deceptively solid: a lake that she would melt with her desire and then fall into.

With the movement of Brandon joining her on the bed, maneuvering his hand critical inches from her thigh, Kelly lost all hope of reliable linear logic.

Barely breathing, she watched Brandon struggle out of his sweater, then toss it casually across the room. *Déjà vu.* Another fiery fragment of a fantasy. She actually recognized his tan, hairy, and well-built chest as he took off his shirt. It was exactly as she had imagined.

Tell him to stop taking off his clothes. It was her inner voice again, in command. How embarrassing if she waited until he had stripped off all his clothes before she told him that she was leaving. Was she leaving? For godsakes, Kelly, make up your mind. Fast. *For godsakes, Kelly, you can't stay.*

"Brandon." Kelly had found her voice. Thank goodness. Brandon was looking at her sympathetically again. He hadn't unbuckled his belt yet. He was moving over to undress Kelly first. He was helping her out of her little silk jacket—her top was already unfastened, and she quickly clutched it closed and squirmed away.

"I can't," she said.

He kissed her shoulder, still trying to slide off her jacket. Velvety kisses. Velvety skin. She pulled away more insistently. He didn't believe her.

"I loved today," she began. "It was a wonderful birthday present. But I just can't go through with this."

Brandon looked at her skeptically, then kissed her

107

hands, which were holding on to her top for dear life. When she moved her hands away from his lips, he kissed the soft mounds of skin that overflowed from her lacy bra.

"I'm a nonrefundable birthday gift . . . I told your friends that," he persisted, sliding his hand up her dress, into her panties, and rubbing the curve of her ass. Kelly felt the wetness between her legs and tried to jump up. He held her down gently.

"Kelly, nobody will ever know about this. The crime is in getting caught. And you won't. If you're uncomfortable about your friends, tell them you couldn't go through with it."

Kelly considered what Brandon was saying. Tempted. Tremendously tempted.

"Relax. Just relax," Brandon advised, keeping his hand in place and kneading her rear. Easy. Suave. Hushed. "Just relax," he purred again. "I'm going to make you feel so fine, you're going to forget all about everything else. I'm going to make you feel things you've never felt before."

Like what? Kelly wanted to know. Brandon's techniques were probably legendary. Suave, handsome, bachelor. She was curious—in how many other places had his peripatetic penis been? What was happening? Kelly felt panicked. None of these uneasy feelings or complications had ever muddled her fantasies before. She was a pistol in her fantasies. A red-hot siren. But what had been wild and sexy with her eyes closed and her sexual imagination spinning was feeling somehow cheap in the real-life setting of a hotel room.

Brandon was unhooking her bra, massaging her breasts, when she sprang to her feet, frustrated.

Dammit. Why couldn't she relax? Why couldn't she make love to him? She was furious with herself, embarrassed. As she began putting herself back together, she groped for an explanation. Brandon was looking at her, but she forced all of her visual concentration onto the process of hooking her bra and buttoning up her camisole.

Before she said anything, she looked over at the bed; they had all gone to such effort for her. Then she glanced down and saw the note. She wanted to reach down and retrieve it as a souvenir, but a souvenir of what?

"I'm really sorry, Brandon," Kelly said, picking up her purse and kissing Brandon one last time.

What was he thinking? Why didn't he say anything? Was he angry? She almost wished that they hadn't talked. That they had just climbed into bed together and made wonderfully steamy love. But that was a fantasy again, she thought angrily, upset, nervous, and exhausted. She felt as if her surprise had been ruined, and indeed it had been.

Shirtless, Brandon walked her out to the door of his bungalow. Neither of them said anything. Kelly wanted to, to either thank him or explain herself, but words would only have trapped her. They would have sounded hollow, reflecting the deep well of emotion that existed beneath it all, echoing her conflict in trite tones. *Forget it, Kelly.*

"Well, Red," Brandon said, his tone neutral, as he kissed her on the lips. "You've either got more willpower than anybody I've ever met . . . or something's definitely wrong with you."

Kelly looked at him, surprised.

Now his voice was light, cute, friendly. "If you ever change your mind, or decide to change your house . . ." He smiled at her, then closed the door.

Kelly thought about remodeling her willpower and wondered if she'd ever see Brandon Michaels again.

Brandon poured himself a fresh glass of champagne, then cut himself a slice of the raspberry tart that they had forgotten all about.

Biting into a generous forkful, he picked up the phone and dialed Angela Jamerson. Angela was always available for a no-notice quickie. She was a writer friend of his who, he knew, would be only too happy to steal away from her typewriter for a good screw. Research, she called it. She was an author of highly pornographic pulp fiction, and she said that Brandon inspired some of her best work. He doubted that that was true. Angela was like one of her characters—the multi-orgasm type, and exactly what Brandon needed right now before he would be able to concentrate on his work again.

"Hello, Angela . . ."

She knew his voice.

"Busy?"

She was working on a chapter that was causing her nothing but grief. Brandon was precisely the inspiration that would carry her through. She would be right over.

Brandon hung up the phone and went back to his raspberry tart, thinking of Kelly.

He was already so aroused that he decided he couldn't wait for Angela.

After a quick but satisfying orgasm, he picked up the phone again. This time he called the florist and ordered flowers to be sent to the photography studio where Kelly had said she worked. He was going to amuse himself with a little old-fashioned courting.

Chapter Seven

THEY HADN'T GIVEN HER A "FLING" FOR A BIRTHDAY PRESENT, they had given her a dilemma. Kelly couldn't get Brandon Michaels off her mind. Something inside her had snapped. Her obsession had been brought to the surface. Brandon's kiss had felt distinctly different from Ron's. It had evoked wildly disturbing sensations in her. She wanted to lie beside him. To lie naked in his arms. To feel his skin against her skin. To inhale his scent. She fantasized that she was at the Bel-Air Hotel, presenting herself to him. It was candid and erotic. He was tearing off her clothes. They were fucking. It was torrid. It was passion. And it was creating complete havoc in her mind.

It was as though Kelly's conscience had declared civil war—splitting off into two diametrically opposed factions, with one side archdefenders of the fort, her family, defending as though this one brief affair would shatter her life and mark her as an indecent person. A cheap woman, branded forever with the sin of adultery.

In direct crossfire against those thoughts that banded together in harsh reprimanding negatives was another coalition, a more reckless alliance of thoughts devoted fervently to the concept of going back to the Bel-Air Hotel to consummate the affair she longed to consummate.

The following morning, when Kelly arrived at the health club, she realized she was feeling apprehensive about seeing Kirstin and Ericka. She thought about why, as she walked down the narrow aisle of the locker room, her eyes scanning the already crowded room, bustling with women chatting, dressing, undressing, and stretching their limbs to warm up for the early-bird aerobics class. Was she embarrassed? Or was she afraid that her friends would be disappointed? Kelly was surprised that they weren't already there. She had imagined them rushing to hear how her birthday gift had played out.

Like a fabulous firecracker her gift had played out—a Roman candle bursting off into the air with the promise of a many-colored waterfall of fire and glow that suddenly fizzles and falls to the ground—a dud. But of course that was Kelly's fault. Kelly was the dud.

As she crammed her purse and tote into her locker and began pulling off her sweats, she wondered if they actually thought that she would go through with it. Would either of them have done it?

A voice sounded above the noise, announcing across the intercom system that class would begin in five minutes.

Kelly was sitting on the bench working leg warmers up over her tights when she saw Kirstin, wearing a white suede-cloth warm-up suit and making her way through the room like a blizzard of energy. Only Kirstin would own white suede sweats. Ericka followed close behind, dressed more appropriately in nondescript jogging clothes, lugging an armful of clothes to change into, and grinning expectantly.

"Well?" Kirstin asked, a demure dimple forming as she bent down to retie the bow on her hand-painted white ballet shoes. "How was he?" she prodded gaily.

Kelly felt a blush betray her.

"Okay, poker face," Ericka teased, opening the locker below Kelly's. "What's a vicarious thrill . . . *without* the vicarious thrill? Was he as good as he looked?"

Kelly grinned, feeling like a teenager—enjoying the suspense she was creating. Was this how young boys felt when they lied about their conquests? Kelly was tempted to lie. To smile in that satiated way and say foxily, "Thank you! Thank you for the best birthday present ever!" Her meaning would be clear. She would stretch her limbs like a contented cat and glow.

"It was a fabulous gift," Kelly heard herself saying tentatively, as she grasped her hair back into a ponytail for the exercise class. That was true. It had been a fabulous gift.

"You really did it?" Ericka's unmasked surprise came as a relief to Kelly. So they hadn't necessarily expected her to go through with it. "I don't believe it! Good for you," Ericka continued. "I thought for sure you'd chicken out. Kirstin, looks like I owe you a lunch."

Kirstin smiled radiantly. "Tomorrow . . . at the Bel-Air?" she asked. "Look, let's play hooky today. I don't feel like exercising. I want to hear all the dirty details."

Kelly was beginning to feel uncomfortable with her implied deception. *Enough playing, Kelly . . . own up. Dud.* She wanted to tell her friends what had really happened, but she couldn't find the right words. Her head seemed so crowded just then, a harried whirligig of thoughts. She was still wrestling with the prospect of going back to the Bel-Air Hotel. Would she call first? Or just pop in on him? She had rehearsed the scenario both ways.

"How does a chocolate croissant sound?" Ericka was asking.

"Infinitely better than exercise." Kirstin pulled Kelly's things out of the locker and handed them to her. "But not as good as a lover . . . eh, Kelly?" she teased.

"Well, to tell you the truth," Kelly began earnestly, stepping back into her sweat pants and pulling the drawstring closed. But she was interrupted by a telephone page for Ericka.

"Oh hell," Ericka said. "Hold the story, Kelly."

116

Well, that would be easy enough. Kelly watched Ericka run over to the phone. It was probably her office calling. What fun to be a powerful studio executive with your office hunting you down all the time for important questions. *Should we send the script to Redford? Spielberg called; he wants to know if you're still on for lunch.* Important questions like that.

"Okay, I have a question for you," Ericka said returning, seemingly incensed about something that had been said on the phone. "Could you become instantly infatuated with a man who was not at all good-looking if he was brilliant and dynamic? By infatuated I mean hot sexual attraction. Chemistry."

"Well, personally I'm into good bodies. . . ." Kelly laughed. Ericka was always trying out these hypotheses on them. Most likely she was having another argument with one of her writers or her boss.

"For me it's power," Kirstin said. "I don't really care what he looks like. I like high-energy men."

"And I go for psychotic-type intellectuals. I think Woody Allen is sexy," Ericka said. "Anyway, there's a terrific actor that the director and I want for the male lead in this film we're doing. His name is Joel Eagen. He's wonderful. But the head honcho at HBO, who has *casting* approval, is having a fit because he doesn't think Joel's 'sexy' enough. Now, our female character is not the kind of woman who is only going to fall for brawn. She's going to fall for the magnetism of the man."

"Who do they want?"

"Cameron Scott—according to HBO, he's going to be *hot*. He looks a little like Tom Selleck, so they don't care that he can't act. The guy at HBO says *that's* the kind of man that *all* women are attracted to. Now, *I'm* a woman and yet *he's* the authority on what attracts women. He's telling *me* how a woman would feel."

"But it's subjective," Kirstin said.

"Of course it is!"

"Why don't you find someone else to play the role?" Kelly asked. But then Ericka looked at her as if to say . . . there *is* nobody else.

"We sold the project to HBO based on a concept, then, *again* with their approval, we selected a writer. When the script was completed, they sent it back all marked up. *A woman wouldn't say this. A woman wouldn't feel this way. . . .*"

"Did a woman write the script?" Kelly asked. "Or a man?"

"A woman. But the guy at HBO thinks he knows more about women than either of us."

"Maybe the script was too honest for him," Kirstin observed.

"Personally, I think it was. But Julia, our writer on the project, thinks he just doesn't understand women. She says it's like Erica Jong wrote in *Fear of Flying*— for years she thought something was wrong with her because her orgasms didn't measure up to Lady Chatterley's, and then one day it occurred to her! Lady Chatterley was really a man—Lady Chatterley was D. H. Lawrence!"

"So," Kirstin said, amused. "HBO wants to define *your* lady's orgasms—isn't that what this really comes down to?"

118

*　　*　　*

The story of Kelly's birthday gift was still on hold as the three of them walked noisily into the newly opened, always jammed croissant shop located across the street from the health club. Only a year ago it had been a yogurt shop. But now croissants were the trend, and the ordinarily diet-conscious chic appeared to be overlooking the fact that they were loaded with butter and calories.

"This is the thirty-one flavors of flaked and puffed pastry," Kelly remarked, inhaling the seductive scent of the freshly baked bread, and noting the slick high-tech design of the croissant shop. The theme reminded her of graph paper: a series of thin perfect lines, horizontal and vertical, intersecting and forming squares that were too sleek and contemporary to be interpreted as checks. The graph design was everywhere—painted in slim red bars on the expansive glass wall that fronted the building, printed, also in red, on crisp white paper bags and paper cups, and even subtly grouted in between shiny white tiles that gleamed as the predominant surface of the room. The croissant shop's clientele appeared to be largely supplied by the health club; at least half the customers were in warm-up suits and leotard combinations, consuming calories that they would work off again to jazzercise or aerobics. They didn't appear to mind, and neither did Kelly as she looked up at the enormous blackboard posted near the sparkling new stainless-steel ovens. Listed on the blackboard were an awesome variety of croissants, ranging

119

from *croissant aux amandes et confiture* to *croissant aux épinards et champignons.*

Kelly ordered a chocolate croissant, Ericka lemon, and Kirstin blueberry. They all ordered café au lait, then brought their trays over to a small round table in the corner of the room that was just being vacated.

"I chickened out," Kelly admitted softly. Regret hung heavily over her, like a weighty winter coat.

"What?" Kirstin asked, as though not quite believing her.

Kelly nodded, her eyes suddenly filling with tears. She reached for the little glass ashtray in the center of the table and dragged it over to spin it around nervously.

"Well," Kirstin said sympathetically, "you learned something anyway."

Kelly nodded again. She supposed she had. Then she looked over at Ericka, who was sitting back in her red lacquered chair taking small bites of her lemon croissant. "Looks like Kirstin owes you a lunch, Ericka," Kelly said.

"What happened?" Ericka's heavily lashed dark eyes flashed concern.

"I just couldn't go through with it," Kelly said, wanting to explain to them how she was feeling. Ever since she had left the hotel her thoughts had been impossibly tangled. "I feel like such a jerk."

"But what happened?" Ericka insisted.

"I just couldn't do it," Kelly said, fiddling with the sugar dispenser and looking up to the ceiling, where an exposed metal air-conditioning system was painted fire-engine red.

"Did you want to?" Ericka asked thoughtfully.

"Of course I did," Kelly confided softly, uncomfortably aware of the close proximity of the other tables. "But there was just something inside me that wouldn't let me do this to Ron."

"It's called your conscience," Kirstin said, sipping at her café au lait, careful to keep the white foam from dissolving into the rest of the drink. Then she lifted her gaze to meet Kelly's. "What did you think when you saw him?"

"I was shocked."

"Good shocked or bad shocked?"

Kelly smiled, drawn into the memory. "Good shocked." She could still hear his voice, and her heartbeat sped up as though she were actually there with him again. "But scared to death! I was terrified."

"But you didn't just get up and leave, did you?" Ericka queried, adding some more Sweet 'n Low to her coffee.

"No. We had some champagne. We fooled around a little." She blushed. "Then we had lunch. We talked."

"So you really stayed quite a while. . . ." Ericka looked surprised, encouraged.

Kelly nodded halfheartedly. The details were just too damn embarrassing for her to talk about. Yet she felt obliged to do so. After all, *she* was the one who was always so open about sex, always talking about how she wanted a lover, and they had gone to such trouble for her she felt she should at least tell them about it. After a few moments of silence, Kelly continued, full of emotion and conflict. "The *reality* of being there with him was so entirely different

121

than any fantasy I've ever had," she confessed. "When I fantasize, it's with complete abandonment. It's free. Safe. I'm not hurting anyone. I'm not risking anything. I'm only playing. But with this—" Kelly exhaled deeply, looking intently at her friends. "This was so *real*. There I was with this *stranger* . . ." Kelly remembered the sensation of his hands on her skin—her skin that had been the exclusive territory of her husband. "I did *want* to do it, don't misunderstand. It was exciting. *He* was exciting. But at the same time it was like I was paralyzed. I kept thinking about Ron. I kept *seeing* him. I thought, this isn't fair at all. Ron doesn't deserve this. What's the *matter* with me?" Kelly locked her fingers together, then rested her chin thoughtfully on the surface she had created with her hands. She felt every muscle tighten with anxiety. "I felt so enormously guilty. I can't believe how *close* I came. . . ." Kelly shook her head and sighed again, trying to disrupt the image of them together in his bedroom, with his hand inside her panties and her camisole undone. It seemed to be imprinted indelibly on her mind along with so many other images. In retrospect, Kelly was actually amazed that she had escaped, and acutely relieved.

"I really feel terrible," Kirstin said guiltily, frowning and pushing away what was left of her croissant.

"Why?" Kelly stressed, bewildered by the ruffled expression on both Ericka's and Kirstin's faces. "Why should you feel terrible?"

"We just didn't think!" Ericka said, obviously galled with herself. "It seemed fun—outrageous—giving you a *fling* for a birthday present."

122

"But it *was*!" Kelly insisted.

"No! It was stupid," Kirstin corrected. "Totally irresponsible."

"Oh, c'mon, you two. Be fair. It's not as though you dreamed this up completely on your own." Kelly looked through her purse for their note she had saved. When she found it she slapped it onto the table in front of them, reciting its content. " 'Our dearest Kelly, we know there is only one thing that you want for your birthday. . . !' That was exactly right. Cologne would have been nice, but not nearly as nice as a lover!"

Ericka laughed through a frown.

"That's what I wanted," Kelly argued, bursting into tears, laughing and crying alternately. "Why am I crying? I'm not sad."

Ericka reached for Kelly's hand and squeezed it compassionately.

"I feel like some kind of pimp . . . supplying a guy for you like that," Kirstin said harshly.

"Wait a minute. Are you trying to take credit for the great *find* of Brandon Michaels? *I* found him," Kelly responded, wiping away tears from her eyes.

"But it was so wrong to interfere with your life like that." Kirstin seemed consumed with guilt. "Look at you."

"I'd have done this sooner or later, with or without you two."

"I don't think you would have," Kirstin contended. "I think you're a big talker. And I think we pushed you."

"No you didn't."

"Would you stop defending me for crissakes and let me apologize.'

"Does that mean I'm off the hook for a thank-you note?"

"Kelly, you're incorrigible!" Finally Kirstin smiled and Kelly felt rewarded.

"God, there's so much tension at this table, and I didn't even go through with it." Kelly slouched against her chair and took a deep breath, for the first time conscious of the New Wave music that pounded energetically through the speaker system, lending a pulse to the room. It was jumping music. And it made Kelly want to dance or bounce to aerobics. She had all this nervous energy that she suddenly needed to vent.

"Was he angry when you left?" Ericka asked curiously.

"Not at all."

"What'd he do?"

Kelly shrugged. "What could he do? I was so nervous. I'm sure he thought I was nuts."

"You've made me remember something amusing," Kirstin said, smiling with the recollection. "When I was about sixteen I had a boyfriend that I was dying to lose my virginity to. I wasn't in love with him, but I *hated* being a virgin. All my friends were having sex, and talking about it, and I felt very left out. . . ."

"Fast times at Stockholm High," Ericka remarked.

"Well, there wasn't anything else to do. The weather was always gray and damp. Anyway we were in bed, with no clothes on, it was really exciting, and then suddenly he said to me, 'Kirstin, are you sure you feel comfortable about this?' Well ... I was so upset. His question implied that I shouldn't feel comfortable. . . ."

Kelly couldn't picture Kirstin ever being that unsophisticated. She and Ericka laughed sympathetically.

"I felt so lousy afterward," Kirstin said. "Here I'd been dying to do it, and then couldn't because I had to feign virtue!"

"I thought things were so open in Sweden," Ericka said.

"Well, that doesn't make it any less scary."

"But you were a virgin," Kelly said, unconsoled by Kirstin's parallel plight. "I'm supposedly an adult."

"A married adult," Kirstin emphasized. "But I *do* remember how traumatic that was."

"So who'd you finally do it with?" Ericka asked.

"His best friend," Kirstin said. "He was less honorable."

Ericka laughed. "Kids are so mean."

"It was all right. I did it with him a year or so later," Kirstin said.

"I should have grown up in Sweden," Kelly said. Then, looking over at Kirstin and Ericka, she felt a wave of warmth and appreciation. "San Diego, where I grew up, just wasn't progressive enough. Or dreary enough," she continued. "Too many sunny days forcing us outside. *You* got to screw. We got to sail and water-ski."

"On that note," Ericka said, rising and looking at

her watch, "I'm going to have to run." She slung her purse over her shoulder. "I've got two tickets to a screening tonight, if either of you would like to go. The new Reichman film. I've already seen it. It's pretty good."

"Leonard hates his films. They're awfully heavy-handed."

"Ron hates anything that has subtitles."

Ericka laughed. "David too. In fact, I'll have to ask David about that—men not liking to see films with subtitles."

"Perhaps they're too lazy to read," Kirstin proposed, and Kelly followed behind her as they exited single file, weaving through aisles bulging with tables, chairs, and the constant flow of customers. Once out the door, Kelly gave each of her friends a tight squeeze.

"I'm sorry it didn't work out," Ericka said, with a conflicted expression.

"Me too," Kelly said.

"It's probably worse now, than before, but there's always your *next* birthday," Ericka teased.

Her next birthday! Was this obsession to go on and on, hovering over her life like a fog? Ericka was right, it wasn't this bad before. It wasn't this acute. It had been an amusing fantasy and now it wasn't amusing anymore. And the worst part of it was that it was like everything she did—she had quit before she got to the real soulful test of it. The commitment of it. It was why she had never really gone after a serious photography career. All those dreams of hers of being a world-famous photographer—flying across the continent documenting events and landscapes to appear on the covers of magazines. Brandon's Cuna Indians flashed through her mind. A snapshot she recalled that she hadn't even seen. It was that imagination of hers, tricking her into situations, tempting her, but then falling away because she lacked whatever it was that allowed others to go through with their dreams.

"Let's just say this was a dress rehearsal," Kelly said lightly. "Maybe I'll do better next time."

After leaving Kirstin and Ericka, Kelly hurried over to the photography studio to meet Bob Kaufman and gather up their props and camera gear. Today's assignment, Bob had said, was going to be a tough one to coordinate. For the shoot they had selected a rustic green setting in the Santa Monica Mountains for chiffon-clad beauties to pose elegantly among the trees.

"Have you a suitor. . . ?" Bob Kaufman teased as Kelly rushed in through the door of the photography studio. Bob was pointing to the most exquisite arrangement of exotic flowers. He bent down to sniff the floral design, delivering an exaggerated sigh at its scent. "The guy's got class," Bob allowed.

Kelly walked over to her unexpected gift, looking for the card. She was certain the flowers were not from Ron; Ron thought flowers were a waste of money. Were they from Brandon Michaels? The thought sizzled through her. No. Couldn't be. They had to be from Ron. Still, Kelly couldn't find a note.

"Well?" Bob pried.

"I hate to dash your glorious fantasies, but they're from my husband," Kelly emphasized, wishing that she could find out who *had* sent them. She didn't dare ask Bob about a delivery receipt or anything. She wasn't about to confirm his suspicions.

"Sure, Kelly. Just don't get caught," Bob was saying. "It was very smart of whomever to send them to you at work instead of your house. Your secret's safe with me." Bob winked and tapped her on the rear with the lens case he was holding.

"And your son called from school," he continued. "Forgot his poster board."

"Jason?"

Bob nodded.

Jason was always forgetting one thing or another, but this time Kelly was not going to run home, hunt for the poster board, and bring it to him at school. He would just have to do without it.

"How long is it going to take you to run it over to him?" Bob looked at his watch.

"I'm on strike. I'm not going this time."

"Good for you."

"But I do have to make one call before we leave." Kelly was dying to call either Kirstin or Ericka and tell them about the flowers.

"Don't make it too mushy," Bob advised. "Act cool. Act as though you're quite used to being pursued and sent flowers."

"I'm calling my girl friend," Kelly insisted. But Bob didn't believe her. He walked whistling out the door and into the other room, closing the door to extend her privacy.

With the door shut, Kelly picked up the phone to call Ericka. She was in a meeting. Then she tried Kirstin.

"Hello." Kirstin's voice was smooth and cheerful.

"Hi," Kelly said. Then she lowered her voice. "Someone just sent me flowers."

There was silence on the other end.

"Did you hear me?"

"Yes. Brandon?"

"I don't know. There's no card."

"How do you know they're not from Ron?"

"I don't."

Silence again. "Can't you find out?" Kirstin asked.

"I don't even know which florist they're from," Kelly said anxiously. "What would you do?"

"Well, it depends. Does Ron ordinarily send you flowers?"

"No."

"Never?"

"Never."

"Well, then I'd say they're probably from Brandon. If Ron does say anything . . . say you never got them. That's all."

"Hey, Kel—let's get a move on it!" Bob called out. "Say good-bye to lover boy."

"Also, I forgot to tell you," Kelly added quickly. "I guess I was a little distracted, but your proofs are ready from the party. I think they're fabulous."

"Great, when can I see them?"

"I thought I'd bring them by your house tomorrow morning after I drop the kids off for school. Around nine o'clock."

"What about the flowers?"

"I gotta run," Kelly said to Kirstin. "Coming!" she shouted to Bob, and zipped out the door, forgetting her gear. She rushed back in to get it. Those flowers were making her crazy.

Chapter Eight

KELLY ARRIVED PROMPTLY AT NINE O'CLOCK THE NEXT MORN-
ing to deliver her photos to Kirstin as promised. She
followed Kirstin up the long and winding staircase
and into her bedroom. Kirstin, who went in for
frivolity, fashion, and the theatrical, was dressed in a
gossamer-light white cotton peignoir set. The padded butterfly jacket was piped in blue satin. The
matching gown underneath was slit to the panty line
and edged in the same satin piping. The design,
Kelly thought, looked oriental: freeform flowers appliquéd in different colors of satin—cobalt blue,
magenta, and sea green. The effect on Kirstin was
stunning.

"Do you always look like this in the morning?"
Kelly asked, tossing the large packet of pictures onto

Kirstin's angular glass desk and looking about the expansive, exquisitely furnished room with its distinct atmosphere of languor.

Kirstin smiled easily. She did.

"You know what I looked like this morning?" Kelly said. "Tennis socks and a flannel nightshirt."

Kirstin looked aghast. "No wonder you complain about your sex life. That hardly sounds rapable."

"Ron keeps our room like an icebox," Kelly explained.

"So sneak over to the control unit and turn up the heat for godsakes."

"I do. All the time. But Ron sneaks back over and turns it down again. He claims that you sleep better in a cold room. He sleeps better. I turn up my electric blanket."

"Well, turn it up even higher, but don't go to bed with socks on, whatever you do."

Kelly thought that Kirstin would have still managed to look sexy in a flannel nightshirt and socks.

"So what happened with the flowers?" Kirstin asked.

"They must have been from Brandon. Ron never said anything."

Kirstin's eyebrow arched. "And there was no note?"

"No note."

"Any other admirers I don't know about?"

Kelly couldn't think of any.

"I wonder what his next move will be," Kirstin speculated. "If he calls, what will you say?"

"I'll say, 'Thanks for the flowers. Wanna screw?' "

"Sure you will."

Kelly opened up the envelope containing the photos she had taken documenting Kirstin's lavish party preparations and spread them out for Kirstin to see. "What do you think?" she asked.

"I think you should forget about your mystery-man architect, since I don't think you're of the cheating mold, and I think you should concentrate on your husband. I think you should go to bed without any socks on or quit complaining about your sex life." Kirstin looked through the pictures Kelly had taken, impressed.

"Why am I not of the cheating mold?" Kelly asked, disappointed. She had half hoped that Kirstin would say that she should call Brandon to say thank you.

Kirstin regarded her. "You're too guilty. You take it all too seriously. Too much to heart. Look, Kelly, for some people affairs are great. They thrive on them. I have friends whose marriages are better because they do have extramarital affairs. I think with them it alleviates some of the pressures of their expectations from their spouses; they're more satisfied and consequently they have very happy marriages. Of course, they're discreet, or feelings would get hurt and battered egos would climb into the picture. And I have other friends who have had that petite cheat. Which is what yours would have been. Maybe they do it once. Maybe they do it twice. Or maybe they stagger fifteen petite cheats over the course of several years."

"Where do I fit in?"

"You flunked your petite cheat."

"That's not fair. And what about you?"

"Me?" Kirstin's lavender eyes twinkled. There was

no way in the world that Kirstin would ever cheat on Leonard. She had worked too long and hard to get where she was to jeopardize all that now. Why put herself in such a vulnerable position? An affair was like chocolate cake—delicious, but gone so soon that it was hardly worth the penalty. Kirstin had the kind of unique willpower that actually quelled her desires. It was useful. "No burning desire to have a lover," she said to Kelly.

"Do you think Ericka's cut out for it?"

Kirstin considered Kelly's question. "Yes," she decided. "But I don't think she's interested. Her mistress is her career, as they say."

"What if it were with that old boyfriend of hers, that cute playwright?"

Kirstin smiled a broad gorgeous smile. "Ah . . . now that's a horse of a different color. But that's dangerous. That's love." Kirstin went back to the pictures. "Kelly, these are really good."

Kelly looked over to see which one in particular Kirstin was admiring.

"The Calendar section is doing a spread they'll need some pictures for," Kirstin said. "They only need a couple of shots, and they'll be black-and-white, but you've got yourself another assignment, if you'd like."

"That's great. Thanks. What's this one on?"

"I just organized a new playhouse. Performances for and by children."

"I should send my daughter over to you. Marlo's dying to be an actress."

"How old is she?"

"Twelve."

"We'll be putting the group together in about six weeks."

"Where's it going to be?"

"You can read about it. Let's talk about those socks instead."

"Would you lay off my socks," Kelly said, walking over to the carved gray stone fireplace to get a better look at a small bronze reclining figure atop the mantel. "I don't usually like sculpture, but this is beautiful."

"Henry Moore's easy to like," Kirstin said. "We've been collecting bronzes for years, but this is really one of my favorites."

Then Kelly noticed that there were quite a few bronzes in the room. A pair of intricately carved bronze horses flanked the fireplace. A lumpy-looking bronze sculpture stood tall on a Lucite pedestal. There was even an interesting-looking bronze light fixture, rounded and almost molded to the combed white plaster walls. Kelly thought the bedroom looked as though it had been designed around Kirstin's extensive art collection, and the effect, she thought, warranted a feature spot in _Architectural Digest_. She'd have to ask Kirstin if it had already been done.

This was a room you needed to take time in, Kelly thought. There were so many things to look at. On the marble-topped light oak night table three Baccarat obelisks in varying sizes caught Kelly's eye where a mosaic of varying colors flickered intensely off the hard-edged forms. Perhaps it was the high vaulted ceiling that kept the room from looking cluttered. The room was all open and white, with white fabric on the bed, stark white walls, and whitewashed wood. The only color came from the profusion of flowers everywhere, and the art seemed to match the flowers— beautiful works from the French Impressionist school. The overall effect was serene, with the feeling of unencumbered space—exactly the opposite of Kelly's own helter-skelter master suite. It didn't matter how much time Kelly spent straightening up her bedroom, there were always toys to trip over, one of her twin son's dirty tennis shoes in the middle of the floor where he forever kicked them off, and stacks of things to read by her bed—books, magazines, mail order catalogs. Kelly couldn't believe that Kirstin had found a *place* for everything. And even if Kelly's room *were* neat, which it never would be entirely, their furniture was a discordant mix-and-match arrangement—some dating back to when she and Ron first got married. End tables donated by Ron's grandmother . . .

A knock at the door interrupted Kelly's thoughts. It was Matty delivering coffee and dainty little Danishes.

Kelly helped herself to a cup of steaming coffee and tried three different kinds of Danish. "I could get used to this kind of life," she said, looking over at Kirstin. "But you look comfortable here. I'd look awkward. You look like you were born to this."

"No, I just got used to it very fast," Kirstin said. "I was born on a farm, actually, the eldest daughter of a very large, very poor Swedish family. My mother worked from morning to night until the day she

136

died. She drove our tractor. Worked in the fields. My father drank. It was hell."

Kelly took this information in with some surprise. She couldn't picture Kirstin poor.

"Did you work on the farm?"

"We all had to work on the farm. I hated it. Then I got a job at one of the local movie theaters. It was great. That's how I learned to speak English."

"From subtitles?"

"Some subtitles. Some dubbed. My accent was all screwy—from Hayley Mills to Audrey Hepburn to John Wayne. . . ."

Kelly laughed—Kirstin learning English from John Wayne? "How old were you when you came to the United States?"

"Well, I always had this vision of coming here," Kirstin began, her past stirred up in her mind. "I was twenty-two when I left Sweden and came to L.A." Kirstin began looking through the photographs again—without really looking. This was an uncomfortable topic for her and she wanted to veer away from it. "They're going to use about six or seven shots," she said, holding up one of the pictures Kelly had taken. "One they'll blow up to a full page, the rest will be smaller, points-of-interest shots."

"There's one of your kitchen that might be good for the blowup." Kelly got up and walked over to the desk. "How'd you finally leave Sweden?" she asked, while trying to locate the particular photograph.

"I saved up enough money and then moved." Kirstin had just leaped over the vast quicksand stretch of her past with relative ease. That muddy ground

137

she had skipped over, if touched, could engulf her. By day it was a secret. By night it was a ghost. The story of how she had come to the United States was one that not even Leonard knew. She had wanted to tell him everything. It would have been such a relief, but she had been afraid, certain that he wouldn't marry her if he knew. . . . He was too prominent a figure in the community and she wasn't driven to test him. So Kirstin maintained the same consistent story she had used from the day she had entered this country, one that protected both her and her two children from the past.

"Did you come over alone?"

"No. I had two children. . . ."

"Two children?" Kelly looked astonished. "I didn't know you had kids."

"Well, we're kind of estranged from one another." Kelly still looked baffled, so Kirstin went on to explain. All of this was true, but she still found herself choosing her words. "When I left Sweden, they were babies."

"Did you leave your husband?"

"No," Kirstin said sadly, remembering with sharp clarity the call she had received. "No, he died in a car accident." They had asked her to come over to the hospital to identify her husband. Routine. She had prayed it wasn't him. She had denied it so fervently in her heart that she had been sure that through sheer concentration and will she would get to the hospital and find out there had been a mistake. And then when they'd pulled the coarse gray blanket off his face, and it had been him, she had been *sure* that he would open his eyes. That he couldn't be dead. She was still moist from having made love with him that morning. For all she knew there was a baby growing and forming inside her—his life—his seed— his love. And then they had covered him up again and her heart had lurched. She had felt it crushing, deep inside her. She was dying along with him. He was the only real family she had ever had. The accident had been a fluke. If her husband hadn't been a diabetic, they told her, he would have been fine. But he'd gone into insulin shock and died immediately.

"God, I'm sorry . . ." Kelly said, floundering. 'How old were your children?"

"They were just babies. Peter was eleven months, and Ingrid was almost two. About six weeks later I found out I was pregnant. But I miscarried."

"How awful for you."

"I didn't handle it well at all."

"How'd you meet Leonard?" Kelly asked.

"I was working at Rusers. On Rodeo, where Van Cleef and Arpels is now. I wanted a new, rich life, and it seemed that an exclusive Rodeo Drive jewelry boutique might be just the place to find a husband. I was right. Leonard came in to pick out a gift for a girl friend and I helped him."

"I'll bet you did." Kelly grinned.

"He was so funny. He was so insecure about his taste in jewelry—although I could tell that was the *only* thing he was insecure about. We must have looked at fifty different items. We spent so much time together, he left for lunch, then came back again, and we started flirting with one another."

"So much for the girl friend."

"I thought he must have been pretty serious about her to be buying her such an expensive gift. I was hoping she was already married. All these crazy things ran through my head. I had this *feeling* about Leonard. Anyway," Kirstin continued after a brief pause, "after lunch he spent another couple of hours at the store."

"He was stalling."

"I showed him another three hundred pairs of earrings, then finally he asked me which piece *I* liked best. 'Well, if it were for me,' I said, flirting at this point so outrageously that I was getting looks from my manager, 'I'd love this pair.' Each earring curved into a delicate vine of marquise emeralds, interspersed with diamonds. They were smashing."

"So . . . he bought them for you . . . ?" Kelly asked. And Kirstin laughed, remembering.

"He wrote out a check, had them gift-wrapped . . ."

"Did you *know* they were for you or did you think they might be for the girl friend?"

"I knew. Of course, I was thrilled out of my mind when I received them the next day."

"What happened to the girl friend?"

"He never really told me. I'm sure there were *lots* of girl friends, which was why I had to work so hard."

"What'd you do?"

"I tried my best to be different from what I'd guessed Leonard's other girl friends were like. I had to stand out. Had to dazzle his friends. You know how men are."

Kelly rolled her bright green eyes.

"I remember going to dinner with two of Leonard's friends. I did a lot of research beforehand. One of them owned a football team. The other one was in oil. Leonard, of course, is in real estate. Their common denominator was local politics. I had five days' notice to prepare and spent every waking hour when I wasn't working reading. I read everything I could get my hands on about football, everything about real estate. Everything about oil. And everything about local politics. I had made up my mind that, instead of being an underpaid shopgirl, I was going to be rich and work as an overpaid wife!"

Kirstin noticed Kelly glance down at the twelve-carat emerald-shape diamond that dominated her slender hand.

"From Rusers?" Kelly asked, indicating the ring.

Kirstin fluttered her ring finger and nodded.

"I don't understand, Kirstin. You're bright. You're capable. If you'd have concentrated all that energy and strategy into a career, by now you could be head of your own empire. You could buy yourself anything you wanted without having to perform constantly." Kelly picked up a *Forbes* from out of the magazine rack. The subscription label had Kirstin's name on it. "Do you really read this?"

"Absolutely. What issue are you holding? Is it the latest?"

Kelly looked for the date. "Yes it is."

141

"Okay, you want me to repeat the content of the 'Computers Versus Aliens' article?"

"You memorized it?"

"Let's just say I have an odd retention capacity. And that I make it a point of utilizing that capacity to keep myself interesting for Leonard. A task which I enjoy. Listen, I've worked hard my whole life. There's nothing glamorous or appealing to me about working or a career. I don't have the need to prove anything. Besides, I love Leonard, and if 'performing' for him, as you put it, assures me of keeping him, then I'll do it for as long as I can."

"Sounds like a full-time job."

"Ahh," Kirstin pointed out, "but a well-paid one."

That's true, Kelly thought, as she watched Kirstin walk gracefully over to the silver coffeepot and pour herself a fresh cup. Kelly was wondering about Kirstin's children—how had they become "estranged" from her? But if Kirstin wanted to tell her she would. Kelly wouldn't ask.

"So what *will* you do if Brandon calls you?" Kirstin queried. "Will you see him again?"

Kelly wavered. Now it was *she* who was on the hot seat. Yes. No. Sizzle. In her mind, she had already had that conversation with Brandon a thousand times. "No," Kelly said finally. "I don't think it's a good idea."

Kirstin took a slow sip of her coffee, then looked up at Kelly as though she'd just been imbued with a wonderful idea.

"C'mere," she said.

Kelly followed Kirstin through a mirrored archway

and into her dressing area. Kirstin and Leonard each had their own bathroom. Leonard's floor, shower, and countertops were all made of a handsome lapis-lazuli-colored granite. Kirstin's floor, shower, Jacuzzi tub, and countertops were all done in richly streaked white polished marble. Reflected in the great expanse of mirror shone their finely chosen accessories— biscuit jars, china pieces, all collected in a harmonious festival of many-colored blues. Hyacinth blue, faded-blue-jeans blue, sapphire blue, robin's-egg blue, and bluebell blue—teamed together with snowy white. This was definitely Kelly's favorite room in Kirstin's house.

Across one full wall of Kirstin's enormous walk-in closet, creating a rainbow of luscious colors, hung her collection of lingerie.

Kirstin scanned the rack and pulled down a vivid pink satiny negligee set. "I just bought this," she said. "It's by the same designer as the one I have on. Natori. She's my favorite."

"It's gorgeous," Kelly said, fingering the appliquéd design on the back of the robe. It was a lavender bird flying into a vibrant aqua sun and a bright white cloud.

"Try it on!" Kirstin urged, pulling the robe off the hanger. "Consider it part two of your birthday gift."

"Kirstin, I can't take this."

"Why not, it hasn't been worn," Kirstin joked.

"That's not what I meant."

Ignoring her, Kirstin said, "Let's see if your husband doesn't rise out of his indifference, both literally and figuratively, to attack you."

Kelly began taking off her clothes, excited to try on her gift.

"If we want to be seduced, you know, we have to be seductive," Kirstin said, handing Kelly the slippery gown to pull over her head. "I'll bet you wouldn't go to bed with Brandon wearing flannel nightshirts and socks—you would *perform*," she said snidely.

Kelly conceded, laughing and maneuvering the gown down over her head. For Brandon she would have fresh, fragrant, just washed hair. She would have luxuriated in her favorite bath oil. She would have a manicure. A pedicure. All-new silky lingerie.

Once Kelly had smoothed the nightgown around her hips, she was disappointed to see that it looked awful on her. The cut wasn't right. She looked over at Kirstin, who by her expression didn't like it either. Kirstin's shoulders were broader than hers. Kirstin was longer-waisted. And Kirstin's breasts were about three sizes larger than Kelly's own, although well-shaped, small ones.

"Well. You tried," Kelly said, regretfully pulling up the spaghetti straps that were way too long.

"Can you wear Sanchez?" Kirstin asked.

"What's a Sanchez?"

"Next best thing to Natori. Only they never fit me right, I'm too busty, but there was a picture of this one in a Bonwit catalog and I had it sent out to me on that off chance that it might fit differently. I was sending it back because, of course, it didn't." Kirstin stooped down in her closet and pulled up a purple-flowered Bonwit Teller box. She opened it and pulled

144

out a shimmering vanilla-colored gown and matching kimono-type robe.

Kelly slipped it on. She smiled brightly when she saw that it was perfect, then changed her expression to a more demure one. "How's that?" she exclaimed, whirling around and loving the feeling of the cool fabric against her skin. That's why it was sexy. It *felt* sexy. She looked in the mirror again and admired the slinky lace and satin design that hugged her hips before flaring down to the ground. It resembled a long sleek Harlow slip, and Kelly felt like a million bucks as she wrapped the robe around herself. The robe flowed!

"Now say thank you and get the hell out of here or I'll be late for my goddamn meeting," Kirstin said. Then she laughed and asked *quickly* to see the kitchen photo Kelly had suggested for the full-page blowup.

Chapter Nine

ALL DAY LONG KELLY FOUND HERSELF THINKING ABOUT THE seduction she was planning for Ron. He would arrive home to find no kids, a ban on TV, candlelight, classical music, and Kelly dressed to kill in her sensuous new Sanchez gown. With amusement she remembered a scene from a movie, where the leading man walked into his living room, noticed background music, then noticed a sleek bare leg rising suggestively into view from the love seat where his mistress was concealed from his view. Kelly, of course, wouldn't go that far, but she would play with Ron. She would flirt with him, tease him, and challenge him. She would make a fuss over him, take off his shoes, offer him his slippers, loosen his tie, and get him a drink. She was going to make him feel like the most incredible man in the world. She wanted an evening charged with passion and quivering sensations. She wanted to feel with Ron what she had felt with Brandon.

At work Kelly wasn't able to concentrate. She was too busy trying to coordinate her vision of a sexy dinner menu. Brandon's luncheon menu had been sexy. There was something sexy about caviar. Maybe it was just extravagance that was sexy, like expensive satin and lace panties. Or then again, maybe it was Brandon. Kelly tried to expunge Brandon from her thoughts, to concentrate instead on her husband. The evening she was planning for him was beginning to take on symbolic significance. It would confirm that she didn't need to have an affair with anyone other than Ron. It would mean she was safe. But every time the phone rang, Kelly became even more jumpy than she already was, wondering if Brandon was calling her. She had moved the now wilting flowers Brandon had sent her into an area of the photography studio she seldom went into, for they were a reminder of what she was trying to blot out.

Kelly channeled her thoughts back to Ron's menu as she opened up a jug of developing solution and poured it into a plastic tub. Scotch salmon to start, she thought, sloshing the grayish liquid into the tub. A light salad of watercress, thinly sliced mushrooms, and pecans, tossed with a raspberry vinegar and walnut oil dressing. Then shrimp al pesto as a main course, she decided, examining a strip of negatives. Ron loved pesto sauce. As she decided on a negative and inserted it into the enlarger, she wondered about a praline soufflé for dessert. Then she changed her mind. She would be dessert. No point in being too full to make love. Kelly laughed and finished setting up the machine, adjusting the enlarging paper, setting the timer, then flicking the switch. She would measure out all the ingredients for the soufflé so that after they made love they could come downstairs into the kitchen and cook it together.

Kelly was in great spirits as she rushed about after work, marketing, finding places for her kids to spend the night, then depositing them, organizing a list for herself, and straightening up the house. With energetic efficiency, she swept up great piles of toys and stuffed them into the kids' toy cabinets. At the market she had splurged on bright bunches of flowers, greatly inspired by the flowers in Kirstin's house. The market where she did her shopping stocked a year-round selection of fresh flowers and potted plants that were as good as almost any florist's. Kelly unwrapped the blooms from their cellophane cones and laid them out on the counter to begin her flower arranging. The bluish purple hyacinths with their narrow channeled leaves and spikes of fragrant, bell-shaped flowers Kelly put into a round, small-mouthed bowl. She selected a handwoven rattan basket for the large showy clusters of pink, white, and blue hydrangeas. And for the dining room table she had bought white hybrid daffodils, iris, and ranunculus, which she balanced into four small hourglass-shaped vases. Delighted with the results, she moved on to attempt the culinary challenge of making a memorable dinner that would take only forty-five minutes to master. Thank goodness for *Bon Appétit's* "Too Busy to Cook" section.

Finally Kelly settled into a steaming hot bubble bath and closed her eyes, inhaling the fragrance of Chloé and luxuriating in the suds. She had set the table with wedding presents that she only rarely had occasion to use. With their not-to-be-put-into-the-dishwasher Minton china, their Lunt silver, Waterford crystal, and Val St. Lambert candlesticks, the table did look beautiful.

Kelly was in the process of tossing the salad when Ron walked in, surprised at the sparkling candlelight all over the house, the flowers, the classical music, and Kelly dressed in her newly acquired nightgown and peignoir. She couldn't wait for his reaction.

"What's going on?" he asked, puzzled, inhaling the aroma of the sauce Kelly had just made.

Kelly kissed him warmly, then took a bottle of champagne from the refrigerator and handed it to him.

"Where's everybody?" he asked, putting down his briefcase and reading the label on the champagne bottle.

Kelly waited for his eyes to meet hers again, then responded with a mysterious smile. "Dispensed with."

Ron looked at her dubiously. "You killed them like Medea? What's going on?"

"I love you," Kelly said.

"I love you too," he answered, even more perplexed. "What are we celebrating?"

"We're celebrating *us.* Marlo's at Lacy's. The twins are at your folks'."

"Oh." Ron loosened his tie and removed the lid of the skillet to see what Kelly had cooking inside.

"Shrimp al pesto," she said, pronouncing it as though she were describing some great sexual act she was going to perform on him.

"Smells good."

"Smells *great!*"

"I didn't think you knew how to use the stereo." Ron walked over to the stereo cabinet to inspect it.

"I decided that we've been living here for six or seven years, and that it was time I figured out how. Turns out it's pretty simple."

Ron was inspecting his expensive high-tech equipment to make sure Kelly hadn't destroyed anything. It was obvious from his tight expression that he wasn't pleased with her mechanical accomplishment.

"It's so stupid to be intimidated by things like that," Kelly continued, refusing to be intimidated by *Ron*. "Like all your electronic gadgetry." She brought two long-stemmed fluted glasses over to him. "Why don't you pour the champagne."

She saw him examining the label again and was ready for his next remark.

"Expensive." They said it together.

"But we're worth it, I decided," she said.

"You decided."

"That's right," she said amiably. "Since I now get a paycheck, I decided." Kelly had gone to great care in choosing the champagne—selecting one that was expensive enough to be indulgent, but still not as expensive as Dom Pérignon.

"That's fair," Ron conceded, opening the bottle.

151

As he did so, Kelly's thoughts regressed into a clear picture of Brandon Michaels opening the bottle of Dom Pérignon as casually as if he'd been opening Perrier or Diet Pepsi. No, she told herself, concentrate on Ron. But she couldn't help conjecturing about how different it would have been with Brandon. He would have told her how ravishing she looked, ravishing her as he told her. He would have chased after her as she finished cooking dinner, and then interrupted it all to make love on the floor. *Think of Ron, Kelly. Not Brandon*, she thought, guiltily accepting the glass Ron was holding out to her. She was looking into his eyes, trying to slow him down enough to be romanced.

Before Kelly could propose a toast, she saw that Ron was already drinking his champagne.

"It is good," he said, going for a second taste.

"How about a toast?" she asked.

"Oh, sorry." But he had nothing further to say. So he settled comfortably on a smile, clicked his glass to hers, took his second taste, and walked over to the TV set to turn on the news, and then over to turn off the stereo.

Kelly tried not to get upset. After all, after so many years of marriage, to suddenly introduce romance into their lives, well, she had to expect that Ron wouldn't know what to do. Besides, *she* could have been the one to come up with the poignant toast, if that's what she wanted. Kelly took another sip of her champagne, then walked over to the TV set. Snapped it off. Touched the button of the stereo set. Switched her classical music back on. All this movement Kelly executed with a careful grace. Elegantly. Sexily.

Ron started to protest, but Kelly silenced him, kneeling on the floor in front of him, wriggling off his shoes, beginning to massage his feet through wool Argyle socks.

"You saw an expensive outfit that you want . . ." Ron speculated, stroking Kelly's hair and enjoying the massage. Kelly wondered why he hadn't mentioned the new outfit she had on.

"No." She pressed her thumbs deep into his heel and smiled when he murmured pleasurably.

"Jewelry?"

"No."

"You talked to the travel agent . . . they've got some package to China you're going to try and sell me on."

"No. Although that does sound good." Kelly worked on his ankles and calves for a couple of moments, then jumped up and headed for the kitchen. She returned carrying a cheese board laid out with French and Italian cheeses, crackers, and two flowers.

"Is it something to do with the kids?" Ron prodded, getting up and walking toward the TV.

"No," Kelly said, intercepting him and pulling him back over to the couch. "Just relax," she said.

"Why can't I relax to the news?"

"Because I don't want you to."

"You're awfully bossy."

Kelly laughed. "Why? Because we're doing it my way tonight?" She picked up the champagne glass he had set down and placed it in his hand.

"Why didn't you buy some good Swiss Emmenthal?" he asked.

Kelly found it difficult to contain her frustration. But she was not going to fight over the cheese. She went to the refrigerator, removed a brick of Swiss cheese she had bought for cooking, and plunked it down in front of Ron.

"I just thought it would be fun to experiment," she said.

Ron was cutting into the pale brick, ignoring Kelly. If only her expectations hadn't been so pumped up.

"Please, Ron," she began, her voice strained and unnatural. "I really miss the fact that we have so little romance in our relationship. It *really* bothers me. So I'm *trying* to do something about it. It will be nice for you too. I promise. So could you please help me out a little bit?"

Kelly was surprised to realize how near tears she was. She was pulling everything out of perspective, she decided, and trying too hard. It wasn't fair to Ron. She was trying to use him to blot out Brandon, and because it wasn't working she was exploding. Stop it, she told herself. Ron now had his arms around her. He was holding her close.

"Are you pregnant? Is that what this is about?"

Why did he have to think this was "about" something—something extraordinary? Was their marriage so lacking, so mixed up, that they couldn't just have an intimate evening together? For Kelly it wasn't enough. She needed more. Why was Ron so damn satisfied?

154

"We should start paying more attention to each other," she said.

"*Are* you pregnant?"

"No."

"Well, stop being so mad at me, then. You've invented some kind of script for tonight and you're pissed because I'm not following the lines you wrote for me. Kelly, I don't know those lines. I never saw your fucking script before. This is all new."

"I'm sorry. You're right. Let's just have dinner."

Ron was quiet as they ate their salads, and Kelly blamed herself. She had made him uncomfortable. He was probably afraid he would say the wrong thing. She tried to come up with something light and conversational.

"So how was work today?" she asked.

"Fine."

"Has it picked up at all? Before, you said it was so slow."

"Picked up a little."

"Are you getting along any better with Sam Thorton?" Sam Thorton was one of the senior partners, and Ron had almost left the firm because of him.

"Not really."

"Do you talk to one another at all?"

"As little as possible."

"So, any new exciting cases you're working on?" Kelly was trying, but Ron's dead-end answers were making her feel an enormous strain. She decided to try harder, to pretend they were on a date, imagining that she barely knew him. She wanted to create

155

that breathless feeling, that high-pitched sense of discovery.

Kelly traced her finger provocatively along the low-cut neckline of Kirstin's gown. Her skin was baby smooth, and she wondered if he noticed. "There was a terrific article in *Forbes* about 'Computers Versus Aliens,' " she said, trying to make herself sound more interesting and regretting that she hadn't asked Kirstin what the article was about. "Did you happen to see it?"

"Since when are you reading *Forbes*?" Ron asked.

"Shouldn't I?" she teased. But it was ridiculous. When would she have time to read business magazines? At eleven o'clock at night, after a manic day, they put her to sleep.

"Yes, I think it's great. But I think you should read *Newsweek* first."

"I do read *Newsweek*."

"You mean you look at the pictures."

"Ron, that's not fair. I just have trouble retaining some of it. I guess I'm not interested enough in politics or the Middle East. I wish I were."

"Well, you should be interested."

"I know," Kelly said, agitated. "But I'm not." Some date this was turning out to be. "I read the words but they never penetrate." She was sorry that she had brought up the *Forbes* article, but that was how hard up she had been for something to say. "I don't have any frame of reference for any of that. In fact, I really hate it all. I hate wars and governmental power plays that have nothing to do with the people whatsoever, except for the criminal exploitation of them. It frustrates me so much that I figure why even bother with any of it. I don't have any control anyway."

"You should keep informed."

"Why? So I can say, 'Oh . . . no, I'm *against* the terrorizing going on in South America. *Against* the bombing in Lebanon. *Against* Mitterand's *fucking* up France!'" Kelly was unable to control her anger. She had tried to put the lid on every which way, as on a Tupperware container, only to have it continually pop off, anger seeping out with air.

Ron shrugged.

Kelly cleared the salad plates and served them each their shrimp al pesto.

"You sure made a lot of food," Ron said, instead of complimenting Kelly on how wonderful everything was.

Kelly stood up, furious. "What do I have to do? Drug you? Feed you aphrodisiacs? I can't do this alone. You're impossible!"

"All of a sudden *you* want to be romantic and I'm supposed to just blend right into your fantasy."

"That's right. I would have been thrilled . . . flattered, if this had been reversed."

"Maybe. Or maybe you'd have been too preoccupied with the kids, or distracted by something else."

"I got rid of the kids."

"I just don't *feel* romantic right now. You want me to fake it?"

"I fake it for you sometimes."

"Oh! Well that's good to know!"

"You didn't even notice my new negligee!"

"I did so. I was wondering how much it cost, but I was afraid to ask!"

"That figures." Kelly felt tears welling up.

"As long as you brought it up. How much?"

Kelly couldn't tell him that Kirstin had given it to her to improve their lackluster sex life. "None of your business," she cried.

"Oh, that from your paycheck too?"

"Yes!"

"Well, why does your paycheck go to frills for *you*, and my paycheck, to *bills* for *us*?"

"You may be right, Ron Nelson." Kelly was crying now. "But you're also *very* wrong. Practicality and logic are not the most important things in this world. Not *always* they're not—so just go to hell!" With that, Kelly threw her hand-embroidered linen napkin down on the table and ran up the stairs crying into her bedroom.

She slammed her door shut, wanting to scream out in rage. And panic shot through her. Admittedly what she had set up for Ron had been artificial. Although they loved each other, they simply didn't have romance in their relationship. Kirstin was wrong. It had nothing to do with Kelly's lack of effort or complacency. And even if it did, Kelly sensed that it was too late to do anything about it. I'm still young, she thought in heartfelt protest. I'm only thirty-two. I want to be wildly *in* love. I want passion. Dammit—I don't want that part of my life to be over.

The next morning Ron awoke before the clock radio went off. He looked over at Kelly, still sleeping soundly. Ordinarily they would not have gone to bed without at least trying to resolve their argument. But Kelly had been asleep by the time Ron came upstairs, and he had taken care not to awaken her.

Noiselessly Ron made his way into the adjoining bathroom, where he began his daily getting-ready-for-work routine. First the toilet. Then the shower. Shave. Blow-dry his hair.

As the water in the shower beat down on him, he thought guiltily about Kelly. She *had* gone to a lot of trouble to create a special evening for him. But it was plainly unfair of her to expect him to just fall right into step with her mood. He had had other things on his mind. He had needed to relax. She didn't understand the kind of pressure he was under at the office. Work had been a bitch that week, with his secretary supposedly out sick and a deal of one of his clients on the brink of falling through. His client had insinuated that it was Ron's fault for having taken too tough a stance on the negotiations, but Ron knew he had *had* to take such a tough stance. Had he not, the deal wouldn't have made any sense. Unfortunately, his client just wasn't sophisticated enough to understand it. In the end, Ron believed the deal would not be broken and his client would make a bundle. His reward, he thought bitterly, would be that his client would think he'd been unreasonable. He would never even appreciate the kind of deal Ron had made for him.

As Ron shut off the shower and rubbed a Sardoette into his hair-matted skin, he directed his thoughts back to Kelly. She would be up any moment and he wanted to be ready for their confrontation. If she had really wanted to create the smooth, intimate wife-mistress atmosphere she seemed to be trying to create, she should have done things differently. To begin with, she should have let him unwind by watching the news in peace. She was the one that liked champagne. Not him. He could have used a stiff bourbon. Then he would have been relaxed enough to have enjoyed the dinner she had gone to such trouble to make. And why did women think they needed expensive nightgowns in order to look sexy? Kelly had a great body. Why cover it up? The only reason he felt bad about it was because she *had* tried and because he could see that, as usual, her expectations had been so great. Kelly let herself in for these disappointments all the time by expecting too much from other people, Ron concluded, stepping out of the shower and securing the towel around his waist. He picked up a can of shaving cream, gave it a commanding shake, then squirted out a handful of thick white foam.

Suddenly noise infiltrated Kelly's deep dream state, and she awoke slowly, heavily, into consciousness as the radio talk show hosts bantered lightly back and forth, signaling to Kelly that it was time to get up.

She opened her eyes reluctantly and looked in the direction of the bathroom filled with the sound of Ron. The portable TV was on. Ron's blow dryer. And in the midst of all that, Kelly could hear the rustling of the newspaper. Ron was not only on

160

schedule this morning, she thought resentfully, but ahead of it.

The nightgown Kirstin had given her was twisted uncomfortably around her thighs and she yanked at it as she got out of bed, reaching for Ron's terry robe and wrapping herself in it. When she saw her reflection in the mirror, with the expensive vanilla satin gown hanging down below the worn terry-cloth robe, her depression deepened. She took it off and put on the matching Sanchez robe instead. Just last night the iciness of the fabric against her skin had felt glorious, rich and indulgent. Now it felt only icy, and she rubbed her hands together, trying to stimulate some warmth into her system. Failing to do so, she grabbed for Ron's robe once more, thinking the hell with this. Then she walked over to the thermostat and turned it up.

As she was doing so, Ron turned off the blow dryer and called out to her. "Kelly?"

Did he have hidden cameras planted around the room? she wondered. Why did he *always* catch her turning up the heat? After moving the little arrow a notch lower to where any complaint from him would be unwarranted, she answered stiffly, "Yes."

"You awake?"

Obviously she was awake, she thought, taking a deep breath and heading for the bathroom.

"C'mere," Ron said, moving toward her, his voice containing a concerted niceness. "I'm sorry about last night," he said. Kelly felt his freshly shaven cheek against her own and she weakened, relieved that he understood. "I love you," he said, hugging the tension out of her and smoothing her hair. His body felt warm and familiar. He had a little piece of Kleenex attached to his chin where he must have nicked himself shaving. "You're just too tough on me."

"I'm not tough on you."

"Yes you are," Ron said, breaking away from their embrace to get dressed. "I'm a great husband," he continued, taking a suit out of his closet and hunting busily for the right shirt and tie. "You just don't appreciate how terrific I am."

"I never said that you weren't a great husband," Kelly argued, unscrewing the cap from the toothpaste and squeezing a neat line onto her toothbrush.

"And I'm a *great* father."

"You're *a fabulous* father. . . ."

Kelly leaned over the sink, brushing her teeth and listening to Ron as he went on extolling his virtues to her, all solid points that reminded her of the checklist she had carried around in her head when she married him. It was what she hadn't thought to put on the list that bothered her now, as she rinsed her mouth and then inspected her teeth. They were pearly white from her just having been to the dentist.

"Are you trying to make me feel guilty?" she asked.

"I'm trying to put things in proper perspective for you—"

"That has *nothing* to do with what I was trying to do last night."

"I'm supportive of your career . . ."

"Sure. Because I don't let it interfere with your life. Ron, you're not *listening* to me!"

"I'm listening, Kelly. I just can't give you every-thing you want. Why don't you grow up?"

"What does that have to do with anything?" she asked, seething at his superior lawyerlike tone and slamming her dental equipment back into the drawer.

Ron shot her a patronizing glance, then moved over to the mirror, where he began winding his tie into place with irritating precision.

"I want to know what you mean by '*grow up*,'" Kelly demanded. "Are you implying that we're too *old*?"

"Look, Kelly, we've been married for fourteen years," Ron emphasized, as though that said it all.

"So that makes it okay for you to be a boring lover?" Kelly snapped at him angrily, turning on her bathwater and then with pointed extravagance pour-ing her most expensive bath oil into the tub. What the hell was "grown-up" anyway but a dull façade of control and acceptance that, in a "grown-up" like Ron, could become so thick that it could crush all joy and spontaneity.

"You think I'm a boring lover?" Ron asked, as though she'd slapped him.

Good, she had gotten to him. But now she felt sorry. "I think you're a *lazy* lover," she said.

Ron looked furious. "We did it in the pool the other night. Wasn't that creative enough for you?"

"Sure, after a monumental fight! What do I have to do? Storm out of the house in the middle of the night nearly naked to inspire you?"

"Give me a break, Kelly. You can't expect it to be like it was when we first met. We can't make it *new*."

"We can try to make it *seem* new," Kelly insisted.

"That's ridiculous." Ron impatiently looked at his watch and increased his pace. He scooped up some loose change from his night table and dropped it into his pocket. "What you're trying to set up, Kelly, is completely artificial."

"Why does being romantic have to be artificial!"

"This is real life, Kelly. Not a movie. Not one of those junky books you read—"

"I still say that doesn't give you license to take us for granted. And to be a lazy lover."

"What do you want me to do? Send you flowers?" he asked sarcastically.

"Some men do," Kelly said pointedly, thinking about Brandon for once without any guilt at all.

"You *know* how I feel about flowers."

"I'm not talking about flowers, I'm talking about—"

"I mean, it's *your* money too. You want to waste it on flowers—"

"I'm *not* talking about flowers."

"Give up some of your clothing budget and I'll send you flowers every week."

"Oh, shut up!" Kelly shouted inanely. She watched Ron take a concentrated deep breath, his fists clenched against his thighs.

Turning off the bathwater, Kelly pulled her gown up over her head and let it drop into a silky puddle on the floor. "It's just that I want our relationship to be . . ." She hesitated, catching her reflection in the mirror. "Am I still sexually exciting to you?"

"We've been married for fourteen years—"

164

"You said that already." Kelly felt her chest constrict. Damn him. And damn the institution of marriage.

"Am I still exciting to *you*?" he roared.

"Yes," Kelly lied, wishing with all her heart that he were, and sure that he could be if he would just make some effort.

"You still turn me on," Ron admitted.

Kelly worked the bar of soap up into a lather, then dressed her body with it.

"Kelly, I love you," Ron said. "I like it the way it *is*. I like having a relationship. And a family."

"And you don't want more than that sometimes?" she asked him, inserting her hand into the loofah mitt and scrubbing her legs.

"What do you want from me?" he pleaded.

"I want you to *want* me."

"I *do*, for chrissakes."

"Like a goddamn great-looking girl with big tits that you've just seen for the first time in an elevator?" she asked.

"Kelly . . . your fantasies are beginning to grate—"

"You're all *alone* in the elevator and she gives you a little half smile as she catches you staring at her tits—"

"I don't think that's how you want to be wanted, Kelly," Ron said coldly.

"What's the matter with raw sexuality?"

"Before, you were talking about romance."

"So now I'm talking about variety! Orgasms by candlelight!"

"Kelly, when you want to talk about this rationally, let me know." Ron turned his back on Kelly, whose eyes began to burn as they welled up with tears. She deserved that. She *wasn't* being rational.

"Look," Ron said. "I've got to go."

The door seemed to slam on Kelly's heart.

Chapter Ten

"DAMN HIM," KELLY SAID OUT LOUD. PUSHING HER SHOUL-
der against the thick glass entry door of the building
across from where she worked and shoving it open
with her weight. She was balancing a pair of Ron's
large black loafers that needed to be repaired in one
hand, along with her purse, and two large manilla
envelopes of proof sheets in the other. One of the
loafers fell from her grip and smacked down noisily
onto the terrazzo floor. "Damn," she cursed, kneeling to pick it up, and then also dropping one of the
envelopes. Proof sheets spilled out of the envelope
onto the floor and, with trembling hands, Kelly
pushed them back in. This was definitely not her
day. Definitely not. And for the third time that
morning, she burst into tears. First with Ron—scat-

tered tears spread out over the course of their argument. Then the dishes. Kelly had forgotten all about the dirty dishes from the previous night's failed seduction dinner and she had broken down at the sight of them scattered all over the dining room and the kitchen—as though the evening itself hadn't been insult enough. Fortified with rage, she had stripped off the new sweater dress that she had put on for a presentation she and Bob Kaufman were scheduled to make to a potential client that morning, and cleared up the dish-strewn disaster with surprising speed. Here she had thought she had been early as a perquisite of having no children to get ready for school, and now it was obvious she was going to be late. So much for the gift of time she had thought she had gained. It wasn't until she was all through that she had allowed herself to collapse on the sofa crying, an indulgence because of which she had incurred an additional fifteen-minute delay to fix her makeup and calm down.

Blinking away a fresh onslaught of tears, Kelly ducked into the ladies' room. She dropped her armful of items on the counter and took several deep breaths in an effort to contain herself. Then, looking in the mirror, she began separating her long lashes, which were clumped together with tears, grateful to see that this time her makeup hadn't smudged too badly. Thank goodness for waterproof mascara—with a minimal amount of dabbing she looked fine. Her green eyes were rimmed with turquoise that matched the electric color of her dress, and she was relieved to see that she looked quite good in spite of how she felt. It was the first time she had worn this outfit and she was cheered somewhat by its effect. The sales-clerk who'd sold her the dress had emphasized the need to look "put together" and in doing so had succeeded in selling Kelly an expensive lizard belt, the color of the cashmere, with an ivory and silver buckle, along with pounded silver earrings shaped like big buttons to match the belt, and a fun ivory ring. Luckily she already owned bone shoes and stockings, or the clerk might have lured her into buying those as well.

Kelly emerged from the ladies' room and resumed her before-work errands. She walked briskly into the copy center across the hall and placed Ron's shoes on the counter. There were two young guys operating what was called "the Miracle Machine" because it spat out copies and collated at a phenomenal speed, and they looked at Kelly with amusement.

"What'd you want?" the shorter one asked her, indicating Ron's shoes with his index finger. "Three copies of each?"

Suddenly embarrassed, Kelly scooped up Ron's shoes and headed out the door toward the shoe repair shop where she had originally *intended* to go.

"You want 'em collated?" the youth shouted after her, laughing.

This was definitely not her day.

"You're late," Bob Kaufman said in greeting Kelly at the door of the studio. She brushed past him and

169

moodily dropped the envelopes of proof sheets on his desk.

"Had to pick up these," she explained.

Bob's face brightened. "I didn't realize they were ready."

"They called yesterday."

Eagerly Bob opened the envelopes and reached for his proof loupe, a small cone-shaped magnifying tool.

"What time should we leave?" Kelly asked, looking at her watch. Their meeting was at eleven o'clock in Century City. Not a long drive from their own Sunset Boulevard location, but the way Kelly's luck was running, the traffic would most likely be bad.

"In fifteen minutes," Bob answered, absorbed in his viewing of the proofs. "These are great! I was worried about the lighting, but there's only a couple that aren't right. So far."

"Do you have any idea how many other photographers are up for this job?" Kelly asked nervously.

Bob shook his head no.

"D & S Construction Company, is that right?"

Bob shook his head yes.

"What would we be doing? Shooting pictures of their model homes?"

"For their brochures. It's not a big job. But it's easy. Fast. And helps pay your salary."

"Very funny," Kelly said, wondering if Pollock's Planned Communities, Kirstin's husband's company, could be a potential account and making a mental note to ask Kirstin about it. "If I were to bring in a job . . ." Kelly hesitated. "Would I get any sort of percentage?"

Bob looked up at her. "Ambitious," he observed.

She looked back at him. "Why not?"

"Artists aren't supposed to be so *business*-oriented."

"Spare me," she said, coming to stand close behind his chair and peer over his shoulder at the proofs. "So what kind of *incentive* program would you have for me?"

"Artistic reward. You can say you're responsible for having brought this . . . client in. That's a nice thing to have on your résumé."

"Oh, bullshit." Kelly laughed, beginning to feel better for the first time that day.

"I'm not interested in partners," Bob complained. "Who's this great contact anyway?"

"Twenty-five percent," she insisted, deciding to withhold the name of her source.

"Lunch at the Bistro."

"Bullshit."

"Dinner."

"Ha!"

The phone rang and Kelly answered it. She nearly fainted when she heard Brandon Michaels' voice on the other end of the line.

"Hi," she said a moment later, picking up the extension in the other room. She pressed the palm of her hand flat against her chest, trying to soothe the erratic flutter.

"How's my favorite redhead?" Brandon's voice was smooth. Butterscotch pudding with no lumps.

"You probably say that to *all* your favorite redheads," Kelly teased, flushed from his call. She picked an index card up from the desk and began to fan herself with it.

"Did you like the flowers?"

"There was no note. . . ."

"Well, I wanted to be discreet. . . ."

"You sound experienced."

"I am."

"I mean with married women." Kelly clenched her hand into a fist. Why did she say that? How stupid.

"Actually, I never go out with married women," Brandon said. "The threat of overwrought husbands scares me off. Overwrought husbands with shotguns."

"We have a shotgun. But no shells."

"Well, see that your husband doesn't get any."

Kelly smiled, nervous. There were a few beats of silence before Brandon spoke again.

"Do you like raspberry daiquiris?" he asked.

"Yes," Kelly answered tentatively. She realized that she was holding her breath and forced herself to begin again. Reset. Breathe.

"And piña coladas?"

Again Kelly said she did.

"I thought so."

"Why?"

"Well, I'm going to tip you off to a specialty of Freddie's. . . ."

Here it comes, Kelly thought. "Who's Freddie?"

"The bartender here."

"At the Bel-Air Hotel?" Kelly tried to suppress another smile. It didn't matter that he couldn't see, he'd sense it. And a smile meant yes—I'll meet you at the Bel-Air Hotel for a drink. *Frown, Kelly, frown.*

"How about four-thirty, five o'clock?"

"Brandon, I *can't.*"

"Freddie will be disappointed. I've told him all about you."

"Honestly. I'd love to. But I *really* can't." Kelly was worried that if he kept asking she'd say yes. She felt as though she were on some kind of ledge and on the other side lay the valley of sin. She was teetering, dangerously, ready to fall over, but fighting dearly for balance. And Brandon was the wind blowing great blasts of temptation at her. With his final gust, she found herself saying yes. As she fell over into the commitment of an appointment—four-thirty sharp at the patio bar of the Bel-Air Hotel—she braced her fall with qualifications. *Only drinks. No more.* He promised. But how could she hold nature to a promise?

The drive to the Bel-Air Hotel was such a beautiful and serene one, with sunlight bright and streaming through trees, that it should have relaxed Kelly, but it did not. Apprehensively she entered the grand wrought-iron gates that opened to the exclusive Bel-Air and surveyed the winding streets that stretched out majestically in front of her. She couldn't get the phone call she'd had with Ron off her mind. Damn him. Why did he have to be so stubborn? So unmovable. So dense. Didn't he sense that she was on the verge of cheating on him? All he would have had to do was show some slight sign of recognition or understanding of what she was going through. But he didn't. Their phone call had been a disaster. Sharp words exchanged. Cold stone walls. Ron just didn't understand. He probably never would. Simmering, Kelly had finally told Ron that she wouldn't be home until late. They had a night shoot to do, she explained. Courage inspired by pain. Then, in a tense voice, she went on. There was bockwurst in the refrigerator. Nate 'n' Al's onion rolls. Plenty of salad stuff. And though the kids wouldn't eat it, she had a jar of *Rotkohl,* the German red cabbage he liked, in the pantry. When he said *fine* and hung up, she felt thoroughly disconnected. Her nerves had snapped— loose, frayed wire within her.

After passing through a shadowed wooded area, Kelly came upon a sculpted metal sign shaped like a swan with an arrow pointing in the direction of the hotel. Well, here goes, she told herself, seeking composure, and continuing on past sprawling estates with imposing gates and tennis courts obscured by greenery. The backyards resembled golf courses. And in some cases the backyards *were* a golf course, or at least appeared that way, because they backed up to the Bel-Air Country Club. Rodeo Realty signs were sprinkled throughout—an indication that the houses were priced at over a million dollars, because Rodeo Realty handled only over-a-million-dollar houses.

With a mixture of relief and freshly jumbled consternation, Kelly veered her car into the driveway and turned it over to one of the parking attendants. Her hands were shaking as she accepted the parking ticket handed to her and she felt an uneasy flutter in her chest.

Just drinks, she told herself, crossing over the stone bridge and glad for the breeze that rustled through the dense junglelike atmosphere. The running water in the stream below and the whispery sounds of the waterfall seemed to melt in the air. Kelly stopped to listen, hoping to absorb the tranquillity. Birds chirped, first just faintly audible, then in great swells of melodious sound pierced by exotic calls. All this, laced with the sweet fragrance of tuberose, worked to soothe Kelly. She continued along the path, thinking about her last visit to the hotel. The surprise party. The mysterious note. And Brandon, coming upon her unexpectedly from behind the door. This hotel would forevermore conjure up visions of Brandon. Years later she would be able to come and visit him here, safe, without his ever knowing, because already his ghost was a clear and vivid presence. Then she thought, what if her daughter were to decide to be married here, under the lacy white iron gazebo. Kelly would stand as the mother of the bride, entranced with her blue-eyed apparition. She stepped up her pace, passing bright bursts of flowers. Red, white, and purple impatiens, magenta azaleas. And lots of red clay pots full of lipstick-red geraniums. Why was she thinking of Brandon in terms of the past—a ghost in the future? She was on her way to see him now.

She had to smile when she saw him, standing with his arms outstretched in greeting and a wicked grin lighting up his face.

"Don't you look gorgeous," he said, giving her a smooth kiss on the cheek and putting his hand on her waist as he appraised her. "Great belt," he said, studying the ivory and silver buckle with his fingertip as though trying to determine how to unfasten it. Just his touch brought back all the feelings she had been trying to repress, and she could tell by the way he was observing her that he sensed her response. This was how she had wanted to feel last night, with Ron.

"I'm glad you came," he said, his blue eyes intense.

"I am too," Kelly answered awkwardly, then slid into the chair beside his, grabbing on to the salmon cushions as she pulled herself up to the table. It was the first time she had seen Brandon not dressed in jeans, and she liked the way he looked in his pepper-and-salt blazer and dovegray slacks. Underneath he was wearing a stark white cotton shirt open casually at the neck.

"This is so beautiful," Kelly said, looking up at the bougainvillea, which grew up a wall, then cascaded over the area to form a lush and colorful awning. "I've never been here for drinks before." Lining the patio were pink planters containing masses of wild white daisies. The tables and chairs were a slate-green wrought iron with salmon-colored cushions, and from the middle of each glass-topped table rose a bamboo post with a natural canvas umbrella opened wide. They looked like the kind of umbrella one would see in an Italian marketplace.

"I love it here. I'm going to be almost sorry to

176

move," Brandon said, his gaze still fixed on Kelly. "Hotel living is so easy."

"When will your house be ready?"

"In another couple of months." Brandon smiled at her as though reading her thoughts. She was contemplating his face, trying to figure out what it was about him that made him so appealing to her—so magnetic. She decided it was his eyes. They were powerful eyes. Eyes that held you fast in a glance. Eyes that could make you blush. Eyes that could make you laugh. They promised paradise, then threatened to tickle her.

A waiter appeared with a bowl of nuts and offered to take their order. Kelly was relieved. She needed a drink.

"Tell Freddie to make us up two of his Jungle Zonkers," Brandon said and winked at Kelly.

"Jungle Zonkers?" Kelly repeated, amused.

"They're great." Brandon leaned in closer to her. "And you smell wonderful. Opium?"

Kelly smiled, surprised that the Yves Saint Laurent fragrance that she had poured into her bath that morning still lingered.

"Hmmm. My favorite."

Kelly looked at Brandon skeptically. "And what if I'd been wearing Chloé?"

"My other favorite."

"You have lots of favorites."

"That's true."

"So you actually expect me to drink something they dare to call a Jungle Zonker?"

177

"To tell you the truth, it's really just a Midori daiquiri."

"Which is?" Kelly asked.

"It's made from a Japanese melon liqueur—Midori. An ounce of that. An ounce of white rum. An ounce of sweet-and-sour mix. Blended with crushed ice. Daiquiris have become so common that Freddie wanted to give it a name with a little more punch. *New York* magazine just did an article on these concoctions. The fashionable firewaters of the Hamptons."

The waiter placed two frothy green drinks down in front of them.

"Pretty " Kelly brought the drink to her lips and ventured a taste.

"To the most tantalizing redhead I've ever met," Brandon said as he clicked his glass to Kelly's. She demurred before drinking to his toast, licking some froth off the rim of her glass and returning his level stare. Their eyes played like that for a while, neither of them smiling, passing messages back and forth. Intense. Desirous. Anxious and exacting. It was an exciting manner of courtship and Kelly felt her nipples become erect beneath her dress. She wasn't wearing a bra and the sensation of her bare breasts against the cashmere was now suddenly erotic. Finally she swirled her straw around in her glass and took a long, contemplative sip.

"So tell me about your photography work," Brandon said, tossing off a third of his drink.

"Well, today we landed a major real estate account," she answered, trying to focus on their conversation.

Brandon's knees were up against her own, and they sent a strain of excitement up her thighs. "Maybe you know them," she continued, as his foot grazed hers. "D & S Construction."

Brandon grinned. "Nine three four seven Avenue of the Stars. Twenty-third floor."

"That's exactly right!"

"I designed the building for them."

"You're kidding! What other buildings here have you designed?"

"One downtown—the Western Savings and Loan Building. And another one in Century City, the one that looks like a tall glass coil, near the Shubert Theater. . . ." Brandon took a pen from his pocket and drew a quick sketch on a napkin. Kelly watched his large hand in creative motion, a spiral of staccato movement. His fingers were long but thick. They were the color of burnt honey and matted with hair. She recognized the building immediately. She wanted to save the napkin.

"So you work for a commercial photographer?" Brandon asked her with keen interest.

Kelly nodded, taking another sip from her drink, which had already diminished to almost all froth and ice. "Bob Kaufman, the man I work for, is really diverse. One day it's ice cream sundaes for an ice cream chain. The next day it's naked ladies in emeralds for a jewelry ad. I like it a lot."

Brandon smiled at Kelly, amused. "There's a show you ought to see at the Otis Parsons Art Institute. I'm on the board there and I just went to the opening."

179

"Who's the artist?" Kelly interrupted.

"Issey Miyake."

"Who?"

"He's an avant-garde Japanese fashion designer. I've been collaborating with another Japanese artist on a design for a hotel in Tokyo. It's been an incredible experience. They have such grace in their designs. And they're so damn innovative."

The waiter replaced their emptied drinks with two fresh ones.

"There's a quote of Issey Miyake's in a new book I just got, dedicated to the show." Brandon's eyes sparkled with enthusiasm. "'I want my work to become a detonator that will set off the explosion of change.' There's a lot of ego in that, admittedly, but there's also a hell of a lot of passion."

Kelly looked up into Brandon's eyes again and what she saw there was unsettling to her. It was ungovernable passion, and she found it madly irresistible.

Leonard Pollock poured another splash of soda into his Crown Royal and, using his finger as a swizzle stick, gave the ice cubes a quick discreet spin. The man opposite him was discussing property acquisitions, but Leonard had tuned out because a few tables away from him sat a beautiful redhead who looked disturbingly like his wife's photography friend, Kelly Nelson, engaged in a very obvious and exceedingly intimate tête-à-tête. Leonard was certain it was she. And he was equally certain that the man she was with was *not* her husband but rather her

180

lover. The flirtation he was witnessing was too familiar a scene. They were literally head to head, shoulder to shoulder. And didn't they realize that the
people all around them could see the games their
knees were playing? Leonard thought it was appall-
ingly cheap the way Kelly Nelson encouraged her
dress to hike up, revealing her long lean legs and
then showing them off by rubbing her hand provocatively along one extravagantly exposed leg. All the
while they were laughing giddily, as though sharing
a great secret—the secret of lovers up to no good.

Leonard agreed with a strategy that the man he
was with was mulling over, then looked over at Kelly
Nelson again, wondering whether or not Kirstin knew
about Kelly's infidelity. If she did, what did she think
about it? Did she disapprove? Or did she take it
lightly—as he took it when his own friends discussed
their mistresses? Sure that his blood pressure was
rising, Leonard reached for his drink.

"Mainly, I want to get the property tied up,"
Leonard's guest was saying, extracting a paper-thin
calculator from his coat pocket and punching an
equation into it. Leonard's guest, Manuel Ruiz, represented some large money interests from Mexico,
where currency was being secretly siphoned out and
protected in American investments. Ruiz was to get
25 percent of the deal they were discussing as a
finder's fee and for raising five million of the down
payment. Leonard was to arrange for the rest.

"When will you get the green light from your
investors?" Leonard asked.

"I need four days." Manuel Ruiz slipped his calculator back into his pocket. "Have *your* lawyers begin the negotiations. Tell them ten million down, but it still works out to a fourteen percent cash on cash return if we have to go as high as twelve million."

Plucking three macadamia nuts out of the assorted-nuts dish, Leonard thought about what Ruiz was saying—he knew damn well that he was going to get stuck with coming up with the additional two million. It had been hard enough for Ruiz to raise the *five* million, and with the time pressure there was no way Ruiz could do it. Under the circumstances, he felt that Ruiz's finder's fee should be brought down accordingly. "That's another two million cash," he said. "If I have to come up with it, your percentage goes down"—Leonard stopped to figure the calculations in his head—"to twenty-two point five percent," he said shortly.

"That doesn't affect my percentage," Manuel Ruiz argued.

"It sure as hell does."

"Look," Ruiz said amiably. "I brought you the deal—"

"From one of *my* brokers."

"I was at the right place at the right time . . . what can I say."

Leonard straightened up angrily and drained his glass. He couldn't help but wonder if Manuel Ruiz hadn't paid off his broker in order to get the deal and *then* bring it to Leonard. Leonard had been doing business with this particular broker for years. It was just like Ruiz to snake his way in there. He looked over at Kelly again. She and her lover were deep in an impassioned dialogue and Leonard wondered what kind of relationship they had. It appeared that the lover was well off. He was signing his check with a thick Mont Blanc pen. It looked like he was wearing an expensive watch. And the sport coat he had on Leonard recognized as one he himself had almost bought. It had been priced at $850. Was Kelly his mistress? Had they been doing business together? That was one of the problems with women working. When women stayed home, did charity work, planned parties, and shopped they were reasonably insulated from the kind of sexual opportunities or temptations that a working woman encountered.

In need of another drink, Leonard hailed the waiter, thinking about how ridiculous people look when they're on the make.

"So do we drink to it?" Ruiz asked, following Leonard's gaze over to Kelly.

Leonard didn't respond. He was annoyed with his broker. He was annoyed with Ruiz. And he was especially annoyed with the conspicuous behavior of Kelly Nelson and her lover, their amorous glances, their subtle fondling of one another. It was making Leonard increasingly nervous about Kirstin. Maybe *all* of her friends fooled around. Maybe they thought nothing of it. According to statistics, women were now playing around just as much as men were.

"Tell you what, Leonard," Manuel Ruiz said, fingering his moustache. "If you can figure out a way to throw her into the deal, I'd agree to go down to *twenty* percent." Ruiz laughed and continued to stare along with Leonard as Kelly and her lover rose from their seats. "What a great ass. I'd even go as low as fifteen percent," Ruiz joked.

Leonard frowned and gulped down most of the Crown Royal the waiter had just set down in front of him. This time he didn't bother to dilute it with soda water.

The sun seemed to have suddenly slipped down toward the horizon and Kelly noticed that the garden patio had been magically transformed. The lanterns at all the tables were lit, though she didn't recall the waiter lighting theirs, and there were tiny white lights strung through the trees. An almost imperceptible evening chill had crept into the air, but it was checked with strategically placed outdoor heaters.

"Well," Brandon said caressingly, "do you want to walk around the grounds? Have dinner? Or do you want to make love?"

Kelly fell hard into his blue eyes. She felt sensually intoxicated under his spell, warm with the glow of alcohol and warm with the glow of him. They were standing very close—their noses were almost touching. She could feel his breathing. They were breathing together. A synchronized rhythm of sexual anticipation. If only he would put his arms around her and kiss her for reassurance.

"I want to make love with you." Brandon's voice was a tender command and Kelly felt dizzy, her mind and body in chaos, as she looked at him, his broad virile form outlined through his elegant clothes. She had every right to be nervous. Like a magnet, he drew her to him. It was completely out of control. He had stirred something in her that she had to keep after. She wanted him right then and he knew it. He was looking at her with clear hungry recognition.

Once inside Brandon's bungalow, Kelly felt as though they had just closed out the rest of the world. She saw that his suite looked different without daylight. The room was veiled in a melon-colored dimness as evening light filtered through the room, so that objects were visible yet quietly muted.

Finally, Kelly thought as Brandon drew her tenderly toward him. He pushed impatiently out of his sport coat, then held her tight again. She felt faint from pleasure as his arms wrapped around her, strong and well defined. Squeezing her. Embracing her. The sensation of his shirt warm from the heat of his body fused extravagantly through the thin cashmere of her dress, warming her breasts that were loose and appetent beneath it. It was a feeling she realized she had been longing for, and she pressed her chest against his, thinking how marvelous it would be skin against skin.

She was breathing unnaturally and she clasped her thighs together, feeling moist and uncontrollably aroused. Every nerve ending was taut and waiting, grateful for his touch that was in itself an aphrodisiac. As Brandon's hand began massaging her neck, moving easily inside her wraparound sweater-dress, Kelly felt it rest temptingly on her bare shoulder. Then he slid the V neck off her shoulder and began sucking her skin softly, then harder. With his other hand he was touching her chin and tilting it up toward him. She felt the pressure of his hardness against her as his mouth covered hers in a pentrating kiss. She felt him tasting her lips and a tortured thrill shot through her as he pressed more strongly against her, his erection growing harder. His tongue traced above her teeth, exploring beyond, and she caught it gently, guiding him. She felt him respond with new force and they grappled together, unfastening her belt so that it shimmied down over her hips and onto the floor, and unbuttoning his shirt because she needed to have her hands on his chest, all the while their lips intent on never parting.

Kelly's lips curved into a smile that only slightly altered their kiss as Brandon scooped her up in his arms and carried her toward his bedroom—her legs weak and her body anxious. As they moved like shadows across the darkened room, through the fizzing silence, Kelly clung to him. Her hands explored the fullness of his shoulders through his now wilting white cotton shirt, adventuring over the curves of his back.

Brandon eased her down gently onto the bed. His chest felt overpowering and her hands wanted to venture in every direction. His skin was hot. She felt transported as he caught her into his impassioned embrace and attacked her lips with his own. His kisses were wild, voracious, and Kelly found herself kissing him back with the same unbridled intensity, as though their lips were joined in a savage dance, with Kelly improvising to Brandon's lead.

It was nearly impossible for her to believe that she

was actually there with him—that this was all real. She opened her eyes and saw his face, tight against her own, with his eyes squeezed shut into a narrow line of dark lashes, his slightly stubbly beard, and his marvelous profile. The room around her was large and beige. It was Brandon's room and she inhaled the scent of him.

"You have such scrumptious skin," he murmured, moving his mouth over her shoulder down toward her breast, and pushing aside the soft cashmere of her dress. She willed him to continue and he did, licking pleasures over the soft curve of her skin. Then he went deeper to the hollow point between her breasts, at last treating her to the warmest delight, his tongue lifting below her breast, traveling, teasing and not quite tickling the smooth line leading down toward her waist. She felt herself falling deeper into the contours of the bed, barely conscious as he pulled off her panty hose. She could scarcely breathe when his kisses fashioned a belt across her waist.

He was driving her crazy and her skin felt on fire. Finally she drew away from him and sat up to pull her dress over her head, shaking her hair free and creating a slight breeze with it. As she did so, she pulled off her clip earrings and set them aside. His eyes scanned the length of her while in a slow smooth motion he brought her thick red hair all to one side, kissing the back of her neck.

His soft sounds of approval were like waves in the Pacific, sweeping over her and carrying her out into its infinite pleasure. She wanted this seduction to last and last. She wanted to be drowned in divine sensations. And then she wanted to make love. With the illicit thrill of a lover—not with her spouse.

Lying naked in each other's arms, they were a labyrinth of limbs entwined, active molten flesh. Kelly felt wet and ready as she rubbed her whole body luxuriously against Brandon's, her breasts passing across his chest and her nipples grazing his. Then he lifted her over onto her back, crushing her under his weight. She could see from his lips the state of desire he was in: they were quivering, restless. As he slid himself into her she felt his mouth on her neck and she pushed her hips up to meet his. God. The feeling of him inside her. Finally. She tightened all of her muscles around him, squeezing, trapping him. Then slowly she released, and he moaned, his mouth still on her face and throat and hair. She tightened again and he grasped her slightly swelling hips. She became a moving target. Their stomachs slapped together—hot—sweaty and eurythmic, until they were both out of control.

Kelly was lying with her eyes closed, listening to Brandon's breathing, and to the musical trickling of the fountain in the courtyard outside the room. She was on her side, curled into Brandon's snug embrace, experiencing the aftermath of their lovemaking.

Her body felt mellow, relaxed. Her thoughts were still out at sea, lolling loosely like a leaf that has been picked up from the shore by a wave, then rushed out on its crest and carried out into fluid blue space. She had the distinct feeling of motion. And the distinct feeling of depth beneath her. But for now, all she had to do was float, stay peaceful, and enjoy her buoyancy.

The bed bounced softly as Brandon got up and padded across the room. Kelly could hear him placing an album on his stereo, and she smiled peacefully when the music of Brahms swallowed her up. When he slid quietly into bed beside her she giggled as he blew on her toes. Then he switched on the bedside light and looked at her.

"You all right?" he asked. It was the first time they had spoken since they had begun to make love.

Kelly pulled the quilt up just over her breasts, then smiled at him. It was a tiny smile, one that conveyed satisfaction, but one that also hinted at how complicated all this was.

"Hungry?" he wanted to know, diving under the quilt and kissing the velvety plane of her stomach, then putting his ear to her belly as though listening closely for famished gurgles.

Kelly hesitated, wondering if she should go or stay. Just as she was about to reach for her watch, Brandon intercepted her. "How long can you stay?" he asked. "How long do I get to keep you here with me?" He kissed her delicately on the lips.

"I should go," Kelly said, distressed by the tension that had suddenly taken hold of her.

"You're not going to make me have dinner all alone, are you?"

Kelly laughed, tempted to stay. She had told Ron she would be working late. Coming home now would probably seem suspicious. It hadn't been dark long enough to complete a night shoot, and Ron would know that. They were probably just now cooking their dinner. Marlo would be making the salad. Ron would be barbecuing the bockwurst. And the twins would most likely be playing with the new video game while snacking on pretzels because Kelly wasn't there to tell them not to. The evening, Kelly realized, was now blocked out for her. She should simply enjoy it. Feel guilty later. Not now.

Brandon moved over to the telephone and dialed. "You don't feel like going out, do you?" he asked her. "I'll light a fire. Order some great food. . . ."

Kelly rolled over to the edge of the bed where Brandon was on the phone and put her arms loosely around his neck. "I guess that means I'm staying."

"Correct," he said, turning his head to kiss her. "Do you like pizza?"

"I love pizza."

"I'm calling Spago's. I'll have one of the bellmen run by there for us."

Kelly listened, surprised, as Brandon placed his order. Takeout was unheard of from the fashionable Hollywood restaurant, but since Brandon was such a regular customer, they reluctantly agreed to accommodate him. The chef there was renowned, Wolfgang Puck, formerly of the fashionable Ma Maison restaurant. This was innovative cuisine that catered to the stars.

Kelly wrapped herself in one of the hotel's white terry robes, adjusting the kimono-style drop shoulders and cinching the sash. Since the hotel supplied the robes in only one size, Kelly's hung down around her ankles, while Brandon's came to just below his knees. They stood with their arms around each other, laughing at their reflection in the mirrored closet that covered the width of one wall.

"We make a cute couple, don't we," Brandon said, leading Kelly out of the bedroom and into the living room, where he took a bottle of Poire Williams from his bar and poured out two glasses. Before closing up the bottle, he inhaled the fragrance. "This is sensual poetry," he said.

Kelly arched an eyebrow as she accepted the crystal liquid, clicking her glass to his. She took a sip of the unusual nectar, swirling it around in its squat goblet before swallowing. The burning sensation it created on the inside of her cheeks and then down her throat felt delicious. "Strong!" Kelly said, examining the bottle, which contained a large pear. "How do they get the pear inside?" she asked, looking at the small opening. It reminded her of those ship models, formed inside glass bottles. The same mystery, and one she had never figured out.

Brandon bent down beside the fireplace, crumpling up wads of newspaper and stuffing them in and around the logs. "The bottles are tied onto the tree when the pears are just beginning to form. They actually grow inside the bottle," he explained, striking a match and throwing it in. "I remember driving down a road in France and all over the place I saw trees with these bottles fixed to them. Really looked strange." Lighting up a couple more matches and encouraging the popping flames with the poker, Brandon finally backed away.

Kelly looked into the fire and thought of hell.

Would she go to hell for what she had just done? *Thou hast sinned.* She sat down beside Brandon on the floor in front of the fire. Then she stretched out onto her side, dipping her tongue in to lick the smooth surface of her brandy, afterward diving in for another taste. But what glorious sin, she thought, savoring the brandy's perfume.

Brandon moved over to her, stroking her hair.

She smiled, wanting to ask him why a rich, gorgeous bachelor like himself would bother to pursue her.

"What . . . ?" he asked, lifting her chin toward him and trying to draw out her thoughts.

"Nothing." She smiled again, looking over at the glass castle on his coffee table that she remembered from before, then looking up at the art on the walls.

"What do you want to say that you're not saying?"

"Am I that transparent?" she asked, noticing how dark his chest looked against his bright white robe.

"Very transparent," he said, nibbling her ear. "And you just did something that you've been wanting to do for a *very* long time. I'm sure your head's bursting with thoughts."

"That's true." Kelly went for another dip into her brandy. "It's funny. I've never been a private person before. I've always been totally open. Suddenly I have a secret."

"How does that make you feel?"

"I don't know yet," Kelly mused. "A little older. A little more complicated. A little guilty. But also somehow proud of myself." She looked at Brandon, needing to explain herself, hoping to get the answers

192

from his eyes. "I don't know *why* I feel proud of myself. I shouldn't. I should feel terrible."

"Maybe you feel proud of yourself because you did something you needed to do. You conquered a fear. A curiosity."

"But it was wrong."

"Who knows? Who *really* knows? There's another quote of Issey Miyake's in that book I told you about." Brandon stood up and went over to where he had a neat stack of large art books and returned with one, flipping through the pages as he sat down. His robe was open across one strong hairy thigh and Kelly felt herself becoming aroused again.

"Here it is. . . . 'One should always be curious,' " Brandon said, reading the words as though they were his own. " 'Not a passive curiosity but an aggressive curiosity that compels one to seek things out and ascertain them for oneself.' " Brandon put the book down on the coffee table. "You've just done that," he said, running his fingers lightly across her cheek.

"Making love with someone other than my husband—I'm not sure that's a noble enough curiosity."

"Noble. That's bullshit. It's *curiosity*. It's *real*. . . ."

"You could justify anything with that."

"I probabiy could," Brandon said, polishing off the rest of his brandy. "That's exactly how I justified robbing a bank last week. I was *very* curious," he teased, looking over at Kelly's neatly tied sash. He reached over for one end of it and pulled so that it came undone with a tiny tug.

"You're very good at that," Kelly observed, looking down to see exactly what had become exposed as a result of his maneuver.

"I couldn't resist," he said, obviously pleased with the sight of her. "I was *curious*."

"You're abusing that quote!" she scolded, laughing and clutching her robe closed.

"And *you're* obstructing my view!" Playfully Brandon tackled her onto the ground, yanking her robe so hard she thought it would tear.

"What a waste!" he exclaimed, sucking hungrily on her lips.

Kelly looked up at him questioningly.

"All this paradise for one man! I can't stand it," he growled and kissed her some more, running his tongue along her teeth. "You have perfect teeth, Kelly Nelson," he said. "You should do toothpaste commercials. They're just the right size. Straight, hard, and sexy."

Kelly laughed, then sighed as his warm breath traveled down to her breasts, his tongue flirting with her nipples before he took them into his mouth. It got so that she could no longer tolerate his teasing her with foreplay. She wanted to feel his nakedness above her again, his hardness inside her. Her hips, she realized, were moving to the turbulent rhythm of Brahms and she reached for him, conscious of the crackling sounds from the fireplace and the smell of burning wood. She was urging him to enter her, but he just kept thrilling her with his mouth, working in smooth circles on her skin, manipulating closer and closer to the point of destination—the very wet and pulsating prize between her thighs.

Finally he entered her, and they came together in a loud and powerful orgasm, completely out of breath.

Just a moment later the doorbell rang. "Oh, my God, the pizza. I forgot," Kelly said, still unable to catch her breath.

Brandon kissed her eyelids, then raised himself off her and got into his robe. Kelly reached for hers and slid around behind the couch, embarrassed.

As Brandon laid out their feast like a picnic in front of the fire, Kelly studied him. His hair was tousled and free. His beard was getting heavier. Like the sun settling down below the horizon, the shadow on Brandon's face marked the passage of time— precious time that was melting too quickly away. It all seemed so illusory to her anyway.

Spago's pizzas, Kelly agreed with Brandon, were unique. They were small individual rounds about nine inches in diameter and their toppings were different from any Kelly had ever seen. Brandon had ordered four different kinds so that she could taste them all. One was a duck sausage pizza, another was prosciutto and artichoke, the third shrimp and leek, and for the fourth selection he had chosen Spago's very special calzone, which was like a pizza pocket containing ham, cheese, and onion. In addition to the pizzas, Brandon had ordered a light salad of radicchio, escarole, arugola, and endive.

While everything tasted superb, Kelly found herself unable to do anything other than sample. She was too stimulated, and again as he talked about how he loved his work, she had the feeling of wanting to climb into Brandon's pocket and go along with him.

He was always traveling, working on projects in France, in Israel, in Japan. Soaking up knowledge and making interesting friends. How exciting to be married to someone like that.

"Have you ever been married?" Kelly asked him shyly.

"No," Brandon said as though marriage were a trap he had steered clear of.

"And you never wanted to?"

"When I was thirteen I wanted to get married. I was in love with my friend's mother. God, she was gorgeous."

Kelly looked at him curiously, drinking some more brandy.

"I used to send her flowers. Candy. I even bought her a bracelet once from Cartier."

"You're kidding. Did she keep it?"

"It was strange. She called me up. Told me to come over. Nobody was there that day. . . ."

"You must have been so nervous," Kelly said, thinking of her own children and trying to imagine Brandon as a young boy.

"I was." Brandon smiled a faraway smile. "Anyway, she seduced me. And afterward she handed me an envelope. I thought she was returning the bracelet. But she wasn't. She wanted to keep it as a memento. The envelope was filled with cash. She just didn't want me to pay for it. She said the gift was that I had given it to her."

Everything about Brandon's world was so overwhelmingly different from Kelly's. Her own life was so normal. It reminded her of a clock—a mechanism

196

that worked in an order designed so long ago, that changed with progress, but only to accommodate that which constituted efficiency. It had nothing to do with romance. And Brandon's had everything to do with romance.

"What happened to your seductress?" Kelly asked, stretching her legs.

"She died six months later. Nobody knew it at the time—she hadn't even told her husband—but she had cancer."

"I'm sorry," Kelly said. "That's awful."

Their mood changed after that. First Kelly showered. Then Brandon. They dressed in silence. It was all very strained for Kelly. Here they had just made love, twice, shared passion on that divine plateau of abandonment, and now she felt as though they were strangers. She was being modest with him again. Hiding behind terry-cloth towels. Hurrying to get her clothes back on.

Afterward they walked together, holding hands, through the moonlit grounds, crossing over bridges and saying little. They stopped every now and then in the hotel's botanical gardens to read the plaques illuminated by scattered spotlights. Specified were the genus and species of the many exotic plants and trees. The male fig tree, or *Ficus roxburghii*, was the most fascinating to Kelly. It was huge and gnarled, with inedible figs growing ominously all along the trunk. The huge leaves resembled Chinese parchment fans.

As they continued on, Brandon began to loosen up again. He put his arm around her and asked if she was cold. When she said she was, a little, he wrapped his jacket fondly over her shoulders. Then he plucked a gardenia free and buried his nose contentedly into the blossom. Afterward he tried to fix it in Kelly's hair. She kept catching it as it fell out. Finally they gave up and she had to hold it in her hand.

"I'd take you down to see the swans," Brandon said. "But for the first time in the history of the hotel a baby swan was born, and the ninety-pound mother swan is overdoing it with protective maternal instinct. She knocked someone down the other day because he got too close."

Kelly couldn't imagine violence from such a graceful-looking creature.

"Are you kidding?" Brandon said. "Their wings have a lot of force. She could knock me over with one bat of her wings if she thought I'd hurt her baby."

"You're not afraid of tigers," Kelly said, "but you're afraid of a swan." She laughed and kissed him on the cheek. She was wondering if she would ever see him again.

"That's right," he said. "Now you know my vulnerability." He pressed up against her.

"I'd better go," she said.

"I want you to stay." Brandon pulled her hair to one side and began kissing her neck.

"I can't," Kelly said, arching her neck into his kisses and wishing that she could. Wishing that she were free to spend the night with him, without responsibility. She imagined the two of them sleeping late, waking up to make love drowsily, falling back asleep, making love again. They would eat breakfast out on the private patio, dressed snugly in their matching terry bathrobes and listening to a cheery rendition of Gilbert and Sullivan.

"When can I see you again?" Brandon asked.

"You can't," she said sadly.

"One more time. I know you want to see me again."

She did want to see him again. But she was afraid it would not be just one more time.

"Then come back to my room with me and let's make love one final time." Brandon began steering her in the direction of his room.

Kelly looked at her watch, torn. It was already ten o'clock. "I have to go," she insisted.

"Then you'll see me again."

"I can't."

"Do you want to?"

Kelly looked closely at him. His eyes looked so lively, she was sure he had no idea what she was going through.

"Why?" she asked.

"I want to be with you again," he said levelly.

"Why?" It was the question that she had wanted to ask him before. There had to be so many women. Why her? Then she guessed that it was just chemistry. It was the way he was touching her. The way he was responding to her. Their bodies seemed locked together. There was a power that wouldn't let them part. They were kissing again, and she loved the way he kissed. His coat fell off her shoulders and onto the ground as he pressed her up against a wall and

she could feel his erection against her thigh. She wished they could make love right there. This was insane. He was making her crazy again. Dammit. Why couldn't she feel this way with Ron? Why couldn't she feel the crazy urgency with him? Damn this desire. Their rhythm was mounting and Kelly put her hand in between his legs, massaging the fabric there, moving back toward his rear. She couldn't stop, she was so close to having an orgasm. What a mad way to have an orgasm. And what about Brandon? But she couldn't think anymore. Her excitement erupted in climax and she sank back amazed against the wall, feeling the delirious aftershocks of orgasm. Feeling sweaty. Hot and cold.

"My God," Kelly said when she could speak, embarrassed.

"I wish you didn't have to go," Brandon said, his breath heavy against her neck.

She noticed that he still had an erection.

"I'm sorry," she said, her cheeks burning with color. She felt she now owed him one and figured that this was exactly how he wanted her to feel.

Brandon didn't say anything. He touched her hair, then bent down and picked up his jacket.

"When will I see you again?" he asked.

Kelly's heartbeat was racing. "You *are* tenacious," she said with a little laugh.

He smiled. "Look at your schedule. I'll call you tomorrow at your office."

"Brandon . . ."

"Sleep on it."

Chapter Eleven

BY THE TIME LEONARD POLLOCK PULLED HIS ROLLS-ROYCE into his driveway, he had thoroughly convinced himself that Kirstin had been unfaithful to him. She had been tried and convicted on the grounds that her girl friend Kelly Nelson was having an affair, and there was nothing Leonard could think of to persuade himself otherwise. After all, what did Kirstin do in the daytime when he was at the office, he wondered, suspicion mounting within him. How many hours could a person spend at the health club? Or at lunch? Or at charity meetings? Or shopping? And the fact that she was friends with someone who was as flagrant about her affairs as Kelly Nelson was showed terrible indiscretion on Kirstin's part.

Leonard slammed his car door shut and strode up

the walkway to his house, trying to clear his rage so that he could think more clearly. There was an evening newspaper in his path and he bent down to pick it up. Before he said anything to Kirstin, he would have another drink. He definitely needed another drink, he decided, stretching the rubber band off the newspaper and then opening it. The stock market was down. Israel was getting another bum rap. And there was a second-stage smog alert in the L.A. basin.

Kirstin was in the kitchen when he found her, going over some notes with their cook. She stopped what she was doing when she saw Leonard and went over to greet him with a kiss. "Hi, darling," she said, taking his briefcase from him and handing it to their houseman, who had just walked in. "You look exhausted."

Leonard felt his muscles tense as Kirstin put her arms around him, steering him out of the kitchen and toward the study. She was wearing a new perfume, he noticed. It was light and fresh and the change struck a discordant note in him. He was always dubious when a woman began changing her perfume, or her hairstyle, or started losing weight. Too often it meant she was trying to please somebody. Somebody new. Men were the same way. He watched her vigilantly as she led him over to his leather chair and pushed him lightly into it. "You look like you could use a drink," she said, already on her way to fix him one.

What a good mood she was in, he thought, observing her uncertainly as she poured out a stream of

Crown Royal into a heavy crystal glass. And how stunning she looked. Her skin was flawless. Clear and creamy. She had the kind of skin he could never resist touching. And it never changed. Never looked tired, not even around her eyes. Then his eyes traveled down to her ass, which was outlined in a snug-fitting gabardine skirt. Ever since she had started exercising he had noticed a pleasing difference in her figure. She had always been slim, but her shape had never been as sensuous before. Now her ass was tight, and lifted. It was pert. Her thighs were smooth, soft but firm. Her waistline had gotten smaller. Her breasts had been perfect to begin with. And the thought of somebody else touching her was driving him insane.

"I saw your photographer friend, Kelly Nelson, today. At the Bel-Air Hotel," Leonard said, waiting for Kirstin's reaction. He looked levelly at her as she handed him his drink.

"You saw Kelly?" Kirstin's eyes opened wide.

"With a man," Leonard continued.

"With a man?" Kirstin repeated. So that was what was on Leonard's mind. She looked at him appraisingly, with caution, noting how intensely bothered he was. Then she opened a split of champagne for herself, waiting for Leonard to go on.

Was it Brandon Michaels that Kelly was with? It had to be. She didn't want to respond one way or the other until she had determined exactly how much Leonard knew.

"She's definitely having an affair." Leonard's voice was dense with emotion. His posture was angry.

"Having an affair?" Kirstin sat down on the edge of the couch, facing Leonard. "Are you sure it was Kelly?" She watched Leonard take an impatient pull from his drink.

"I'm positive," he said.

"What did the man look like?" Kirstin asked, trying to analyze what her best tack would be.

"Nice-looking. Tall. Dark hair. Graying. Expensively dressed." Leonard paused. "You don't look surprised," he observed.

"Look, it's nothing." Kirstin stood up. She could feel Leonard's eyes on her legs as she paced anxiously back and forth in front of him. What a mess this was turning into. Obviously Brandon had called Kelly up and she had agreed to see him. But how was it that Leonard was so certain they were having an affair? Knowing Kelly, it was possible that she had only met him for drinks.

"How do you know it's nothing?" Leonard exclaimed heatedly. "You didn't see them. I did."

Kirstin drew a quick intake of breath. She couldn't go any further into this conversation without revealing the truth. "Look," she said, trying to reassure him, "I've never lied to you before. And I'm not going to start now." Kirstin felt her nerves pinch with the flat inaccuracy of her words. She *had* lied to him once, if the sin of omission could be held as a lie. But that was all so long ago. Before they were married. And the distance with which Kirstin viewed that fragmented portion of her past was analogous to a novel or film whose effect upon her had been so great that it had blended in with her own reality. Like having read Ibsen's *A Doll's House*. Or Selma Lagerlöf's *The Wonderful Adventures of Nils*. They were experiences shared and muted. Fiction touching fact—fact touching fiction—blending and becoming obscured. "Kelly needed a little romance in her life. A little spark. When she got married she was very young—"

"What does this have to do with you?" Leonard interrupted harshly. Beyond his mask of anger Kirstin detected fear, or insecurity. It was an emotion, however, she knew she could not address. Leonard's pride and his sense of power were too thick. He operated only on levels on which he had supreme control, sheltering his vulnerabilities from the world and most likely even from himself.

Kirstin stepped back into her story, being as cautious as she could possibly be while still being truthful.

"Leonard, just let me finish."

"Go ahead," he said tightly.

"Kelly was *so* young when she met her husband that she was never able to have any sexual experiences with anybody else."

"So I still want to know what that has to do with you?"

"Well," Kirstin went on gamely, "Kelly was always talking about sex. You know how Sidney Grossblat is always talking about women?" Kirstin was referring to one of Leonard's golf cronies. "Well, that's how Kelly talks about men. She's obsessed with sexual curiosity. But in a funny way. Or funny to us because that's Kelly's personality. . . ."

Kirstin stopped for a moment, searching out Leonard's reaction. When he didn't say anything, she continued. "So Kelly made this birthday resolution. By the time she turned thirty she was going to have an affair—"

"That's what you girls talk about at the health club?"

"Is it any different in a men's locker room?"

"Very. We don't go around making birthday resolutions to cheat on our spouses."

Of course you don't. You just go cheat, Kirstin thought. "Anyway," she said, "at the time it seemed funny. We joked around about it a lot. Kelly, another friend from the health club, and myself. Thirty came and went uneventfully, as did thirty-one, and then just before Kelly was about to turn *thirty-two,* she met a man with whom she was dying to have an affair." Feeling very uncomfortable, Kirstin went on. "So, for Kelly's birthday, the other woman from the health club and I called this man up and asked him to be Kelly's birthday present—"

"You what?" Leonard's face became a deep red and he was yanking at his tie as though he were suddenly being strangled.

"It was a mistake. I *know* I shouldn't have done it. That *we* shouldn't have done it. But at the time it was really only a joke. A prank."

"That's supposed to be funny? Interfering with someone's life? Kirstin, I just can't believe—"

"It just happened."

"It just happened?!"

"I made a mistake. And anyway, they didn't *do* anything," Kirstin argued, as Leonard knocked back the rest of his drink and went to pour himself another, consuming half of it in one angry swallow.

"Kelly met him at the hotel for lunch. Thinking that she was meeting us. They had room service in his bungalow, and before anything really happened, Kelly chickened out."

"And you believed her," Leonard said with a slow derisive smile.

"Of course I believed her."

"Well, that's *bullshit*, Kirstin. She's having a hot affair with this guy. I saw them out on the patio having drinks together and they looked like they couldn't wait to jump back into bed."

"That may well be, I have no idea what's going on with her now. But I'm telling you the truth. Three days ago they hadn't even made love," Kirstin insisted. "Kelly's not the type to lie."

"She'd be stupid not to lie. Why would she want you and that other woman to know? She tells you she chickened out and meanwhile she's fucking her brains out with this gigolo."

Kirstin shook her head in disagreement. "Kelly's not like that."

"Why the *hell* would you set her up? *That's* what I want to know!"

Kirstin tugged aimlessly at a book on the bookshelf. Now *Leonard* was pacing back and forth, and she listened to the sound of his heels obdurate against the planked oak floor. "It just happened," she said again, nervously. "I told you it was only a prank."

"You call that a prank!" Kirstin was afraid that Leonard was going to hit her when he grasped her by the shoulders and yanked her around to face him. "And what if this *prank* had been played on you? What happens when it's *your* birthday?"

"The prank wouldn't have been played on me."

"Why not?"

"Because I'm not interested in having an affair. Kelly was."

Leonard looked skeptically at her.

"I'm telling you the truth!"

"Sure."

Kirstin winced and tried to pull away from Leonard's grip. He was holding her with such force that he was hurting her. Finally she tore herself away from him and saw that he was shaking with rage.

"Can you tell me honestly, Leonard, that you've *never* gotten a girl for a guy before? Or that *none* of your friends have?"

"That's different," Leonard said vehemently.

"Explain to me why it's different."

"I don't care what you say, Kirstin, I don't care what kind of liberated crap you give me. It's different with a man! It always has been and it always will be. With a man it is *purely* sexual."

"With Kelly it was purely sexual—"

"You said that she wanted *romance*," Leonard said quickly.

"But it was still sexual."

"A man doesn't *need* romance. He needs a good warm hole to stick it in."

"*Romance* in Kelly's case was part of the foreplay," Kirstin argued, ignoring Leonard's crude remark.

"How do you think it makes me feel, Kirstin, that you instigated this?" Leonard asked her pointedly.

"I was wrong." At this point Kirstin's only objective was to put an end to Leonard's fury.

Neither of them said anything for a while. Kirstin was waiting for Leonard to cool down. He picked up a newspaper and began scanning it, but it was clear to her by the way he was clutching the paper and by the tightness of his jaw that he needed several minutes alone. Kirstin turned and started out of the room.

"Where are you going?" Leonard asked roughly.

"To see about dinner."

"What are we having?"

"Patrale sole."

"Fish again?"

"You like patrale sole," Kirstin reminded Leonard affectionately. After his last physical the doctor had telephoned Kirstin. Leonard's cholesterol was higher than it had ever been and she was advised to limit his intake of red meat to once a week. Although Kirstin went to great efforts to disguise this new regime by calling up the best spas, such as La Costa and the Golden Door, to procure their best recipes, Leonard continued to battle with her. It wasn't simply that he would like to eat a good New York steak seven nights a week, although that was part of it, but mainly he couldn't deal with having rules imposed on him, rules that emphasized his weaknesses. His human frailties. Not only did Leonard desperately want to remain virile and powerful forever, but this restrictive diet acted as a gnawing reminder of the eighteen-year age difference between him and his wife. Sensitive to this, Kirstin did her best to play it down.

By the time Kirstin was able to leave the dinner table and go upstairs to undress she had a throbbing headache. Throughout the course of their meal, Leonard had been impossible, at first sitting in stony silence, then grilling her maniacally about what precisely she did during the day. Her answers were never enough for him. They seemed to pass right through him—rejected words. They were not what Leonard was looking for. No, Leonard was looking for guilt. He was looking for a lie. He was looking to trap her. His face was pinched with distrust and accusation. He was a zealous prosecutor and she was the defendant, responding wearily to his unrelenting firing of questions.

Kirstin headed straight for the medicine cabinet in her bathroom and took two aspirin. Kelly's birthday present had cost her a great deal. Too much, she thought, unzipping her skirt and stepping out of it. She had never seen Leonard so enraged with jealousy, and she was concerned that it might be a while before he recovered totally. She would have to give some serious thought to distracting him. Maybe a party. Or a big trip. It would be a good idea for her to be working on something that she would be discussing with him, so that he would know for certain what she was doing during the day, without actually having to account to him. A vacation was a good idea. Leonard loved to travel. He had been talking about going to South America, and the research they would do before they went would be extensive. It always was. Before their departure, Kirstin would most likely be an expert on the whole damn continent.

She smoothed out her skirt before hanging it up in her closet. She was so exhausted that she felt as though she were moving in slow motion. Everything she did seemed to require too much energy. Unbuttoning the tiny buttons on her silk shirt, then taking it off and arranging it on the lightly scented Porthault hanger. Removing her jewelry and storing it in the safe. Shoes. Stockings. Makeup. When it came time to select a nightgown to wear, she decided cautiously on the most virginal one she had. It was a delicate halter gown. The fabric was hand-painted and it resembled a Pissarro. Impressionism on silky satin.

As she carried the gown into her dressing room to put it on, she became aware of Leonard's presence, bulky in the doorway. He was gazing heavily at her as she unhooked her bra and let it drop to the floor, pulling the gown quickly over her head. He stopped her midway, intercepting the fabric with his hands to get a grasp on her breasts. The last thing Kirstin wanted to do now was make love.

"You sexy bitch," Leonard growled, forcing her nightgown up over her head and throwing it aside. His beard felt like sandpaper against her skin and there was liquor heavy on his breath as he maneuvered her hand onto his swollen crotch, murmuring a slurred snort of pleasure and rubbing his cheek harshly against hers. Then he pressed harder on her hand, demanding more friction, and drove his tongue deeply into her mouth, tasting distinctly of Courvoisier.

Kirstin didn't say a word as Leonard commandeered her over to the bed. He was breathing in impassioned gasps as he tore at her panties with his hands and at her skin with his mouth. His own clothes were off in a moment, thrown haphazardly onto the floor. She felt his anger in the heat of his hand pressing firmly between her legs, demanding what belonged to him. He applied a mounting pressure, thrusting his palm against her. His eyes contained violence and she knew by the cold flash of a smile that passed over his lips that he felt her trembling. Immediately he was on top of her. No hint of love. Just the weight of him crushing her and the force of him entering her.

In and out. In and out. After a while Kirstin felt herself getting so dry that Leonard's thrusts were beginning to hurt. She looked around the room for something to focus her attention on—a readily available distraction. The flowers in the vase near the bed needed to be replaced. The irises that had been fresh and colorful just that morning were now wilted and dull. Then she realized that something else had wilted, something far more serious, as she felt Leonard go soft again inside her. Was it her fault for having lost interest, she wondered guiltily. For thinking about limp flowers? Had he sensed her silent wish that he hurry up and roll off her? She had been moving in rhythm with him, feigning interest. Now all Kirstin could do was remain rigid, her unexcited body held beneath Leonard's as he forced her hips up and down. She never quite knew if she should move or not because his orgasms were uneven and

212

silent. Sometimes she would stop, thinking he had already come, and then after a few moments, just when she was ready for him to push off, he would begin fumbling with her hips, begging for motion, for some sort of satisfaction. This isn't how it should be, Kirstin thought, becoming aware of Leonard swelling up inside her again. She glanced at the clock impatiently. If only she could put some raunchy images into his head. She would try concentrating on X-rated scenes—concentrate so hard that Leonard would have to see them, feel them, go wild with exquisitely fleshy females and their insatiable lust and get his blessed rocks off! C'mon, Leonard, eight women all at once! You get to screw a whole goddamn whorehouse!

My God, this is sick, Kirstin thought. She felt sexually dead. It had never been right with Leonard, but she had thought it would change. Certainly she had been dazzled, even overwhelmed by his adoration when they first met—his attention, his flattery, his money, his power, and the concern he lavished on her. She loved him. He loved her. They just needed to become accustomed to each other. That was what she had thought when she had married him. But the sex never did change. At first she had been frustrated. Now she was numb. But it was all right. After all, life was a series of trade-offs, and basically Kirstin had what she wanted. Then she thought about Kelly. What was happening with Kelly? Was she having an affair with Brandon? And what had happened with the nightgown she had given her—with the seduction of Kelly's husband? Kirstin wondered whether or not Kelly would tell her about Brandon. Before, she thought there was no doubt Kelly would. But now Leonard had made her uncertain. Most likely they would be seeing each other at the health club in the next day or so. Her hunch was that "Brandon" would be one of the first words out of Kelly's mouth.

In the midst of Kirstin's speculating, she became aware of Leonard moving even more frantically. Then he collapsed against her, spent. If only she could preserve him in this condition, she thought. It had been so different with her first husband. She used to spend hours in bed with him, locked in his arms, warm and safe. It was a time reserved for intimate chatter and affectionate laughter.

But not a chance of this happening with Leonard. He was up in a flash and back to business. Sex was supposed to be a marvelous unwinding device, but with Leonard there was some kind of infallible spring that bounced him immediately back into action. He was already crossing the room, dabbing a Kleenex to his penis and heading toward his briefcase, which Kirstin knew would be filled with his industry periodicals.

"Do you want a dish of ice cream, darling?" Kirstin asked him, rolling over onto her side and trying to read his mood. Ice cream before bed was a ritual with Leonard, an indulgence that Kirstin told his doctor she couldn't take away from him, cholesterol or no cholesterol.

He turned to her, still naked, wearing his reading glasses, holding his open briefcase. His body was sagging, but not too badly for a man who was about

214

to turn sixty-three. He had only a slight paunch, some comfortable love handles, but his legs were strong and shapely. It was too bad that they had never had children together. They would have had wonderful legs. But it had been a subject about which he'd been adamant. Leonard removed his spectacles to look over at Kirstin, then rubbed his eyes. He was tired, Kirstin could see that. "Did you buy chocolate almond?" he asked. Sex and ice cream were two things Leonard wouldn't turn down under any circumstances.

Chapter Twelve

KELLY WOUND HER CAR DOWN AROUND THE PARKING RAMP
on her way to the health club, entering on the designated level. She needed desperately to talk to Kirstin
and Ericka and hoped they would be there. Even at
this early morning hour she had a difficult time
finding an available space. Finally she maneuvered
her Volvo station wagon in next to a black Ferrari
and found herself wondering what kind of car Brandon drove. A black Ferrari somehow seemed appropriate. As would a Maserati. A Porsche perhaps, but
as she walked toward the escalators, and noticed that
there were lots of Porsches, she decided that Brandon would drive a car that was more unusual, even if
only because the price tag made it so. Imagine,
Porsches commonplace, when some of them cost al-

most as much as a condo. Well, that was L.A. for you.

Kelly hiked anxiously up the narrow escalator. She wasn't in the mood to stand still. Brandon was so much on her mind that even trying to read the newspaper that morning had been impossible. Like attempting to read in a doctor's office when she knew she was going to be called in any minute for a shot that would definitely hurt. And struggling to act normal around Ron or the kids—that was like trying to act sober after having had too much to drink.

The night before had been like a crazy dream. Patchwork. Hazy. Not just like a voyeur watching intimate moments on a movie screen. And not just passion on a page, hot words and steamy passages read between the covers of a book. But between the sheets of a lover's bed—under a satin coverlet. It was a fantasy enacted. Unforgettable. Body heat. Multiple orgasms. Now she understood. Words suddenly evoked new meanings—and Kelly was reeling from them.

As she walked toward the entrance of the health club, her mind was popping with recollections— kernels sizzling in her dilemma, then bursting and cooling into new forms. Abruptly Kelly flashed on last night. She remembered feeling the residue of Brandon dripping ominously into her bikini underwear as she had stood at the threshold of her bedroom, seized with panic—what would she do if Ron wanted to make love?

"How'd it go?" Ron had asked, looking up at her, his tone mellow, friendly. He was sitting at his rolltop

218

desk surrounded by paper work and Kelly squirmed worriedly. The TV was on, providing company for him like a faithful old dog, and at the sight of Ron and his electronic friend Kelly felt an immense wave of guilt.

"Fine," she had responded, a bit belatedly, her voice unsteady. She was worried about having to fabricate details. She was worried about sleeping with him. Not only was she acutely conscious of incriminating evidence, moist and alarming between her thighs, but she was concerned that she might be carrying the scent of sex. She couldn't even let him get close to her. "I'm exhausted," she exclaimed, in hopes of closing their exchange and postponing it until tomorrow. "And so grungy. I think I'll take a hot bath. Then crash."

Ron tossed his pen onto the desk and turned around in his chair. Kelly waited, holding her breath, feeling jumpy.

"Do you want to talk?" Ron asked calmly, his arms crossed over his chest. He looked as he had looked ten years ago, studying for the bar exam. Sleepy. Young. Logical.

"No. It's okay," Kelly said, escaping toward the bathroom. Brandon was an imaginary presence trailing overhead, soaking her underpants beneath. Airy fantasy. Sticky reality. How in the world could she carry on a conversation with her husband?

"Because if you want to talk . . ." Ron offered, entering the bathroom behind her, closing the lid of the toilet to make a seat for himself as Kelly turned on her bathwater.

"Do you?" Kelly asked. An old message from Psych 1 in college: turn the question around.

Ron shrugged as Kelly poured Vitabath into her tub. She felt too guilty for the indulgence of her more luxurious bath oils. Vitabath felt wholesome. Kelly needed wholesome. The kids' Mr. Bubbles would have been just right.

"Okay," Ron said pleasantly, standing up and rubbing his eyes. "I've got another couple hours of work."

"Do you want me to make you some coffee or anything?" Kelly asked in a small voice.

"No thanks."

"Do you need any typing done?"

"I thought you were exhausted."

I am, Kelly thought. But anything to redeem myself. Blueberry pancakes for breakfast. Fresh orange juice. Homemade syrup. You name it.

Then, after her bath, charged with guilty redemption plans, which were spliced with thoughts of Brandon, and sure that she was never going to be able to fall asleep—Kelly had fallen asleep.

Before moving on into the gym Kelly stopped at her locker. She was anxious to find Kirstin or Ericka, but it was fifteen minutes before the early-bird aerobics class would begin and it was unlikely that either of them would be here this early.

In the gym, Kelly looked around at all the women working hard at this ambitious hour, following specified routines on the various muscle-toning machines. What discipline, she thought. Leg lifts. Twenty-five repetitions. Check. Pectoral press. Twenty-five repetitions. Check. Kelly retrieved her own exercise card from one of the floor attendants. Before she began her program, she limbered up, lifting a five-pound weight up over her head toward the ceiling, then bending down to pull it through her legs. The stretching movement felt great, reaching up and out, releasing, stretching out thick knots of tension. *Did last night really happen? Will he call today? What will I say? I've got to take the kids to the dentist in the afternoon. Will I see him again?* The knots of tension unraveled into questions, balling up again and relocating. If she were a computer, she decided, her indicators would flash in bright red warning signals—*emotional overload!* Excited. Guilty. Happy. Sad. Nervous. Confused. Conflicted. Falling in love. Depressed.

Kelly moved to the leg pulley and adjusted the chrome weights. Her card indicated five pounds, but she felt like adding an additional two and a half. As she buckled the strap onto her ankle and rolled over onto her hip to begin, gearing up for thirty-five repetitions, she saw Ericka approaching her.

Without makeup Ericka looked years younger, more like a high school student than a high-powered studio executive. She was wearing UCLA jogging shorts and a man's tank-style undershirt, thick socks rolled down into neat little cuffs and Adidas running shoes. Her hair was in a ponytail. "Boy, do I need to work out," Ericka said, patting her thighs. "I was just in Montreal for a few days and the food there is incredible."

"What were you doing in Montreal?" Kelly asked,

wanting to tell Ericka about Brandon, but deciding to wait and see if Kirstin showed up.

"We're talking about shooting a film there," Ericka said, picking up a couple of two-and-a-half-pound weights and beginning to work on her arms.

"What kind of film?"

"A comedy-thriller."

"Why in Montreal?" Kelly asked, tightening her buttocks and thighs and swinging her leg back and forth.

"We'd be cofinancing it with a Canadian film company. They've got it all set up there." Ericka stopped to look up at Kirstin, who was walking toward them. Kelly was relieved to see her. "Well, well, well. Look at you," Ericka teased. Kirstin was wearing a shimmery silver-gray and yellow leotard, with a deep scoop back, and matching tights. Around her waist she had on a skinny gray patent-leather belt. Kirstin had the largest, most innovative exercise wardrobe Kelly had ever seen. Leotards. Lingerie. Actually, that was all Kelly had ever seen Kirstin in, now that she thought about it.

Kelly switched the weights to her other leg. One. Two. Three. She strained.

"Well?" Kirstin strapped herself into the metal contraption next to Kelly.

Kelly smiled, not sure where to begin. "I saw Brandon Michaels again," she said nervously.

Ericka's mouth opened wide. She looked shocked. She looked delighted.

Kirstin's expression was grim and Kelly wondered why.

"Where?" Ericka asked, putting her weights on the floor and sitting down. "What happened?"

"Well." Kelly grinned uneasily, finishing her leg lifts, then unbuckling the strap. "The day after the Bel-Air, he sent me flowers." Kelly turned to Kirstin. "You knew that." Kirstin nodded and Kelly went on, her mind spinning again. "Then he called and wanted to get together." Kelly stopped for a moment and looked over at Kirstin. "The seduction was a disaster," she explained.

"Wait a minute, what seduction?" Ericka interrupted. "I go away for three days and—"

"I was going to seduce Ron," Kelly said. "I decided that I wasn't cut out for an affair, and since I wanted more romance or more sex or both in my life, I'd have to initiate it."

Ericka looked over at Kirstin and laughed. "I think I know who had a hand in that plan," she said, amused.

Kelly noticed that Kirstin was not amused.

"So what happened?" Ericka asked.

"It was terrible. Nothing went right," Kelly said, remembering. "I looked *so* great," she said to Kirstin, then explained to Ericka, "Kirstin gave me a fabulous peignoir set. I made a romantic dinner. You know. The whole bit. Ron was in a lousy mood. And all we did was fight."

Nobody said anything for a moment. It was announced over the intercom that class was to begin and Ericka asked Kelly if she would rather pass.

"Do you mind?" Kelly asked them both. She was grateful that they did not.

"Anyway," Kelly went on, "the next day at the office, Brandon called."

"Boy, does he have good timing," Ericka intoned.

"Perfect timing," Kelly agreed. "I was incredibly depressed."

"So he asked you out . . . you said no. And he said, 'Just drinks.' " Ericka took Kelly's hand compassionately.

"I know. You've already made this movie," Kelly said laughingly, tears coming to her eyes. She felt comforted by Ericka's easy acceptance of all this. It was Kirstin's reaction she couldn't understand. Was it disapproval she sensed? Kelly couldn't help but feel resentful, whatever it was. After all, Kirstin had led her into this in the first place. All of a sudden she was going to be prudish about it? Maybe it had to do with the nightgown she had given her. Maybe Kirstin was offended because Kelly hadn't thanked her afterward, or called, or anything.

"Many times. But it's always different," Ericka said, squeezing Kelly's hand. "So . . . was it wonderful?"

Kelly noticed Kirstin's expectant look. It wasn't judgmental, she concluded. It was just subdued.

"Wonderful," Kelly said, her voice low. At that moment she wanted to be back in Brandon's arms. She had such a clear picture of him.

"I can't believe it," Ericka said. "How do you feel?"

"Crazy," Kelly said, trying to describe her chaos. She was dying to ask Ericka if *she* had ever had an affair. There was something in Ericka's eyes that translated as understanding. Kirstin, on the other hand, was acting so remote. "What is it?" Kelly finally asked her.

Kirstin put her hand to her mouth and drew a deep reluctant breath. Her neatly manicured nails were the color of cherry stains. Her large diamond ring flickered and Kelly's jittery state increased.

"God, Kelly. I don't know how to tell you this," Kirstin said regretfully. "I knew you were with Brandon. Leonard was at the Bel-Air Hotel yesterday having drinks and he saw you there with him."

Kelly froze, unable to say anything, unable to process what Kirstin had just said.

It was Ericka who picked up the ball. "Wait a minute, Kirstin. Leonard saw Kelly? What did he say to you?"

Kelly listened numbly as Kirstin told them about Leonard. Good God, somebody had been watching her. The thought had never even occurred to her. Being out on the patio with Brandon, Kelly had felt apart from the rest of the world. They had been in a private garden, in paradise. She tried to re-create the scene. The tables. Where had Leonard been sitting? She hadn't seen him, but she hadn't looked. Was he there the whole time? She felt violated. Naked. She felt ridiculous. She felt as if the whole world had just turned upside down.

"Kelly, I'm sorry," Kirstin was saying, putting her hand on Kelly's shoulder. "I was just glad that it was Leonard and not someone who might say something to your husband."

Kelly felt tears stinging her eyes. There was anxiety coursing through her. She was wearing melon-colored leg warmers. There was a loose thread and she pulled at it.

"How did you leave it with Brandon?" Ericka asked Kelly gently. "Did you say you'd see him again?"

It took a moment for Ericka's question to reach Kelly.

"He's probably going to call me today at the office." Kelly hesitated. "I can't stop thinking about him," she admitted in a whisper. "I was going to say no, if he asked to see me. But I guess I was hoping he'd be persuasive enough to . . ." Kelly's voice trailed off. She didn't know what she thought. Part of her was afraid that if she did continue to see Brandon, she'd fall in love with him, and another part of her was saying how marvelous that would be.

"Look," Kirstin said, just as Kelly let loose a flow of tears. "You don't have to worry about Leonard. I wouldn't have even told you, except that I want you to know how careful you have to be."

Kelly looked over at Ericka, who was biting her lower lip and looking as though she wished she could say something. "I really can't talk about it any more now," Kelly said, standing up and blinking away fresh tears. "I'm being overly emotional. It's not just Leonard. It's everything all at once. I can't think straight. . . ."

"If you need to talk at all," Ericka said, "I'll be at the office all day."

"I'm fine," Kelly said.

"And I'll be home," Kirstin offered. "I've got some work to do at home."

"I'm fine," Kelly repeated, feeling foolish. And not feeling fine at all. A palette of too many colors mixed into a muddy gray—too many emotions mixed into a muddy gray depression.

Chapter Thirteen

IT WAS LATE WHEN ERICKA ARRIVED HOME FROM THE OFFICE that evening. She had had one meeting after another, and her five-thirty went on until after nine. There were phone messages piled up on her desk that she hadn't even looked at. She was hungry and tired and wanted to get home. Then she realized that Kelly might have called. Dammit. The day had been so manic she had forgotten all about Kelly. Most likely she hadn't called; they rarely made contact outside of the health club. But what if she had? Some friend she'd think Ericka was! And she'd be right.

Ericka closed her front door, kicked off her high-heeled pumps, put down her briefcase, and hurried through the house. The glazed terra-cotta tile floor felt cold beneath her stocking feet.

She found her husband eating popcorn and drinking Grolsch beer in front of the television set.

"Hi, sweetheart. I'm sorry I'm late. I hope you got my message," Ericka said wearily, going over to David and kissing the top of his head, then ruffling his curly brown hair. It was thick and soft and smelled of coconuts—a fragrance she recognized as the hair conditioner from the tennis club. David, she surmised, had played tennis and then showered at the club. He was wearing cotton khaki pants, a lemon-yellow cable-knit sweater, and a striped polo-style T-shirt underneath. Ericka put her arms around him as he reached up to squeeze her hand. He looked relaxed, tan, and handsome. His eyes, she saw, were fixed on the TV, where a player was sprinting across the football field with the ball tucked close to his gut, his head held low as he avoided his attacking opponents. The large padded players collapsed into a heap, and as they did so David turned his head to Ericka and kissed her.

"Good game?" she asked.

"Shitty," he said, stroking her cheek. "You look beat."

"I am." Ericka sighed, scanning the headlines of the evening newspaper spread out across David's lap. Her cheek was resting against his.

"Rough day?" David asked, snapping off the TV and tossing the newspaper aside.

"Long."

"Did you have dinner?"

"No. Did you?" Ericka came around to take a handful of popcorn, stepping over one of David's tan-colored Topsiders on her way. She noticed the shoe's mate under the coffee table.

"There's butter on it," David cautioned abruptly, as though he were warning her that the popcorn she was about to stick into her mouth contained poison.

"I didn't eat all day," Ericka said, unconcerned about the calories she was consuming. She was looking at a lithograph David had just acquired, done by a contemporary Indian artist named Fritz Scholder, and thinking how well it tied in with the red, green, and orange of the Navajo area rug. David had designed the interior of the old Spanish-style house himself and was quite proud of it. He had started about five years ago, after attending a psychiatric conference in Santa Fe. New Mexico had so enamored him, with its flourishing artistic life, its piñon-studded landscapes, and its spectacular skies, that David had begun to immerse himself in its culture. He had started collecting southwestern art, Pueblo pottery, Hopi Kachina dolls, New Mexican santos, until finally he had decided to do their entire house in that look. Since the architecture was Spanish to begin with, everything fitted right in. The Spanish colonial three-legged stools made out of sun-bleached wood. The hand-worn altar table. The iron frame furniture. The pots and baskets. Cactus plants. Many of the pieces David had procured were from trips he had taken deep into the mountains of New Mexico, where he and a friend had gone to barter. They brought back all kinds of things, one of David's favorites being a weathered fragment of a cantera column, which he upended to be used as a small table next to a grandly oversized leather and splint "basket" chair.

The art investments David had made had been substantial. Indian alabasters by Doug Hyde. A small Remington sculpture. One of David's crazy, very wealthy patients who wintered in the fashionable ski community of Vail, Colorado, and was treated long distance by David through forty-five-minute telephone sessions, three times a week, contributed to David's collection. Every year, as an expression of extravagant gratitude, in addition to paying David's steep bills, she sent him an expensive little red clay pot. These pots, with intricately etched figures of wildlife, were creations of Joseph Lonewolf, a talented Indian artisan from Santa Clara, New Mexico. They cost about three thousand dollars each and were purchased from an exclusive store in Vail, specializing in Indian art, called the Squash Blossom. This particular patient was unusual, however. Baseball tickets were a far more common token of a patient's appreciation.

But David looked right somehow, Ericka thought, in the warm, easy surroundings he had created. Had it been up to her, the house would have been starkly contemporary.

"You'll have to do an extra twenty minutes' worth of exercise tomorrow," David teased, taking some more popcorn himself and putting his feet up on the big wooden coffee table that had once been an old stable door.

"I don't go to the gym tomorrow," Ericka said, taking off her suit jacket and hanging it on the nose of a turn-of-the-century carrousel horse she had bought David as a birthday present. On location in Mexico, filming in the small town of Puebla, about two hours from Mexico City, one of the crew members had taken her to a shop called Chapis where Mexican antiques were sold. The sculpted wooden animal caught Ericka's eye immediately. It wasn't a shiny colorful horse, gaudy with brightness and lacquer—instead, it was primitive-looking, worn with the patina of time and faded down to a dull weathered wood. Ericka had been delighted when David had loved the horse just as much as she had.

"Then forty minutes the *next* day. Get your jacket off my pony."

"Give me a break!" Ericka sat down on the sofa, sinking into the cocoa-colored cushions and putting her feet up on the table next to David's. He tickled her foot with his own and she giggled, noticing how perfectly matched his Argyle socks were with his outfit.

"I love your body just the way it is," David said, pushing her skirt up over her thighs and examining them.

"So how was *your* day?" Ericka asked him, resting her head on his shoulder.

"Great. Saw four patients. *Changed* their lives. . . ."

"You're that good a doctor, huh?"

"The best. You just don't take advantage of me," David said, squeezing her thigh. "I could change your life too."

"I like my life."

"Because you don't know any better."

"I'm perfectly happy."

233

"That's what they all say."

"Yeah—until you dig in there and show them all the misery they're covering up. . . ."

"Of course," David teased.

"I think I'll pass on that kind of psychoanalytical surgery." Ericka took another handful of popcorn. "So did you play tennis?"

"Great tennis."

"What about dinner?"

"I stopped for sushi on the way home." David took a swig of beer, then looked over at Ericka again. "What kind of meeting were you in that lasted so long?"

"We had a meeting with the studio lawyers."

"On the Hindson story again?"

"They're driving me crazy on this," Ericka said. The Hindson story was a fictional account of a true story about a boy in Texas who joined a cult, was brainwashed, and began robbing banks to get money for the cult. First the lawyers had driven Ericka crazy in the writing of the script. Now, after the script had been completely approved by them, and then filmed, they were driving her nuts again. They had received threats from Hindson's father's attorney and they were nervous.

"I thought you had a release."

"No. We were advised not to. If we had asked for a release from Hindson's father and he had turned us down, according to our lawyers we would have been in even bigger trouble. All the research we've done on the film has been from interviewing people outside of the family, taking public-record incidents—"

"But the film's already been shot."

"Yes, and they want us to edit it down so much, all we'll have left is a twenty-minute short!"

"That's a pretty costly short subject."

"Only about thirty-five million. The whole thing is ludicrous. We may have to add some scenes. Do some reshooting—I don't know! Then I had another problem: we had a location set up for another film, a big old hotel in Louisiana. The guy called today. . . . I think they're backing out."

"And you like your life?"

"Well, this wasn't my favorite day."

"Poor baby, you worked so hard on that Hindson story. You must be pretty upset." David pulled Ericka up off the couch and began steering her down the hallway in the direction of their bedroom.

"I *hate* lawyers."

"Good! Get that anger out," David coaxed, massaging her neck and shoulders as they walked.

"They're ruining my movie."

"What do you think they should do about the situation?"

"They should go fuck themselves."

David and Ericka both laughed. Ericka felt close to tears.

"*Good,*" David said, encouraging her.

"That feels *so* good!" she said, climbing the stairs and rolling her head to the side as he worked on an especially tight muscle at the base of her neck. "You have the best hands. Hmmm."

"I have the perfect remedy for you. . . ."

"I'm hungry," Ericka protested as he directed her into the bedroom.

"First I'll relax you. . . ." He gave her a little shove and she stretched out on her stomach on the bed. He straddled her, continuing the massage. "Then I'll spoil you with one of my famous omelet creations. Do we have any avocados?"

"I think so."

"Cheddar cheese?"

"Uh-huh."

"God, you're tight," he said, working on the left side of her back. "How can you function when your body's so jammed with tension?"

"I don't know," Ericka murmured. "I guess I'm afraid if I were loose I wouldn't be able to function. I'd be like cooked spaghetti. . . . I wouldn't be able to stand up straight."

"So instead you're brittle, like *uncooked* spaghetti . . . the thin, fragile kind—capellini." He lifted her blouse up from out of her skirt and unhooked her bra. His hands felt warm against her skin. Large, protective, and warm. "Now, if I can just get you to *al dente* . . . you'll be perfect."

Ericka arched her back, then rolled over, knocking David onto his side. "Stop talking about food, David, I'm famished," she said, kissing his neck and unbuttoning his shirt.

"Hmmm . . . you're at your *best* when you're famished," he said playfully, unzipping her skirt and wiggling it down over her hips.

"Your stomach is flatter," he observed, running

236

his tongue down around her belly as he stretched off her panty hose. "And you're more *passionate*."

They continued undressing one another, then pulled aside the bed covers to make love.

Afterward they lay in each other's arms for a while not saying anything. Ericka was looking up at the old wood-beamed ceiling, rehearsing in her mind what she'd say to the hotel owner in Louisiana if he backed out of the deal, then thinking about the pile of phone messages on her desk. She should have looked at them. Or have brought them home with her. She'd need at least an hour in the morning to return phone calls before her ten o'clock meeting with promotion. And she had to remember to call Kelly. Ericka sat up in bed and reached over to the night table to get a pen and paper. David intercepted her move.

"Can't you *ever* just relax?"

"I need to jot something down," Ericka said, trying to maneuver around him.

"What?"

"I have some things I want to remember in the morning."

"Like what? I'm curious," he said, handing her the paper and pen. "What's so urgent that it preys on you like this?"

"It's not a matter of urgent. I just don't want to forget."

"But you'll write *these* things down. And then in a few minutes you'll be springing up with some more. You ought to learn to contain them."

"I wish I could," Ericka said, beginning her list. (1)

Check phone messages and return calls. (2) Have Lilly set up lunch with Rick Mayhew. (3) TT Kelly Nelson. (4) TT Louisiana. (5) Review memo from Hindson meeting. (6) Check the dailies on *Manhunt.* . . .

"Who's Kelly Nelson?" David asked, looking down at Ericka's rapidly growing list.

"Wait a sec," Ericka said, trying to concentrate. There was something she had been thinking about earlier. . . .

"You should just sit down every evening and write all these things down at one time."

"David, shhh—wait—I've got one more thing . . . dammit. . . ."

"I'm telling you, the best way for you to relax is to organize this in one shot. Do it just before you leave the office. That's the best way."

"Oh, come on, I can't think when you're talking."

David was quiet for a moment. Ericka still couldn't remember what it was that she needed to write down, so she put the list aside.

"It's really a good method to just sit down at the end of your day and make an organized account of all the things you need to do the next day. You'll discipline your thoughts that way. Instead of having them out of control."

Ericka looked at David. "My thoughts aren't out of control. They're just active."

"They're hyperactive."

"I'm under a lot of pressure." Ericka reached over for the paper and pen again, remembering the item she had forgotten. *Check artwork on* Manhunt *before*

238

meeting with promotion. Then another. *Have Lilly call Writers' Guild,* she put down. *Credits on Jonathan Avedon.*

"Feel better?" David asked.

"Much. Actually, I usually do get to do this at the office before I leave. Today was total anarchy."

"Who's Jonathan Avedon?"

"A writer I'm meeting with in the afternoon."

"Who's Rick Mayhew?"

"Does completion guarantees."

"And who's Kelly Nelson?"

"A friend I got into a jam."

"What happened?"

"It's a long story. Girl talk."

"I hear girl talk all day long. Seventy percent of my patients are girls. And the other thirty percent have problems with them."

"You get paid to listen to their predicaments."

"So Kelly we'll handle pro bono. You got her into the jam. I presume you're planning on getting her out of it."

"It's really me and another friend from the health club."

"Is this the one that wanted to have an affair?" David asked, stroking the back of Ericka's neck.

"Kelly is."

"And I take it she did."

Ericka adjusted her pillow against the headboard and sat up as she told David all about what had happened with Kelly. How she and Kirstin had set it up. How Kelly, after all her excessive dialogue about how she was dying to have this affair, had not been

239

able to go through with it. And then finally about how Kelly *had* gotten together with Brandon Michaels and how she had been seen by Kirstin's husband. It was a relief telling all this to David, and as she did so she felt especially close to him. He really cared about her work, her problems with her friends. How nice to have your husband as your *best friend*. Finally she felt relaxed. He had a way of unwinding her for which she was really very grateful.

"I feel terrible about it all," Ericka said, remembering the look on Kelly's face when she had left her this morning, and reaching for David's hand to squeeze. But he pulled roughly away.

"You should," he said sharply, suddenly stone cold. Ericka was stunned by his reaction and waited for him to say something else. "I think we should deal with this from the point of view of *your* motivation. *Your* subliminal desires," he said abrasively.

"This has nothing to do, David, with my subliminal desires—"

"Sure it does."

"Don't give me that psychoanalytic crap," Ericka said. The tension that had left her came flooding back into her system.

"You obviously did this because *you* would like to have an affair—"

"That's not true."

"That's basic, Ericka."

"That's bullshit."

"Look. You may be a movie expert. But *I'm* a *head* expert. I *know*."

"You don't know! Kelly wanted to get laid and we

240

arranged it for her. Period. Cut. No analysis necessary."

"Not for Kelly. That's commonplace enough. But for you and this other friend of yours . . . that could use some looking into as far as I'm concerned."

"Oh, David. Just forget it."

"I can't forget it. I need to talk about it." David jumped out of bed and stepped into his Jockey shorts. He went downstairs to get a diet cola and returned a few moments later still seething.

Ericka was tempted to rage right back at him as he sat down angrily on the edge of a chair. *He* was the one who had been cheating on her throughout their eight years of marriage. What right did he have to get wild at the thought of her *wanting* to have an affair? Which she didn't. What kind of crazy hypocrite was he?

"David, I don't think we should get into this any further," she warned. She didn't want to discuss *his* infidelities and she imagined he didn't want to either. His breathing was quick and shallow, like that of a fighter being held back in the ring, and Ericka suddenly realized that she had hit David where he was very insecure. She could tell by his eyes how threatened he was. His affairs, she realized, were different from the single affair that she might have. Because her affair would evolve from an entirely different need. David's liaisons were sexual and nothing more. Quick and ego-gratifying. They were flings in the true sense of the word. But the affair that Ericka would want to have *would* be threatening to David, and she supposed that they both knew that. Of course, her affair would be a love affair. With Jamie Sterling, she thought, her subliminal desire suddenly rocketing to the surface, disturbingly clear.

Ericka got out of bed and pulled on David's shirt. She went over to where he was sitting, his arms locked around his chest in angry meditation, and took a sip of his diet cola. A modern-day peace pipe, she thought, only instead of puffing she sipped.

"I'm sorry," she said, realizing for the first time how vulnerable David really was. The fear of the unknown. His territory previously unshared—shared. Since David had cheated on her before, she was *familiar* with what that felt like. It was lonely. A kind of dull aching pain—that made her acutely aware of a void that existed within her. In her life. In her marriage. It was like a nagging reminder that things weren't as they should be. But that was all. The dull aching awareness was relatively easy for Ericka to block. Work was an efficient block. The distraction always took over. But David had no idea what the pain of his wife cheating on him would be like, and his fear of it appeared to be monumental. Ericka wanted to say to him, *Don't worry, David. It doesn't hurt that badly. I know.* But she couldn't. It would hurt David very badly, she thought, if her cheating on him led to his losing her. And that, she sensed, was what he was afraid of.

Ericka's teeth were nearly chattering and all over she was trembling. *Jamie. She wanted to have an affair with Jamie.* The acknowledgment of that was like skiing down a glacier. It was exhilarating, terrifying. She wouldn't stop until she had reached the bottom.

The momentum was on, mounting. A speed reckless and driving like a drug. Would she fall? Would she crash? Would she break all her limbs—or her heart? She *was* going to have an affair with Jamie. Not just an affair, but somehow she was going to go after him. When she gave Kelly the fling, it was really giving her the opportunity to live out her fantasy. As Ericka *wished* that she could live out her own. David was absolutely right. Yes. She did want to have an affair. An affair that would put their own special relationship, their friendship, their marriage, into unbelievable peril. Ericka felt a hot guilty string of tears as she touched David's back, trying to soothe him. After all, he hadn't really betrayed her when he had fooled around with other women. His extramarital affairs were consistent, she thought, with their philosophy—David's philosophy. Romance as an illusion. Romance as an avenue for suckers and dreamers—a definite dead end. Their marriage was a bond of a more logical brand of loyalty. The kind of loyalty that wasn't endangered by brief encounters. But Ericka couldn't help but wonder whether with Jamie her life might be different. She was a dreamer *and* a sucker ready to march down the avenue David called a dead end. Maybe it was really just a lovely cul-de-sac. With kids. And bikes. Stray roller skates and love.

Just then the private line in Ericka's office rang. "I'll be right back," Ericka said reluctantly, running to catch the phone in the other room.

It was Hart. Ellis Hart. Her writer-director discovery who had turned into a hot Hollywood "element."

She could tell immediately from his lilting tone of voice that he was completely drugged out and she hoped he hadn't tried suicide again. Hart was supposed to leave for Italy in a few weeks to direct a film Ericka was associate-producing, and as before every picture, he was panicking.

"Ericka . . . I'm so glad I got you in. . . . I just wanted to tell you that I . . . I love ya, baby, and your . . . fucking big mouth . . . and I fucking swallowed a whole bottle of . . . I'm fading fast, love . . . five mil . . . twenty-five fucking capsules. . . . I can't go to Italy and work with that asshole. . . ."

The "asshole" Hart was referring to was the line producer the studio had hired to work on the picture. Ever since they'd started working out the budget, the two of them had been warring with each other.

"Hart, listen, Hart. Start throwing up. I'll be right over."

"Ericka, baby, angel, sweetheart . . ."

"Cut the crap, Hart, and stick your goddamn finger down your goddamn throat!" Ericka slammed down the phone and hurried back to David to explain.

"I wish that yo-yo director of yours would just get it over with. His goddamn suicides are getting real boring," David said. "The idiot only swallows just enough pills to get himself good and sick, but never enough to get it over with."

Ericka hesitated. She could see that David was still angry with her. "I know that, but what if I don't go and this time he really means it?" she asked him.

"You'd be doing us all a great favor."

"David . . ."

"Maybe I should try offing myself. Maybe then *I* would get your attention."

"And what would you do with all that attention, David? You're a very active man."

"Well, there's always half time or a seventh-inning stretch." David was beginning to get his sense of humor back.

"That's what I was afraid of."

"Oh hell, go rescue the suicidal fruit. Just keep him alive long enough to get him on the plane to Italy next week or whenever it is he's supposed to go."

"That's what I love most about you, David. Your sensitivity," she said, throwing on some clothes and kissing him. "I'll call you if it looks like an all-nighter."

"At least take an apple with you or something. That bastard will survive, but you'll die of starvation."

Ericka's hunger had passed.

"KING OF HARTS" in screaming yellow letters flew from a flagpole to the right of a gray stone entrance as Ericka pulled her car into the driveway.

"Crazy fool," she said out loud, standing in front of an enormous red-lacquered heart-shaped door. Ericka expected Hart's usual sarcastic retort to come crackling out of his hidden intercom system. Hart liked to eavesdrop while unsuspecting visitors murmured their comments at the door. But tonight it was too quiet, and Ericka felt a quick wave of fear. Maybe this time Hart had done something more serious. What was the idiotic password? Oh yes, "Key to my heart!" Ericka cried, and the door opened slowly.

Ericka headed through the door and up the floating spiral staircase. Suddenly she was in Wonderland. The king was dying on the enormous heart-shaped bed, covered with a white rabbit fur spread. The bed was on a raised platform. Ericka stepped up and sat down on the bed beside Hart.

"You all right?" she asked.

There was silence.

"Hart." Ericka became frightened. She shook him gently. Then harder.

"Fuck off," Hart mumbled.

"Hart. It's me. Ericka."

"Oh, hi, Ericka. Fuck off."

"Hart, are you all right?"

"Shit. I thought I'd be en route to heaven by now. I'm tired of earth. It really sucks. You know."

"Yeah, Hart. Really sucks." Articulate Hart. Boy genius reduced through his artistic temperament to a four-letter-word vocabulary.

"Hart, did you throw up like I told you?"

Hart looked at Ericka. Sly. Childish.

"Hart! Yes or no?" Ericka demanded.

Hart began to laugh hysterically. Then abruptly he ran into the bathroom, his hand clutching his mouth. Ericka could hear him retching and moaning from the other room.

She walked around his fantasy boudoir, carefully studying all the detail. The room was dark, except for a lighted Lucite case that majestically exhibited Hart's collection of crystal crowns. Steuben. Lalique.

246

Baccarat. Tiffany. . . . And then she looked up at the glowing portrait of Hart that hung above the fireplace. He was dressed as the King of Hearts. The eyes were spooky; no matter where you stood in the room, the eyes were watching you. Coolly. At one angle, they even winked. Ericka puzzled over how it worked. She touched the paint lightly and a mocking cackle sent her reeling.

"Goddamn it, Hart," she said, catching her breath when she realized it was another crude trick of the wired funhouse portrait. "He'll make it through the suicide attempt, and I'll drop dead of a heart attack," Ericka said out loud as she walked shakily over to his bookshelf, thumbing through the titles and extracting an ancient volume of Chaucer that would have looked more romantically authentic caked with mounds of poetic white dust. The book felt peculiar, and Ericka opened it noisily. Ahh. A secret box. How delightful. Inside it were stashed nearly ten vials of cocaine . . . alas, the poetic white dust . . . along with a Tiffany spoon and a gold razor blade. Ericka closed the book and filed it away under *C*. She could still hear Hart making vile noises in the bathroom, and she tapped softly on the door.

"Ericka, I'm dying."

"Do you want me to call the doctor?"

"No. Will you get me a ginger ale?"

"Ginger ale?"

"In the icebox. In the bar. Near the bookshelf. See it?"

"No." Ericka looked around. She saw a light switch and turned it on. The room went black except for some bright green and shocking-pink strobe lights that cascaded across the room.

"Hart, I can't see a thing." Everything was moving weirdly. "Some of your *fercockte* strobe lights just went on."

Ericka peered through the flashing strobe. The frenetic distortion of lights was dizzying.

"Where's the friggin' ginger ale?" Hart complained, emerging from the bathroom. He made a dramatic scene of opening up the refrigerator and taking out his ginger ale.

"Spare me." Ericka collapsed onto the big bed. "Hart, you're such a jerk," she said, clamping her eyes shut.

"Well, at least you didn't call me a faggot." Hart administered himself into an oversized chair; it was a Lucite throne with purple velvet.

"Good night," Ericka said, all at once overwhelmed with fatigue. Her body felt as though it had been shed decades ago. Her mind was slipping off into some other dimension. A feather blown high into the air. She smiled dreamily, thinking what a pain Hart could be, but somehow grateful to him for having rescued her from her confrontation with David.

Thoughts of Jamie floated into her head. Ericka and Jamie running along the beach the day of his graduation from college. She was sixteen and trying to seduce him. That picture stayed with her more than any other. Sometimes a fond happy memory, sometimes a dark bitter one. Tonight it was happy, free of the details and emotions that would have made it otherwise. Then another picture: Jamie sitting in the exact same chair that he always sat on in her parents' house. Her father's favorite student. Sweet, intellectual Jamie. Complicated Jamie. Talented Jamie. The Jamie that she would love for the rest of her life. Like it or not. That Jamie.

Ericka opened her eyes to see Hart standing over her, his hand posed moodily on his hip. He had two black eyes where his mascara had smudged below his lids from the trauma and hysteria that must have led up to his suicide attempt. He looked ridiculous.

"Hart, really, when you're going to die, the least you could do is wear waterproof mascara. You look like a goddamn panda!" Ericka teased, surprised by her feelings of affection for him.

"Jeez, you're an unsympathetic bitch!" he answered, irritated. "Ericka, I'm dying." He fixed her with a dirty look. "I'm glad you think it's so funny."

"I don't. But I think you're like a cat with nine lives."

"Well, maybe I'm running out of chances . . . like I think I'm on the eighth one or something. . . ."

"Just remember that, the next time you go to down a bottle of whatever it is you take."

"Ericka, you're a real cunt. You know that?" Hart said.

"Why, because I care about saving you from yourself?"

"You just care about your pictures."

"That's not true," Ericka said, defending herself.

"I'm an element you need. That's all."

"That's not so," Ericka was close to tears.

"I want you to get the studio to buy me that book. *End Resolve.*"

"I've talked to them about it."

"What'd they say?"

"I've told you. They think it's a hard movie to do."

"I can do it."

"It's risky."

"It's *good.*"

"Hart. I promise you. I've got a project meeting with Norman tomorrow and I'll really give it my best shot. Okay?"

"I'll go to Italy without any problems," Hart offered, his thin body shaking. "I'll be sane. I'll stay on budget. I want to make that book."

Ericka took Hart in her arms and rocked him softly. She tried to console him, but his gentle sobbing grew and grew, a crescendo of pain that seemed to tear right through Ericka. With resignation, she realized she'd have to be there with Hart the rest of the night.

Ericka awoke to apricot shades of amber, cast by sunlight that was welcoming an easy day. Everything seemed so different in the morning, she thought, rubbing sleep from her eyes and stretching her muscles awake. The sky was a dazzling blue and the day felt promising. Ericka touched Hart's frail body. He had his thumb in his mouth. She removed it, as though that might help him grow up.

Now Hart was breathing in soft, even tones, purring tranquillity against a restless world. He chewed on some air and swallowed it as though he had tasted better. Bringing the covers tenderly over him, Ericka brushed her lips against his cheek. She blew some of his hair out of his eyes and he pawed the warm breeze like a puppy.

Then a tall brass sculpture, sleekly designed as a giant rabbit, flashed a warning of the hour to Ericka. Nine-thirty A.M. and she was late. Quietly she tiptoed out.

Ericka watched her boss, Norman Ross, World Wide Pictures' president in charge of theatrical releases and miniseries, as he packed down the tobacco in the bowl of his Sasieni pipe with a gold tamper at the end of his Colibri lighter. His office was always fragrant with the oaky vanilla aroma of his Dunhill A21000 pipe tobacco displayed in its tin atop his old English partners' desk. It was a terrific office, Ericka thought, warm and reflective of Norman. The carpet was a beige wool Berber, his executive chair a taupe leather that was coordinated handsomely with the taupe sofa. The occasional chairs had heavy tubular Lucite arms and legs and were upholstered in the same taupe fabric as the sofa. Built into an antique armoire was Norman's well-stocked bar. And all over the room there were photographs of his wife and his family, and photographs of Norman posed cheerfully alongside political figures and Hollywood stars. There were also stacks of screenplays and plenty of clutter, both personal and business from what Ericka could see. But what she most liked to look at was the Oscar he had won, the elegant bronze symbol that beckoned seductively.

"It's not so much that the book's risky," Norman was saying to her. "Because I think with Hart on it—with his outrageous way of looking at everything—it could be made commercial. Intelligent *and* commercial, which is a rare duet these days. But it's the author's mother! She's crazy. She's never going to sell that book."

Ericka sat back in her chair, determined to sell Norman on the project. They were discussing *End Resolve,* the book she had promised Hart she'd push. The author of the book had died in a plane crash shortly after the book's publication. The rights had been turned over to his mother, his only living relative. Many attempts had been made by studios and independent producers to buy the rights to the commercially unsuccessful but well-reviewed book. The mother, however, had been impossible to deal with and finally the project had been forgotten. All that Ericka had intended to do about the book was mention it briefly and only because she had given her word to Hart that she would. But as she had sat in the studio commissary during lunch, reading the short hard-bound volume, she found herself so engrossed that she was late for her two o'clock meeting with Norman. With the endless amount of reading Ericka's job required, the book had faded in her memory, filed away with the thousands of rejected projects she had encountered through the copious stream of treatments, new manuscripts, old books, galleys, "pitches," magazine articles, and newspaper clippings that came into the studio. Her file cabinets were packed with coverage on these would-be blockbusters. But this book struck Ericka as something special—no wonder Hart wanted to do it so badly. It was a tragic, provocative story about a group of elementary and junior high school national science fair winners who are on a field trip in a space shuttle when the earth is destroyed through a nuclear war. Unable to return to Earth, they are forced to reestablish their lives, creating a new civilization on another planet. The book dealt with social and moral problems—reminiscent of *The Lord of the Flies*, but updated. As impossible as Hart was, Ericka knew he was the right director for the project.

"What if I could convince her to sell us the book?" Ericka asked, sitting forward in her chair, crossing her legs, and leaning toward Norman's desk.

Norman laughed. "Ericka, you're shrink-by-night for Hart, politician-Fuller-Brush-salesman by day."

"My husband's a shrink. My aunt was an Avon lady. I come by it naturally. C'mon, Norman, give me a shot at it. I'll make you a bet. Send me to New York and within three days I'll win this woman over. That is if you're certain you want to buy the book."

"God, the special effects on this would be a killer," Norman said. "Where the hell would we film it?"

"Arizona."

"Maybe."

"Open space is what you need."

"I forgot. What's this planet like? Is there water? Ocean? Mountains?"

"That's not really a problem. If you want to make *Lord of the Flies* in space, you should buy this book. That's all."

"You willing to take responsibility for it?" He chewed on the bit of his pipe.

Ericka drew a quick breath. "Yes," she said, her pulse racing. *Why are you doing this? Is it because you love the book that much? Or is it because it means you'll be in New York and you can look up Jamie Sterling?* The thought had crossed her mind—clouded it, was more like it. *Don't think of Jamie,* she told herself in a silent command. *You've got to be objective about this book. The book. You're going out on a limb for it.* But it was too late. Norman had stood up and was leaning over his desk, his arm outstretched to shake Ericka's hand on the bet she'd proposed.

"What's at stake here?" he asked, grinning, ready to conclude their deal. "Dinner? Your virtue? A nickel?"

"If I get the rights—you owe me a raise," Ericka said weakly, standing up and extending her hand.

"How much?"

"Twenty percent."

Norman laughed again, his bushy eyebrows moving. "Ten percent," he said. "And if you don't?"

"I don't get the raise."

"Wait a minute. . . ."

"It's fair. If I get the rights, I deserve it. You said it was impossible."

"A shrink, a politician, a Fuller Brush salesman, *and* you're as tough as an Arab camel trader," he teased.

"That's why you hired me, I guess."

254

Norman took Ericka's hand and gave it a firm shake, thereby sealing their deal.

When she returned to her office her thoughts were moving in nervous succession. Jamie. New York. And the challenge she had just set for herself. What in the world was she doing? Why would she be able to sell this woman on parting with the rights to her son's book if nobody else had been able to? Had she done this to create an opportunity for herself to be in New York to see Jamie, or had she done it because the book was really that special? The answer, she thought, was convenienty, fortuitously, insanely *both.* But she had better make some phone calls quickly and find out exactly why this woman was supposed to be so difficult. World Wide Pictures had considered the book, but they'd never made an offer. She did have a friend at Warner Brothers who might know.

Ericka buzzed her secretary, Lilly Carson, to come into her office. Lilly appeared carrying a green steno pad along with a fresh stack of telephone messages. "If only these were dollar bills," she said, throwing her long strawberry-blond hair over her shoulder.

"Those all since lunch?" Ericka asked, distraught.

Her secretary nodded. "You should feel very secure. Everybody needs you."

"That's just about when I begin to feel insecure," Ericka said, glancing quickly through the messages and noting that Kelly had returned her call from this morning.

With a staggering amount of things left to do that day, Ericka began issuing instructions to her secretary.

Chapter Fourteen

WHEN THEY PUT THE WORD *INSECURE* IN THE DICTIONARY, they did it with men like Leonard Pollock in mind. Deep down, Leonard had always questioned Kirstin's love for him. He had never been able to put away his suspicions that she had married him only for his money and the security of their relationship. Experience had taught him that everybody wanted something from him.

Leonard hesitated before picking up the telephone, looking first around the great expanse of his office. There was a consuming tightness throughout his entire muscle network, a binding pressure of nerves and a sensation of swelling across his chest into his arms. He felt confined by his fifteen-hundred-dollar custom-made suit—as though he might burst right out of it. He had had that feeling ever since seeing Kelly Nelson at the Bel-Air Hotel two days ago.

It was a premonition, spiraling in him, he thought, smoothing his hand along the rounded corner of his English oak-burl desk and looking down at its stainless-steel base. Rich and powerful. That was the look of his office. That was the taste he needed in his soul. He was wearing Rossetti shoes, tapping one of them on the teak and travertine floor. Power—which translated to him as control. Leonard tried to buoy himself up against his instincts. His instincts had always been his map, his guide. They had directed him out of poverty and into this position of great wealth and power. Those same internal commands, those psychic light bulbs were now pressing Leonard to pick up the telephone and investigate his wife. She had been *too* calm throughout their confrontation. She was *too* good to him. Too perfect. What was she covering up? Was she making a fool of him? Lately he'd noticed the difference in their bodies. Her flesh was young. His flesh was old. Hers was fair and clear. His was spotted with age. Small patches of hair had disappeared on his legs, down around his shins, probably from where his socks had rubbed for so many years. Kirstin must have noticed. When he had married her, he had been in top physical condition. His thighs had been like thick steel rods. His chest had been imposing. But now, he knew, he was getting soft from so many years behind a desk. The only muscle he used lately was his brain. At least that was still in first-rate form.

Leonard sat down in his tan buttery-leather chair,

gripping the icy chrome arms that curved down into the base of the chair as he swiveled around to look out reflectively at the Century City skyline. Some men did their unwinding by smoking a pipe. Some by playing squash. Some by listening to music. And some by a quick spin over to their mistress's apartment. Leonard preferred his own meditative method, which soothed his mind and helped him clarify positions. His point of focus, his center as some people called it, was the great panoramic view afforded to him by his superbly situated corner office. It was in this manner that he was able to think things out, instructing his secretary to hold all calls. Several minutes of productive peace.

Brand spanking-new buildings soared into the sky. They were the new landscape. Originally prairie land, later transformed into movie sets and then, in the early sixties, swept over by the storms of economy, the land had been revalued and sold profitably as real estate. Real estate that was now a mecca of concrete and steel. The buildings appeared cold and sure of themselves, like the baby-faced executives, swathed in Brooks Brothers clothes, who were delivered as graduates out of the wombs of the East Coast institutions ready to take over the world.

But Leonard had come up the hard way. And he remembered the world as it was. You had to fight to make a living. You weren't "groomed." You ran like mad, working as many jobs as you could, saving, juggling, and outsmarting.

Leonard had been born in Indianapolis to poor Russian immigrant parents as the youngest of seven children. In 1932, at the age of twelve, he had had to drop out of school to help support his family, making money any way he could. He sold telegrams for Western Union at the train station, running around the bustling complex with a telegram pad and hustling business. The messages he carried over to a central Western Union office, where they were processed and then wired. Also at the station, he carried suitcases for the tips. Weekends he worked at newsstands. And in the evenings he supplemented his income working as a movie theater usher. The telegrams proved to be the most lucrative method of making money. The train passengers were always harried, having to rush to make their trains and needing to place their messages quickly. Leonard found it easy to take advantage of the pressed-for-time senders by overcharging them and pocketing the extra money. When ten words sold for thirty cents, Leonard was able to get away with charging sixty cents. When they sold for sixty cents, he would charge ninety. It was skimming in much the same manner as Leonard's parking lot attendants now skimmed from him in several parking structures he owned across the state. Leonard and his friends had called it IIG, which stood for if it *goes*. IIG money could add up to a lot.

After two long years of this, Leonard was able to fulfill his dream. Everybody in his family deposited their earnings into a special jar that would provide for the family's expenses. But Leonard had secretively held back a portion of his weekly earnings to save for his dream of bringing his family to California to find a better life. At the age of fourteen, after two years of trading one uniform for another— Western Union boy by day, movie usher by night— Leonard had saved up enough money to accomplish his goal.

The manager of Indianapolis' Western Union, who had befriended Leonard, had a relative in California who owned a shoe factory in Los Angeles. A letter was written on Leonard's behalf, landing him a job that would pay sixteen dollars a week. Leonard was elated. He was now on his way to making his fortune.

He began by working daytimes in the shoe factory, nighttimes again in movie theaters. On Saturdays he worked for a florist, and in the evening he ran over to the amusement pier in Santa Monica, where he'd sell ice cream bars. By the time the Depression started, the box under Leonard's bed as well as his pockets was bulging with cash.

It was around 1938, when he was eighteen years old, that Leonard made his first real estate endeavor. One day at the shoe factory a friend of his needed a place to stay, so Leonard took him in with his family as a boarder. A couple of weeks later he took in another friend, then a third. When he heard that the people living next door were being foreclosed on by the bank, Leonard went to the bank and made a deal to take over the house. With his boarders from the shoe factory, he told them, he could easily fill the house with tenants and be able to make the monthly payments. After that acquisition, he worked closely with the bank, buying up houses and filling them with tenants, until he found himself in the boarding-house business. With a taste of the money that could be made in real estate, Leonard decided to focus his energy in that area and found that he didn't have to limit himself to buying houses. Hotels, office buildings, commercial properties—they were all being foreclosed on, and Leonard was able to pick them up for ten cents on the dollar. For the big deals he put together groups of investors.

After the Depression Leonard found he was able to refinance the buildings and obtain great amounts of cash to buy even more buildings. From that his operation expanded. Some of the small hotels that he had bought cheaply he sold to the Hilton chain, taking stock as his payment—a valuable payment indeed.

After the war Leonard went into construction himself, building tracts of houses. With all the men in service coming home from the war and needing places to live, Pollock's Planned Communities quickly thrived, putting Leonard Pollock on the map as one of the largest builders in the country.

The alternate rise and fall of fortunes in the real estate business made it a precarious one. It was a roller-coaster ride, and over the years Leonard had watched many of his friends who had made it big go under. Somehow Leonard had managed to hold on through the unpredictable economic cycles, weathering governmental and environmental controls, suddenly monstrous interest rates, and other ebbing trends resulting from too much product on the market. Leonard attributed his success to several factors: brains, timing, hard work, and luck—not necessarily in that order. From his Russian heritage, where it was nearly impossible for a Jew to own land, Leonard had acquired a great drive to possess property. In his case it became a valuable heritage.

In the midst of his reverie, Leonard noticed a tall, well-dressed blonde crossing the bridge over Avenue of the Stars. He was too far away to be able to determine whether or not it was Kirstin, but it reminded him why he had told his secretary to hold all calls. The blonde was carrying a shopping bag, swinging it back and forth, and his thoughts took on a corresponding rhythm: Should he or should he not make his call?

Then, with his decision suddenly made, Leonard picked up the telephone and dialed Patrick Delaney's office. Patrick Delaney was the private investigator Leonard had been using for several years to do asset searches for him, to check out potential partners. Once Leonard had begun using the former FBI agent's services, he discovered more and more areas in which to apply them. Now he was about to subject his wife to their expert scrutiny.

Patrick Delaney was on the telephone when Leonard's call came through. His secretary had scribbled Leonard Pollock's name on a little piece of paper in front of him. Seeing it, Delaney immediately wound up his conversation and lit one cigarette off the butt of another, before punching into the line where Leonard waited. Leonard Pollock was an important client and Patrick Delaney made a point of responding quickly to all his assignments.

This, Delaney sensed, was not going to be an ordinary assignment. He could tell immediately from Leonard Pollock's unusually rapid speech that this case was personal. He put on his best bedside manner and listened as Leonard told him that he wanted his wife checked out. Leonard didn't say much, but Patrick Delaney had no trouble grasping the situation. While his investigation agency rarely took on messy domestic cases, Patrick Delaney was clearly going to have to make an exception, and he began jotting things down as Leonard spoke. The call lasted only a few minutes, as did all communications Delaney had ever had with Leonard Pollock.

A moment later, Delaney was organizing the probe. He called up two of his best surveillance stringers and put them on the case. Then he called in a member of his staff and told him to run a basic computer search on Kirstin Lindstrom Pollock. He'd seen pictures of the beautiful blonde Swede and was actually curious himself about what might turn up. Younger knockout woman. Older man. Probably she *was* cheating on him.

Chapter Fifteen

ROXBURY PARK BUSTLED WITH ACTIVITY DURING THE AFTER-
noon. There were children with their parents or
housekeepers screeching on the swings in the sandy-
surfaced play area, on the long winding slides, and
on the jungle gyms. Kites. Frisbees. Dogs. Jocks throwing footballs. Lovers lazing under trees. Kids riding
bikes. Little old men playing on the bowling green
lawns. And tennis players waiting for the crowded
courts.

Kelly walked through the park observing all this,
on her way to the twins' Little League game. The
game was probably half over, but Kelly wanted to
catch what she could. She tried her best to be at as
many games as possible.

What a perfect afternoon, Kelly thought, pulling

her sweater up over her head and tying it around her shoulders, as she looked out across the field for her boys. There they were: Jason playing second base, Joshua out in left field. Kelly took her place in the bleachers designated for the parents of the Reds, looking around briefly to see who was there, smiling a few quick hellos. Ordinarily the same parents were at each game, and she recognized just about everybody there.

"Top of the fourth. Three to two," said the mother beside her.

Kelly glanced up at the score displayed across a big wooden billboard recently made electronic. Strikes, balls, and outs lit up in bright red. The numbers and innings were flipped by a press of the button by the announcer, a cute kid of thirteen who was enclosed in the green wooden booth outside of the chain link fence announcing with all the style of the major leagues. Top of the fourth. Three to two. Three balls. Kelly smiled at the mother who had offered her the score. Annabelle Sherrer. Annabelle Sherrer appeared at every single game, always bringing a jug of wine and plastic cups, which she cheerfully distributed among the other parents. Was she an alcoholic? Kelly wondered, thinking that she might be. She was always so eager to get everyone to drink along with her.

Making a rare appearance and sitting on the bench below Kelly was one of the "celebrity" parents. Every year there was at least one. This year it was rock star Spike Donner. He'd arrived in his big black limo with his chauffeur. On most days the chaffeur came in his place.

Then Kelly noticed off to her right Sheila Klein, dressed to kill as usual in the latest designer clothes. Today she was wearing an electric-blue suede coat dress and shoes that looked dyed to match. Her stockings were tinted subtly in the same hue. And she had on sculptural gold jewelry. A smashing look for a magazine layout but definitely out of place at a Little League game. Maneuvering himself close to Sheila, drinking a cup of Annabelle Sherrer's wine, was Marshal Jolton, one of the single fathers who came to the games partly to watch his kid play— mostly to pick up on the mothers. What a cast of characters the parents of these Little League teams composed, Kelly thought.

Making a great ruckus from behind Kelly was the team's gung-ho mother, Nancy Ladd, who always wore the team color, red, and asked the other parents to do the same during play-off games. Kelly half expected Nancy Ladd to tap her on the shoulder any minute, to reprimand her for having worn a lavender sweater. But at the moment Nancy Ladd was too busy shouting a cheer: "Give me an *R* . . . give me an *E* . . ." and Kelly looked out toward the field again to see what she had missed. Jason and Joshua were waving to her as they ran toward the dugout along with the rest of their team.

"Watch!" Jason mouthed angrily, waving his hands and arms to help him get his point across.

Kelly mouthed back that she *was* watching as Jason came up to bat.

Positioning himself, Jason worked out a grip on the bat and kicked the dirt under his feet a little with his cleats. He bent his knees and looked intently toward the pitcher. What a perfectionist, Kelly thought, aware of the concentration on Jason's small face, the way he was grinding his teeth while waiting for the pitch. He was a miniature Ron, carbon copy. Joshua also looked like Ron, but he really had more of Kelly's temperament. *"Ball!"* The pitcher shuffled his feet and exercised his arm before heaving a second pitch toward Jason.

"He's so cute!" said the gung-ho mother, Nancy Ladd, from behind Kelly, tapping her on the shoulder.

Kelly nodded, without taking her eyes off her son. C'mon, baby, she thought. Hit it towards the klutz on third base. *"Strike."* Kelly saw Jason muttering something, frustrated. She realized her own hands were clenched into fists and she smiled. This time Jason's bat made contact with the ball, sending it hard and long into center field. The center fielder ducked away from the ball, which was coming too fast and directly at him. Kelly jumped up and cheered for her son, who had just made a triple. All right, Jason! The parents of the Reds applauded. Nancy Ladd sang a cheer. Sheila Klein smiled and adjusted her designer sunglasses. Marshal Jolton patted Sheila's thigh. Annabelle Scherrer poured herself another glass of wine and hooted. And Spike Donner looked up at Kelly, surprising her with a big smile that told her he knew that Jason was her son. She smiled back at him, then looked quickly over at Jason, blowing him a kiss and making a victory gesture. Jason was in a crouched running position ready to sprint home at the first opportunity.

Kelly sat back down, accepting a cup of wine from Annabelle Scherrer. Next up to bat was the token girl on the team. Each Little League team had one girl player, and Kelly looked over at her father, who was leaning against the fence in a three-piece suit. This was the son he'd never had, and he never missed a game, coming directly from his law office for the last hour or so of each game. With her long hair hanging down from under her batter's helmet, she whipped around, missing the ball. She tried again, missing again. On her third swing she bunted, sending Jason home and bringing herself to first for a single. Jason was ecstatic as he dashed into the dugout, exchanging "fives" with his teammates.

A slight breeze had kicked up and Kelly pulled her sweater back on, adjusting it over her jeans and lifting her shirt collar out over its boat neck. She took a sip of her wine and looked up at the clear blue sky that probably wasn't as clear as it looked; she was just used to it. Smog in L.A. was a presence that never really went away; it merely lessened at times. A clear blue sky was the sky she would have had if she had been free to take Brandon up on his invitation. The notion of joining Brandon in Sardinia sent a fresh chill through Kelly and she took another sip of her wine, grinning at the preposterousness of it all. And then imagining what it would be like.

Brandon had called her just as he'd said he would the day before. Nervously Kelly had managed to dodge his calls, using Bob's answering service as a screening device. She hadn't wanted to talk to him. He was a fantasy lived out and filed away in her memory. She couldn't chance saying yes to him again. There was too much at stake—having been seen by Leonard Pollock had really brought her down to earth. And besides, she was too vulnerable. Too susceptible. Too in need of him now. Ever since their night together she'd been unable to get him off her mind. It was as though she were charmed, drugged, craving the feel of him. His voice. His eyes. His mouth. Like a Goya portrait, they haunted her. Safety was Ron, the kids, work. They were a blanket of familiarity under which she could hide. To peek out and expose herself was to risk seduction again. It would take time for the effects of Brandon to wear off.

There hadn't been time, however. Today Bob had been in the office with her and she had had no choice but to take all calls. When she actually got on the phone with Brandon, she was a nervous wreck.

Brandon, in that caressing voice of his, began their conversation in a light amusing way, as though he was already completely aware of the state she was in. He was affectionate, familiar, linking right into where they had left off. They were on intimate terms. He was her lover. They'd shared a very special secret together, and for some inexplicable reason talking to him made Kelly feel better about it. She told him all about how Kirstin's husband had seen them together, how awful she'd felt afterward, and how she really shouldn't see him again.

Brandon had been warm, understanding, in response. Even sympathetic. He told her he'd make it all better by taking her away with him to Sardinia. He was leaving tomorrow for about a month to begin preliminary work on blueprints for a hotel he and a group of partners were putting up.

It was a perfect technique, ignoring the guilty reality—playing instead with the fantasy. It relaxed Kelly, made her laugh as he attempted to lure her into accompanying him by painting marvelous word pictures of what her month would be like if only she could go. If only she *could* go.

It didn't take much to activate Kelly's imagination. Brandon spoke of Sardinia as one of the last unspoiled wildernesses of the Mediterranean, with its rugged coastline of granite cliffs falling steeply down to emerald waters and secretive beaches, where one could almost envision Ulysses sailing around one of the rocky points in search of sirens or the Cyclops. The countryside he described as a carpet of wildflowers with dwarf iris growing densely over the tumbled headlands, smothering the landscape in every conceivable shade of purple.

Porto Retondo was the pristine village where Brandon stayed, an exclusive development put together by two aristocratic Venetian brothers as a private playground for Italy's very rich, very inbred high society.

It was plainly paradise, he told her, describing the sailing they could do together on the sea that was flat as a mirror. The waterskiing. The scuba diving. The hobnobbing with the whole top layer of Italian industry as well as with a multitude of counts, countesses, princes, princesses. . . . Late in the evenings they'd go dancing together in Sardinia's most unusual nightclub, Ritual, which was a cave converted into a swank discotheque. But best of all, Brandon told her, in a voice that promised pleasure, was the unsurpassable lovemaking the Italian island inspired. Just the air there, he told her, was an aphrodisiac. Cool breezes working in harmony with the sun. The sun sending down sultry rays of smoldering passion, melting down every sensation into lazy desire. *Have you ever made love in a grotto?* he had asked her outrageously.

Joshua Nelson looked over at his twin brother, Jason, for support, then went up to bat. It was the bottom of the last inning. The game was tied. He had to get on base—he *couldn't* get out. In his back pocket he carried along with him a Steve Sax baseball card for good luck and fast inspiration, and just before getting into position, Joshua brought out the baseball card, managing a discreet look. Steve Sax was Joshua's idol. If Josh could be anyone, he'd be the hustling, base-stealing Dodger. The pitcher was getting restless, so Joshua hurried up his movements. He'd wanted to look over at his mother, but it was too late.

With a loud crack he sent the ball sailing, foul by inches. He felt his throat constrict as he heard the umpire behind him shouting *Foul ball. Strike one.* He shouldn't have swung, he thought tensely, mad at himself. The ball was definitely outside. Frustrated, he readied himself for the next pitch. *Stttrrrike two.* That was low. Joshua was sure. He looked over his shoulder at the third-base coach, who nodded that

272

the umpire's call was correct. Determined to make this one go, Joshua bunted the ball, running safely to first and letting out a sign of relief. Shortly after that, the next batter walked, sending Joshua automatically to second. When he got there he crouched down, anxious to steal third—the image of Steve Sax clear in his mind.

Joshua was halfway between second and third when the catcher, holding the ball, saw him. From the position Joshua was in, it was easier to run to third than to run back to second, so he ran toward third base as fast as he could. The catcher's throw went to the third baseman. Joshua was sure he was out, until the third baseman stumbled and dropped the ball. Fired up with his opportunity, Joshua raced home, sliding hard into the plate a split second before the ball.

Kelly was brought abruptly out of her reverie by all the excitement around her. Everybody was standing up and cheering, waving their arms. Kelly looked out at the field to see what had happened. A few of the parents were looking at her and smiling. Spike Donner turned around and told her what dynamite boys she had. Team mother Nancy Ladd patted her on the back.

Joshua, she saw, had slid into home plate. She watched him stand up and dust himself off. When he looked over at her, she applauded him, wishing she could ask someone what had happened but feeling too embarrassed. Hoping for a clue, she looked up at the scoreboard. Bottom of the last inning. Reds 7, Pirates 6. Whatever had happened, Joshua had apparently won the game for his team. Usually it was Jason making the heroic plays. Kelly was glad to see that this time it was Joshua, and she wondered if he'd hit a home run. If he had, it would have been his first. Then she noticed that he was limping.

"You didn't even see." Jason said hotly, running over to the bleachers. Joshua was limping close behind him. The joy that should have been in his eyes was clouded by tears.

"Yes I did," Kelly responded guiltily, going over to Joshua and hugging him. "That was great, baby! Looks like you're the new team hero!"

Joshua blinked his eyes several times and smiled tentatively. It was obvious that he was holding back the great pride he felt. He was waiting to make sure that Jason was wrong—that his mother had seen his victorious slide into home plate.

"What happened?" Jason asked Kelly in accusation. "What?"

"If you saw, then what happened? I looked over and you weren't paying any attention."

Kelly hesitated, her arm around Joshua, looking uncertainly at Jason. "Don't talk to me that way," she said, feeling immensely guilty, trying to distract him from the situation by directing her attention to Joshua's leg where the white cotton pant was rubbed heavily with dirt. "You okay? You were limping."

"I'm fine," Joshua said shyly. Kelly hugged him tightly to her. He was so sweet, and she could tell that his feelings were hurt. If only she'd asked someone what had happened, she could have reassured

Joshua. But now there wasn't much she could say to redeem herself.

"Well, I think this calls for a celebration," she said, trying. "Both of you played great. Spike Donner turned around to me at the end of the game and said how terrific you both are."

Joshua smiled, ready to believe her. But Jason's face was full of the injustice he felt they'd been dealt.

"Let's go," Kelly said uncomfortably. "I've got to get dinner on. You guys hungry?"

Jason hesitated for a moment, then looked up at Kelly. "Can we go by Häagen-Dazs and pick up some ice cream?" he asked, his eyes full of the devil.

"Sure," Kelly said, making her peace with him.

"And their chocolate fudge cake?"

Jason would go far in life.

Chapter Sixteen

BUDDY NAZIO AND LISA WELLS STOPPED BY MCDONALD'S TO pick up Egg McMuffins and coffee on their way to the Pollock residence. It was their second day on the job. Having been contracted by private investigator Patrick Delaney for a surveillance assignment, they were busily comparing hunches about their Swedish subject, Kirstin Pollock.

"I'll bet ya one day's pay that she's gettin' it on the side," Buddy said, adding some more sugar to his coffee.

Lisa watched him tear open his third packet of sugar and shake it into his Styrofoam cup. Buddy was cute, if you liked the all-American football type, with his big round blue eyes, sandy hair, and large athletic build. But he was always on the make. "I hate being put on assignments with you, Buddy. It always costs me. I work too hard for my money. Go find yourself another sucker." Lisa looked up at the food counter, tempted to take along an apple Danish with her for lunch, then deciding against it.

"I'll settle for payment in kind," he said, letting his eyes roam down to her chest and grinning wickedly.

"You never give up."

"It's just that you've got the best tits I've ever seen and I'm dying to squeeze them."

Lisa polished off her coffee and stood up to go. Buddy was incorrigible but harmless.

"You think she's straight?" he asked, referring again to Kirstin, tapping his fingers on the small rectangular Formica table.

"That's what I'm here to find out."

"Girl's got no imagination!" Buddy said, shaking his head at his petite but well-built partner. When he'd first met her on a case they'd shared a few years back, he'd been taken by surprise. She just didn't fit his image of what a female private eye should look like. She looked so much like Sally Fields. "Bet ya an apple Danish?"

"And be in your debt. Never!"

Buddy was parked in front of the Pollocks' Tudor estate. Lisa was stationed at the corner, her communications radio tuned for word from Buddy. They operated as a team, alternating their tail of the suspect and keeping in constant communication through radios and walkie-talkies.

Buddy looked at his watch. Leonard Pollock had

left the house twenty-eight minutes ago. From Buddy's experience, the wife usually left about thirty minutes after her husband, in which case Kirstin Pollock could be expected to pull out of her driveway at any moment. He snapped the cap back onto his pen, then took the *Racing Form* that was spread across his lap and threw it into the backseat of his borrowed black four-door Caddy. One of the things about working ritzy assignments for Patrick Delaney was that he lent you classy company cars to drive. After all, Buddy's own beat-up Buick might look suspicious parked for such long periods of time in these fancy locales. Caddies, Mercedes, Porsches, BMWs and Audis were camouflage cars of the trade that blended in with the Bel Air, Beverly Hills, Holmby Hills scenery. When he'd worked on protection for President Ford in his Secret Service days, before going out on his own as a private investigator, he used to ride in limousines all the time. But that had been a lousy way to make a buck. All the traveling had been fun at first, trips to Vail, Colorado, where President Ford went skiing, and that spread he used to go to in Palm Springs, but after a while it got too familiar. Finally his wife grew fed up with it all and left him, taking his kids and hitting him for alimony and child support.

"There she is," he said into the radio, starting up his engine as he saw Kirstin Pollock's silver-blue Corniche pulling out of the long stretch of driveway. He waited for her to get to the corner before he took off after her. What a looker, he thought.

A couple of blocks later, Lisa picked up the tail. Buddy was following on a parallel street ready for word from Lisa. When Kirstin's Rolls turned east onto Sunset, Buddy was behind her again. *Piece of cake.* Kirstin drove like the lady of leisure she was. Slow, steady, and perfect. He wondered if she fucked like she drove. Slow, steady, and perfect. These jealous-husband-checking-out-wife assignments always aroused him. Especially when the wives looked like this one.

Kirstin made a left turn off Sunset into the parking lot behind the row of fashionable Sunset Plaza shops.

Lisa followed her into Ole Henriksen of Denmark, looking around the stylishly furnished skin care center and waiting briefly before going up to where the elegant Kirstin Pollock was standing at a mauve Formica counter, wearing a leopard-patterned silk blouse that had a caramel background and was tucked loosely into a pencil-straight black skirt. It was an old look that, from recent issues of fashion magazines, Lisa had noticed was reemerging in a big way. Leopard *anything* just a year ago she would have considered tacky. On Kirstin Pollock, however, the look was sensual and chic.

"Good morning, Mrs. Pollock. You're here for a facial today . . . is that it?" asked the girl behind the desk.

"And an eyelash dye," Kirstin said.

Lisa watched Kirstin walk down a hallway and disappear through a doorway. She returned just a moment later, having shed her outfit and put on a rose cotton smock. It was a bad break that Kirstin was there for a facial instead of a manicure. A facial room was private, offering no opportunity for Lisa to eavesdrop and take notes.

Back at the appointment desk, Lisa asked if there were any manicure openings. While waiting for a reply she noticed, in a Lucite frame atop the counter, a picture of Victoria Principal shot nude to the waist from the back, with the glamorous actress looking over her shoulder. It was an ad from *Harper's Bazaar*, plugging "Makeup by Marja." Just across the room was another mauve Formica countertop, this one being a display unit and makeup station for Marja herself, who was busy working there, applying makeup on a Japanese woman in a white warm-up suit that was dribbled with pink, teal blue, and green paint, like a pastel version of a Jackson Pollock painting. On her feet were teal-blue moccasin-type loafers and on top of her head teal-blue sunglasses. She was wearing big diamond stud earrings that Lisa thought had to be four carats each.

"You were interested in a manicure?" Lisa turned toward the petite blonde and nodded, following her over to her small table, also mauve Formica, that was covered with the supplies of the trade.

Once seated, Lisa extended her right hand, observing with reserved pleasure the manicurist working on it. Manicures were something she rarely treated herself to. They didn't last long enough for her to justify the expense. When they fitted in with her surveillance scheme, however, she was delighted. She'd turn the receipt over to Patrick Delaney. It was a legitimate expense.. While Kirstin was in the other room getting her facial, Lisa could wait for her without arousing suspicion. A facial took an hour, a manicure thirty to forty-five minutes. With drying time it would work out just right.

By the time Kirstin emerged, Lisa was standing blowing on her nails to hasten the drying process and looking bewildered at the one-hundred-dollar-plus purchases she had made. Lipstick and a new kind of smudge stick eyeliner pencil from Marja. And then an assortment of Ole Henriksen products. A lemon cleanser. An anti-wrinkle night moisturizer with RNA-DNA and jojoba. An eye-throat cream with avocado, jojoba, and aloe vera. A cucumber clay mask. A spot lotion for blemishes. And cellular collagen ampules. This was promising to become an expensive assignment. But if she came out of it with her complexion looking even half as good as that of the woman who had sold her the products, it would have been well worth it. Hell, she could write it all off.

Now it was Buddy's turn, and he waited while Kirstin drove her Corniche up into the driveway of the Beverly Hills Hotel. This was it. Too bad schoolteacher turned FBI lady turned private eye Lisa hadn't taken him up on his bet. Only two days on the job, and he was about to wrap it up. Classy dames like this didn't rendezvous in flea-bag motels. They got laid in three-hundred-dollar-a-day suites with caviar and Dom Pérignon as foreplay.

Wondering what Delaney's office had come up with on Kirstin through its in-house computer check and then the follow-up report that would have resulted, Buddy got out of his car and accepted the ticket handed to him by the parking attendant. When he went into the office later in the afternoon to turn in his surveillance report he'd ask Delaney's cute little secretary about it. Women used their female charms as bartering devices all the time—why shouldn't he profit from his own adorable baby-face charm, he thought with a chuckle, trying to dream up a new line to deliver to her. He'd never actually taken Delaney's secretary out. That, he'd learned, was the quickest way to spoil a source. Invariably he'd make the wrong move, and presto, the lady didn't know you.

Buddy took his sport coat from the backseat of his car where he had it hung up neatly on a hanger and, putting it on, headed in the direction of the legendary pink stucco building—the Beverly Hills Hotel. Over the walkway, he noticed, was a green-and-white-striped canvas porte cochere. It reminded him of the awning at the Turf Club at Hollywood Park, and he checked his watch again, anxious to get to a phone to call his bookie. He had had a hot tip on a horse called Native Princess and he wanted to make sure to get his bet in on time.

There was lots of activity with all the people flowing in and out, some in business suits, some in designer tennis clothes ... silk dresses ... jogging suits. A distinct air of the privileged pervaded the atmosphere. Bellmen were busy wheeling in cartfuls of prestigious but not necessarily attractive luggage.

The position Buddy chose for himself afforded him an easy view into the lavishly furnished hotel, which had recently been done over by some big-name designer, preserving the hotel's original glamorous forties look.

First checking the pink and green plastic cushions and then dusting them off, Buddy sat down on a black wrought-iron love seat on the porch outside the lobby doors. He had already spotted Kirstin standing at the front desk talking to a man dressed in a navy-blue blazer wearing the hotel's crest over his right breast pocket. After a moment Kirstin left him, walking through the bustling lobby and nodding to one of the bellmen who had waved at her. Curious, Buddy thought. Either her lover lived here or stayed here a lot or she just did *business* out of the hotel. Wouldn't it be something if he found out she hooked! Some women got their kicks out of charging for it. Kirstin Pollock could be one of them.

Oldest trick in the book, Buddy thought as he got up from his seat and walked into the hotel where Kirstin had gone into some fancy dress store. If somebody happened to see her in the hotel, her explanation would be that she was shopping. He sat down on one of the pink print sofas across from a marble fireplace. Above the fireplace was a beveled mirror set in a wooden molding. Through the mirror he was able to keep a watch on the entrance to the hotel's promenade shops. Most likely Kirstin would stay in there about ten minutes, then come out and go to where she'd planned on going all along. Sin City. As predicted, close to ten minutes later, Kirstin was back in the lobby. She'd even bought something. That was fast work. Probably just a little something to legitimize it all. Swinging her glossy tan shopping bag back and forth, she crossed over to where the elevator was located, then continued past it down a corridor. What luck that the room she was going to was on the first floor, Buddy thought, passing a bank of phones and hoping he'd be as lucky with Native Princess. The logistics of an elevator tag were far more complicated. Buddy stayed a good distance behind Kirstin but close enough to see which room it was that she went into. He watched her knock, straightening her hair that didn't need to be straightened, and smoothing her skirt that didn't need to be smoothed. The door was opened immediately, but Buddy was unable to get a glimpse of her host. She extended her arm to him, and was drawn in out of his sight. Holding his position for about thirty seconds, Buddy looked around. No hotel guests to give him suspicious glances. Just the big green banana leaves of the wallpaper that he thought of as indigenous to the grand old hotel. He waited a moment, then hurried down the hall to make a note of the room number.

After making a quick call to his bookie, Buddy got hold of Lisa on his walkie-talkie, filling her in on what he'd seen so far. "I'll let you know when she leaves," he said. "You take over, I'll stay back and check out the turkey in 108."

"Gotcha." Lisa's voice crackled into his walkie-talkie.

"Looks like nooky-nooky," he said.

"Just do your job, Buddy."

"Roger, baby. Over and out."

An hour later, Kirstin was walking thoughtfully through the lobby. She looked as though she were trying to figure something out. To make a decision. Her face was very serious and Buddy wondered if there'd been a fight.

"Subject leaving premises," he said, wiring into Lisa.

Then he went over to one of the house phones to begin his probe. "Hello," he said when a man answered on the first ring. "Yes," he continued, "this is room service, we've got an order for you but we've got some confusion. . . . I apologize for the—"

"I didn't order anything from room service." The man had a thick European accent.

"Is this Room 108?" Buddy asked, making his voice sound confused.

"Yes, it is."

"There must be some mix-up. . . . What's your name?"

"Mr. Bernard."

"Are you registered as Mr. and Mrs. Bernard?"

"No, just Mr. Bernard." The man was extremely polite.

"I see. . . . Sorry. We have two Bernards registered at the hotel. Our mistake."

On a small spiral pad, Buddy made some further notations. Room registered single male. Bernard co-suspect.

Chapter Seventeen

IT WAS HOT INSIDE KENNEDY AIRPORT AS ERICKA SQUEEZED into the jungle of passengers hovering over American Airlines's baggage claim. Watching her suitcase and tote traveling around the carrousel for the second time, Ericka managed to yank her luggage off the machine, bumping it awkwardly to the ground.

She was dying from the heat and wishing she hadn't worn a silk blouse and wool gabardine suit. As soon as she stepped outside, she would be blasted with frigid air and her sweat would dry, producing a cold grainy chill and leaving her handsome ensemble limp and unwearable.

By now Ericka had deep-rooted reservations about this trip. To begin with, the research that she had done, utilizing her best studio informers, had turned up disconcerting reports on Mrs. Beall, the woman with whom she'd be negotiating on the book rights she was here to acquire. From everything she had learned, Mrs. Beall was a craggy old lady, reclusive, and dead set against parting with the rights to her late son's "science fiction masterpiece." Apparently the fact that Ericka, on the telephone, had succeeded in persuading the old woman to meet with her was a major coup. When Norman had heard about it, he'd come into her office and offered his congratulations. After their meeting together he, too, had done some further checking into the situation, and he said he felt as if he were sending her off on a mission to sell the Pope on a pro-abortion petition for the Catholic Church.

Also tearing away at Ericka's composure was the dilemma she faced about whether or not she should call Jamie. Before she'd gotten onto the plane it had been crystal clear that she would. But as she soared across the three-thousand-mile stretch from her coast to his, her courage dropped away. Just that morning, packing for her trip, and winding up loose ends on the phone, she'd been fueled with wondrously romantic notions. But now as she literally came down from the clouds, the realities of the situation felt as if they were closing in on her, suddenly claustrophobic, and Ericka felt trapped in a stifling rash of doubt.

Why was she doing this? She'd asked herself on the plane, trying her best to concentrate on a story treatment she was reading and failing to absorb its content. Because she wanted to get Jamie out of her system once and for all, she answered herself. Kirstin Pollock had once pointed out to her that perhaps she didn't *want* Jamie out of her system, and now that the test was so near, it occurred to Ericka that Kirstin could be right. Getting Jamie out of her system would be like saying good-bye to a memory that had in some odd way become a part of her. She almost wouldn't know what to do without it. Then she worried how that particular exorcism would affect her relationship with David. If, without Jamie, she wanted David more or loved him more, in all probability she would need him more. That was not at all what their relationship was about. It never had been. And at this particular moment that realization had Ericka feeling completely undone.

Unable to get a skycap, Ericka maneuvered her luggage toward the exit.

With the long, fat line leading out of the airport finally behind her, Ericka welcomed the cool breeze and stepped into another line, impatient to hail a taxi. Tallying up how many people were ahead of her, she noticed a cab pulling up to the curb, and getting out of it, she was certain, was Jamie Sterling. In an opaque daze, Ericka watched him scuttle up to the main entrance, catching a quick glimpse of the tortoise-rimmed glasses that had always distinguished him, and then the familiar blue oxford cloth shirt she always used to tease him about. To this day she couldn't see a blue oxford cloth shirt without thinking of Jamie. Strapped over his shoulder, she saw, was a tan carry-on luggage case, and the nondescript raincoat he had on flapped loosely behind him, unbuttoned and billowing, like a beige version of a matador's cape.

Ericka was still reeling with shock when she realized that if she didn't act quickly she could kiss her fantasy good-bye.

Her first dilemma was what to do about her bags. Locating a skycap standing nearby, she nearly attacked him with a twenty-dollar bill, imploring him to send her bags on to the Mayfair Regent Hotel without her. The twenty dollars was his tip. She told him to tell the taxi driver to charge the cab fare to her hotel room, they knew her there and wouldn't give him any problems. When the skycap said he couldn't do that, she convinced him by stuffing another twenty into his hand. After scribbling down her name for him, she ran off after Jamie.

Confused by the clutter and chaos of the airport, Ericka agonized over which direction to take. There were three paths that Jamie could have taken: right, left, or straight ahead. Her mind was spinning with options, with images of Jamie hurrying down each path. If she didn't make a choice soon, she would miss him altogether, so she would have to just walk fast and pray.

Taking a deep breath, Ericka charged off down an undetermined aisle, feeling out of step with gravity. To have gotten so close to him, and then to have him vanish like a mirage. Where the hell was he going? Where the hell was he going without her?

When she spotted him about twelve yards ahead of her, she tried to overtake him, wondering what she would say to him after all these years. He passed through the X-ray security check and she followed, quickly flashing her own ticket jacket, dropping her purse onto the conveyer belt. As she retrieved her purse and continued on, she let out a sigh of relief that she hadn't been stopped for any questions. Then she stepped up her pace; her thoughts dismantled into a curious flutter. After thirteen years, this was not how she had envisioned their reunion—herself harried and a mess from her long flight. She had planned on looking stunning. Crisp, chic, and sensational. In her ever-present scenario she took his breath away and then melted him down with passion.

In an instant the man in the blue oxford cloth shirt broke off from the flow of the crowd and walked over to a bank of public telephones, his back still toward her. She watched his fingers deposit a dime into the round metal cutout, then punch out a number and retreat.

Aware of the increased pace of her heartbeat, Ericka hunted for her compact, smoothing her hair and skirt at the same time. She pulled the compact out of her shoulder bag, discreetly turning her back and inspecting her ravaged reflection. She pulled out a tube of lipstick and smeared it quickly on her lips, then added a smudge to her cheeks for color. After a few pats of face powder and several whips of her hairbrush, Ericka felt sufficiently renewed and turned back toward Jamie.

As she did so, he turned toward her. Their eyes made contact and Ericka, trembling with emotion, ready to run up and throw her arms around him, to claim him once and for all as hers, nearly cried out.

It was the first time she'd actually gotten a frontal look at him, and she felt all at once like a complete fool when she saw it wasn't Jamie at all. How could she have let her imagination get so out of control? He didn't even look like Jamie. He had a prominent nose, a pointy chin.

Ericka felt like a balloon that suddenly deflated before the knot was in place. The force of her disappointment was so great and disorienting that she made her way over to a nearby bench where she collapsed in order to collect herself.

If this had been a movie, that would have been Jamie.

Mad at the perfect scenario that had just been blown, Ericka looked up and noticed Jamie's lookalike boarding a plane to Barbados. Maybe it was his hair. Golden brown like autumn leaves. Tight curls streaked with colors.

If only it *were* Jamie, and she were boarding along with him, she thought.

"Last call for Barbados." The announcement brought Ericka out of her reverie and she sighed heavily, wondering if her luggage had made it to her hotel or not. It would serve her right, she thought, if it hadn't. That had been a dumb thing to do.

Sitting in the backseat of a yellow Checker cab, avoiding the torn portion of the black vinyl upholstery, Ericka closed her eyes. She was totally drained and decided to utilize the forty-five-minute ride into the city for a much needed catnap.

But her mind was her worst enemy, like a video

game that she couldn't shut off—with little bleeping mutants of anxiety racing back and forth and interfering with her peace, sabotaging her efforts toward relaxation. Recalling how David was always telling her to concentrate on a calming image, she conjured up the beach on a gray day. Rough gray waters. Gray sand. Sea gulls soaring across a gray sky. It was romantic. Soothing. Conducive to introspection. Gray and moody. Intense. The perfect backdrop for *calm*.

Once focused on the somber gray beach, Ericka allowed another image to enter. It was Jamie superimposed on her most frequent memory.

The day still seemed so vivid to Ericka, the details set permanently in slow motion, dancing on instant recall. She was sixteen, Jamie twenty-two. It was his graduation day from UCLA. Everybody was celebrating but her. Jamie had been like a son to Ericka's father, a relationship that had begun Jamie's first quarter. Ericka had fallen in love with her father's favorite student the first time he'd come over to their home. Her father was a theater arts professor at UCLA, and having students over for stimulating "coffees" was a long-standing Thursday night tradition. Ericka had been allowed to stay up through the first hour or so of these sessions, at which point she was always tired and glad to go to sleep. Until Jamie. For four years Ericka's love for Jamie had never wavered, only grown stronger and more obsessive. When her girl friends were busy worshipping Paul McCartney, Ericka secretly worshipped Jamie. At twelve years old she had already stopped wondering who her prince charming would be and was instead plotting his seduction.

When Jamie would talk about philosophy, Thomas Hobbes, or John Stuart Mill, Ericka would run to the UCLA bookstore, buy their entire works, and then inhale them so that she could discuss them articulately with Jamie, mostly relying on Cliff Notes she'd buy to help her understand the complicated texts. It was always fun and challenging. Far more so than the fun magazines her friends were reading. Ericka loved projects and especially loved the high she would experience when Jamie's eyes would light up in surprise. She wanted so badly to be his equal, for him to take her seriously. He was really responsible for the better part of her education. He had been her impetus.

She remembered the day they raced along the beach, charged with sexual energy. Ericka had just gotten her driver's license and Jamie had promised to let her take him for a ride. It was after his graduation ceremony and Ericka had stolen him away from his friends, insisting that he hold to his word. She drove him to the beach.

"You're too fast for me," Jamie had hollered out, catching up with her. She slowed her pace, letting him tackle her in the sand. They were out of breath. And their limbs were tangled together. Ericka let her hair fall into the sand, resting on Jamie's forearm.

"Don't you just love this part of the day, when it begins to grow dark like this?" she cried breathlessly.

"I shouldn't have you out here this late," Jamie responded, looking at his watch.

"What's wrong, do the sea monsters leap out of the ocean once the sun retreats?" Ericka knew that Jamie had a date that night. There was a graduation party and he was probably worried about being late for it.

"Does your father know how precocious you are?"

"Do you mean does my father know that I want to sleep with you?"

At that Jamie had sat up. "You're crazy. You're a little kid," he said uncomfortably.

"I'll be your Lolita," she replied, bringing her lips to his.

Jamie stood up, brushing the sand off his jeans. "Does your father know you talk this way?"

"Leave my father out of this. I'm sixteen, Jamie. I'm not a little girl anymore. You're six years older than me. Big deal. My father's *eight* years older than my mother."

"Six years is a lot now," Jamie explained.

"You're embarrassed, that's all. Embarrassed about what it would look like to your friends if your girl friend was sixteen."

"Barely sixteen."

"Admit it!" Ericka had felt herself growing angry. "If we were the same age you'd go to bed with me in a minute."

"But we're not."

"I know you find me attractive, Jamie. When you've left our house late at night and I've come to kiss you good night, in my less than decent nightgowns, I've seen you react. I bought those nightgowns with you in mind. You've seen my body take shape. When I

297

look in the mirror and notice the changes I think of you!"

"Ericka, don't. . . ."

"Other kids my age are sexually involved with each other—"

"Let's go. . . ."

"They aren't sleeping together yet, but they're making out a lot, experimenting."

"That's natural—"

"But not me! I won't let anyone touch me but you. Whether you like it or not, Jamie, I'm in love with you."

"You're too goddamn young to know what love is," Jamie said, frustrated.

"Am I? Give me one good reason why."

"Tell me why you're in love with me," he said.

"Because . . . I adore you."

"That's not a reason."

"You're just using my age against me again. You give me one good reason anyone is in love with anyone else."

At that, Jamie grew silent. Ericka knew it was a difficult question for anyone to answer and she watched him struggle. How do you say *why* you love someone? The reasons, once articulated, all sounded so frivolous, so silly.

He was looking off into the ocean, and Ericka didn't know how to interpret his mood. She cradled his cheeks in her small hands.

"Do you know what it's like to want someone, so much so that they're never off your mind? That you find yourself living for their reactions? Isn't that love, Jamie, doesn't that count as love?"

Jamie was cupping the sand in his hand and letting it pour out slowly, sifting the tiny grains.

"I'm sorry. I guess I've put you in an awkward position," Ericka said, watching him closely.

"It's not your fault."

"Just tell me this, and then I'll leave you alone. Do you think you could ever fall in love with me? In a year or so?"

"Erickish . . . you're very special to me."

"Jamie, please. I have to know. Tell me the truth. I won't hold you to it. I won't announce it as some proclamation you've made . . . I'll keep it to myself. While you're away at Yale, and I'm here, I just need to know. Do you like me that way? Am I attractive to you?"

Jamie put his arm around Ericka. He looked flustered. She suddenly felt older than he was.

"When you grab on to some courage and can speak clearly, let me know, Jamie Sterling. I may be young, but at least I'm old enough to articulate what's on my mind."

With that, Ericka ran toward the ocean. Running fast, hearing him shouting her name behind her, Ericka ran crying into the sea. She let the water engulf her, her tears the same salty substance as the sea. It seemed poetic and her tight fists drove through the water, smashing out her anger. The massive stretch of water was glistening with moonlight that should have been romantic.

Had she ruined everything with her brashness?

With her aggressive, cutting remarks? But she'd had to say what she'd said. She couldn't let him go off to graduate school never knowing how she felt about him. She heard Jamie sloshing toward her, shouting her name out loud over the sound of the ocean.

He had picked her up, carrying her, weightless in his arms, toward the shore. He was kissing her and his kiss melted through her entire being. For the first time in her life she felt like a woman, full of desire, yearning for her desire to be fulfilled. Her thin cotton dress was soaking wet on her body. Jamie pulled off his shirt and told her to take her dress off and put on his dry shirt or she'd catch pneumonia. At the same time he was kissing her wildly, her lips, her cheeks, her neck, her wet shoulders. His hands were roaming across her body, giving new sensations to her hips, her rear, her breasts. She was muttering that she loved him, that she was sorry. She was crying. And laughing. Deliriously happy. The feel of him was incredible. His groans of pleasure were divine.

Would he make love to her? Her mind was still working, quickly, nervously. His hands were massaging her thighs and she thought he would. She felt her crotch wet and excited. She *wanted* him to move his hands over to between her thighs. He must feel her wanting him. How could he not? She felt frustrated from her desire. His tongue was penetrating her mouth, running along her teeth, setting her on fire.

And then he pulled back. Abruptly. His cheeks had felt hot against her own.

"My God, Ericka, I'm sorry!" he said.

Ericka only looked at him, confused.

"I don't know what came over me," he continued, moving the wet strands of her hair from her face. "I'd better take you home."

"Jamie, don't apologize," Ericka said, unbuttoning her dress and noticing the way he was looking the other way as she stood up and stepped out of it. She unhooked her bra and tossed it across the sand. His glance dropped to the discarded item. The only thing she had left on was a pair of skimpy panties, still wet from the ocean, but she was too embarrassed to strip down to nothing. She reached for Jamie's shirt and put it on. It hung down to just above her knees. After gathering up her mound of sandy, sea-drenched clothing, she took his hand and they headed toward the car.

When they pulled up in front of her house, after a silent drive, she looked tearfully at him. "I guess that's good-bye," she said.

Jamie gave Ericka a long kiss on the lips, breaking away from her slowly.

"Will you write me from Yale?" she asked.

"I'm not much of a letter writer, but I'll try," he said.

"I'll be applying to Yale undergrad."

"That's a couple of years away."

"Just two. Don't you think I'm worth waiting for?" she asked, smiling sadly at him.

He kissed her again, this time on the cheek. Ericka took a deep breath, opened her door, and blurted out that she loved him. That was the last time she'd

seen or spoken to him. She had saved the blue oxford cloth shirt.

The yellow Checker drove down Park Avenue,
past a long stretch of vivid yellow tulips. Every season the Park Avenue gardens were dressed up with
different lively blooms and Ericka always found herself looking forward to the surprise of them.

Located on Sixty-fifth, between Park and Madison,
was the hotel where Ericka always chose to stay. She
liked the elegant but intimate atmosphere of the
small, by New York standards, Mayfair Regent Hotel.
Especially she liked the location. A short walk to
Bloomingdale's. Just down from the Whitney. And
Madison Avenue, with its glorious line-up of designer boutiques. Missoni. Ungaro. Kenzo. It was a
good thing Ericka rarely had time to shop. The
money she'd spend could easily exceed the money
she'd earn.

Once in her hotel room, Ericka kicked off her
shoes and fell across the bed, wishing she had time
to go to sleep. There was a small box of courtesy
chocolates on the dresser and she went over to them,
deciding the quick fix of sugar would do her good. In
the condition she was in, she didn't know whether or
not the sugar would really take, but they tasted delicious and she went for a second try. Her luggage,
she noticed gratefully, had been stored safely in her
closet, her hanging bag thoughtfully unfolded and
set up on a heavy brass door hook.

Trying to motivate herself, she took off her jacket
and began to unpack.

First she pulled out a black long-sleeve Sonia Rykiel

sweater of a wool-angora blend. Scattered at random over the front and sleeves of the sweater were reflective royal-blue and black paillettes, small shiny ornaments the size of a nickel. The paper-thin metal disks were sewn together one color overlapping the other, creating a deep shimmering effect. The back of the sweater was plain, while the back of each sleeve repeated the blue and black spangle design. To wear with that, Ericka had brought along a straight black wool skirt. Tonight she was going to see Jamie's play, *Restless Fires,* and on the off chance that she might see him there, she decided to wear this newest acquisition. After laying it out carefully across the bed, she went back over to her hanging bag and took out a second Sonia sweater. This was completely different from the first. It was simple, soft and feminine, cranberry-colored, with black trim and ruffles. She'd brought it to wear with the black skirt for her meeting the following day with Mrs. Beall. It was a good outfit in which to do business, she thought. Graceful, unaggressive. To roam around the city in, Ericka had packed a red pinwale corduroy jump suit, gray leather pants with an oversized gray leather jacket, and an assortment of coordinating tops so as not to be defeated by unpredictable weather.

When she was finished unpacking, she took a hot revitalizing shower, washed and dried her hair, and reapplied her makeup. She had decided to pass on dinner and go straight to the theater, giving herself a little more time to relax.

In one of the drawers, Ericka had noticed a telephone book, and she pulled it out now, curious to see if Jamie was listed. Readjusting the small white towel around her torso, she sat on the bed flipping through the cumbersome directory, stopping to take a deep breath when she came to "Sterling." In Manhattan there were three S. Sterlings, two James Sterlings, and one J. R. Sterling. "James" sounded strange to her. She'd never heard Jamie refer to himself as James. He didn't look like a James. Could be J. R., but Ericka couldn't remember ever knowing Jamie's middle name. Robert. Jamie Robert Sterling. Did that sound familiar to her? No. Robert, Reginald, Ross, Ronald, she tried every name she could think of beginning with *R*, hoping that it would sound familiar, but none did. Then she thought maybe it was S. Sterling. Maybe *S.* stood for his middle name. A more discreet listing. Samuel. Steven. Seth. Sergio. Oh, God! Ericka pulled the phone over toward her. Just call all of them, she told herself. What have you got to lose? The number she began dialing belonged to J. R. Sterling, but she stopped in the middle, realizing how unprepared she was. What if a woman answered? Should she just act cool? *Hi, my name is Ericka Wallace . . . I'm an old friend of your husband's.* She imagined the woman on the other end of the line listening dubiously. *Hi, my name is Ericka Wallace. I'm in love with your husband.* Husband, was Jamie really somebody's husband? She'd never thought of him that way—as belonging to somebody else. He was a character in her fantasy world, unencumbered by the realities of his everyday life. Did he have children? Had he changed? Would he laugh at the same jokes? What were his politics like, now that he was actually voting and earning a living? What were his vices? Did he drink too much? Many writers did. Did he do drugs? Had he been through therapy? Did he still wear blue oxford cloth shirts?

Trying to put a stop to this stampede of questions, Ericka picked up the phone again and punched out the J. R. Sterling number as quickly as she could. A woman answered. But it was a machine. "Hi, we're not here right now, but if you'll leave your name, the date, and time of your call, we'll get right back to you. 'Bye!"

Ericka hung up the receiver, writing "J. R. Sterling" and the telephone number on a pad, then following it up with a question mark. She went through the rest of the Sterling numbers without any success. Then, staring at the Bell contraption, trying to think of what to do next, she was startled when it rang. She picked it up nervously, as though it could be Jamie calling her. Of course it wasn't. It was the hotel desk clerk calling to tell her that her car and driver were downstairs.

After fifteen minutes of fussing, Ericka was finally dressed. Her new outfit looked sensational on her and she felt her spirits soar. There was nothing quite like a flattering reflection in the mirror, she thought, nothing like a brand-new outfit to make that reflection flattering. She continued looking in the mirror, pretending it was Jamie's image in front of her.

"So you wanna have an affair, Sterling, or what?" she asked, pursing her lips in rehearsal and mugging for the pose.

Jamie wouldn't say anything for a moment. He'd be stunned.

She'd smile at him, a slow closed-mouth smile. Savvy. Sultry. How would he be able to say no? Unless he were gay. Please don't let him be gay, she thought. Better that he was only married.

The theater district was mobbed. Ericka negotiated her way through the throngs of people waiting to see Jamie's play. *Restless Fires* blazed from the marquee, and Ericka felt special somehow—connected to it. Connected to the man who had penned it.

When the curtain went down at intermission, Ericka had tears in her eyes and a terrible constriction in her throat. The play was every bit as good as the reviews had said it was. But it was so strange seeing Jamie's work up there on the stage. She found herself trying to read into the content of the play and the emotion behind it. She needed the play to somehow be familiar to her, to be reminiscent of *him*. But it was a political piece, dealing with the Irish struggle against the British crown, and she had no idea how to translate the drama of that into a romantic projection.

Feeling suddenly confined, Ericka stood up and pushed her way up the aisle and through the lobby. She struggled out of the smoky chaos toward the ornate bronze doors that were open for intermission.

"Ericka!"

Her heart seemed to plunge down to her toes at the sound of her name being called out and she whipped around expecting to see him.

"Who's holding down the fort at World Wide while you're gone?" teased a nice-looking guy who would have been nicer-looking if he hadn't been losing his hair. Stan Fox was a business friend of Ericka's, a Hollywood agent whom she'd known since the mailroom days. "I never have time to catch dinner when I'm running the theater circuit," he said, holding up the Hershey bar he was eating. Ericka thought Stan Fox didn't look as though he missed many meals. He was cute, but definitely stockier than he used to be. Too many expense-account dinners now that he was one of the little Porsche-driving agents with CTA on his license plate. CTA stood for Creative Talent Agency, currently one of the most powerful entities in Hollywood.

Stan talked nonstop and Ericka listened loosely, her mind still on Jamie, until the lights flashed and the chimes sounded signifying the close of intermission. "So what are you doing afterward?" Stan asked.

Going back to my hotel room to cry myself to sleep, she thought. But what she said was "Going to bed."

"I'm going to a party in SoHo. Why don't you come?"

"I've really got a big day tomorrow," Ericka answered. "Thanks, though."

"Come on. It won't be that late. Besides, you should *be* there. Martin Sheen's invited. Steven Spielberg. It's *business*," he urged jokingly.

"Yeah, and what makes Sammy run?" Ericka asked. Although Stan Fox wasn't exactly who she'd had in mind for the evening, going to a party with him seemed preferable to going back to her empty hotel room where all she'd do was think about Jamie.

"Money. Sex. Fame."

"In that order?"

"Depends what I've had last." Stan Fox was a character and Ericka had always gotten a kick out of him. She watched him finish off his Hershey bar, roll the wrapper into a tight ball, and toss it into a nearby trash basket.

The party was in full swing when Ericka and Stan Fox arrived. They had hiked up a long flight of stairs and were both out of breath when they entered the expansive avant-garde SoHo loft. The old building's original elevator, with its newly painted grillwork and upholstered bench, had been attractive, but out of order. Ericka had taken one look at the sign hanging on the elevator door and had laughed with resignation. *Out of order. Not functioning. This is not your day. Pass Go, but do not collect two hundred dollars.* Stan didn't think having to climb to the sixth floor was the least bit funny, but he said he was glad Ericka was so easily amused.

"Whose place is this?" Ericka asked, catching her breath and following Stan as they squeezed through the tangled cliques of people into the room. The music was very New Wave, and very loud. Ericka had to practically shout to be heard above it.

"Joel Morris. He's a Broadway producer."

"It's huge," Ericka said, looking around the sparsely furnished room, which was one large space without any partitions.

"There's two additional levels." Stan pointed to a stainless-steel staircase that wrapped steeply downward. "He's got sleeping quarters on one floor, his office on the other."

"I've always wanted a loft."

"Just *sounds* romantic, Ericka. But sometimes these old buildings can be a nuisance. Look at the elevator."

"So I'd do *stairs* instead of aerobics. C'mon, let's get something to eat. I'm starved."

Set up near the high-tech kitchen that reflected a chef who liked to cook was a colorful buffet of antipasto and pasta salads. On another table was a dessert buffet. Ericka filled her plate before she followed Stan over to be introduced to her host. She was relieved that the New Wave music had been replaced by the more mellow sound of jazz.

"So where's Spielberg?" she teased, finally not having to shout. She took a bite of cold eggplant, then a forkful of spinach pasta.

"He's in Madrid making a movie. Don't you read the trades?" Stan said devilishly, stabbing his fork into a corkscrew-shaped rotelle bathed in red sauce. They stood for a few minutes talking and finishing off what was on their plates before continuing over to their host.

Just as Ericka was shaking hands with the heavyset Broadway producer, who looked as though he liked to eat at least as much as he liked to cook, and telling him how terrific his place was, she saw Jamie standing with his back toward her. This time she wasn't hallucinating. She was positive it was him. She recognized his posture. His build. His hair. Whatever it

309

was about the man whose back she was staring at, she was sure it was Jamie Sterling. He had on a tweed sweater and cords. When he turned around and she could see his profile, she felt her whole body tense. The tortoise-rimmed glasses were the same. So was his nose, which was small and angular. She'd always loved his profile. But then again, she'd always loved everything about him.

A waiter came by and collected her empty plate. She thanked him quickly before stealing a careful look at the four people standing next to Jamie. Two women. Two men. There was an odd man out and Ericka hoped that it was Jamie. Maybe he was the single. Maybe he'd come alone. But what about his wife?

There were no hand holders in the group, no demonstrations of affection that would allow Ericka a clue as to who belonged to whom. Both of the girls were attractive. Youngish. Tall. They could have been twins, they looked so much alike. Probably they were models. They were so tall Ericka didn't want to have to stand next to them when she went up to say hello—which she would do in just another couple of moments. She needed to watch him a little longer, figure out what to say to him. What if he didn't remember her? Ericka decided she needed a drink. One glass of wine to mellow her anxiety. But there wasn't time. If she were to make her way across to the other side of the room where the bar was, only to come back to find Jamie gone, she'd never be able to live with herself. She told Stan Fox she'd be back in a moment and crossed over to where Jamie was standing. She was terrified.

The room was so crowded and Jamie's group was clustered in such a tight circle that it was difficult for Ericka to get his attention. She felt foolish trying. Finally one of the women touched Jamie on the shoulder and with a grin pointed to Ericka.

At first he looked at her blankly. Then recognition spread over his face.

"Ericka?" he said tentatively.

Ericka laughed in relief and threw her arms around him. He hugged her for a moment, then pushed her gently away. "I don't believe it," he said. "God. It's been so long! How are you?" His hazel eyes were sparkling. She could tell he was happy to see her and she relaxed a little.

"Great."

"You look great!" Then he paused, his face growing more serious for a moment. Ericka thought he might be remembering their last night together, maybe feeling guilty about it. Or the wedding invitation he'd sent her that had been his only communication in the thirteen years since they'd last seen one another. But then the grave expression passed. "Are you living here? In New York?"

"No, I'm just here on business." Her voice, she thought, sounded shaky. She was nervous again.

"Business!" He looked at her affectionately. With surprise. "What kind of business?" She could tell he still thought of her as a kid.

"Film business," Ericka answered, holding herself back from boasting of the early success she'd had

311

and wondering if she'd ever be able to stop needing to impress him.

"Film business? Hollywood? Your father's an intellectual. How could you go Hollywood?" he teased. Before her response, he asked her how her father was, her mother.

"Great," she said smiling, thinking fondly of her parents. "Crazy. Dad took a sabbatical and they're living in Alaska."

"Alaska! What are they doing there?" Jamie laughed. "Whose idea was that?"

"I think it was collaborative craziness. Daddy keeps writing in his letters that it's the Wild and Woolly West all over again. He's living out a Western frontier fantasy of the old gold rush days. People carrying guns in holsters, old-fashioned saloons, of course mixed in with modern buildings, barroom brawls—and there are drunken Eskimos on the street instead of Indians."

"What about your mom?"

"She's really into photography—was she doing that when you were in L.A.?"

"No. She was into cooking for Thursday nights. Making her own preserves and chutneys. Baking bread. Do they still have Thursday nights?"

Ericka chuckled, picturing a younger Jamie, her parents' house, herself. "They left for Alaska on a Friday, and, typical Dad, he didn't miss his Thursday night 'coffee.' They had suitcases all over. Boxes. And Dad's latest group. . . ."

"He's something else. They're both something else."

"Anyway, Mom's photographing everything. She's

really good. She spends half her time on Kodiak Island, off the coast near Anchorage, photographing bears. She has some amazing close-up shots that make me kind of nervous—even with a telephoto lens it looks dangerously close."

They were both quiet for a moment after that. Ericka realized she felt safe talking about her parents. Now Jamie was looking at her in a way that made her uneasy all over again. But she remembered that that was just his way. He was intense. He always had been. She'd be joking around with him about something and then he'd stop, as though jarred by a deeper level of consciousness. His friends, she noticed thankfully, had closed the two of them out of their circle.

"You look sensational," Jamie said suddenly. "Are you happy?" It was an abrupt question. Strange in the context of their conversation. Ericka wasn't sure how to answer. Was he asking the question as a big brother would—cutting through small talk—exhibiting brotherly concern? Or was he asking from the point of view of a man who had passed by the one woman who he now realized loved him more than anyone else ever had? To know if she still needed him because he now needed her? *Doubtful*.

"That's an awfully broad question," Ericka said finally. "Can you give me a simple answer? Are you happy?"

"Yes."

"That's simple enough." Ericka looked at him surprised. Hurt. How could he be so completely, unequivocally happy, without her? Then she realized that she was taking it all a lot more seriously and certainly a lot more personally than she should be. Jamie was thirty-five years old. A successful New York playwright. Good-looking, in a pale, New York intellectual way. Why shouldn't he be happy?

"You look disappointed," he observed, lifting her chin and looking quizzically at her.

His eyes had always changed color depending upon what he was wearing, like the ocean mirroring the mood of the sky. Tonight they were flecked with the autumn colors of the sweater he had on, olives, grays, and tan. Tonight they were autumn eyes and she felt the most overwhelming urge to run her fingers through his soft curly brown hair. But for all she knew, one of the tall pretty women standing so close to them was Jamie's wife.

Jamie's hand was still under Ericka's chin when she turned her head to point discreetly to the group he'd been with when she'd come up to him.

"Is there a Mrs. Sterling I should meet?" she asked, trying to brace herself.

"No."

"*No?*" Ericka realized the relief she had shown, and both of them broke up laughing.

"No," Jamie reiterated, putting his arm around her. "Unless you want to meet my mother. . . . My God, Ericka, that was a schoolgirl crush—don't tell me . . ."

"Wrong. You *thought* it was a schoolgirl crush."

"You were fifteen years old."

"Sixteen. And the key word there is *old*. Old for my age."

"*Just* sixteen. You'd gotten your driver's license, I think, two or three days before I left for Yale."

"You remember that?" Ericka said, happy that he did.

"Perfectly. Graduation, that night, the beach. You know, I was young too."

"You were twenty-two," Ericka argued, then laughed immediately. "That is young. At the time you seemed so old."

"I felt awful—"

"*You* felt awful!"

"You were seducing me. . . ."

"You weren't easy to seduce."

"That's what you think. I was going nuts. I was scared to death that I was going to end up raping you."

"But I wanted you to. . . ."

"You were a little kid. You didn't know what you wanted. You were infatuated with me—"

"No, Jamie. I was in love with you."

"You've got to be the most stubborn person I've ever met. Do you realize what would have happened if I had made love to you?" Jamie threw his head back as though the mere thought of those repercussions made him nervous. "You were underage for one. Your father was like a father to me." Jamie let out a short breath.

Ericka took his hand and squeezed it. She felt unbelievably happy to learn of the effect she had had on him. Before, it had all been in her head. Now they were talking about it as adults reminiscing about their shared history. It was very intimate and very uplifting for Ericka.

"I hadn't had all that much experience myself, if you want to know the truth," Jamie continued. "You're smiling. It's true. And I was horny as hell. There you were, in a soaking-wet dress, perfectly formed underneath it, perfectly visible. . . ." Jamie groaned.

"What?"

"Well, let's just say you filled a young man's fantasies for a while."

"You're kidding." Ericka was delighted.

"I thought that was sick, if you want to know. I thought I was doomed to like little girls for the rest of my life."

"I always guessed that you hadn't had a lot of experience."

"That's not very flattering, Ericka."

"You were so sensitive. Kind of shy. You weren't an operator like some of the guys that used to come over."

"Like Sandler?"

"Exactly like Sandler. I wonder what ever happened to him."

"He was going to NYU film school when I was at Yale. But I think I heard that he married some rich girl and went into her old man's business."

Ericka was dying to ask Jamie who *he* had married and what had happened, but it was a subject from which she wanted to stay clear.

"So you never got over me?" Jamie looked glad about that. If egos could glisten, his would have.

"Never," Ericka said, flirtatious and honest at the

316

same time. They were smiling hard at each other, both filled with questions to ask, exuberant, when Stan Fox came up to Ericka and put his arm around her. "You ready to go?"

Ericka was paralyzed for an instant. Ready to go? How could she go? She had waited years for this moment. This moment that was better than any she had ever even imagined.

"Jamie, this is Stan Fox. Stan—Jamie Sterling," she said, trying to think quickly. Jamie, she noticed, was sizing Stan up. The two men shook hands, Jamie with reservation, Stan brightly, with a friendly jerk to his wrist. Jamie, she could see by the sudden strain in his expression, had assumed that Stan was her date. A complication for him, but, Ericka realized, an opportunity for herself. If Jamie thought that Stan was her date, then it would follow that he would also think that she wasn't married. What a relief. Marriage was something that she absolutely didn't want to have to think about this weekend. She was certain that David wasn't thinking about his marital contract with her. He was away at one of those trendy retreats he went to every year or so. One year it had been Esalen, est another. Whatever was the newest fad retreat, David tried it out. This time it was some kind of transactional analysis session in Santa Barbara, where the group was totally isolated for seventy-two hours. Ericka was certain that, when David attended or led these intense therapy sessions, he conveniently managed to misplace his wedding vows over the three-day period. This weekend she had the feeling she would be doing the same.

Stan's interest perked up. "The author of *Restless Fires*?"

"Yes, as a matter of fact."

"You're kidding, we just saw it," Stan said. "Ericka probably—"

"You did?" Jamie looked at Ericka, obviously wondering why she hadn't mentioned it.

"I didn't get a chance to tell you," she said, embarrassed.

"You didn't get a chance to tell me a lot of things." He looked over at Stan. "Ericka and I are old friends."

"Your play was stupendous," Stan said.

Jamie thanked him, then turned back to Ericka. "For how long are you here?"

For as long as you want me. For the rest of my life, she thought, exalted. "I'm staying through the weekend."

Jamie looked at Stan again. Stan said nothing. She felt Jamie wanting her and she didn't know what to do. It seemed as though all of her passion had stopped for her at the point of this one man—like a needle on a broken record, her romantic self was stuck in the crevice of an old groove.

"I'm at the Mayfair Regent," she volunteered. "Call me. Okay?" Ericka gave Jamie a kiss on the cheek, holding him to her as she did so and savoring the way he felt. Why didn't he ask her to stay with him? Why didn't he whisper something in her ear? She was tempted to tell Stan to leave without her, but she couldn't manage the words. She needed Jamie to make the move. She had always made *all* the moves.

Reluctantly Ericka let go of Jamie. There was a

318

nervous energy coursing through her that she guessed was panic. What if he didn't call her?

When she got back to her hotel room from the party, it was already two in the morning. Wearily she called the front desk to request a seven-thirty wake-up call. Her bed covers, she noticed, had been turned down for her, and after getting undressed, she climbed in between the fresh white sheets, elegantly monogrammed with the hotel's insignia. As her head touched the pillow, which crushed softly against her cheek, she felt her eyes suddenly suffused with tears. She was wondering what on earth was going to come of all this. There were so many conceivable scenarios. And yet as she tried to force herself to sleep, she thought about the complications that would arise as a result of every single one of them. As she tossed and turned, it was with one recurring hope in her heart—that Jamie would not disappoint her again.

It seemed as though she had only just settled into slumber when the phone began to ring. For the longest time she had been replaying in her mind the reunion she'd had with Jamie. She'd been trying to analyze it. In her dreamlike state the same fuzzy quandaries kept recurring to her unresolved, then decomposing just as she was about to have a revelation.

Ericka reached for the blaring telephone receiver without fully opening her eyes. She was groggily trying to calculate how much longer she could sleep if she were to skip breakfast. Her meeting with Mrs. Beall was set for nine-thirty.

"Hello," Ericka said twice, having to clear her still-sleepy voice. She hadn't had a drop of alcohol the night before, and yet she felt hung-over.

"Ericka?"

At the sound of Jamie's voice—when instead she had expected the hotel operator's "Good morning, this is your wake-up call"—Ericka bolted into an alert sitting position. Her pulse was racing.

"Hi," she said, trying to sound awake.

"Are you alone? Because if you're not, I can call you later—"

"I'm alone," Ericka interrupted.

"Good," he said, and she smiled. "Sorry to call so early, but I was afraid I'd miss you—"

"I'm *glad* you called," she assured him, looking around the room, so glad to be in New York. The early morning traffic was noisy beneath her window and she reveled in the sound of it that was so typically Manhattan.

"I'm going to the Hamptons for the weekend," Jamie said, causing Ericka's heart to fall. "But I'd like to see you before I go. What are your plans today?"

"I've got a meeting this morning," she said, flustered, crushed that he would be leaving. *The Hamptons!* Not this weekend. Not when she was here.

"How about lunch, then? Can you meet me at the Russian Tea Room?"

Ericka hesitated. She had no idea how long her meeting with Mrs. Beall would last. But she wouldn't *not* see Jamie. "Is one-thirty too late for you?" she asked, trying to conceal her disappointment.

His long pause disturbed her.

"There's a good chance I'll be done sooner," she went on, frustrated. "But I really won't know until we're into it. What time were you planning on leaving?"

"Ericka—do you want to just come with me?" Jamie said abruptly.

Ericka closed her eyes and held her breath for a moment, feeling as if a prayer had just been answered. Did she want to just come with him? More than anything in the world.

"I love getting out of the city on weekends," he added. "What do you think?"

"I think it sounds great!" Ericka said.

"Instead of hassling with a big lunch, we can grab a bite on our way out," he said, continuing on, making plans, telling her about the Hamptons and the place he had there in East Hampton, and then finally telling her what she really wanted to hear, which was how glad he was that she was going with him. Ericka was so excited, she wondered how she'd possibly be able to contain herself through her meeting with Mrs. Beall.

Ericka looked up at the ornate clock as it signaled the hour. It was one o'clock and she'd been sitting in the same spot, in a flowery armchair, across from Mrs. Beall since exactly 9:30 A.M.

The old lady didn't seem to want her to leave. She didn't seem to want to do business either, and Ericka suspected that she rarely had company. Her apartment was old, in a dingy-looking building, but inside, the small quarters were neat as a pin and furnished like a quaint old dollhouse. The walls were scattered with a tiny floral print. There was lots of lace. Delicate china pieces. And the furniture was antique.

What Ericka had learned in their hours together was that Mrs. Beall had not gone off her rocker, as everyone Ericka had talked to had said. She was just lonely. Bereaved. The pictures Ericka saw set in dainty little frames around the room were all old. Ericka had an awful feeling that the majority of these people had died.

Mostly Mrs. Beall wanted to talk about her son, and she talked about him as though he were still alive. Ericka had learned on her own that the son had died in a plane crash. The tragedy had happened a couple of years ago on his way out to Los Angeles where he had a meeting with one of the studios to discuss writing the screen adaptation of his book. After that, Mrs. Beall had been approached on many occasions to sell the rights she'd inherited, but she had flatly refused. She had been certain that if "crass commercial Hollywood" got hold of this "fine esoteric masterpiece" it would be bastardized. It was bad enough that she had lost her son, but to chance also losing his only legacy to her was unthinkable.

As Ericka listened to the lonely old lady rambling on about the only son she'd had, and so late in life, Ericka felt great pity for her.

"Do you have any children?" the old woman asked, catching Ericka off guard.

"No."

"I see." The puffy eyes were filled with despair. "Are you married?" She was looking down at Ericka's unadorned ring finger.

322

"No I mean *yes*," Ericka corrected herself uneasily. The word "no" had just popped out. Like calling a friend accidentally by another friend's name. The old woman was looking at her skeptically, piercing Ericka with her wise old glance.

"Why don't you wear a ring?" she persisted.

Ericka thought of Jamie and then immediately after of David.

"We just never did," she explained unsatisfactorily.

Anxious to redirect the conversation, Ericka sat up in her chair and looked at Mrs. Beall. Before she could say anything, the old lady spoke.

"You're the first person to come to me—not on the phone."

"I've never liked discussing things of this personal a nature on the telephone," Ericka said truthfully.

"Are you sure you don't want some cookies?" Mrs. Beall asked her again.

"No, thank you." Ericka was feeling very frustrated and was just about to go on about the book when the old woman dissolved into tears.

"I'm sorry," she said, sobbing and looking embarrassed. "This is very painful for me."

Ericka got up and found her way into the bathroom, bringing out with her some tissues, which she handed to Mrs. Beall.

"You see, my son loved movies. I didn't. My husband didn't. But my son did. He wanted to write the screenplay. . . ."

"I know."

"But that would have been *different*. He wouldn't

323

have sacrificed the power of the book, the human visions. . . ."

Mrs. Beall went on a while longer, talking about the book that she felt was a parable of their times. When she was through, Ericka took over, intent on convincing her that the film they would make *would* preserve the integrity of the book. It would be a memorial to her son. A tragic, provocative tale that would be important on screen. On screen as her son would have wanted.

Mrs. Beall had stopped crying and there was a sad look on her weathered face. She sat back for a few minutes contemplatively grasping the upholstered arms of her chair. It was obvious that this was an agonizing decision for her. She said that she believed Ericka. That even if the film didn't remain true to the book because of the money machines of the industry, she believed that Ericka would try and that that was what her son would have wanted. But the old woman still didn't seem ready to commit. She looked tired. Emotionally spent. Ericka felt it would be unconscionable for her to push this any further. The old woman appeared to like her. To trust her. If she were to sign away the rights to her beloved son's book, Ericka felt it would be to her—to World Wide Pictures. Now it was a matter of sleeping on it, before making the monumental surrender. And it was time for Ericka to shake hands and say good-bye. Time to move on to the more pressing personal matter of Jamie. To be sitting snugly by his side driving away from reality on the way to finally living out her long-awaited fantasy of the two of them together.

Jamie looked handsome and relaxed sitting behind the wheel of his Jaguar when he picked Ericka up at the hotel. He said that she looked like a splash of paint, having changed out of her skirt and sweater and into her red corduroy jump suit.

The two-and-a-half-hour drive to the Hamptons whizzed by, broken up by a quick stop at a mom and pop restaurant along the way, and nonstop talking.

When they finally arrived, Jamie ran around the car and opened Ericka's door for her. It was a romantic gesture and they both laughed, with Ericka glancing, enchanted, toward the nineteenth-century barn that had been converted into a house. It was a white shingle-sheathed box with a gambrel roof and eight-paned windows.

"What do you think?" Jamie asked her, setting down their luggage on the plank floor after they'd entered the house.

Ericka smiled at him, feeling like the bride who had just been brought to see the new house her wonderful groom had bought for her. A dated fantasy for such a modern woman, she thought happily, looking up to the high vaulted ceiling, struck by the cool planar geometry of the house. There were functional-looking rough-hewn posts and beams painted white going off in all directions as structural braces. In fact, the entire barn had been painted a stark white, creating an immense volume, which she found peaceful. There was colorful contemporary art on the walls. Very little furniture. It reminded her of the loft from the night before, except for its warmth. She loved it. She loved Jamie. She felt she could move right in.

Jamie gave her a quick tour of the downstairs, then took her up the ladderlike railless stairs toward his bedroom.

"This is my favorite room in the house," he said, taking Ericka's hand.

"I'll bet." She laughed nervously.

"Have you ever been in a hayloft before?"

"No."

He tackled her onto the bed, which was built on a platform. "Never rolled around in a hayloft?" he asked, taking all of her in, in a long, lustful glance.

"No," she answered, enjoying the feel of him above her, their closeness. But he turned her head with his hand, and she saw what he was talking about. Jamie's bedroom *was* a hayloft, minus the hay. There was a low Plexiglas sheet as a guardrail so that nobody could fall, and a hayloft view of the entire living area below. Ericka could easily imagine herself poised at the edge, ready to leap down to a thick mattress of hay.

"Now look up," Jamie said, changing his position from on top of her so that he was no longer obstructing her view.

There was a skylight built in above the bed, into the sloping roof, and Ericka looked up to the darkening sky that would soon be splattered with stars.

"I can't believe I'm here with you," she said, overwhelmed. It was incomprehensible to her that this was not just another fantasy. His lips were sus-

326

pended above hers, ready to make that long-awaited contact. They were both breathing harder now, quick shallow breaths. Finally they were kissing, holding on to one another. It was the kiss that Ericka had been waiting for all these long years, and the impact it had on her was like a matchstick struck and touched down to a long line of gasoline, instantly ignited and then blazing down its course into a rough and stormy fire.

Together they were caught up in a great spiral of passion, tearing off their clothes, impatient for their bodies to be interlocked, skin touching skin.

The sexual hunger Ericka felt raging within her was the kind of high-voltage excitement she had worried that she was incapable of feeling. She cried out in relief as Jamie's hands roved boldly over her now naked body. For years she had worried that there was something seriously wrong with her. David always felt that *need,* that primitive kind of craving that put everything else out of his mind. It came easily to him. But until now Ericka had never experienced anything even remotely like it. She had always been so ambivalent.

They rolled over so that she was on top of him and she let her glance draw an obvious path down his body and then up again to look into his intense tigerlike eyes. Kissing his neck, she swept her flushed breasts lightly back and forth against his chest, reaching down to clasp the fleshy part of his thigh with her hand. He moaned and his eyelids fell heavily, creating a half-moon of spiky lashes across his high cheekbones. Almost shyly, Ericka moved her hand over to encircle his penis, which she felt hard against her belly. He moaned again as she continued giving him pleasure, and without words he directed her. Until finally he lifted her, turning her onto her back, then guiding himself into her. She arched up clamorously to merge with him, so he could love her more completely. With all of himself.

Welding her to him firmly, he was changing tempos. Driving her harder. His fingers were traveling the length of her spine in concert with his lovemaking. She tried to focus on pleasing him, but her intentions were lost to sensation. She was on the brink of having the most resplendent orgasm. Then finally, holding on to Jamie's shoulders in a feverish grip, she came with an abandoned cry.

For some time afterward Ericka was incapable of saying anything. Her eyes were still closed, and she was taking her time about regaining consciousness. She was reveling in the aftershocks of her voluptuous orgasm and relishing the phenomenon of Jamie lying beside her.

"Funny how things work out," Jamie said softly, breaking the silence.

"I know," Ericka agreed with a happy smile. "I've waited thirteen years for this! Seventeen if you count back to when I first fell in love with you."

"And in all those years you never fell madly in love with anyone else?"

"No," Ericka answered, without having to lie, but praying Jamie wouldn't get any more specific. This weekend was so important to her, she didn't want it to be complicated by the realities she would have to face when she got back to L.A. It was an idealistic interlude to exist out of space and time—apart from her real life. For now.

Chapter Eighteen

KIRSTIN WAS IN AN EXCELLENT MOOD WHEN SHE PUSHED open her massive front door and entered the house. It had been a busy day. She had met Kelly at the gym, and after class they had gone to the children's theater, where Kelly had shot the L.A. *Times* Calendar layout. Lunch was at Hillcrest Country Club with one of the directors of Litton Industries, to discuss a fund-raising event she was chairing. Then there was a series of errands. The one Kirstin enjoyed most had been to Leonard's tailor, to pick up a tuxedo and shirt she'd had made as a gift.

Still holding Leonard's gift, she began thumbing through the mail on the entrance hall table. She passed over the bills in favor of a large envelope addressed in a scarlet-edged silver ink. Most likely an invitation. But she decided not to open it. Instead she took *New York* magazine, with its feature story about the unusually big season Broadway was having, and went upstairs with it, wondering whether Ericka had found her Jamie.

Kirstin dropped the magazine on her desk to look at later. Then she headed through a mirrored archway toward Leonard's dressing room, where there was an island containing a bank of light oak drawers. The countertop was a vibrant blue lapis-lazuli granite that complemented the design of his bathroom. Everything was compartmentalized, as in a store. There were shelves stacked neatly with sweaters. A cleverly designed built-in tie rack that made Leonard's dozens of ties easily accessible. A floor-to-ceiling display of shoes with a small library ladder for the difficult-to-reach pairs he seldom wore anyway, stained in the same honey-blond shade as the cabinetry. There were also racks of shirts, slacks, suits, golf wear, and tennis clothes.

Unzipping the bag she was carrying, she removed the elegant gray silk mohair tux and hung it up. The fine silk lapels, Kirstin thought, were just a bit too narrow, but Frankie Vairo, Leonard's tailor, had insisted Leonard liked them that way and Kirstin had decided to rely on his judgment.

After putting the ice-gray cotton shirt she'd ordered to go with the tux down on the granite countertop, centering a bow tie at the base of the collar, she knelt down to a safe that was concealed in one of the drawers and removed a black velvet box, which she opened delicately. *This* was why she'd had

332

the tux made. About a month ago, Kirstin's jeweler, Victor Van Houghten, who had become a dear friend of hers over the years, had called from New York to tell her about two exceptionally rare pairs of cuff links and studs he was on the brink of acquiring from an estate. He had described them to her over the telephone as best he could, but said that he should have them in a few weeks and would be flying out to L.A. anyway, so she could see them then. They would cost her a king's ransom, he warned, but added that they were worth it.

Kirstin had been enormously excited about the prospect. It wasn't easy to buy a man like Leonard a gift, and whenever she actually came upon something, she was thrilled. It was to show off these extraordinary cuff links and studs that she had had the tuxedo made, having decided that only a brand-new tux would do.

It was a kind of unveiling as Kirstin held one of the six-carat star ruby links up to the light to marvel at the gem's clarity.

As Kirstin was bending over to replace the case, she noticed a piece of paper on the floor around the corner of the bank of drawers. She picked it up. It was a list that startled her into recognition.

9:07 A.M.—*subject left Flower Fashion Florist.*

9:46 A.M.—*subject entered William Ernest Brown Stationers.*

10:28 A.M.—*subject left William Ernest Brown Stationers.*

10:45 A.M.—*subject entered Bruno and Soonie Hair Salon.*

11:45 A.M.—*subject left Bruno and Soonie Hair Salon.*
11:59 A.M.—*subject entered Bistro Garden Restaurant.*

Her hands were trembling and she felt a mounting tension within her as she began puzzling over how long this surveillance might have been going on. What did Leonard know? What was he trying to find out? Kirstin was becoming increasingly upset and frightened. Could it be that this was all an outgrowth of the episode with Kelly—or had he discovered something else? Something from her past?

She continued to stare bitterly at the piece of paper through tear-filled eyes.

The next morning Kirstin left the house shortly after Leonard. She hadn't said a word to him yet about having found the surveillance log. She hadn't recovered enough from the shock of it and had decided to wait until she felt more in control for what was sure to be a severe and highly charged confrontation. Leonard's behavior, now that she was thinking back and analyzing it, did seem more strained than usual, but he got that way even when it had nothing to do with her. Pressure at the office often made him remote. Suddenly elevated blood pressure made him irascible.

As Kirstin pulled her Rolls out of the driveway, she looked up and down the street, feeling paranoid and wondering if there was already a car there waiting for her. She noticed a red Corvette. A sable-colored Mercedes. And a black Cadillac.

She looked in her rearview mirror as she passed

all three cars, driving slowly, anxious to see if one of them would pull out behind her. But the streets of Holmby Hills were winding, and in a moment all the cars were out of her view. She continued on at a snail's pace, sure that one of the three cars would catch up with her. When they didn't, she put her foot down hard on the gas pedal and drove too quickly in the direction of the Bonwit Teller department store.

As Kirstin drove her car into Bonwit Teller's parking lot, she looked again in her rearview mirror to see if another car had pulled in behind her. None had. A parking attendant opened her door and, feeling skittish, Kirstin stepped out, putting the ticket that was handed to her in the pocket of her gray flannel slacks.

She walked up the tawny tangerine-color carpeted steps that led up to the department store, holding on to the railing and pausing before she opened the glass doors to look at two cars that had just pulled in. The devil you know is better than the devil you don't know, she kept thinking. One car was a navy-blue Jaguar, the other a white Peugeot. Both drivers were women. The driver of the Jag was elegant, tall, and slender. Middle forties with red hair. The other, cute, petite, with shoulder-length brown hair and a bounce to her walk as she collected her ticket and then started for the store. Neither of them looked like what Kirstin imagined a private investigator would look like, and feeling foolish, she exhaled deeply, finally entering the store.

The interior walls looked as though they had been

freshly painted. They were a pale cinnamon shade. Sophisticated and new-looking. They made an excellent backdrop for the long glass and mirror jewelry display case Kirstin noticed to her left where contemporary silver jewelry was attractively arranged.

"Hello, Mrs. Pollock." Kirstin was startled at the sound of her name being called out and she turned with rapid reflexes to the woman behind the jewelry counter to her right, who was waving at her.

"Hi, Rose," Kirstin said, recognizing the saleswoman, walking toward her, and then turning again to look at the entrance door. It was early, so there wasn't much activity in the store.

"You're going to love it!" the saleswoman exclaimed, stooping down to the cabinet behind the jewelry display case. Kirstin had ordered a necklace that she had seen advertised in *Town and Country,* and Rose had called her a couple of days ago to say it was in.

"Isn't this marvelous? I just love all this new *faux* jewelry," Rose said, unfolding the tissue paper and then holding up a big glass emerald-colored ornament set into a silver flex band. Kirstin put it on while looking in the mirror.

"We also got in matching earrings," the saleswoman went on. "Would you like to see them?"

Kirstin glanced over at a man with a cane pushing open the glass doors.

"They're clip-ons," the saleswoman was saying, handing the earrings to Kirstin, who removed her own ivory ones and put the flashy new pair in place. The last thing she felt like doing now was buying jewelry, but she handed Rose her charge card, trying hard not to think about her predicament.

Next Kirstin went to the hosiery counter. Again she looked around to see if someone was watching her. This time she noticed a wiry-looking man with a swarthy complexion, thick black-rimmed glasses, and shiny gabardine pants. Gripped with fresh panic, Kirstin turned away. The sleazy-looking son of a bitch. How dare Leonard, she thought, suddenly angry at the insult of it all. She dropped the pair of stockings she was looking at and walked over to the escalator. She rode it up to the second floor, staring at the white moiré walls along the way, trying to think of what to do. When she got off on the second floor, she waited, feeling chased. She was determined to see if he would follow her up.

Two little old ladies mounted the escalator chatting and stepping gingerly off when they arrived at the second floor, where they hurried off toward a rack of dresses.

Kirstin continued to wait a while longer and then took the elevator down, curious to see whether someone would jump in at the last minute behind her.

Walking out of the elevator past cases of Judith Leiber evening bags, then past Estée Lauder, Clinique, and Stendahl, Kirstin found herself exiting the store through the front entrance onto Wilshire Boulevard. She turned left, compelled to repeat her activities in Saks.

She knew she was being followed. It had been documented down to the minute. And she could sense it as well. But that wasn't enough. She needed to see whoever it was peering at her. She needed to be sure.

She felt as though she might break into tears at any moment.

Later that evening, Kirstin twisted her wrist to look at her diamond-faced watch. She had fifteen minutes before Leonard would be home. And then another fifteen minutes before her well-rehearsed confrontation with him would begin.

Her stomach tense, she made a final inspection of herself in the mirror, hoping she didn't look as distressed as she felt. First she checked her eyes. The Visine drops had cleared them and they looked bright and surprisingly trouble-free. They were a pale lavender blue, edged by the charcoal-brown fringe of her lashes. Because of what she was wearing, her eyes gleamed like an accessory. They were the only color on an otherwise cream canvas. Kirstin had changed into vanilla-colored silk charmeuse lounging pajamas with a long, narrow tunic top. Wound around her neck was a waist-length double-strand pearl necklace with a simple diamond and platinum clasp. Her teardrop earrings had been designed to match subtly.

In the study, where all this had begun with Kelly, Kirstin set her stage for the drama that was about to be played out. She noticed the lilies all leaning one way in the tall Lalique vase and went to adjust them. Otherwise the room looked perfect: in order and as gleaming as a study should be with its book-lined walls, its his-and-hers rich raisin-leather chairs and ottomans. The fine oriental rug was without a ripple, all four corners matched up and exactly in line. Kirstin looked up at the long, gaunt face of the Modigliani over the carved wood mantel of the fireplace and then down to the bright orange and yellow flames leaping and crackling behind the etched glass screen.

Everything had to be perfect, especially her performance, because that was what she felt she had to give tonight—a performance. She had to mask the great quivering fear she felt inside and project instead a velvet calm. It was true that she was deeply hurt that after all these years of absolute devotion to Leonard he should strike her this way with the low blow of a sleazy private eye, but that injury was a mere bruise compared to the brutal wound she felt could still be inflicted.

Never again would she allow herself to be in such a position. Her past was an albatross around her neck. If only she could have the courage to rip it off and suffer the consequences. But she couldn't. What had happened was so long ago. Buried. And she refused to believe in the power of ghosts.

Kirstin was startled when Matty, the housekeeper, knocked quietly before bringing in the hors d'oeuvre she had requested. When she heard Leonard at the front door, it was like the curtain rising, and she experienced genuine fright. She collected herself and waited for the inevitable cue, which would be Leonard calling out her name. She closed her eyes until she heard it.

"*Kirstin.*" A word delivered like a line. *Kirstin.* It

339

was a complete sentence that implied more than it said.

As Kirstin started out of the study, she saw Leonard walking toward her. His eyes looked tired and she imagined she knew why. With a voice reflecting a calm she certainly didn't feel, she said hello, going up to kiss him affectionately, touching his cheek a moment longer than she ordinarily would have.

She helped him out of his jacket, handed it to Matty, who had suddenly reappeared, and went to the bar to fix him a Crown Royal and soda. Her intention was to relax him thoroughly, to get everything off his mind before she confronted him. She couldn't possibly wait until after dinner, though she would have liked to. Her stomach was in knots and she could only pretend calm for so long.

Leonard loosened his tie and sat down in one of the leather chairs. She tried to keep a steady grip on the cold crystal glass as she handed it to him, but her hand was trembling and the ice cubes knocked against one another.

Leonard appeared to notice, but said nothing.

Completing their cocktail ritual, Kirstin opened a split of champagne for herself.

Leonard seemed so very tired, she just wanted to run over to him and tell him the truth. All of it. She wanted him to hold her tight, comforting her. To whisper gently that she needn't worry. That she should have told him the truth to begin with. And as her imaginary words tumbled out they didn't sound half as bad as they sounded trapped in her head.

But Kirstin waited until Leonard was ready to

begin his second drink. Then, at last, she felt it was time. She took another fortifying sip of her champagne and fixed her attention on the task that lay ahead, knowing she had to avoid putting Leonard on the defensive. She needed him to *listen* to her first, to gain his sympathy.

She lowered her eyes and began. "I discovered something yesterday that hurt me very deeply. I feel—completely undone about it. I feel so disillusioned and disappointed to learn that someone I love more than anybody, in whom I've always put my complete faith and trust, doesn't trust me." Kirstin paused for a moment, looking into Leonard's eyes. He looked away and she continued telling him about the paper she had found.

Leonard finally interrupted her, obviously shocked that she knew, probably furious with himself for having been so careless. He looked embarrassed. Blood rushed to his forehead. It was anger, but not purely anger.

In a raised voice that was both accusatory and defensive, Leonard justified what he had done. Kirstin was relieved to learn that he had been having her followed because of Kelly and not because of anything else. The fact that she had actually fixed Kelly up, that she had so little regard for marriage and all that that union should imply, had sent him into an utter tailspin. He couldn't rationalize it away, he told her. He *had* to know if she was disloyal to him. He had to be sure, or it would eat away at him. He just couldn't understand what she had done.

Then it was Kirstin's turn and she turned on him

with rage in her eyes and conflict twisting in her heart. She told him she was horrified that after so many years of marriage and devotion and loyalty to him, he thought so little of her.

"Have I *ever* given you any reason to distrust me?" she asked.

"Not until this asinine birthday present!" Leonard howled. "But I thought I obviously didn't *know* you very well after that—I was shocked that you would do such a thing."

"I told you I thought I was wrong. That it was stupid. But, Leonard, I've been a good wife. For one stupid mistake that had *nothing* to do with us, for you to take such an extreme position—my God—having me followed like I was some kind of . . . cheap . . . I don't think I deserved that, Leonard—"

"I had to know, dammit."

"It was a betrayal. A violation."

"Was it?" Leonard stood up abruptly and slammed his drink down on the table. Kirstin held her breath—terrified. This is it, she thought, watching Leonard storm out of the room. She waited, too tense to even speculate. He returned a moment later with the familiar sheets of paper, crumpling them as he began looking for something he wanted to read aloud. "10:20 A.M.—subject enters *Beverly Hills* Hotel," he said viciously. Kirstin thought, my God, is that all, and she prayed intently that it was as he continued. "Subject *leaves* Beverly Hills Hotel 11:20 A.M." He paused to look at her as though suspecting the worst. He turned to the next page, running his finger down it again, before speaking. "2:30 P.M.—subject enters

342

Beverly Hills Hotel. 3:35 P.M.—subject leaves Beverly Hills Hotel. Five minutes longer this time!" Leonard raised a thick graying eyebrow. He had worked himself up to such a heated state that his color seemed permanently blood-red.

Kirstin knew it was imperative for her to disguise the immense relief she felt. Without missing a beat, she looked directly at him. "So when you found that out, why didn't you just *kick* me out," she said hotly.

"I wanted to know more. I needed to be holding a full house."

There was so much pain in Leonard's expression that Kirstin felt a wave of pity for him. But he had been wrong to do to her what he had done and he deserved to feel the full impact of this lesson. This time *she* stormed out of the room. She went upstairs into the bedroom, into Leonard's dressing room, and to the safe. From out of her jewelry case she again pulled the small velvet box containing the star rubies. Then she closed the safe. She hurried into her dressing room, retrieved Leonard's tux from where she had hidden it, and rushed out of the room and down the stairs.

"What the hell is that?" Leonard asked virulently.

Kirstin handed Leonard the velvet box. "A gift for you," she said coldly.

He immediately pushed it back at her, without opening it.

"*10:07* A.M." she fired at him. "Subject entered Beverly Hills Hotel to look at a pair of star ruby cuff links to buy for her husband."

"Don't give me that—"

"11:07 A.M.—subject left Beverly Hills Hotel because she couldn't decide between the star rubies and diamonds."

"Kirstin—"

"2:30 P.M.—subject entered Beverly Hills Hotel *serious* about making up her mind, but *slowly* because it was such an *important* decision! Because she loved her husband so much she wanted—"

Leonard grabbed the box from her and opened it roughly. "How do I know these were for me?" he asked skeptically, his face softening but his distress just as great.

Kirstin shoved the tux at him. "Frankie Vairo. *Your* tailor. *Your* measurements." With that, Kirstin swung around and headed out the door.

"Where are you going?" Leonard asked, stopping her, grabbing hold of her arm and turning her around to face him. His eyes were actually welling with tears. He looked awful. "My God, Kirstin, I'm so sorry. I don't know what possessed me." He hugged her to him, throwing the tuxedo onto the chair. "Jealousy, obviously. Crazy, insane jealousy. That damn Kelly thing . . ." His voice trailed off. Kirstin held him tightly, relieved. How she loved this man, and thank God he was going to call off the investigation.

Buddy Nazio was in Patrick Delaney's office discussing the Pollock case and a couple of others when Leonard Pollock's call came in.

Buddy noticed the way Delaney cleared his voice as well as his manner before picking up the line, dropping his tough, ex-FBI-guy act, trying to sound like a big-shot businessman instead. Their conversation was short and Delaney didn't get to say much more than a few scattered but pretentiously issued phrases. Buddy counted three "I sees," two "No problems," three "I understands," one "Of course," and then a closing "Anytime."

When Delaney hung up from the call, he pulled the Pollock file in front of him, opened it, and began tapping the top sheet with his pencil several times as though trying to make a decision.

"Hey, yo!" Buddy said, reminding Delaney of his presence. "What'd the big gun want now?"

"Pulling the old ten twenty-two," Delaney said, still tapping his pencil. "1022" was FBI jargon for calling off an investigation.

"Just when I was beginning to have fun," Buddy complained, thinking about the voluptuous blonde. "What are ya gonna do, stick me on some boring insurance checkup now?"

"Most likely."

"Oh shit." Buddy slouched in the shiny white Naugahyde chair, looking over at Delaney, who was swiveling pensively in his matching executive one. Guy thinks he's hot shit with all this companion Naugahyde crap, Buddy thought, eyeing the matching vinyl couch and nearly snorting. If *he* were making the kind of bucks Delaney made, he'd be swiveling in the best buttery leather money could buy, with a buxom blonde under the table applying favors to him. *Kitsch*, he thought, that's what President Ford's hot-shot Washington groupies would have called this office back in Buddy's Secret Service days. Totally *kitsch*.

The carpet was a bordello red. The grass cloth wall covering a tacky washable plastic. The desk was in glaring bad taste, slick and oversized, with phony marble accessories. Even the view was the pits—a flat composition roof that was the top of a lower building next door. The only impressive thing about this supposedly high-class private eye's office, with his fancy Beverly Hills clients, was his fancy Beverly Hills highrise address and the size of the room.

"So what's the problem?" Buddy asked, lighting up a cigarette and pulling an ashtray already crowded with ashes and cigarette butts toward him.

"Just something I thought maybe I ought to have mentioned to Pollock but didn't."

"What's that?" Buddy asked, always eager to hear more about a case.

"I don't know," Delaney said evasively. Then he shut the file and pushed it aside. "What the fuck. Nobody ever appreciates it when you tell them something they really don't want to know anyway, right?"

Buddy shifted in his seat. Delaney was so fucking uptight about discussing the details of a case. It was really annoying. Really arrogant. "Does he know about the Beverly Hills Hotel?" Buddy asked, fishing.

"Yeah, he's got the surveillance report." Delaney smoothed his hair. "It's the background search I was putting together . . ."

"If you don't tell Pollock and he finds out on his own, won't he be pissed off?"

"Maybe. But the guy's been married, what—fifteen, twenty years? If he doesn't know now . . ." Delaney concluded his sentence with a gesture. "It's like tell-

346

ing your buddy you saw his wife playing around on him. You think you ever really get *thanked* for being the bearer of sour news? Bullshit." Delaney leaned over and pushed the intercom button for his secretary. He pushed it three more times and when he got no response he stood up irritated. "Next time I hire a secretary I'm going to make sure she has a bigger bladder. Every time I need her, she's in the john." Walking out of the room, Delaney told Buddy to sit tight, he'd be back in a few minutes. He wanted to photocopy some papers for him on the insurance case and then they'd wrap it up.

With Delaney gone, Buddy stood up and looked around the room again. He stretched out his long thick legs and yawned, then, feeling somewhat curious about what it was in the Pollock file Delaney had been deliberating about, Buddy turned the folder around and went quickly through it. What he learned was that Kirstin Pollock had a couple of AKA's. Born Kristina Lund, changed to Kirstin Lindstrom when she moved to this country, changed to Kirstin Pollock when she married old man Pollock. Odd that she would elongate her name when she immigrated instead of shortening it, but that wasn't any big deal. Then he saw that Kirstin had had a quickie Las Vegas marriage and divorce. Most likely to get her green card, he thought, taking in the fact that she hadn't changed her name with that marriage. There wasn't much else on Kirstin but there was quite a bit on the ex-husband. Holy shit, Buddy thought, skimming the incriminating rap sheet as fast as he could. John Clark . . . number of arrests 32. 2-28-53—Run-

347

away Juv . . . . 4-28-55—shoplifting. Paid fine $75. 7 days in Juv. Correction unit. . . . 10-14-55 D.W.I. Hit and Run, Remanded to Juv. Court Center 30 days. . . . 5-10-56 GTA Grand Theft auto—1 year supervised probation. . . . D.W.I. Reckless driving, dismissed. . . . Buddy read on. Poss. of marijuana, dismissed. . . . Probation violation, 18 mo. AZ State Prison. 9-6-72—Forgery. . . . 1-12-83—carrying a concealed weapon. Buddy shut the file, whistling low to himself. It was amazing to him how you could always find dirty laundry under everybody' s bed, no matter how fancy the sheets. And this wasn't necessarily the end of it. Interpol in Sweden was already working on the Pollock case, and the facts they would be accumulating would continue to roll right in.

Buddy looked over at the rows of file cabinets in the corner of the room that were packed with valuable scorching goods on all kinds of influential people. He wondered if Delaney had ever been tempted to retire on threatening to expose one of these hidden secrets.

But then Delaney walked into the room shaking his head and muttering something about his secretary and Buddy thought, *no chance.* Delaney liked to act tough because he worked in a macho kind of business, but basically he was soft and straightlaced, a rule follower with a knack for getting along with people who had a lot of money.

Chapter Nineteen

THERE WAS AN ENERGETIC PULSE TO DOWNTOWN L.A., KELLY thought, riding the elevator up to the twenty-third floor to Ron's law office. She was meeting him to sign some papers that had to be notarized. When the heavy metal doors parted, Kelly stepped out of the elevator and directly into the lobby of Ron's law firm, which accounted for two full floors of the building. The lobby was decorated in hunter green, with lots of dark wood paneling and Charles Bragg sketches on the walls. Six years ago, when the offices had been remodeled, the look had been great, but now Kelly thought it was awfully dark and could use some updating.

"Can I help you?" asked the receptionist, a tall black woman with pretty skin.

"I'm here for Ron Nelson—"

She was already punching some buttons into the board in front of her. "Who can I say is here?"

"His wife."

The black woman looked up at Kelly, interested in getting a better look. "Oh. Hi," she said.

Kelly had spent more time putting herself together this morning than she ordinarily did. She was wearing a long navy double-breasted cable-knit cardigan with a shawl collar, cinched at the waist with a narrow navy reptile belt. Underneath she had on an ivory silk shirt and with it a pair of classic pinstriped trousers. With an extra ten or fifteen minutes allotted to her makeup and hair, she thought she looked terrific. On the rare occasions when she came to Ron's office, he always liked to show her off. He would take her down the halls, peeking into everyone's office, reintroducing her to his old associates and to any new ones who had recently joined the firm. Most of the lawyers' secretaries were young. They were always bubbling over with enthusiasm when they spoke to her, but she always wondered whether they gossiped about her afterward. When Kelly was in college, she worked part time as a secretary. She remembered clearly what it was like after visits from wives. The cuter the man, the more of a target his wife became. But now it was different, she supposed, with the growing number of male secretaries and the growing number of female lawyers.

Ron was on the phone when Kelly appeared at his door. He motioned to her to have a seat. Before he was off the call, they were joined by a petite blonde holding a stack of papers. She grinned at Kelly, who wondered whether this was the new secretary Ron had told her about. Kelly thought Ron looked handsome.

"Kelly, this is Lana," Ron said, finally ending the call. "Lana's our notary public."

Lana put down her stack of papers in front of Ron, who indicated to Kelly where she needed to sign. When they were all through, Lana took the papers and departed.

"Where's your new secretary?" Kelly asked.

"She had a dentist appointment."

"She as cute as Lana?"

"Oh, cuter," Ron teased, standing up and straightening his tie. "Ready to make the rounds before lunch?"

"Do I have a choice?" Kelly asked earnestly, not looking forward to being paraded around, to shaking hands and making stiff small talk.

"Not really," he said, taking her arm and directing her out the door in front of him.

After the thirty-five-minute tour—Kelly had timed it—Ron told her they'd have to have a fairly quick lunch because he had a lot of work to do.

"Look, I got off work today to come downtown to sign these papers and have lunch with you. I want a romantic leisurely lunch. Screw your work. Who *doesn't* have a lot of work to do? Pretend I'm your mistress," she said, linking her arm through his and leaning up against him as they rode down in the elevator. "Can't you make an exception?"

"Where do you want to go?"

"Rex."

"Very funny."

"C'mon Ron. Be a sport. It's supposed to be so beautiful and so romantic, and the food is supposed to be phenomenal."

"So are the prices."

"I thought we'd split something so that it wouldn't cost so much."

"I'm hungry. I don't want to split something."

"Where's your romantic soul?"

"When are you going to accept the fact that I don't have one—"

"Never," Kelly said, smiling at him undaunted. "How much can it be if we just order pasta? That's what's supposed to be so good." Kelly pulled a restaurant review she'd clipped from out of her purse and began reading it to him, describing the pumpkin pasta, the pasta with truffles, and the reviewer's favorite, hay and straw pasta served with a creamy caviar sauce. She pointed out that the fine old architecture and the exquisite design of the restaurant, which had originally been a haberdashery, rated two long paragraphs. "And the pièce de résistance, as far as I'm concerned," she said, following Ron out of the elevator to the noisy street, "is their 'bride's cookie,' or, as the reviewer preferred to call it, their 'kissing cookie'—"

"What is a *kissing cookie*?"

"I put one end in my mouth, you put the other end in your mouth, and we bite through it, until our lips come together," she said, demonstrating without the prop.

Ron laughed.

Disappointed and feeling defeated, she asked Ron where he wanted to go. When he told her the deli down the street, she felt like shoving him to the ground. The deli was not at all what she'd had in mind for today.

"How about Chung Fu's Kitchen?" she asked.

"How about the deli?"

"How about you have lunch by yourself," Kelly said, angrily walking away from him. Now she was hurt. Then she turned around, afraid that he wasn't going to come after her. "Look. I come downtown, what, twice a year? I took the day off from work because you asked me to. I spent an extra fifteen minutes putting on my goddamn makeup to make *you* look good, and I think the least you could do is—"

"I don't feel like spending a hundred bucks! Is that so hard to understand?"

"We don't have to go to Rex, but I'd at least like to go somewhere we can sit down and relax. And talk!"

"Where do you want to go, then? You want to go to Chung Fu's? Fine."

Not really caring anymore where they went, Kelly nodded. They walked to the restaurant in absolute silence.

"So what did you want to talk about?" Ron asked after they'd ordered. He poured a cup of tea for her and handed it across the table.

"I hate that," Kelly said. "It really puts me on the spot when you ask me that kind of question. I just want to talk. Don't we talk anymore?"

"Relax!" Ron looked self-consciously around the small room occupied mostly by businessmen.

Kelly took a deep breath. She was thinking about Brandon, imagining the two of them at Rex together, sharing the kissing cookie without finding it silly, talking easily without having to try so hard. Probably, if Kelly had agreed to go to the deli, they would be finished eating by now and Ron would have considered it all just fine.

A waiter brought over the two bowls of sizzling rice soup they'd ordered.

"Smells good," Kelly said, lifting the big plastic spoon, not wanting to fight.

"I'm sorry, Kelly," Ron said, reaching over and taking her hand. Immediately her eyes filled with tears and she bit down on her lip, trying not to cry.

She'd been feeling so frazzled lately. So high-strung. Brandon's image had been hanging over her like a presence she couldn't shake, making so many things in her life that had once been fine now seem inadequate. When Ron didn't notice the sexy new underwear she'd bought a few days ago, after she'd deliberately paraded in front of him, she dwelt on how Brandon would have reacted. With Brandon, she wouldn't have had the television set as competition. And then she felt guilty because it really hadn't been Ron at all she was thinking about when she'd bought the lingerie in the first place. And the pedicure appointment she had made was close to when she thought Brandon would be back in Los Angeles. She'd recently gone for a makeup lesson, and an eyebrow arch, and gone to get her hair conditioned, and all this she knew she was doing for Brandon, even though she kept telling herself that if he called she would tell him that she absolutely couldn't see him. But a day didn't go by when Kelly didn't think about him. When she didn't play out a soothing fantasy in her head. Many of those fantasies, she discovered, were retaliations for small, inconsequential arguments she'd had with Ron.

"I'm sorry too," Kelly said, meaning it. Sorry for comparing him constantly to Brandon and then for being angry with him when he didn't measure up.

"I don't know what you want from me. I'm a good husband. I'm a good father. I love you. We can't keep getting into this all the time."

"I know."

"I'm getting really tired of it."

"I know you are."

"I work hard. I'd like to be able to relax when I'm with my family. I shouldn't have all this pressure from you."

Kelly finished her soup in silence. She felt guilty. But not *wrong*. "I'm going to say one more thing. And then we'll drop it." Kelly ignored Ron's impatient look, waiting before she continued, as the waiter cleared the soup bowls and put down a bamboo basket of steamed dumplings. He served them each two, pointed to the ginger condiment, and disappeared. Kelly took a sip of her tea, then went on. "Ron, I may be overreacting somewhat, but I'm not the only culprit in this. I'm legitimately frustrated."

"What are you so damn frustrated about?"

"Our lives are so busy and we're running so fast all

the time taking care of things we can't neglect, and we're neglecting *us*."

"What do you want from me, Kelly?"

"Just a little bit of effort. That's all. You do love me, don't you?"

"Of course I love you."

"Well, then think a little bit about trying to make me *feel* loved." Kelly looked at Ron, spreading some of the shredded ginger onto her dumpling and then dipping it into the reddish orange chili oil. He was trying so hard, and she knew he had no idea what she was talking about. He was being patient while feeling that she was being unreasonable. Maybe she was.

In desperation, she reached into her purse and pulled out two brochures that described two different summer camps she thought might be good for their twins. One specialized in computers. The other was a good all-around camp with a wide variety of activities.

"I think I'd pass on the computers," Ron said, glancing through the glossy literature Kelly had handed him. "I don't know, it just doesn't seem like camp to me."

"The twins really want to go."

"They hate doing their homework. This will be like a month of nothing *but* homework."

"Not really. They think of the computer as play."

"I can't relate to that as camp."

Kelly smiled, knowing exactly what Ron could relate to as camp. He laughed as though reading her thoughts. The two of them had *met* at camp. Kelly had been an eighteen-year-old counselor in training, Ron a twenty-one-year-old counselor serving his last year at the camp he had attended since he was a little boy.

"What about Marlo?" Ron asked.

"Wherever there are boys, Marlo will be happy."

Ron grimaced. "Maybe we should send *Marlo* to computer camp."

"She's too excitable, I'm afraid."

"These kids are just so *fast* nowadays," Ron said, clearly worried. "Have you had a talk with Marlo?"

Kelly knew how concerned Ron was about the call they'd gotten a couple of days ago from Marlo's P.E. teacher, cautioning them about how Marlo's class was the most sexually aggressive she had ever experienced. The girls were driving the boys crazy with taunting comments like "I'm not wearing any underwear," and doing things like daring or inviting the boys to touch their breasts.

"Marlo said the P.E. teacher was exaggerating. I think the kids are so overloaded with sexual messages from the media that they talk about it more than we did. But I *think* it's basically innocent."

"I'd like to believe you're right."

"I asked Marlo what kinds of games the kids play at their parties—"

"And you expect her to tell you the truth?"

"I can tell when she's lying. She's a lousy liar."

Kelly told Ron she didn't think the games and the silly shy reactions had really changed that much since they were kids. Marlo's seventh-grade gatherings sounded identical to the ones Kelly had had. If

357

anything, Kelly thought she had done more kissing than these kids were doing. There were a few wild girls in the class, but according to Marlo they were the more developed ones, being sexual to be popular, and the kids all regarded them as sluts.

"When Marlo's fifteen or sixteen, then we can start to worry," Kelly said, trying to reassure Ron. "I have such mixed feelings," she admitted. "I'm going to have a hard time advising her. On the one hand I don't want her to ever be taken advantage of. But on the other hand I want her to have a healthy amount of sexual experience and a free, unencumbered attitude." Like I wish *I'd* had, Kelly thought.

"That's bullshit," Ron said.

"Why?"

"Because it sounds great in theory, but she's not even old enough to understand the theory."

"Well, what are we going to tell the twins?"

"To screw their brains out."

"That's cute, Ron, real cute."

"To be discriminating."

"Then why can't we just tell Marlo the same thing?"

"Kelly, you live in a dream world."

"I just think it's unfair. And I don't like perpetuating a grossly unfair double standard."

"Well, don't go pioneering with my daughter, okay?"

They were interrupted by the waiter clearing away their plates.

"It's so strange," Ron said. "It doesn't seem like it was all that long ago that I was convincing girls how good it was to be sexually free, and now, all of a sudden, I'm the staunchly conservative father, worried about my daughter's virginity."

"And I remember just how persuasive you *were* with that line of argument." Kelly touched her leg to Ron's under the table. "I sure fell for it."

Ron laughed. "You sure did. Now I'm worried that Marlo might be just as gullible."

Kelly looked fondly at him, taking in his boyish good looks. She couldn't remember that he looked any different when she had first met him. His face still had that youthfully eager, almost naïve quality. His attitude was different. His clothes were different. But his face was the same. She could picture their own summer at camp together so easily. Ron had seemed so perfect to her. All her dreams of what the man she would marry would be like seemed to be contained in this one incredible person. He was handsome, bright, from a well-to-do Pacific Palisades family. He was just starting law school. He was a great athlete. Fun to be with. He represented the kind of steadiness Kelly knew she wanted. Her father, great-looking and a chaser, had been a sales representative for a sportswear line. He was always on the road, turning down opportunities to work in one place because he *preferred* to be away. Her mother, a pretty but always tired-looking woman, never failed to let Kelly and her two sisters know of the great burden she felt, being left alone to raise the children on her own, with Kelly's father's meager earnings. She was a bitter woman, trapped in her own self-pity and lack of strength, and Kelly had always felt sorry for her. It was only as she grew older that she let go of the resentment she had felt for her father and began instead to feel pity for him as well.

But Ron was from another world, and it was in his world that Kelly envisioned herself. Their romance was condensed but wonderful, limited by the short time frame of summer camp.

Late one evening after all the campers had gone to bed, Kelly and Ron got stoned together on some grass one of the other counselors gave them. There was a stream not far away and they walked there together, bringing a blanket along with them. Kelly only remembered fragments of this. She had been very high, very loose. She clearly remembered hoping that Ron wouldn't *stop* as she had asked him to on their previous nights together. Until tonight she had satisfied *him* but had been left unsatisfied herself. And soon she understood that this time Ron wasn't going to stop.

The next time they'd made love, it was in a rowboat on the lake. There were no TV sets at summer camp.

Kelly smiled, thinking about what her life might have been like if there'd been no Ron. Maybe she would be married to someone just like him, or maybe she would have waited and focused instead on her aspiration to become a great photographer. Maybe she would have married someone more like Brandon. How very *early* she had chosen her path, she thought, hoping that her daughter would wait until she was older and more aware of the *meaning* of choosing a path.

There were two fortune cookies on the plate with

the bill, and Kelly leaned over to select one. She broke it in half and tugged at the tiny strip of paper that was in so tightly. Then she looked up surprised, taken aback by the message, which seemed to have been planted there as a note of caution to her. *When you commit a sin the second time, you no longer consider it a sin.* The almost ominous words of Kelly's fortune stung her, and she remembered the postcard Brandon had sent her from Sardinia. It was tucked away in her desk drawer at the office. It was a magnificent photograph of a flame-colored sky over the bright blue Mediterranean Sea with its jagged edge of coastline, with an amber sun making its descent, and Brandon had sent it to her with only a short inscription. *Your hair is like a Sardinian sunset,* he had written—*I'll be back in L.A. in another week or so.* What worried Kelly was how eager she was to commit a second sin—one more time.

Chapter Twenty

THEIR LAST NIGHT TOGETHER IN THE HAMPTONS, THEY HAD spent in bed. In love. On another planet. Ericka's memory of her idyllic weekend with Jamie now played over and over in her head, like an unforgettable montage. They had taken long walks along beaches where oatmeal-colored fields blended into ridges of sand heaped into dunes formed by the action of the wind. They had held hands, traded thoughts, shared secrets, and divulged dreams of their projected futures—speculating about whether they would find themselves together.

The weekend had been perfect except for one flaw. She hadn't told him she was married. She'd brought him up to date on everything she'd been doing for the last thirteen years, except for the existence of a husband. She'd edited David out like a character who had to be dropped from a story, tightening all that was around him so the gaps wouldn't be felt. As it turned out, the revisions required to accommodate the extraction of David had been strangely simple. Ironically, David's deep conviction that they lead full separate lives, never dependent upon one another, so that they would remain "whole people," made it possible for her to sound "whole" without him. She wasn't half of a couple accustomed to conversations filled with "we" and "us." She was just Ericka. Ericka, who, it seemed, had never *not* been in love with Jamie. As in a movie theater when the house was dark, all her senses were focused on the fantasy.

Ericka thought anxiously back to the argument they'd had about whether he would come out to L.A. or whether she would return to New York. They had been in bed, in each other's arms. *L.A.?* she'd thought, alarmed. *Her real life was in L.A.* There were unthinkable complications in L.A.

"No?" Jamie had asked her, looking surprised, running his hand along her thigh, watching her face intently.

"I'd rather come out to New York," she remembered saying.

"But it's far more difficult for you," he'd insisted. She had a job she had to show up at. He was a writer. He could write anywhere. Just give him a typewriter and he was happy, he'd claimed, with his hand moving up the contour of her behind.

While sighing from his touch, she'd continued to

argue with him—New York was so much more romantic than L.A. They could go to museums, to the ballet, to the theater. . . .

He had only laughed at her, saying that he'd rather go to bed with her in a great bungalow overlooking the beach. His agent would lend him his place in Malibu. *That*, he thought, sounded much more romantic. They could walk on the beach and make love, and walk on the beach and screw, and walk on the beach and fuck. "Imagine, all that variety," he had concluded tenderly. "Sounds romantic to me."

Ericka was jarred out of her daydream by a loud buzzing from her intercom. Feeling disoriented, she picked up the line to find out what her secretary wanted.

"Norman needs to see you," she was told.

She looked across her white lacquered desk, usually so neat but now made disorderly by a pile of neglected work. "Tell him I'll be right there," she said.

Obviously having Jamie on her mind all the time was taking more of a toll than she had realized. She'd forgotten the meeting with Norman. It wasn't her secretary's fault because *she'd forgotten* to tell her secretary about it. For Ericka, this sort of disorganization was completely out of character. It rattled her terribly.

Sitting back in her chair, she looked up at the David Hockney swimming pool hanging opposite her on the wall. David, not David Hockney but *her* David, had bought her the lithograph as a birthday present that year. He said the tranquil image of water would help to calm her down. From his accredited psychological point of view, the picture of the swimming pool created an image of being relaxed. And the exercise he had prescribed along with his gift was one he used in teaching self-hypnosis. He told her to create for herself the feeling of lying on a raft in the swimming pool, serenely inactive. "Concentrate on the sensation of the water," David had said. "Conjure up the smell of the pool; think it through your senses. The chlorine. The way the sun feels beating down on you. The slight swishing sound of the water as you redirect your raft from the edge of the pool. The feeling of that water on your hand. . . ." Ericka could almost hear David's voice as she went through his technique.

She allowed herself two and a half minutes. Then she picked up a couple of the files she thought she would need for her meeting with Norman and a legal pad.

"Have a seat, Ericka," Norman said, standing up and leaning over his desk. "Having marital problems? Or are you pregnant?" He gazed down to the belly she didn't have.

"You're just used to me being perfect," she teased with a lightness she didn't feel, as they both sat down.

"I am used to you being perfect. Which is why I get concerned when you don't show up for an appointment." Norman lifted his pipe from out of his ashtray and relit it.

When she began apologizing, he cut her off.

"Don't worry about it. Your otherwise perfect record excuses you—it's just that I can see you've been distracted lately. If you want to talk about it, I'm here. Otherwise, shape up," he finished with a grin.

She smiled back at him, confirming in a grateful look that something was disturbing her, but that she didn't want to talk about it. They switched over to business and she relaxed, going over various projects and updating him on their status. He was particularly happy with what was happening with *End Resolve;* Mrs. Beall had finally called to give her consent, and, as promised, Ericka was awarded her raise. There was a screening scheduled for the Hindson story the following afternoon, which Norman wanted her to attend. They were running it for the lawyers and he needed her input.

When she returned to her office she collided with her dreams. Jamie was there, unannounced, waiting for her. She looked at him, stunned, and closed her door. She buzzed her secretary, who'd obviously been bribed, to hold all calls.

Abruptly Jamie put his arms around her, saying, "I missed you," covering her response with his lips. His embrace was tight and passionate, and she wished he would hold on to her forever.

"You look beautiful," he said. "And this is some office. I'm impressed."

"I meant for you to be impressed," she said, pleased as he looked around the spacious room that had been designed for her in pretty pastels. It was simple, starkly furnished, but feminine. "But what are you

367

doing here? When I talked to you *yesterday*, you didn't say a word."

"I finished that project I was working on in the afternoon. Then decided to surprise you," he said with a sly curve to his lips. "If you have another date for tonight, just cancel it."

Trying to think quickly, Ericka remembered that David had said he was working tonight. It occurred to her that he might not be working—maybe he also had a date. Perhaps they'd select the same restaurant and end up sitting booth to booth. Jamie's smile disappeared. "Is he that important?" he asked, looking concerned.

Only my husband, she thought. "No, of course I'm going to be with you tonight. I was just trying to think of where I should take you."

"I've got my agent's place out in Malibu. The weather's so great, I thought I'd barbecue."

That would be safe, she thought.

Just then Ericka's buzzer sounded.

"It's that conference call—New York and London," her secretary said.

Damn. Something else she'd forgotten about. "Tell them to hold just one minute," Ericka said.

"I've got an appointment anyway," Jamie told her. "I'm meeting with a couple of producers about my play."

"To do a film?"

He nodded. "I'll call you later. Plan on dinner at my place about seven. Is that all right?"

"Can I bring something?"

"Just a change of clothes for tomorrow." With that,

he kissed her on the lips, nibbled at her ear, and whispered that he was mad about her.

As she watched him rush out, she took her call, thinking how she had to tell Jamie *tonight* about David. How she couldn't delay it any longer.

"Hello," she said, looking at her watch, sliding into the conversation easily, glad for the distraction. Business relationships were always so much easier than personal ones. They always had been for her.

During the long drive out along the Pacific Coast Highway to Malibu, Ericka blasted her Carly Simon cassette, trying to drown out her anxiety in the tunes. But the melancholy lyrics that were belted out with such heart only increased her awareness of the predicament she was in and she turned the volume down to a more manageable level in order to think.

She would come right out and tell Jamie the truth, she decided. She would try to explain the entire situation to him: how she had always been in love with him, how her marriage was really more of a friendship, and how she would like to let her relationship with him play out and be tested before she made any rash irrevocable decisions. That would give them both a chance to see if what they thought they had discovered in each other was real and lasting.

It all sounded so hollow to Ericka as she reviewed her arguments, and she was desperately worried about Jamie's reaction. The truth was that she didn't really want to threaten her marriage with David. As flawed as their marriage was, she wasn't ready to let go of it, to walk away from a marriage of six years that in spite of its romantic shortcomings worked well for them. On some level they provided something very secure for one another. Perhaps it was the way they always accepted each other's imperfections. There were no fanciful expectations to collide with—no false hopes to be shattered by. No flames to go out. David always said that passion was a flame, and what a bitch it was to sit around waiting for it to go out, because inevitably it would.

She pulled into the private entrance of the Colony and gave her name to the guard waiting for her in the little wooden boxlike structure that was his office. He glanced down at the clipboard he was holding, found her name, then allowed her to pass, instructing her where to go.

Bumping over the speed control hurdles along the paved road, Ericka wound her car around and down the narrow drive until she came to Number 41. She parked, checked her reflection in the rearview mirror, took a deep breath, and then started toward the house. It was tall and angular and constructed out of redwood. The aroma of something being barbecued permeated the air.

Ericka rang the doorbell and waited. She had gone home to change and was now wearing tight yellow cotton jeans and a yellow and white V-neck sweater with the sleeves pushed up to just below her elbows. It was chillier out in Malibu than she had anticipated, and she was sorry she hadn't brought along a jacket.

The door was opened vigorously by Jamie, and Ericka stood facing him, afraid to enter, afraid to reveal to this man who was convinced she had spent her whole life waiting for him that she was married. The threshold of the house seemed to represent the giant step she was about to take, from the safety of illusion to the precarious truth-declaring avowal inside.

"This is paradise," Jamie said, ushering Ericka in. "I'm obviously in the wrong end of the business. Maybe I ought to become an agent. This place must cost a fortune."

"It does. But there are plenty of writers out here—"

"*Screenwriters*, not playwrights," Jamie corrected her. "And I think I've just been inspired enough to begin writing my first screenplay."

The bungalow was designed to take full advantage of all the ocean's moods, the generous glass doors letting in the fresh salt air and the furniture arranged to face the splendor of the Pacific. The walls, Ericka noticed, were bare, with nothing distracting the eye from the magical ocean view. Jamie took Ericka by the arm and walked her out onto the patio, where the railing resembled the detailing of a great ocean liner of the twenties. There was a built-in cast-iron barbecue, which Jamie went over to check, lifting the lid and releasing a sweet smoky fragrance.

"Smells good," Ericka said.

"I do a mean marinade," he said. "I hope you like lamb."

"I love it."

"Good." He put his arm around her. She snuggled up closely to him. They stood quietly watching the water rush in, shattering like white crystal along the ridge of the shore, then slowly retreating, sliding back down into a slick blackness.

371

Ericka listened for a moment to the sounds of the ocean, wishing her own worries would swell up along with the great sea, and then leave her in a great wave of relief. But the tide repeated its mystical pattern, pulling the waves back in, and anxiety welled up inside Ericka once more.

"This is about done," Jamie said, going over to the barbecue again where the butterflied leg of lamb was sizzling. "I hope you're hungry."

"Famished," she said, much too nervous to actually be hungry, but aware that he had gone to too much effort for her to be truthful. She followed him inside and into the small but efficient-looking kitchen, where he began moving about with swift authority.

"When did you become such a chef?" she asked. On the counter were the remnants from the salad he had put together and a blueberry tart he had made.

"I like to eat. I had to learn to cook."

"Fruit tarts?"

"My mother was French. She taught me how to make tarts when I was eight years old."

"I didn't know that."

"There's a lot about me you don't know."

This was a perfect entry into the confession, and Ericka wondered if she should begin. She was trying to decide if she should tell him before or after dinner. But the moment quickly disappeared when Jamie opened up a big lidded straw basket, removing two cloth napkins and place mats, which he handed to Ericka. "You're on table-setting duty," he said, opening the cupboards where the dishes were stacked. "I'll take care of the wine."

This was just as well, she decided, reaching up for two white china plates. After a glass of wine, Jamie would be more relaxed. And so would she. The flatware was whimsical-looking; silver molded into a contemporary shape with a bright blue enamel teardrop inset at the tip of the handle. Ericka finished arranging the place settings, found a matchbook, and then lit the candles. She looked over at Jamie, who was now carrying the lamb in on a big pewter platter. He set it down, then began uncorking a bottle of Chateau Haut-Brion 1961.

"To the second time around," Jamie said, pouring out two glasses, then touching her glass lightly with his own. They each took a sip of the mellow wine.

"Your turn," Jamie said, his glass poised in preparation for another toast.

"I'm not very good at this," Ericka said shyly.

"C'mon."

"I even went out and bought a book once to learn how—the toastmaster's guide to something or other—but I never got past the first page. Whatever I say sounds corny."

"I won't laugh."

To your loving me in spite of what I have to tell you tonight, she thought, looking around the room for inspiration. "To nothing screwing us up this time," Ericka said sincerely, groping. She looked over at an arrangement of pale yellow roses. "To blooming rosebuds unscathed by the thorns that threaten beneath them." Erika started laughing. Nervous laughter. "I told you I was lousy at this."

"Good God, the thorns that *threaten* beneath them? Are things that bad?" He, too, started to laugh.

"Okay, to dinner not getting cold," she said.

After dinner he led her over to three big pillows he had thrown down next to the fireplace, gazing at her intently. "God, you're beautiful," he said, touching her hair. "I couldn't believe it when I saw you in New York. A little girl transformed."

"I never felt like a little girl."

"I know." He was running his finger along her cheekbone, encircling her lips, then moving in to kiss her. Her heart was filled with panic and she knew as his lips moved hungrily over her own that she couldn't let this go on. She was feeling chills down her spine and also feeling slightly off kilter from all the wine, but she had to begin. "Jamie, I have to talk to you," she insisted suddenly. She was absolutely terrified. But his kisses covered her plea, muting the words and making her unsure if she'd actually even uttered them. As in a dream when she called out voicelessly for help, her vocal abilities were frozen in fright. She tried to relax as he pulled her down onto the floor, close to the fire. She would tell him afterward. He was kissing her ardently, glowing under the soft amber light. If I lose him, I'll die, she thought miserably, wishing desperately that she could lose herself in his passion, be swept away in his heated embrace, searing the reality of her predicament into ash—lost forever.

But she couldn't go on. This was wrong. She broke away from him, sitting up and taking his hands tightly in her own. "Jamie. I really have to talk to you *now*,"

374

she began, restlessly, unsure of what to say next. "I'm sorry. I'm really sorry."

"Don't worry about it," he said tenderly, regarding her with anxious concern.

"I love you more than I've ever loved anybody or anything in my life. . . ."

Jamie looked at her perplexed.

"I don't know how to say this. . . ."

"Just say it," he told her calmly.

"You're not going to understand."

"Try me."

"When you sent me your wedding invitation I was heartbroken. I'd just gotten my acceptance to Yale the day before and I remember I'd gotten so crazy, I burned it."

Jamie looked at her stunned. "Ericka, I feel terrible—"

"Every date I ever had I compared to you," she interrupted him. "I tried, but I couldn't get over you. I'd dream about you. And you were always so cruel to me in my dreams. But I loved you anyway. You could have done anything at all to me and I still wouldn't have been cured. Because it had nothing to do with reasoning. It was my heart."

"You're making me feel pretty awful."

"Then, when I was in college, I started dating this medical student. He was doing his residency in psychiatry. We had a lot of fun together. He used to analyze me all the time. He knew all about you. But it never bothered him because he felt it was just part of my compulsiveness. He regarded you as unfinished business for me and that was all. Anyway, we became really good friends. Best friends. He's very bright. Fun. Relaxed. He made things seem not so serious, and after a while we decided to live together. And then a couple of years later—" Ericka paused, barely breathing, looking into Jamie's eyes. "We got married."

Jamie looked completely bewildered and Ericka realized he thought she'd been married and then divorced.

"Why didn't you say anything?" he asked finally. "You knew all about my marriage."

"Jamie. I *am* married. Still."

He stared at her shocked. His eyes were colder than she had ever seen them. "Why did you lie to me?"

"I didn't lie. You never asked—" she responded, trembling.

"That's bullshit!"

"I was afraid. I couldn't bear to have you say no to me without giving us a chance."

"I don't even know what to say. I can't believe it. How could you not tell me?"

"Would you have gone away for the weekend with me if you'd known?"

"Of course not."

"I guess that's why I didn't tell you—"

"You're married!" he said with unusual vehemence. "What kind of a relationship do you have with this guy? What kind of person are you?"

"Well, I'm not the first person ever to have an extramarital affair, so stop looking at me that way. What I did that warrants your outrage was that I didn't tell you. And I didn't tell you for a very justifiable reason—"

"What is this—do you and your head doctor have some kind of open marriage or something?"

"No. I've never cheated on David before."

"Oh, great."

"But *he* has affairs all the time—"

"Terrific. Some relationship."

"Would you stop passing judgment and listen? Whatever kind of marriage I have now is a result of having been so much in love with you that I could never match it. When I married David, I thought that something inside of me had broken, and that I just wasn't capable anymore of feeling the way I'd felt for you. I thought that by marrying him, I would grow to love him. I was young and there was a void inside me that I wanted desperately to fill. When I found that he wasn't going to fill it for me, I got a career."

"Did that do it for you?" Jamie asked coldly.

Ericka shook her head no. "I was still miserable. Jamie, it's always been you. Why are you making this so difficult for me?"

"Does your husband know?"

Again Ericka shook her head no.

Jamie stood up and went to pour himself another glass of wine. "What did you expect to happen after tonight? After you'd told me?"

"I expected that you'd be outraged—"

"Good guess."

"But that you'd realize after you thought about it

that what I'd done wasn't as awful as you initially thought it was—" she continued.

"How long is it supposed to take me to realize?" he asked her harshly.

Ericka didn't respond. She rose to get herself another glass of wine also. There was only a drop left in the bottle, so she hunted instead for some brandy in the bar.

"Ten minutes?" Jamie was guessing. "An hour? Maybe I should meditate on it! Jesus Christ, Ericka. Then what? After I'd realized it wasn't so awful?"

Ericka poured herself a Courvoisier. She took a sip as she turned to face Jamie. "I think we should continue to see one another," she said defiantly. "As though I weren't married."

"But you *are* married."

"My relationship with David—"

"Stinks. Do you sleep together?"

She looked at Jamie, feeling defeated. "Yes," she answered guardedly; wanting to explain how little that meant, how unpassionate their sleeping together was for her, but feeling foolish.

"I'll tell you why I can't do this, Ericka. First of all, by our seeing each other under these conditions, it's going to be completely artificial. There's too much pressure. It's unnatural and it's wrong. If you think you're married to the wrong man, then you'll have to take care of that *before* you start getting involved with someone else. I don't want to be responsible for breaking up your marriage."

"You wouldn't be responsible!" she insisted.

"But I would. Later on, if things didn't work out perfectly between us, you'd blame me."

"That's not true at all. Why would I blame you?"

"You just would."

Ericka set down her drink. "I love you, dammit!" she shouted at him, breaking into tears. "If you don't want to see me because of the way you *feel* about me, I can accept that. But—"

"You'd be a wreck sneaking around. It's cheap, Ericka." Jamie's anger was abating.

"No. It would be worth it."

"It's not worth being unfair to your husband."

"But my husband's unfair to *me*."

"Well, then it's not worth it to me. What about *my* feelings? What if you decide to stay with your husband after all this?"

"Jamie, I love you! I want to marry you."

"You're crazy—one weekend and you're ready to run off and get married," he said, going over to hold her. She cried, unable to stop as he smoothed her hair and muttered soothing words. Then she broke away from him, unable to contain her frustration, suddenly furious.

He pulled her back, trapping her in his arms. She struggled to free herself. "Just let me go!" she cried.

But he held her and kissed her. "I can't," he whispered. They stared at each other, sinking down onto the pillows in front of the fireplace. Ericka listened to the waves crashing explosively onto the shore while her heart beat wildly and all she could think of was the way Jamie felt against her and how badly she needed that sensation, and before she was fully aware of it, they were naked. They made love violently, their bodies thrashing fervidly against one another, unable to part.

Hot and drenched with passion, they showered together. As Jamie was working the soap up into a thick lather and smoothing it over Ericka's back, she turned, slippery in his arms, and began kissing him. Tears washed down her cheeks beneath the spray of the water. She felt Jamie hard against her and she urgently guided him into her. He pressed her against the wall and made love to her as fiercely as he had before. With the warm water rushing at them, they climaxed, kissing wildly throughout the frenzied connection.

When Ericka got dressed to leave late that night, she knew that, in spite of their lovemaking, Jamie was definitely on edge.

"Thanks for dinner," she said, as he kissed her tenderly at the door.

"What are we going to do?" he asked, lifting her chin and brushing strands of hair from her eyes. "I'm crazy about you."

"Well, you know how I feel," she said timorously.

"Call you tomorrow?"

"Okay."

"Do you want to have dinner?"

"Are you cooking?" she asked, ready to start crying all over again—this time out of relief.

"Maybe."

They kissed one last time before Ericka turned to leave. She was keenly aware that if she didn't briskly assess her life, if she weren't prepared to risk her marriage, she would lose him.

David was sitting at Ericka's desk in her small but tidy home office trying to piece together a puzzle that had been bothering him for some time now. Something was amiss with his wife.

He sat almost trancelike for several long moments in her chair, touching her things, as though waiting for an answer to arise psychically from her possessions.

He earned his living analyzing people's behavior and now when he most needed his talents they seemed to be jammed and ineffective. What are you looking for? he asked himself, flipping through the mostly blank pages of the desk calendar that she never really used. A clue. Evidence. Evidence of what? She's having an affair. I'm positive she's having an affair.

David continued this internal dialogue for a while, trying to articulate to himself how it was he felt Ericka had been different lately. Distractedly he went through the four piles of mail on her desk. Bills. Business. Social. And then advertisements and newsletters that she probably considered miscellaneous. After finding nothing there he read the titles of the screenplays he found in another stack. Then he fingered her Rolodex. Still nothing.

Why do you think she's having an affair? he thought. Because I've had so many I know! Ericka, whose behavior was ordinarily consistent—always fairly nervous, compulsive, busy but friendly—was now swinging radically between two extremes. One minute she was unusually warm and attentive, almost guilty. Then she'd be cold, critical, and standoffish. If Ericka had ever, in their relationship together, shown any of this mercurial conduct, David wouldn't have been so suspicious. But this was unequivocally atypical behavior for her.

Now he began to go through her drawers, replaying in his thoughts the argument he'd had with her about her friend she'd set up. Even then, Ericka's reaction had been suspect, as though on one level the gift had almost been innocent, but on another deeper level, as David had pointed out to her, she really did wish that *she* had been the recipient of the fantasy. It was as though while they were arguing heatedly with each other something had clicked in Ericka. She'd gotten strangely silent. Contemplative. And her impatient anger had fallen away, replaced by this same soft, nervous, almost vulnerable, overly warm behavior that was now driving him crazy.

Then he saw it, and everything fitted into place. In Ericka's top righthand drawer, thrown in and lying in plain sight, was the *Playbill* to *Restless Fires*, Jamie Sterling's play. Inside of it was a single ticket stub. *Ericka's fantasy,* of course. And he wondered with a sinking feeling if he hadn't actually pushed the button that sent her off to him.

When Ericka opened her front door, she saw David standing there, waiting for her.

"Did you just get in also?" she asked him uncomfortably, sensing something was wrong. His feet were apart in a stance of confrontation. One hand was on his hip, the other he held behind his back. He had a strained tightness to his jaw and his eyes were cold.

"You didn't mention that you'd seen Jamie Sterling's play when you were in New York," he said roughly, thrusting the *Playbill* at her.

Ericka put her briefcase and purse down on a chair and glanced at the *Playbill,* swallowing deeply.

"No," she said, walking past David, trembling, wondering where she'd left it and then remembering that she'd put it in her desk drawer upstairs. "Since when do you go through my things?" she asked.

"Since you started cheating on me!"

Ericka turned on David, outraged. "Mr. Cool—Mr. Respect for One Another's Privacy goes snooping through my things and then implies that it was a liberty due him because I'd cheated on him. You goddamn hypocrite!" she shouted, feeling torn apart.

"Are you having an affair with him?" David asked. They both knew who "him" was.

"Yes." It was a whisper.

"When did it start?"

"When I went to New York."

"Why?" David asked, shattered.

"I don't know," she replied softly, going over to David and touching her forehead to his chest. He didn't move. He was absolutely rigid. Ericka knew how deeply she was hurting him.

"You don't know?" he asked bitterly.

"I *had* to," she responded heavily. "You're a psychiatrist—you ought to understand all of this perfectly. I certainly don't."

"Is he in L.A. now?"

"Yes."

"Do you think you still love him?"

Ericka's eyes immediately filled up with tears again and she felt a horrible knot in her chest. She looked up miserably at David, feeling panicked, torn between telling the truth and lying. What if it didn't work out with Jamie? What if this were all a lark? What was going to happen to her relationship with David—would he ever get over this?

"Then go to him, dammit!" David raged at her.

She was speechless. Totally unprepared for this kind of response. "You're being unfair, David. It's not as though *you've* been faithful to me. I've never interfered with your little liaisons! For once I'm having one and you go berserk."

"This is different and you know it!"

"Who sets these rules?"

"If you love him *go* to him," David repeated with emphasis. "Just get the hell out of here and go do what you need to do!"

Without saying another word, Ericka went into the hall closet and took out a jacket. She picked up her purse and briefcase, realizing she was still holding Jamie's *Playbill*. She looked up at David, praying that he'd stop her, and when he didn't, she left.

Once again Ericka was racing up the Pacific Coast Highway toward Malibu, feeling like a battered ball. She had no idea what Jamie's reaction would be.

When she pulled her car up in front of his bungalow, she thought about turning around. A small battle had been won when she'd left him before.

They were having dinner together tomorrow night. Now she'd be stirring things up all over again. Presenting him with another bombshell. She sat there for a while thinking, listening to the same cassette of Carly Simon lamenting her woes in verse. So many words seemed appropriate. These songs had been written for her.

Finally she removed her keys from the ignition and got out of the car. She shut the door as quietly as she could so as not to foreclose turning around and chickening out. "Hi," Jamie said, looking alarmed when he opened the door. "Is everything all right?"

"I left David," she said with intense trepidation. Jamie just stood there not saying anything. "Can I come in?"

He apologized and moved aside to let her pass. She watched him stand for a while, facing the door with his back to her. He was fidgeting with the sash on his robe.

"Ericka, I *really* don't want to be responsible for breaking up your marriage—"

"Jamie, *please* don't lecture me," she said, going to him. "I love you. I feel like a broken record already. I've made a decision that perhaps I should have made a long time ago—"

"But you didn't."

She started to protest.

"You didn't," he pressed, "because something about your relationship was important enough to hold you there. You must have been getting something you needed. Something you'll miss if things between us don't work out."

385

"I don't care," Ericka said, going to stand by the window and looking out at the water, trying to draw strength from the waves.

"But you might care later," Jamie was saying.

"I need to do this." She turned to him. "Let's say you'd gone into your dad's business. You'd joined his accounting firm like he wanted you to. You made a good secure living but *inside* you were restless, discontent. All your life you'd dreamed of being a writer. In your heart you knew you could do it and you were bitter that you hadn't. You were withering because in your fantasies you were Tolstoy or Proust or Faulkner, and you needed to make yourself dull in order to live with the disappointment of being an accountant. Then one day your soul acted up. You started writing a play—secretly. Then you found out that in order to live with yourself, you had to make a decision. You could play it safe—you could be a decently paid accountant for the rest of your life. *Or* you could go after your first love."

"Are you finished?" Jamie asked her. She had followed him into the kitchen, where he was pouring them each a glass of orange juice.

She nodded.

"This is not the way to begin a relationship," he said. "If you've absolutely made up your mind that you want to leave your husband, with or without me out there to catch you, then get a place of your own and live by yourself for a while. You can't go from one dependency to another."

"What kind of box are you putting me in? I love you, Jamie. You wanted to stop seeing me because I was married and now you don't want to see me because I'm ending my marriage."

Jamie walked back into the living room. His eyes were dark with concern. "You love your fantasy of me," he insisted. "You don't know me well enough to be sure you love *me*."

Ericka sat down on one of the chairs, extending her legs out far in front of her and letting her head fall back onto the cushion. She listened to Jamie tell her how he couldn't possibly live up to the fantasy she had created of him. He felt it was unfair to even have to try.

"I don't believe this," she said, disregarding his argument. "Look, you made a mistake in your marriage. You're divorced. Why can't you accept that I made a mistake in mine?"

"Because you can't fall on me as a way to salvage your life. I don't want to be in the position of rescuing you. That's just more fantasy."

"So this is it?" she asked, overcome with rejection.

"For now."

"For now—that's bullshit. We're either off or we're on—"

"This is too quick, Ericka—it's hasty."

"Then tell me you don't love me. For once and for all, let me off the hook so that I can forget about you. So I can write you off, finally, and close the book on you. Just tell me that you don't care."

"Of course I care. It's more complex than that. You need to be on your own."

"Tell me you don't love me." Ericka closed her eyes, needing to hear those words come out of his mouth. Maybe they'd cut a wound so deep her love for him would finally die, so she could bury it and get on with her life.

"I don't know how I feel," Jamie said, taking her hands and lifting her out of the chair.

She looked at him resentfully as he continued on logically, coolly, and with just enough conflict in his eyes to make her still believe that she had a chance. It resolved nothing for her. All she heard was that he didn't love her *enough,* and in the middle of his next sentence, she left.

We Never Close flashed comfortingly in bright red neon from the roof of Dolores' all-night coffee shop. Having nowhere else to go, Ericka drove into the well-lit parking lot where the abundant specials were prominently advertised on signs posted in the windows. She had parked directly in front of the *Special of the Day:* Old-fashioned chicken pot pie, butter crust, $3.95—whipped potatoes, garden green peas, tossed salad, roll and butter. Feeling nauseous, she got out of her car and headed toward the bank of coin-operated newspaper dispensers in front of the restaurant, purchasing several different papers to take inside with her.

Drinking coffee out of a heavy mug, Ericka waited for the sun to come up. She tried to analyze her predicament, to make plans, but she knew she wasn't thinking clearly. On a napkin she scribbled a list of the things she needed to do the next day, adding to it every now and then something she remembered that had been a carry-over item of extremely low priority from months before. Phone calls that would be nice to make, but that she never actually had time for.

The newspapers she had purchased were in a messy pile on the seat beside her, and on the table in front of her there was a plateful of crumbs from the blueberry muffin she'd ordered.

When it was time for David to be leaving for his office, Ericka went up to the cash register and paid her bill. Then, numb with exhaustion, she drove home, half expecting that David would be waiting for her. She was surprised to realize how disappointed she was that he was gone. There were so many decisions lying ahead of her. So many biting cold and lonely realities.

She took a particularly long shower, then, unable to stand it any longer, called Jamie. When there was no answer, she tried again, hoping she'd dialed the wrong number. She let it ring an inordinate number of times, thinking he could be in the shower or out getting a newspaper. While she got dressed, she let the phone continue to ring, checking it every couple of minutes in case he had returned from wherever it was he'd gone. Probably he was upset. He could have taken a jog along the beach. Gone out for breakfast.

After twenty minutes of this, dressed and ready to go, Ericka finally gave up. When she arrived at her office half an hour later, she learned from her secretary that Jamie had called to say he was returning to New York.

You schmuck! she wanted to shout at him. *You goddamned coward!*

Her day never got any better. It seemed that there

were magnets attached to each crisis snapping one in after another, surrounding her with miserable news. Then finally, when she was getting ready to leave for the day, David called her.

His voice was low and tentative as he began apologizing at length for his uncontrolled behavior, telling Ericka that he loved her and that he wanted her to come home. She listened with a split reaction. Half of her was overwhelmingly relieved. The other half of her was worried. All of her wanted to cry again. What they had together, he insisted, was good for both of them. Ericka would be foolish to leave him for Jamie.

"You know how I feel about the kind of rainbow you're chasing," he was saying. "And I guess I always knew that this might happen. You're compulsive about everything you do. Why shouldn't you be compulsive about your fantasies?"

"I don't know what to say," she replied, holding her hand to her chest. There was a magnet in her head now, and all those other crises were flying up and attaching themselves to it.

"Say that you'll come home and we'll forget all about this. I got crazy last night. You know that wasn't like me at all."

"David, I don't know," she said, emotionally drained. "We have a lot of thinking to do. A lot of talking to do."

"I agree. But let's do it together. There's no rush. Just come home and we'll discuss everything. If you need to continue to see Jamie, then you should continue to see him, but there's no reason to move out.

We're adults. We have a very frank and open relationship. Above all, we're friends. The way I see it is, you live with someone who is easy for you to live with—but often you love somebody you absolutely can't live with. That's the way I've *always* viewed marriage."

"I know. But is it enough?"

"All that undying love and romance is crap. The only reason you're so in love with him is because you've never really been able to have him."

"How classic, right?"

"Ericka, I'm good for you and you know it. I'm supportive of your career. I've encouraged you to become an independent person, unlike what a lot of insecure husbands would do. I've never stifled you, never said no. I've given you complete freedom."

"He left for New York this morning," Ericka said, beginning to cry again. "He didn't want to break up my marriage."

"He shouldn't! You've got a good marriage. You just don't know it because you're such a goddamn dreamer. Have you *ever* heard of a romance really lasting? Name *one* couple."

Ericka couldn't think of any.

"If I thought that kind of romance existed I'd go get it for myself. But it doesn't. Romantic affection, yes. But we have that. We're best friends. We have good sex. We're supportive. We love each other. We have a hell of a good marriage."

Tears continued to stream down Ericka's cheeks as David went on comforting her with his soothing logic.

She was reminded of their early days together when those healing words had won her over.

"So what do you say? You coming home?" he asked finally.

She looked up at the picture of the swimming pool on the wall and closed her eyes. The sensation of her raft bobbing on the surface of the water. The sun beating down on her. Warming her skin. Melting her tension. "Yes," she said, looking at the bright blue water again. David was good for her. She was just crazy.

Chapter Twenty-One

KELLY ADJUSTED THE OVERHEAD LIGHT AND CONTINUED TO concentrate on the proofs laid out across her desk at the photography studio. She looked at one tempting ensemble after another from Lina Lee, the trend-setting boutique on Rodeo Drive.

"I'll take that one," Kelly said aloud to the empty room. "And that one. And that one." Then she laughed, imagining Ron's reaction if she were to bring home three totally accessorized outfits from this store where movie stars shopped for everything from their Malibu beachwear to gowns for the Academy Awards. Lina, the proprietor of the store that had exploded into the forefront of fashion, was a client of Bob's and had hired him to do a big job for her. In the midst of her going through the proofs, the phone rang. It was Brandon. He had just returned from Sardinia.

"Did you miss me?" he asked instead of saying hello.

She laughed nervously in response, and then an unexpected sadness welled up inside her.

"Brandon, why don't you play with someone more available?" she asked genuinely. She could easily picture him with any of the stunning models posed dramatically in the photographs in front of her. Brandon Michaels would date girls like these: tall, lithe, and draped in expensive fabrics. The rich man's toy.

"I would, except that I can't think of anyone else I'd rather play with."

"Surely your little black book must be as thick as the Manhattan directory."

"When do I get to see you?"

She let out a deep sigh.

"Tonight? Dinner?"

"Did you get your hotel designed?" she asked.

"Six o'clock?"

If only she could say: *That would be delightful. See you then, darling.* Instead, she asked ridiculously how the weather had been. She'd heard they'd been having a heat wave.

"I thought I'd tell you about it over dinner."

"I can't see you again," Kelly said. "I want to. But I'm just not cut out for this kind of thing."

"What are you saying?"

"I'm saying that I'm sorry, Brandon. You're nearly impossible to resist but I have to."

"It's a bitch being married, isn't it? Boy, what

394

willpower. Okay. I'm going to test that willpower of yours one more time. If you *don't* give in, your prize is your fidelity—and if you *do* give in, your prize is me. Sleep on *that*, and think about which award it is you would, in all honesty, enjoy the most."

"You louse," she said as she hung up.

Her hand was still on the phone when it rang again. A tenacious son of a bitch, she thought. But it was Ron.

"Hi," she said guiltily, as though the phone had been tapped and he were calling to have it out with her.

But his voice was too steady. He was in too good a mood. He was calling to tell her he was playing poker tonight, so not to plan dinner for him.

Kelly sat back in her chair for a moment afterward, thinking about the order of fate. Had Ron called first, she wondered if she would have been persuaded to meet Brandon just for drinks.

She was in the kitchen cleaning up the dinner dishes after finally getting the kids to sleep. She had been helping the twins sew backpacks for home ec, and Marlo write her science report. Now at last they were quietly tucked away.

Filling the sink with hot sudsy water, Kelly was thinking about Brandon—wondering what it would be like if she really could lead a double life. Maybe having a perfect balance between husband and children and lover would make her feel so happy, so complete, that she would actually be more valuable to everybody. What a fine justification, she thought.

Too bad her theory had as many holes in it as Swiss cheese. It sounded wonderful. Even practical. Certainly fulfilling. And Kelly envied all the people in the world who were able to handle that way of life. She, unfortunately, was not one of them. As black velvet drew lint, she attracted guilt. And she could just imagine how acute that guilt would be. It would be impossible for her. How did people do it? She remembered the night she had come home from the Bel-Air Hotel after having been with Brandon. She had been scared to death that Ron would want to make love.

It was beginning to seem to Kelly that that magical night had never existed. With every day that passed, the lived-out fantasy grew more diffuse. It was the reverse process of a Polaroid where an image grew from nebulous to sharp. Instead, her image of their evening was growing weaker for her. The picture was disappearing.

Her fling was supposed to have been a one-night adventure, fulfilling all her sexual curiosities with one wildly erotic experience. Without commitment or heartbreak—a fantasy caught in flight and spent. Now she felt greedy for wanting more.

When she had read novels about women who had lovers, if the heroine was basically a nice person, like herself, reasonably sympathetic because one liked her, or because she was passionate (it was difficult for her not to support passion), then she was always brought to tears when everything didn't work out all right. Take Anna Krenina, she thought. She had a lovely husband, like Ron; slightly dull, like Ron, but

396

nevertheless good. And yet one forgave her. There were millions of notorious women with unquenchable passions. History was usually kind to the ones who did it without malice. They were the heroines upon whom we based our fantasies, Kelly thought. Why couldn't she readjust her perspective to envision herself as one of those characters?

She just couldn't. She was overwhelmed by the restrictions of her upbringing, her road map of custom, and she found herself battling to decode her dilemma, questioning that clean respectable choice—marriage with absolutely *no* forays—when what she wanted for just a short while longer . . . was a lover.

Then she began speculating about what it would be like to have Brandon walk through the door instead of Ron. It was a preposterous notion, much too domestic for any scene she and Brandon were likely to play out. Brandon would be disastrously confined by the family frame. He would want to burst right out of it. Her kids and, if they were to have any, their kids would all be stashed neatly away in exclusive far-off boarding schools. Kelly looked across the room again, this time picturing it without her family—without her children. Her line of vision jumped like a magnet, landing on a series of colorful drawings that dressed up the plain white refrigerator, all signed in big scratchy handwriting "To Mommy with love," from Joshua and Jason. Marlo had contributed a collection of pottery mugs that she had made at camp last summer. Could Kelly stand the silence after so many years of noise?

But this was all ridiculous. She couldn't imagine

not falling asleep next to Ron, not waking up in his arms. It seemed to her that he had always been there. She loved having a partner to share everything with. Her happiness or her triumphs would have been halved without Ron. Her losses would have made her feel so alone. So he was irritatingly logical. Precise. Bull-headed. As he had reminded her on numerous occasions, he was also well read, well rounded, and well preserved. They had built a history together. The kids. Besides, Ron had his own laundry list of complaints about Kelly. And most of them were accurate, she conceded, finishing up her work in the kitchen and tossing the damp dish towel into the washing machine. She decided to go upstairs and read a book. Somebody else's fantasies were safer than her own.

Kelly was reading in bed when Ron walked into the room.

"Won forty bucks," he announced, taking off his coat and turning on the TV set.

"Why do those guys let you stay in the game?" Kelly asked, reluctantly putting her book aside. "You're always cleaning them out. They must think you cheat."

"I *really* played well tonight."

"Maybe you ought to up the ante."

"Maybe I should," Ron answered, unfastening his belt and continuing to get undressed. "Clayton Smith was there. He invited us to Touch a week from Saturday night. I thought you'd like that . . . Do you want to go?"

Touch was the newest, most fashionable private dinner club in town and Kelly laughed, smiling at Ron, who knew she would love to go. "What do *you* think?" she teased. "Will you leave me sitting all evening after dinner in the discotheque as a frustrated spectator, or will you dance with me?"

Ron gave Kelly a noncommittal look.

"Who is Clayton taking as his date?" she asked. Clayton was one of their old friends from college who had been divorced for several years and was thoroughly enjoying his renewed bachelorhood. Kelly seldom saw him with the same date twice.

"I don't know," Ron answered, going into the bathroom to brush his teeth.

Kelly got out of bed, untwisting her nightgown, and followed him in. "Did you hear any more about Harold Lipshitz and his actress girl friend?" she asked. Harold Lipshitz was a good friend of Ron's good friend—they were contemporaries, and it bothered Kelly a lot that Harold had dumped his wife and kids and was now being seen regularly with one of the hottest sex symbols in Hollywood. Harold's wife had supported him during his long trek through medical school, internship, residency, and the building of a career as a prominent Beverly Hills gynecologist. Now that he had achieved prominence, apparently he felt free to cut himself off from his wife and kids and play the glamour bit with starlets. This particular starlet had been one of his patients, and Kelly wondered at what point in the examination they'd decided they liked one another.

"Still hot and heavy," Ron said grinning. "George

Simpson must have gotten envious. He's just separated from his wife, what's her name—Susan—and he's dating that great-looking girl in 'Fast Track' —what's her name . . . ?"

Kelly stood up angrily. "Susan gave up a great career for that schmuck. She had four bratty kids with him, and personally I think she's a hell of a lot brighter than he is—and now . . . for what! He's giving her the shaft because he can *afford* to date movie stars! What is this with you guys?"

"You sound a little threatened, Kelly."

"I am," she said honestly.

She turned on the tap and began washing her face with a special French olive oil soap that was supposed to help preserve her, glad that she'd actually had an affair while she was still in her prime. "It's so unfair," she said.

"Kelly! Don't get mad at me! I didn't do anything. I'm not sleeping with Morgan Fairchild."

"Not yet! But you'd like to! You sit around these poker games listening to these society surgeons talk about all the celebrity snatch they're getting, and you're envious! You're impressed!"

"And you're jealous."

"No. I'm mad. Women my age feel gypped! We feel like schmucks! First we're too young—then we're too old. No wonder women are doing things differently now. No wonder women finally revolted and overthrew the double standard." She opened her drawer and began hunting for her nighttime moisturizer.

"Listen, Kelly. It's not exactly a piece of cake for

400

the husband. Susan's going to hit George for one hell of a settlement."

"And the way I hear it is that the wives are coming out shafted all the way around. All the women are ending up broke, because their wonderful rich husbands have managed to get everything so tied up. The men are driving around in their fancy foreign sports cars, living in Beverly Hills, and their ex-wives can't even support themselves. Did you know that divorced women with children constitute the new poor in the United States?"

"Is that so?" Ron said, grinning.

"Yes. Goddammit—where's my cream?" She slammed her drawer shut, realizing that Marlo had probably taken it. Lately she was getting into all of Kelly's things.

Ron got into bed and began flipping through television stations.

Kelly climbed in beside him, picking up her book again. He leaned over to kiss her. "You're cute when you're jealous."

"I'm glad you're not a doctor," she said. "I don't like this new trend of theirs—dating their patients."

"Lawyers just date their clients," Ron teased, kissing her again before she could respond.

She had never considered that before. Clients had always been sexless in her mind. They were clients, without gender. "Do you have any beautiful ones that I ought to be jealous of?'" she asked.

"Not necessarily jealous of—maybe leery of."

"Like who?" She could just hear Ron's poker group

sitting around gossiping like fraternity brothers. What kind of thrill was Ron contributing?

"Let's just say my female client list has grown substantially."

"On what sort of matters? Any on-the-make starlets I ought to be apprised of?"

"A few," he replied, grinning again.

"For corporate and real estate work?"

"Sure—they make a lot of money. Buy houses. Make investments."

"Who?"

"What's the difference?"

Kelly felt like smashing Ron with her book. He was enjoying this too much. He was being obnoxious. "I'm curious!"

"It's attorney-client privilege. I can't tell you."

"Well, what about attorney-wife privilege?"

"You get to spend the money my clients pay out."

"Are some of these women executives?" she asked, rethinking Ron's work environment. "Are they young? Attractive?"

"Some of them."

"I can't believe I live with you and you're not allowed to discuss anything with me."

"Doesn't it make me more intriguing?"

"No. More aggravating."

"Oh, Kelly. Come on."

"I hate feeling jealous," she said, thinking about all the bright, young, beautiful executives and starlets he represented. Imagining what their meetings were like—what kind of temptation Ron felt when he was with them. Was his willpower better or worse than hers? Feeling terribly guilty and terribly hypocritical, Kelly realized she would *never* be capable of extending to a man the freedom she desired for herself.

"As long as you have all these wealthy female clients and my attorney-wife privilege is supposed to be the bucks you make off them, how about spending it on a trip to China? It would be so great to go away together. Just the two of us. It's been ages." She was thinking about Brandon. About getting as far away from him as possible. About falling in love with her husband all over again to eradicate the need for a lover.

"China? No chance," Ron said.

"It wouldn't even be that expensive. I heard about this great tour deal—"

"Chinatown for dim sum is as close to China as we're going to get for a while. Maybe San Francisco."

"For the last four years you've been saying that you want to take a vacation. I've got some money saved up. I'll pay for it."

"Kelly, I've told you that I don't want to go to China until they get some decent hotels. They've got bugs and rats in the rooms. Filthy sheets. It's dusty and dry and I hear the Chinese clear their throats by spitting on the streets. And I don't like what I've heard about their airlines."

"Those stories come from your pampered friends and clients who exaggerate. They want the Ritz wherever they go. They couldn't care less about learning when they travel, or about culture. They only care about luxury."

"What about safety? Or is that too practical a consideration for your romantic soul?"

"I don't want to wait until China has become so commercial that I feel like I'm in the United States."

"Well, *I'd* like to stay in an American hotel, with some American breakfasts available to me every now and then, and some clean American sheets."

"Then why even bother to leave America?"

"Good point. Let's go to Vegas. I can wait another two or three years for China."

Kelly realized she was glowering at Ron with the same frustration she always felt whenever they discussed travel. She wanted to tell him that if she could only get some romance and adventure into him, she wouldn't have this need to go out and find it somewhere else.

She watched him cross his long hairy legs. They were the legs of an athlete with lean muscles—like a runner. His feet were pale and scrubbed-looking, almost delicate. There was something so familiar about them. *Oh, Ron.* She was wrong to be so critical of him. To expect so much. All she had to do was cuddle up beside him and he'd put his arm around her warmly, glad to have her as his. He loved her. He was a good husband. She loved him. Who in the world ever found their fantasies all rolled up in one perfect person? Nobody, of course. Even Brandon wouldn't be the perfect person for her. So she had to stop wanting and needing more.

She put her arms around Ron and kissed him tenderly. "You're one of the good guys."

"Is that how you're going to negotiate with me about China?"

"Maybe. Any objections?"

"You can try."

"Okay. I will try." Kelly put her cheek next to his rougher one. She ran her hand slowly along his chest, playing with a little patch of curls in the center.

"But first let's watch the news," he said, moving her hand away, pointing up to the TV that was always on when he was in the room.

"Don't worry. Nothing earth-shattering has happened since the last report you heard." She returned her hand to his chest, then massaged downward, drawing a line with her finger under the elastic waist of his boxers.

"It's only thirty minutes. Afterward we'll make love."

"I have an idea. Tape the news and let's make love now. You can watch it before you go to sleep."

"Kelly, cut it out," Ron said, moving her hands away again and switching to another news channel. He adjusted his position, moving as far away from her as he could get without falling off the bed. Then he watched the Lite Beer commercial with an intensity that made her furious. "This is a great commercial, Kelly. Look at this guy."

"Ron, I *need* some romance in my life."

"Just let me watch the news. In thirty minutes I'm all yours."

She glared at Ron. His eyes were fixed on the television set and she wished she could throw a rock into it, smashing the intrusion of its droning picture forever. She didn't *want* to need a lover. She wanted

Ron. It was always *another* fifteen to thirty minutes' worth of news or sports that he *had* to see before making love. TV was their foreplay. He didn't understand that it broke the mood.

If only she could have it all. A husband and a lover in one nice, neat little legitimate package. Then she flattened her pillow out on the bed and curled up into a sleeping position. She could hear Ron telling her that it wouldn't hurt for her to know what was going on in the world, to watch the news. Kelly just ignored him. She knew he was oblivious to the tears that were welling up in her eyes and the frustration that was swelling up in her heart. He took her hand in what she supposed was a gesture of peace, still watching the television set where again a commercial was playing, advertising kitchen floor polish. It was so difficult for her to settle for only part of what she wanted. It was so hard not to mourn the part she couldn't have. She wondered how many other people around the world were shedding tears over the same division, the same compromise. Ron squeezed her hand, and she squeezed his back even more tightly.

"I love you," he said, moving closer toward her. "Look at *this*."

She followed his arm, outstretched toward the television. He was pointing with interest to a shootout that was happening on someone's front lawn.

Then he put his arm around her and pointed to the set again.

"It's almost over," he said.

She looked over to where Ted Koppel was broad-casting some cheerier events.

"Then we'll do it."

But now all Kelly was in the mood for was sleep.

Brandon Michaels was sitting talking to Bob Kaufman, watching the red light outside the darkroom where Kelly was working, unaware of his presence. Instead of calling her again, and chancing another no, he had decided to come directly to the studio, first setting up an appointment with her boss to legitimize his visit. What he was talking to Bob about was hiring him to do some photographs of the house he had just finished building for himself, before the furniture was installed. He wanted some pure focused shots documenting the architectural rhythms, capturing the fine details, without the distraction of chairs and sofas.

As he nodded at something Bob was saying, he peered over to the closed door again, wondering what Kelly's reaction would be when she saw him. It could be that she'd be angry. After all, she had said no. He had a slight wavering of conscience, thinking maybe he wasn't being fair to her. She *was* trying to fight this. He had been teasing her about her Herculean willpower, and he realized how clearly bent he was on destroying it. There was something about her he just couldn't resist. She was different from the women he was accustomed to dating. Fresher. More alive. More real. She would have been the kind of girl he'd have wanted to marry back in his naïve youth when marriage was actually a consid-

407

eration for him. Then, soothing his conscience, he reminded himself if Kelly were really so happy at home, none of this would have happened in the first place. She *needed* to have an affair. And Brandon was perfect for her. With him she was safe. They could have a full-fledged love affair, wild in all its extremes, a release from everyday life, and yet Kelly wouldn't have to worry about repercussions. She wouldn't have to worry about having a man falling in love with her and trying to screw up her marriage, which she apparently wanted badly to preserve. No nutty phone calls or crazy declarations of the sort she might get with someone else who wouldn't take it for what it was. An interlude of perfect passion. Sensational sex. Free to have a conclusion, as all love affairs were meant to have. Kelly didn't even realize what an opportunity it was Brandon was offering her. Total secrecy. No chances. No commitments. No heartbreaks.

The red light suddenly went dull and Brandon turned all of his attention to Bob. The wheels were greased and in motion.

Kelly was still drying her hands with a paper towel when she walked out of the darkroom. She gasped out loud when she saw Brandon sitting in the chair opposite Bob, the two of them deep in conversation.

What on earth was he doing here? Was he crazy? What nerve he had, dropping in on her at work. And what did Bob think? Oh, God, what a mess. She was just about to say something when Bob stood up and introduced her to Brandon, as though they'd never met. Kelly listened, dumbfounded, as Bob described the job Brandon was talking to him about.

In the midst of Bob's explanation, Brandon shook Kelly's hand, holding it a little longer than necessary and looking meaningfully at her with those devastating denim-blue eyes of his that matched his jeans. She looked at him as though to say, *what is going on?* Brandon just smiled and pulled up a chair for her, continuing his conversation with Bob, and including her in it.

She didn't say a word, she just watched him, amazed. Was he really going to hire Bob to do his photographic work? Was this all because of her? *Be strong, Kelly!* she cautioned herself, worried and wondering if *strong* was really what she wanted to be. How long could she be expected to resist? There was such a definite gap in her life and Brandon could so obviously fill it. She couldn't go through this again. She had to put a stop to it. For Brandon it was probably an amusing game. She'd said no so often, she figured she'd become a challenge. He was probably very spoiled and very used to yes.

"I've got some more work to do in the darkroom," she said, rising. Then she turned resolutely to Brandon. "It was nice to meet you," she said. His sensuous mouth curved into a smile that was a tease.

"Actually, I've got to run anyway." Brandon also stood up and Kelly wondered what he was going to do next. "Maybe you or Kelly would like to come up to the house with me to get an idea what you'd shoot and how long it would take."

"Sounds good," Bob said, looking pleased. "Kelly, why don't you go."

"You wanted those pictures finished . . ." Kelly began, protesting.

"You'll just be an hour or so—you can get to them later."

Kelly stood frozen for a moment, feeling defeated. How could she go with Brandon to his house, alone, and not give in to him? She had to get out of this. "Bob, why don't you drive over with me, and then we'll get lunch afterward."

Brandon didn't say anything. He looked at Kelly, surprised. Amused at her resistance, at the struggle she was putting up.

"You buying?" Bob asked jokingly.

"It's on me," Kelly replied, dead serious.

"No—you go ahead. I've got a meeting here in about an hour."

It was drizzling outside and Kelly hurried toward her car. Brandon was driving the black Lamborghini Contach parked just a couple of cars away from hers. He had told her to follow him. His car was almost as sexy as he was, she thought, fastening her seat belt and starting up her ignition. His was a cocky car, but she supposed he was looking at her own Volvo station wagon and laughing to himself— she was driving the stereotypical suburban housewife's vehicle. She peeled out behind him, going just as fast as he was along the slick streets, never letting another car cut her off, and never stopping because a light had been yellow too long and was turning red. She could see him looking at her in the rearview mirror and she held up her fist, shouting out her window to him, "You bastard!" A large drop of rain fell onto her nose and she stuck her head back in the car, rolling up her window again. All he did was laugh and speed up. She chased him up Coldwater Canyon, determined more than ever to say no to any passes. If Bob lost the job, that was too bad.

"You're nuts!" she shouted when they finally got to his house. They were standing in the rain and he put his arm around her, rushing her inside. "Shouldn't I see the outside? Bob is sure to ask about it."

"Afterward."

After what, she thought, impressed with his house, in spite of what was happening. The front door alone warranted a photograph. It appeared to be about eight feet wide by ten feet tall, and instead of swinging open, it pivoted at an angle. But it wasn't just its size that made the door so outstanding—it was a work of art, a two-sided relief sculpture formed out of concrete, glass, and steel by Laddie Dill, a Los Angeles-based artist, whose work Kelly knew and admired. Cement washes had been applied to the rough surface, contrasting with smooth glass insets where light red iron oxide pigment shone through. Brandon had told them about the door at the studio.

"What a coincidence, huh?" he said once they were inside, enfolding her in his arms.

"Are you really planning on hiring Bob, or was this all a pretense?" She wished it didn't feel so good to be in his arms, so warm and snug. If only she were free to relax, to let her head fall against his

411

chest. Her heart was racing and she wondered if he could feel it.

"It was a pretense, *and* I'm really planning on hiring Bob. You do good work, right?"

Kelly didn't respond—she tried to struggle free, but he was too strong for her. This was too much of a test for anyone to endure. It wasn't fair. To get chased by your fantasy and to be expected to fight him off—it was absurd.

"From what I saw at the studio," he continued, "I was impressed."

"And what if I *don't* sleep with you?" she asked, keenly aware of the confidence he exuded in every movement. He wore his masculinity with a grace and assurance befitting the legendary big-game hunters of Africa.

"You mean you *might*? That's better than I'd hoped for. Of course I'm using Bob either way."

"Brandon, you're driving me crazy."

"Good. You want a tour?"

"That's why I'm here."

Brandon threw his head back and laughed. There were long deep dimples on either side of his mouth. It was a rugged face, alarmingly compelling, and she turned away from him just as he was about to kiss her. Then she turned back, changing her mind and initiating the kiss.

"If I give in," she began, in between slow kisses, "promise me you'll never call again. This would be it. Finished. No more."

"What about the photography?" he asked, with his

tongue giving pleasure to her neck, untying each little tight nerve and dissolving it.

"We'll do them; I don't have any choice now but—" She stopped, lifting her mouth up toward his lips, shivering and murmuring, distracted from what she was saying.

They went up the concrete formed staircase, then over a bridge that had glass sides and appeared to be floating. Brandon told her how the house worked on a concept of bridges. There were bridges all over. This particular one was suspended beneath a skylight and she looked up at the sudden pelting noise caused by the rain above them. Then she looked down and saw the entrance below, where, except for the doors and structural concrete colunms, the perimeter of the house was all glass, visually bringing in the lush green landscape from outside.

"I'm going to be sorry to see it with furniture," Brandon said when they walked into what she assumed was the master bedroom. His hands were on her waist, sliding down her hips.

"You really enjoy designing and building," she whispered, running her hands over his broad chest, feeling his hair and skin through the pure cotton fabric of his shirt. There was a masculine smell about him that was so enticing.

"I love it," he murmured, leaning over and kissing her passionately, furiously, the fullness of his mouth drinking her in.

She began unbuttoning his shirt, anxious to have her hands on his skin. They were both in jeans and button-down shirts. Both in boots. They looked like

413

an ad for Western wear, she thought as she explored the breadth of his shoulders and looked into his eyes ringed with lashes that seemed wasted on a man. She pulled the soft fabric of his shirt out of his jeans so she could have free rein of his sinewy frame. His chest was wild with dark thick hair and his skin was a deep bronze beneath it.

Then he unfastened her shirt, releasing one little button after the other. She could see her chest rising and falling, the swell of her breasts expanding as she held her breath. As his fingers touched her skin it was an extraordinary sensation, velvety soft and mellow on the surface, charged with electricity within. When he pulled her shirt out of her pants, the way she had done with his, she felt a coursing excitement between her thighs. Her jeans were tight against her crotch and the pressure they created there was unbearably stimulating. They were both now shirtless but Kelly thought they still looked like an ad, a sexier ad. Brandon ran his finger down from the hollow in her neck, slowly toward her cleavage, releasing her bra. As she wriggled out of it and let it fall to the ground, they admired each other in a look. Next Kelly knelt down in front of him, her nose touching his belt buckle. She put her hands on the tips of his boots, then brought them up past his knees, onto his thighs, and finally over the bulge in his pants. With deft movements she removed his belt, sliding it in a long lean motion out of the loops and tossing it aside. She leaned in to apply hot breath to the denim protuberance that was bunched slightly to his left. Then she unfastened his jeans and he

414

helped her pull them down, laughing and tumbling onto the floor together. He had on small, European-cut elasticized briefs, showing off the coarse wiry hair on his belly that she found so sexy. Doing crazy contortions, they finally yanked off his boots as well as his jeans.

Kelly leaned back, supporting herself on her elbows, with first one long leg up in the air and then the other as Brandon struggled to pull off *her* boots. She held on to her lacy lilac panties as he worked her jeans down over her hips and off. She studied his arms as he brought his strong frame down beside her, their thighs touching. Then she raised herself up to kiss him, looking solemnly into his eyes. They were the eyes of a pirate. So blue—so full of laughter and adventure. They both pondered the kiss as though tasting it for definition.

"You know what you reminded me of when I first saw you . . ." He was touching one of her nipples and watching it rise, then touching the other with his tongue. "A grown-up Alice in Wonderland, all fine-boned and graceful, all tangled Titian hair, verdant eyes, and skin that looked like it had been dipped in honey."

"Alice in Wonderland had blue eyes and blond hair."

"Not mine," he said, following the contours of her breasts with his hands.

Suddenly there was a crash of thunder and Kelly reached instinctively for Brandon. She laughed when she realized what she'd done, feeling silly. The drizzle had turned into an out-and-out storm. Pretty soon an arrow of light tore through the sky and Kelly watched it through the window.

Brandon's mouth was on her stomach, sucking hungrily. With his teeth he removed her panties and she squirmed with this dizzying, demanding need as his mouth grazed her furry mound. Kelly matched his movement, also pulling his briefs down with her teeth. The task seemed to be easier for him than for her and she smiled as she worked, trying to maneuver the elasticized band over his throbbing erection.

He was moaning with pleasure as the silky fabric slid to the floor, and when she was all through, he drew her up to him, kissing her anxiously, with his hands exploring every part of her.

When she could no longer tolerate just foreplay, he seemed to know. Crushing her beneath him, he entered her, sighing loudly, relishing his sexual power. His mouth never stopped sucking as he thrust himself farther and farther into her. She was moving her hips and lifting her rear to meet him in new ways. Tightening her muscles to enhance his pleasure, she thrilled at the feeling of his fullness inside her. She listened to the eurythmic charging of the rain, forming a protective sheet around the house, isolating them from the world outside.

Brandon's movements were growing faster as she held on to his back, nearly crying out. She slid her hand downward to encompass all of him. The volume of his sounds increased as they held fast to each other, moving in reckless quest. There was another loud roll of thunder. Another erratic bolt of lightning. She felt her orgasm approaching, making her weak,

416

urgent, on fire. Then, with a wild explosion of the heavens' artillery crashing through the atmosphere, they climaxed, Kelly first and Brandon just after—a climax that blended and fulminated together in one long, intense eruption.

Reluctantly, Kelly and Brandon parted.

"*Never?*" he asked, walking her out to the car, his expression grave. "Never again?"

"You owe that to me. That was part of the deal," she replied, as he opened the door for her. When he closed it, she rolled down the window and he leaned in. There was still a slight drizzle, but the storm appeared to have moved away, leaving behind remnants of dark gray clouds that streaked the sky in silver-edged swirls.

Now she was following his black Lamborghini down the canyon. She could see his face again in his rearview mirror and she wondered what he was thinking. This was probably so simple for him. For her it was harrowing. In no time at all he would be saying "Kelly who?" and yet he would remain with her forever. The affair she once dared to have.

Just then she caught Brandon staring at her. He winked, then turned around to blow her a kiss. They had left it that if she ever changed her mind, she was to call him—no hesitation. Now she felt like crying as she smiled bravely back at him. Was she falling in love? Kelly Michaels. Mrs. Brandon Michaels. Kelly and Brandon. She tried on all the titles, seeing how they fitted. They sounded strange. Kelly and Ron. That sounded right. Easy. But maybe just because it had a familiar ring. "Kelly and Ron" had been a phrase for so many years that she'd gotten accustomed to it. They were a couple. She could see the two of them smiling at her from photographs that had been taken. Kelly and Ron clowning at camp. Kelly and Ron getting married. Kelly and Ron with Ron's hands on her pregnant belly. Kelly and Ron and the kids. Specific snapshots flipped through her mind, making her feel enormously guilty and enormously confused. She looked at Brandon again, who was again looking at her. Didn't he ever look straight ahead? He could run red lights driving this way. She pointed toward him, gesturing for him to keep his eyes on the road. He pretended to swerve, and she got so thrown off, she swerved too.

Was she falling in love with him? Did her heart race with anticipation at the prospect of seeing him? Yes. Did she think about him constantly? Yes. Did she make sure that she looked great for him? Yes. Did she feel the urge to talk about him all the time? Yes. Yes. Yes. How foolish could she be? What it really came down to was did she want to disrupt everything—risk everything—her family, and all that meant—for great sex and romance?

Brandon was strictly a fantasy. There he was in his fantasy car. With his fantasy house. And his fantasy life-style. She could imagine him unpacking his Bekins boxes, coming to one marked—"OLD GIRL FRIENDS." A million love affairs captured in their prime by Kodak. Would she have ended up another memento in that box, if he'd had a picture of her? She even envisioned captions for all those faces that might have

418

existed within the box. "Alexandra Stanford. Wildly successful real estate broker." "Shana Carson—Vassar graduate, a knockout centerfold in *Playboy*." "Kate—with no last name—biggest female rock star in Europe at one time." Then she imagined an eight-by-ten glossy of an attractive girl dressed in a black evening gown with glistening heartshaped lips parted flirtatiously and large black eyes that sparkled. She named this imaginary creature "Nancy Chasen—seventeen. Beautiful. And brazen." Brandon would have dated them all, and she wondered if he'd had a photograph of her how he would have captioned it.

Brandon tooted his horn and waved at her as he turned right when they got to Beverly Drive and she turned left. She let out a deep sigh. It was a potent mixture of relief and regret. The sun was starting to break through and she opened her glove compartment to look for her sunglasses. As she reached into the crowded opening, she noticed the jumper cables Ron had recently bought for her and she felt another surge of guilt. How could she *not* love Ron? As infuriating as he could be, he was always looking out for her. These jumper cables, which operated by plugging them into a car cigarette lighter, Ron had sent away for out of a mail order catalog. It was typical Ron. He was so worried that she would be stuck somewhere with a dead battery and not know what to do. In her trunk was another gadget that would fix a flat tire in no time. Also in her trunk was a first aid and survival kit he had bought for her that contained Mylar blankets that folded up into packets the size of a Wash'n Dri. Space-age light sticks that flooded with fluorescent light when bent in half. Food sticks. Ron knew Kelly was forever driving around a carload of kids, and he wanted her to be prepared in case of an emergency, specifically the God-forbid-dreaded-Killer-California-Earthquake. He was such a concerned husband and father.

Suddenly Kelly realized she was late. She had definitely been gone longer than an hour and she wondered how she was going to explain her delay to Bob. He would be expecting her to finish up the work she had begun in the morning. And her kids would be waiting out in front of school for her at three o'clock sharp. Anxious, she pressed through the traffic, cutting impatiently around slow-moving cars, trying to think of what she would say to Bob. She hoped he'd be too busy to notice the flushed color in her cheeks.

─────────────────Chapter Twenty-Two

BUDDY NAZIO OPENED THE DOOR TO HIS MARINA DEL REY apartment and went directly to the refrigerator to get a beer. Shitty day. Definitely a shitty day. He dropped the papers he'd copped from Delaney's office on the coffee table and began studying them again. So Kirstin Pollock wasn't so lily-white after all, according to the Swedish inquest. Boy, did he know his women. Every time. He had the nose for dirt. An uncanny instinct. So why wasn't he making more money? There was a picture of him with President Ford that took him back to his Secret Service days. The Buddy then was different from the Buddy now. The Buddy then was only a moderate gambler. The Buddy would never have considered blackmail.

He looked at his watch. Three minutes to go before the racing results would be given. He turned the radio on softly and held his breath, getting out of his leather jacket and pitching it over onto the couch. *Come on, Brassy Knave. Don't let me down. It's really critical this time; I'm riding everything I've got on you.*

Buddy had been flying high on a hot streak until just a few days ago, when his luck had suddenly burned out, plunging him into debt. This was something that happened to "stupid gamblers," not to careful, clever gamblers like himself.

The three minutes were up. *Come on, Brassy Knave.* He broke out into a cold sweat as he waited for the sportscaster to announce the outcome of the seventh race. For tomorrow's race he had another tip from an even better source. If Brassy Knave didn't take first place, he wouldn't be able to play it. Then, as the results of the seventh came on the air, he stiffened, turning up the volume and listening intently. Brassy Knave had run a useless second and Buddy's heart was pounding roughly with the loss. Cursing, he picked up the telephone and dialed, preparing a couple of fat lines of cocaine at the same time. He snorted them quickly for fuel.

"Hey, Joey," he said, rubbing the remaining cocaine off the mirror with his finger and applying it to his gums. He felt the numbing sensation almost immediately and ran his tongue along it. "Buddy Nazio here."

"You owe big, baby." Joey had the most sadistic voice.

"No problem. Relax. Give me one more on Lofty

Eagle to win, tomorrow third race. I've got a hot tip." He was trying to sound cool, but his nerves were doing coked-up gymnastics.

"Forget it, Buddy. Like I said, you owe us some big bucks. Pay up, and then we'll make another 'hot tip' bet for you." The cackle that was his laugh sent a cold chill down Buddy's spine. That slimy son of a bitch.

"Look. This tip is for sure. I'm good for it. You don't think so, I'll take my business elsewhere. I'd say you've made some good money off me in the last couple of years. Some real good money. You're always taking free rides on my slick streaks, so now you can afford to ride tight for a little while on this dry one. I'll give ya an extra cut."

"Sounds pretty desperate."

"No, just feeling generous."

"Yeah? With whose money? Corky don't like it when I take bets from desperate, generous boys."

"Fuck off, Joey!" Buddy slammed down the phone. Well, screw him. Buddy would pay him back and never give him another dime's worth of his business. Joey was a prick anyway. Maybe someday he would push someone too far with his sadistic humor and finally get his.

He began looking through his book for Frankie's number. Frankie would take a bet from him.

"Hiya, Frankie. Buddy Nazio here."

"Hear it's pretty heavy for ya," Frankie said.

Buddy took off his college ring and began spinning it nervously along the tabletop. "You guys sure like to gossip. Gossip and exaggerate."

"Hear you're down ten big ones. That don't need much embellishing to make a good story."

"I got a real good tip on tomorrow's race, Frankie. Lofty Eagle in the third to win."

"I don't know, Buddy. How much?"

"One grand. Tim O'Brian's running her."

"A thousand bucks? I can't do it, Buddy. I wish I could, but you're really under now. I'd lend it to you, but I've been running a dry streak myself."

"Frankie. You have to help me this time."

"I wish I could." Frankie's voice sounded tentative. Buddy thought he was making some headway.

"Look, Frankie, I've got some money coming in from another source," he said, looking over at the papers he had on Kirstin Pollock and feeling a tenseness in his gut. "I'll have it in a few days. Cover me just this once until then."

"How about five hundred?"

"I need a grand." Buddy listened to Frankie's hesitation.

"Off the record, I'll do it for you. But keep it between us."

"Frankie, you're a sport."

"I'm a *schlemiel* is what I am. Hope she comes in first for both our sakes." With that, Frankie hung up. Buddy looked at the phone, feeling slightly better. Kirstin Pollock better cross her pretty little fingers, he thought. Lofty Eagle wins, she's off the hook. Lofty Eagle comes in second, or third, or worse, he'd have to come up with his money another way. A way she wouldn't be too happy about. Nor would he. These petty blackmail bits were dangerous and shitty to pull off. He definitely didn't like supplementing his income this way.

Suddenly there were babies everywhere—cute cuddly babies, wrapped in soft fluffy blankets—and Ericka felt as though she were missing out on something. She held open the health club doors for a young woman who was wheeling in her baby girl in a stroller. The young woman thanked Ericka, then began chatting to her infant, holding up a rattle, trying to get the baby to play with it. The health club now offered a nursery as one of its features so that figure-conscious mothers would have some place to park their kids while they worked out. "How old is she?" Ericka asked the attractive mother, whose shape appeared to have shrunk right back to petite.

"Six months." The mother smiled, kneeling down in front of the baby and cooing to her. "Do you have any kids?"

"No," Ericka said, staring down at the baby, wondering if she ever would. This preoccupation with wanting a child had only begun after seeing Jamie again. With David, she had never wanted children. Even discussing them used to make her nervous and defensive. She had her career—no time for parenting. No inclination. No maternal drive or instinct. After being with Jamie, remembering how she felt with him, she realized how untrue all that was. Now her once dormant wants and desires were crystallizing, dominating her thoughts and distracting her from everything else. She wanted a real marriage. A real commitment. She wanted to be in love. And if she couldn't have all that with Jamie, then dammit she'd start all over again and find it with someone else. She hadn't been able to stay with David. Something inside her had been uncovered, feelings raked up, real needs, real wants, and she couldn't reconcile burying all those critical instincts again. Win or lose, she realized she had to go out on the line and try. After just two days with David, that had been clear to her.

"Ahhh," the mother said in response to Ericka's childless state. "This is my first. What a treat."

"I'll bet." Ericka regarded the curly-haired child for a moment longer, then continued on into the locker room. Kirstin and Kelly were leaning against the lockers talking, both dressed in leotards, and they waved at Ericka when they saw her approaching.

"Hi," Kelly said, looking at Ericka and thinking how thin and tired she looked. "How's it going? Did you find a place?" Kelly couldn't help feeling at least partially responsible for Ericka's predicament. In some way, even though Ericka had denied it when she'd confronted her with it, Kelly felt she had triggered Ericka's going after Jamie Sterling in the first place.

"Yes," Ericka said, putting her change of clothes into her locker. She sat down on the bench to retie one of her running shoes. "I just sublet an apartment from a friend at the studio who's getting married. It feels so strange to me—she's going into a marriage, just as I'm coming out of one."

"You're really going to do it?" Kirstin asked, looking skeptically at Ericka.

"I have to." Ericka began retying her other shoe.

426

"How's David handling this?" Kelly asked. "Have you talked to him again?"

Ericka looked as though she was going to cry. She waited until she'd finished with her shoelace before she answered, getting the bow too uneven and having to begin again. "I feel terrible. David just doesn't understand. He's so angry. He thinks I'm being foolish. He thinks I'm screwing up a perfectly good relationship to chase rainbows. . . ."

"Are you?" Kirstin wanted to know

Ericka sighed. "Oh, who the hell knows. Maybe. Maybe not. Maybe I just need a change."

"That's awfully nebulous for someone who's breaking up her marriage," Kirstin observed.

"It's more than that. I'm confused." Ericka's voice broke and her eyes welled up with tears. She blinked several times, trying to fight her emotion.

Feeling a wave of sympathy, Kelly went over to take Ericka's hand, her own eyes moist. *God,* what Ericka must be going through, she thought. To be so unsure about such a terrifying decision. Ericka was taking a great risk, and Kelly admired her for not looking at it that way. She was acknowledging what was wrong with her marriage, with her life, and actually going out and doing something about it.

"I think Jamie was right in some respects," Ericka was saying tearfully. "I really do need to be on my own. I have to figure out what *I* want. Not what my parents wanted for me. Not what David thinks I should want. At first I panicked. Alone—that was such a jarring concept for me."

"And you seem so independent," Kelly said. "You're

successful. You and David had such an independent relationship."

"It wasn't *really* independent. That's why we're both having such a hard time."

"Does David think you'll go back to him?" Kirstin asked, straddling the bench, her amethyst-colored eyes narrowed in thought.

"He said that I have to be careful. He thinks I may be causing such damage to our relationship and to him emotionally that by the time *I've* worked things out, his defenses could be so built up *he'd* be unable to get back together."

"What a thing for a shrink to say!" Kirstin said, surprised. "He should tell you to do what you have to do. To get your head together. Lines like that."

Ericka laughed, clearing the smudged mascara from under her eyes with her finger. "I *know*. Those are exactly the lines he'd give his patients. But he *meant* what he said."

"He was threatening you." Kirstin looked angry.

Ericka nodded. "It's really hard. David only bullies when he's miserable. I've thrown everything off for him and I feel terrible about it. As far as he was concerned, our life was perfect."

"Sure, you let him do whatever he wanted to do." Kirstin shook her head. "I don't know what I would do if I were you. My first instinct is always to preserve a marriage because most people just expect too much. But in your case, you may be right. You're young. You don't have any children yet. I don't know, Ericka."

"I think I'm doing the right thing," Ericka said,

standing up. "But if I'm going to be single," she joked, "I'd better work on these thighs."

Kelly followed behind Kirstin and Ericka, walking through the locker room and then into the gym. Class had already begun, so they decided to skip it and just work out instead on the health club's equipment. They each retrieved their exercise cards, and as they began, Kelly wondered if she should tell them about Brandon.

At first when she'd seen Kirstin she'd been tempted, but something had held her back. She decided now that it was embarrassment. It was different the second time. The second sin. She remembered the fortune cookie she'd gotten with Ron. *When you commit a sin the second time, you no longer consider it a sin.* It *had* been easier the second time. And what would they think? That there might easily be a third and a fourth and a fifth? A string of sequels to follow easily after the first difficult one?

Feeling uneasy, Kelly began her warm-ups. It was true that this last time hadn't cured her. How silly to even think that it could. She'd probably go on wanting Brandon and fantasizing about him for years. She'd begin to forget what he looked like exactly; instead, she'd remember the *feel* of him. The craving he evoked within her.

She looked over at Ericka using the leg pulley and at Kirstin hanging upside down on the gravity apparatus. She couldn't tell them about Brandon; their last time together had been too personal. Eventually she knew they'd ask: Was he back from Sardinia yet? She would respond that he had called, which he had, and that she'd said regretfully that she really couldn't see him again, which was also true. There was no reason for her to expand beyond that.

Going over to get some weights, Kelly began her bust exercises. She flashed on Brandon lying naked beside her on the floor in his bedroom. She remembered so clearly the way their bodies had fitted together. He was taller than Ron, broader. His bulkier frame had felt exciting. More masculine. Brandon had been noisier. More expressive. He seemed to derive more pleasure than Ron ever had. He was one of those men who *loved* making love with women. Loved the feel of a woman's skin. Her scent. Ron never seemed to react, other than to get a hard-on and to perform. But never sensuously—as Brandon had, making her feel like the most luscious woman in the world. Oh hell, that was just the way it was with marriage. The contract obviously bred sexual complacency, and what it all came down to was simply getting off. The truth was, Kelly didn't savor Ron's contours either. Not the way she had with Brandon. If only she could get herself to make more of an effort. If only she could make Ron understand. In any event, it was definitely over with Brandon. He had really proven himself a gentleman when he called Bob to say his assistant would be handling everything on the photographs. When Bob told her about the call she felt relieved and grateful. To have had to work with Brandon would have been murder for her, and obviously he knew that.

"Trying to compete with Dolly Parton?" Kirstin teased. "How many of those are you going to do?"

Kelly looked over at Kirstin and realized she'd probably done fifty bust repetitions instead of the twenty-five indicated on her card.

"Are your pects ever going to hurt tomorrow!" Kirstin exclaimed, beginning a series of advanced sit-ups.

Buddy was parked next to Kirstin's car in the health club's subterranean parking lot, waiting for her to emerge. He took a swig of beer, then looked at his watch again. Goddamned bitch had been an hour and a half, he thought, lighting up another cigarette. How long did it take to shake off fat where there was no fat to begin with? Crumpled up on the seat beside him was yesterday's *Racing Form*. A reminder of why he looked and felt like hell. Angrily he picked up the paper and hurled it out the window. So much for hot tips. Lofty Eagle hadn't even placed. Frankie was probably trying to call him about his grand. They could be waiting outside his apartment; that wouldn't surprise him. Well, before he went home he was going to have to get his hands on some bucks. The thought of what he had to do, as he saw his pretty Swedish lifesaver walking out of the club and toward his car, made him nauseous. His husky legs felt weak and he swore to himself he'd never get into this kind of jam again.

Kirstin was just about to open her car door when a man's hand stopped her. The hand, she noticed, was large and white. Smelled of cigarettes. She was half expecting to feel a gun directed into the middle of her back. She waited, frozen, for her assailant to make the next move.

"Mrs. Pollock?"

Oh, God, he knew her name.

"Yes," she said as levelly as she could, not yet brave enough to turn around. Mad ravaged eyes piercing her might make her scream. The sight of a weapon would make her faint.

"We have to talk," said the voice. It was a low voice. Not insane. But nervous.

"About what?" she asked, turning cautiously. Trying to mask her tear. She noticed he was holding some papers.

"About these. About Sweden. About Kristina Lund."

She knew exactly what he was talking about and a bolt of fear ripped through her. In a way, she had been waiting for this moment for years, ever since she had left Sweden. Especially since she had married Leonard. She looked into the stranger's anxious blue eyes, noticing his unshaven face. This had to be the private investigator Leonard had hired. She had seen him faceless in her dreams and she wished desperately that she could turn back the clock—but to when? This was obviously going to be a blackmail threat, and she wondered how she should deal with this young man who appeared to be just as nervous as she was. Exactly what about her past did he know?

"What is there to discuss?" she asked, trying to sound calm

"Some criminal activities you might want to avoid having exposed."

"Activities?"

"Carrier of illegal money for Sweden's infamous Porno King."

Kirstin stiffened. "If this is—"

"How you got yourself to the United States by neglecting to make the drop on one of those carries and stole away with all the cash—"

"You're wasting your time," Kirstin insisted.

"And what about your marriage in Las Vegas, to a guy with a three page criminal record—"

"You're wasting your time," Kirstin repeated. "My husband knows all of this. He hired you for a completely different reason when he wanted me followed, which is none of your damn business."

"I think you're lying. I think he doesn't know."

"Think what you want," she said, regarding him tensely and trying her best not to look threatened.

"Then let's just call him and ask him," he suggested.

One pair of icy eyes locked into the other. Kirstin couldn't tell if he'd go through with the call or not. Her stomach was cramping with panic. There was a pay phone near the escalator and they walked over to it. She took a dime out of her purse and looked coldly again at the detective. She lifted the receiver out of its cradle and slowly deposited her dime, waiting, praying, for him to shout stop. It began to ring and she handed it to him, sure that he'd throw it down. When he actually cleared his throat and asked to speak with Leonard Pollock, she quickly grabbed the phone and hung it up.

She stared hatefully at the detective, knowing she would never consider paying him. Instead she would finally tell Leonard. She was so embarrassed and so ashamed she didn't know how she'd ever manage to say the words. But after all the anxiety she had been through, the torment of living with a secret that could one day be exposed, she realized the avowal might actually be a relief.

"A hundred G's and you'll never hear from me again." His voice was low, tired. He looked desperate.

Kirstin just walked away from him, ignoring his calls behind her. He was the background cry of her nightmares. The faceless image that had finally surfaced.

Kirstin was holding Leonard's hand as they walked through the lobby of the Century Plaza Hotel. They were on their way to a black-tie charity affair where Leonard's closest friend, George Schwab, was being honored. Leonard was wearing his new gray tux with the star ruby cuff links and studs. She was in a simple black silk faille evening gown that was a backdrop for her jewelry—tonight she was wearing all diamonds. They smiled at several popping flashbulbs, greeting the parade of paparazzi.

She hadn't had a chance to discuss her plight with him. She was anxious to do so, but felt she had to wait until later tonight. Leonard was expected to give a speech on George's behalf and she didn't want to spoil what she knew was a very important night for the two old friends. It was going to be pure agony, sitting up on the dais, being looked at by the seven hundred and more people in attendance, but that would be a mild discomfort compared to the actual confrontation she would later have to face.

The ballroom was mobbed with elegantly dressed couples, speaking cocktail chitchat and nibbling delicacies from the elaborate hors d'oeuvre buffet. As Kirstin and Leonard entered the festive scene, she felt like running out again. There were too many people. Too much noise. The room seemed to be whirling too fast around her and she realized she was close to passing out, when Leonard held her fast by the waist and whispered tightly into her ear, "What's wrong?"

"I'm okay," she apologized, trying to smile. She hadn't been able to eat all day and she decided she had better force herself to have something before she had a drink. She needed to be completely sober and to have her wits as sharp as possible.

"Are you sure?"

"I'm fine, darling."

"You've been acting strangely ever since I got home this evening."

"I'm fine. I love you." She wanted to tell him at least that there *was* something, that she'd talk to him about it later, but she didn't want him to push her to tell him now.

The evening passed in a fog for Kirstin. Physically she was there. Mentally she was miles away. In another lifetime. In Sweden. Where it had all begun.

She hadn't even been aware she was doing something wrong. It had just been good fortune, she'd thought, that fate had delivered as some kind of compensation, at last, to distract her from the terrible blow of her husband's death. For the last eighteen months, Kirstin had been suffering from severe depression—not an uncommon condition in this dreary, predictable part of the world. Sweden just wasn't the same without Gösta, who was so much fun and always created such gaiety wherever they went. Even with their meager income they managed to travel every chance they could, leaving the babies with friends, not worrying. They were so much in love that they didn't need money to make them happy. Nobody in Sweden had any, and they didn't care. But when she was left alone, exhausted, trying to be both mother *and* father to her two babies, working long arduous hours, she grew to hate her life. No more gaiety. No more travel. Gloomy weather. And a dull regimented life. This new job opportunity had changed all that. There had been a three-month training program at the travel agency that had hired her, and after that she began leading tours to other countries. It was a dream come true.

Then one evening Kirstin received a dinner invitation from the man who'd hired her. She was delighted. In fact, she looked forward to the evening as though it were a date. Lars was a good-looking man in his early forties. Not married. Very outgoing. The restaurant he was taking her to, Fem Sma Hus, was one of the finest in Stockholm and known to be very expensive. Their evening together began well. They drank ice-cold aquavit in shot glasses with Tuborg beer chasers to wash down the harsh liquor. Their dinner was exceptional: crawfish, a Scandinavian specialty, to start, and veal Oscar as their main course. For Kirstin this was a feast. Midway through dessert, Lars made his proposition to Kirstin—words that changed her life. She had no idea that when she was accompanying tourists on the agency's trips in and out of the country, what she was really doing was carrying illegal money into Switzerland. Lars revealed to her that the travel agency was in actuality a front, owned by a very high-powered man known as the Porno King. She had been carefully selected and groomed for this position. It was her cool calm manner, he told her, that made her the consummate candidate. After several successful carries, during which she was closely observed, it was determined that she had the right makeup for this kind of work. It was decided that it was time to present her with their proposition. Her carries from now on would be more involved and would therefore require her cognizance. But the rewards, Lars told her, would be great.

Kirstin was shocked to learn what she had been doing. But the way Lars explained everything and then made his offer, it somehow seemed less awful. "Actually you're not hurting anybody," he said lightly. "Just cheating the government a little." In his opinion Sweden's restrictive socialistic government was asking for these kinds of maneuvers. There was no way for any law-abiding citizen to get ahead.

She remembered so distinctly the hot churning sensation at the pit of her stomach as she'd sat back in her chair, sipping her beer and looking carefully at Lars as he told her how much money she'd be making. How easy it sounded, how tempting, she thought, amazed that she'd even consider such a thing. But what she was doing didn't feel illegal. And until she'd started working with the agency, her life had truly been miserable—barely worth living. What Lars wanted her to do would give her the kind of money she'd never even dreamed of making. Enough to eventually save up to emigrate to the United States with her children, where she could give them a life filled with possibilities. Suddenly, in an uncharacteristically reckless spirit, Kirstin agreed.

For about eighteen months her carries went smoothly. Until, one day, hearing about not one but *two* cohorts who'd been arrested drove home the reality of what she was involved in. The prospect of spending fifteen years in a jail was enough to convince her that she was in the wrong line of work. When she told Lars that she was scared and quitting, he looked worried. The next day she was called in for a meeting with the Porno King, whom she had never met. He made it clear that the agency had no intention of losing her. If she refused to continue making the drops, he warned ominously, then they would see to it that *she* was arrested. Kirstin didn't doubt for a minute that they would. Now scared to death, she agreed to continue. As she was leaving the small office with her back to this terrible man, he asked her about her children. How were they doing? Fine, she'd replied, unable to turn and face him. His inquiry was an unveiled threat and one she knew she'd have to act on, though she had no idea how.

Then, on her next trip, she was struck with an

438

impulse—one that had crystallized as a result of days of dire desperation. She asked her cab driver to turn around and head back toward her home, where she scooped up her two children and took them with her. This time, when she arrived in Switzerland, she quickly disappeared without making the drop. Terrified at what she'd done, she boarded a train to get into Italy, where she and her children could hide until the necessary papers were processed for them to go to the United States. She remembered she was so frightened about the money that it took her three days to actually find the courage to open the false bottom in her flight bag and learn how much was there. The sight of all that currency only heightened her fear. Cash in what amounted to thirty thousand dollars in American money.

"Kirstin, you've hardly touched your meal. Are you sure you're all right?"

They were sitting on the dais eating prime rib, roast potatoes, and soggy green beans. Kirstin looked out at the sea of faces, then over at Leonard to her left.

"Do you want me to ask them to bring you something else?" he asked kindly.

"No, thank you, darling. This is fine." She picked up her knife and fork and began cutting into the slab of meat. Her thoughts were still in Italy. That awful *pensione*. That unshakable terror.

"Have you got your speech down?" she asked Leonard, putting her hand on his arm, trying to look unruffled.

"Kirstin, I just gave it. My God, where are you?"

"Leonard, I have to talk to you," she said, trying not to fall apart, willing herself not to cry.

"What is it?"

"I can't tell you here."

"Well, do you want to leave?"

"No, George would never forgive us."

"I've already given my speech."

Kirstin shook her head. "I'm sorry. It can wait."

"What is it?"

"I'll tell you later."

"You look so pale, Kirstin."

"I'm okay."

"Tell you what, honey. Let's go into the bar downstairs. We'll have a drink. You'll tell me what's going on. And then we can come back. If we feel like it, Okay?"

Kirstin started to protest. She wanted to wait until they got home. This wasn't the time or the place, and she was sorry she'd even brought it up. But Leonard was already standing and ushering her out of the room. He wouldn't take no for an answer, and the concern reflected in his eyes made her feel slightly more optimistic. They left the dais and went downstairs.

His face was grave as she told him everything, winding up her confession with her life in America before she'd met him. She had become friendly with several Swedish girls, and they all had similar problems, the biggest of which was managing to stay in the country legally. A common solution to the expiring visa was to buy a temporary, unconsummated

440

mock marriage. So, for five hundred dollars, Kirstin bought herself a husband. But, unfortunately, with her marriage came blackmail. The charade went on for nearly six months. Then, with only two weeks to go before their court appearance for the final approval of her green-card petition, the man Kirstin had married in Las Vegas announced he wouldn't sign the papers she needed unless she gave him additional money. With her green card dangling in front of her, and no time for alternate plans, Kirstin paid the man off. The divorce, she wasn't surprised to find, came at an equally high price. But it was the final payment and Kirstin paid it, anxious to get on with her life.

Leonard went through three Crown Royals, listening intently and not interjecting a word. When she was all through, he fired a series of questions at her. It was as though she were on a witness stand, on trial for her crimes, and he was the prosecutor.

"I can't believe it!" he said finally, aghast, leaning forward, both elbows on the table, thrusting his hands toward her. His voice was low and contained a terrible rage. "I don't even *know* you." The volume of his voice was rising. "First you pimp for your friend. Then you tell me someone's trying to blackmail you because you have a criminal past."

"I was afraid to tell you."

"You should have been. My God."

"I guess I should have known you wouldn't understand." Kirstin's hands were trembling as she picked up her glass.

"I don't. I don't understand at all. I can't believe

441

I've lived with you all these years. . . ." He gripped the table, trying to restrain himself.

Kirstin was devastated by his reaction. "All you're hearing is what I did and not *why*."

"I'm hearing all right. I'm hearing the same damn disrespect for rules and laws and simple, basic moral behavior that had you fixing up your married girl friend—"

"That has nothing to do with this—"

"Laws that don't suit you, you just disregard—"

"I was cheating the government. I felt it was small compensation for the alternatives and the opportunities the socialist government denied me."

"You can justify anything."

"What about the way you *finagle* on your taxes—what's the difference?"

"So *you* just decide what's fair, then?"

"Was it *fair* that I was widowed at twenty-two years old? Left alone with two helpless infants?"

"The victim."

"I'm not asking you to feel sorry for me, dammit, Leonard. I'm asking you to just understand. This isn't black-and-white. I'm sure that in your survival days, when you, too, were broke and trying to rise out of the muck to make a better life for yourself, *you* did some questionable things."

"I was always within the law."

"I don't believe you. No big business gets as big as yours without some—"

"Now you're calling *me* the liar—"

"No. I think you just don't remember. Or never looked upon what you were doing as 'illegal.' What I was doing *never* felt illegal. And when I took the money at the end, well, I didn't know what else to do with it. I was running away to save my life. To save the lives of my children." Kirstin's voice broke. "It was either throw the money away or keep it. My God, that would have been stupid not to keep it! The money belonged to a thief anyway."

"I thought you said he wasn't so bad. He was just cheating the government."

Suddenly Kirstin was angry. Furious. She stood up, unable to take any more. "If you'd have only left things alone—accepted them for what they were— you wouldn't have spoiled our really very wonderful life together. You've been good to me, but I've also been very good to you. We had a good marriage. And now you've ruined everything. I'm sorry, Leonard. I really am. I love you, but I don't see how we can stay together after this."

Leonard's eyes were dull. He didn't say a word.

Looking at him with a great sadness, she began removing her diamond jewelry, putting it on the table in front of him. First her necklace. Her bracelet. Her earrings. Her ring. She had shed about a hundred carats of D flawless diamonds. "I'll walk out of your life as I came into it," she said. "With nothing. But the wonderful years we've had together—*that* nobody can ever take away from me."

No longer fighting her tears, Kirstin took a long last look at Leonard, softly whispering good-bye. Then, with the feeling of weights in her heart, she left.

* * *

Out in front of the hotel, she got into a taxi. He hadn't followed her as she'd thought he might. She put her head back on the seat and closed her eyes, aware that the driver was waiting for instructions where to go. But she didn't know what to tell him. She was too proud to call any of her friends—even Kelly and Ericka didn't know about her past, and she didn't want to have to tell them. Ingrid and Peter, her two children, were her only family, but she couldn't possibly turn to either of them. They had always blamed her for having put Leonard before them. They were probably right. At first she had thought that marrying Leonard *was for them*. But now, the way things had turned out, she honestly didn't know. Maybe more mothering and less money would have made them happier people, would have brought them all closer together. Fancy schools, expensive clothes, and hot wheels hadn't been the answer. And now Leonard had become everything to her. He was the axis on which her world revolved, and now she was spinning lost and out of control. For the second time in her life she had nobody to turn to. Her only solace was that there were no dark shadows lurking behind her—threatening her.

"Hey, lady, this isn't a rest stop. Are we going somewhere? If not, I'm going to have to start charging you for driving in place." The cab driver had turned around, annoyed.

"I need to find a hotel," Kirstin said.

"You're at one."

"A different one. In another part of town." Kirstin put her hand to her head.

"Can't you be more specific? Let's start with north, south, east, or west. Pick one. Any one. If you've got dough—I've got gas."

"Please, just head toward Orange County," she decided, intentionally selecting someplace where she'd remain anonymous. Anonymity was what she needed right now, she thought, rolling down her window. She was beginning to feel queasy. The car stank from cigarettes. And she hadn't been broke like this in *so* long. All she had was a hundred dollar bill in her purse. It was the emergency money she always passed from purse to purse, no matter where she went. She felt insecure without it. Now the hundred-dollar bill would buy her one taxi ride, one night in a TraveLodge, and she'd worry about the rest tomorrow.

The next morning Kirstin awoke to a blaze of light streaming in through her window. Nothing looked familiar. Thin white curtains. Off-white walls. Orange-and-gold-flecked carpet. Where on earth was she? Then, with a terrible heaviness in her chest, she remembered and closed her eyes again, not wanting to know. But even in this groggy state, sharp images of what had happened over the last twenty-four hours came back to her. With great despair she opened her eyes again and looked around. On the nightstand were notes she'd made before going to sleep. They were scribbled emotionally on the cheap motel stationery—covering three sheets of paper, one envelope, and two postcards as she'd tried to bring her thoughts into focus. At one point she'd tried to compose a letter to Leonard, but then decided against

445

it. She had said all there was to say. Now she had to forget about him and think about putting her life back together. So she'd start modestly. She'd done it before. The only way to survive was to look forward. To pause for self-pity was already to be defeated. And her objective at hand was to find herself a job to get started. But before she even got out of bed, she remembered that all she had with her was her evening gown. She couldn't possibly go out looking for a job in a forty-five-hundred-dollar Chlóe gown.

Picking up the telephone, she dialed the front desk, asking the clerk to send a sewing kit and some scissors up to her room. With a blanket wrapped around her, she answered the door, and within twenty minutes she had remodeled her outfit, cutting away about a thousand dollars of it as she hemmed the long narrow skirt. She would still look overdressed, but fortunately the strapless gown had a bolero jacket that went over it, and it would just have to do until she could buy herself something more appropriate.

On her way out the door, as she picked up her key and purse, making a last inspection of herself in the mirror, she realized what she was holding in her hand. It hadn't even occurred to her before. An eighteen-karat-gold Bulgari minaudière that she had bought from her jeweler, Victor Van Houghten. In a store the evening bag would sell for anywhere from thirty to forty thousand dollars. When she had been giving Leonard back her jewelry, she hadn't thought about the purse. This time she called housekeeping to see if anyone who had recently checked out might have left a shopping bag in their room. Suddenly she

446

didn't want to be walking around with such a valuable item exposed in her hand.

Her first stop was at a pawnshop to see what she could borrow against the gold bag. She had no intention of selling it because she knew she'd get next to nothing. Probably not even melt-down value. Besides, as soon as she got back on her feet financially, she would pay back the pawnbroker and see to it that the minaudière was returned to Leonard. She wanted nothing of his. She wouldn't touch her department store charge accounts, nor would she go to their bank. When the pawnbroker finally presented Kirstin with his offer, she looked at him horrified. All he would lend her on the piece was two thousand dollars, and for that he wanted a criminally high interest rate. Having no choice, Kirstin reluctantly agreed.

Next she went to an inexpensive-looking dress shop and bought herself something more suitable to wear. After that she stopped at a discount drug store for cosmetics. Then, feeling hungry, and anxious about getting a job, she went into a small coffee shop, had some breakfast, and began circling employment ads in the newspaper. It was very important to her that she work someplace where people she knew wouldn't be coming in and feeling sorry for her. She also did not want to chance seeing Leonard. Then suddenly she wondered how *he* was managing without *her*. What about his meals? And he had some suits at the cleaners—he wouldn't even know where they were. There were a thousand things, but, oh, God, she had to stop thinking about him.

*　　*　　*

Another bad putt. Leonard's golf game was reflecting his mood. Distracted. Impatient. And overall foul. He walked over to the ball again, conscious of the rest of his foursome ready to go in their carts, watching him. He'd four-putted the last five holes and they were aware that something was wrong. With a slight bend to his knees, he gave the ball a frustrated tap. It crawled toward the cup, rolled over and around its rim, but then didn't go in.

After the ninth hole, when the guys went into the snack shop for a quick bite, Leonard told them he was not going to play on.

His friends looked sympathetic. They'd all had days like this, and they didn't ask any questions.

He drove straight home after that. His house felt disturbingly quiet. Even the help seemed to be tiptoeing around, trying to stay out of his way. Kirstin's absence left everything somber. Cold gray. There was a general feeling in the house of mourning. He went into the study to fix himself a drink, not hungry for lunch. He *could* drive over to the office, but then he doubted he would be able to concentrate on his work any better than he'd been able to concentrate on his golf game. He had to just stop and address his situation—decide what he wanted to do about it. He was mad as hell at Delaney for letting this happen, and he'd told him so. Leonard didn't care that Delaney *himself* hadn't done the blackmailing. Delaney was responsible for whoever it was he put on the case.

But now the knowledge was out and Leonard had to deal with it. Would he ever be able to trust Kirstin again? He took a sip of his drink and then turned on the ball game. Sitting back in his chair, with his feet up on the ottoman, he tried to manipulate his thoughts—to make them calm, unemotional.

He tried to envision the scenes Kirstin had described to him. To understand how she'd gotten into all this in the first place. She was young. Wanted to better her life. Yet what she'd done sounded like something out of a spy novel. Carrying illegal money out of the country. Getting into trouble and then stealing away with it. This was his wife? A fugitive? A mule?

Oh, the hell with all that. The real question was: Could he live without her? Did he want to live without her? The fact was he loved her. She loved him. They had a damn good life together. What did it really matter what she had done back then? So she wasn't satisfied with a mediocre life—would he have anything in common with a woman who would have been? Kirstin had great spunk to her. She was clever. Inventive. Fun. She was warm and cared about him. He couldn't imagine her in the kind of gloom she'd described—and actually he didn't want to.

Damn that Delaney. Leonard wanted his wife back. He picked up the phone and dialed Delaney's office, having no idea where to even look for Kirstin. When he got the detective on the line he shouted angrily at him, "I paid you all this money for fucking up my marriage—now dammit, you stupid bastard, find my wife."

Chapter Twenty-Three

ERICKA FELT COZY IN HER PLUSH TERRY TENT OF A ROBE AS she belted it loosely at her waist with a thick rope. She felt rejuvenated from her shower and, still towel-drying her hair, walked over to the stereo set to make a record selection. The woman from whom she had sublet the apartment had left all her albums and told Ericka to play whatever she liked. Ericka was thinking it was quite a collection as she bent down to make a choice. Billy Joel, she decided, *Glass Houses*. She slipped the large black disk from out of its jacket and set it carefully on the turntable. With the press of a button the quiet room was filled with rich sound. Next she went over to the fireplace. Might as well treat herself to a little romance. Her father had shown her how to get a good roaring fire going when she was a little girl, but it had been years since she'd actually built one herself. She knelt down on the hearth, pulling aside the screen and crumpling up wads of newspaper. She pushed them in between the logs, forcing the paper into place with a brass and iron poker. Then, striking a long matchstick, she tossed it in, setting the logs ablaze. The wood-burning fragrance was almost medicinal, and she sighed, teary-eyed and feeling reminiscent—tempted to call her parents in Alaska and tell them what had happened in her life.

The fire was warm and Ericka moved away from it, considering what her parents' reaction might be. They'll be sad, she thought, going over to the small kitchen and pouring herself a glass of wine. Maybe a little afraid. But so was she. Her father would think she had done the right thing, though he might not actually say so. He liked David, but he'd never been able to understand their relationship. Jamie had been pretty much of a taboo subject. Ericka had always gotten terribly upset when they mentioned him. But they both knew how she felt about him. And there was an unspoken awareness of how, after that, Ericka hadn't ever been enough in love. They would worry that she was too vulnerable. Her mother would be worried that she might be hurt again. The telephone wasn't the right form of communication for something this deep, she thought, something so charged with change and complications. It had been over a week now since she'd been on her own; her thoughts were somewhat in order. She would write to them.

Sitting down at the desk in the living room, sipping her glass of wine, she began suddenly to miss her parents very much. She wanted her letter to be full of articulate introspection, but not overly emotional. She didn't want to alarm them.

The words on paper were like contact for her, and she felt comforted as she began, getting to the heart of what she had to tell them right away.

Then the phone rang and she reached over to pick it up.

"I was wrong," Jamie began, gentle but matter-of-fact. "I miss you.

"How'd you get this number?" she stalled, her heart beating wildly.

"I called your office earlier. You were at a meeting. Your secretary said you'd be here later. How are you doing?"

"Okay." Her voice was strained. She felt unbelievably torn.

"This is so crazy, Ericka. I should have just stayed in L.A. I'm sorry. I want you. I miss you. I want you here with me. Can you come out to New York?"

"I don't know," she said tentatively.

His words grew into an intense plea, as he tried to persuade her. It could have been the exact phone call she'd fantasized about receiving. Except that it was late and her fantasies had realigned themselves. Now all that was around her, what she was experiencing, was suddenly very real. And *real* was what she had decided she wanted. Although she felt lonely, sad, and confused, she remained convinced that above all else she needed time by herself.

"I think you were right in the first place," she said quietly. "I do need to be on my own for a while."

"I wasn't being fair," Jamie argued. "You knew exactly what you wanted and I was too nervous to accept that. To begin with, I was shocked. Also I was overwhelmed."

"Understandably."

"But I've thought about this. A lot—I was wrong."

"But I was doing *exactly* what you said. Going from one relationship directly into another. I did want you to be my 'savior,' as you put it—"

"That's fair, though. You love me—why shouldn't I rescue you from a marriage you got into because of my not being there for you in the first place?"

Ericka let go of the pen she was holding and sat farther back into her chair, shocked that she was arguing with Jamie. He wanted her. Was she crazy? Why on earth, after all this time, was she saying no? "I just *feel* something inside, Jamie. This is wrong. I don't want any more fantasies in my life. I don't want any more illusions. I want a commitment. A marriage based on *more*. With David I was ignoring things I shouldn't have ignored. And if I were to be with you now—"

"All I want is to be with you—no pressure—just to be together. You're building this up all out of perspective."

"No I'm not. For the first time ever, I'm seeing things as they really are. The truth is, I love my fantasy of you—but I don't know you well enough to know beyond that."

"So get to know me."

"I can't. Not yet. I'm confused. . . ." She felt like a yo-yo that had been played with too much—her string was frayed and wouldn't react with the usual command.

"A week ago you wanted to marry me. A week ago you left your husband for me."

"A week ago I was scared."

"You sound scared right now. A week ago you sounded sure."

"I was scared then and I'm scared now. Look, I've been through a lot of emotional blizzards in the last couple of weeks. I can't see or think clearly."

"Why don't I come out to L.A.?"

"No, Jamie. I don't want to see you now. Give me a few weeks to sort all this out—"

"Look, Ericka, I can't hang around waiting for you to—"

"I waited for you."

"Well, I'm not like that. Right now I feel like being with you. You accomplished what you set out to do, which was to make me feel this way about you."

"So you can't wait a few weeks—a month?" Ericka was astonished. Hurt.

"You can't just put me on hold, on ice. If you can't make up your mind now—I'm not going to wait."

"Typical. Things don't go exactly as you want them, and what do you do? You walk away!" she said bitterly.

"I need you with me. Now."

"I can't believe this. I've been waiting for you since I was twelve years old. I *never* stopped loving you and you can't wait three weeks—"

"Well, what the hell do you want?"

"I want you to want me! That's what I want. I want you to want me so badly that you're willing to put up with a little inconvenience. A little imperfection. A little reality, for crissake."

"I need someone in my life. If it's not going to be you, Ericka, it'll be someone else. I meet beautiful women every day. If you want me, you better come out, because I can't make any promises."

"And if you *do* meet someone else, then I say the hell with you—for once and for all, the hell with you, Jamie Sterling!"

She hung up the phone breathless. In a rage. Trying to understand. In one gulp she drank half her wine, then broke down in tears, smearing the ink on her parents' letter. After a while she got up and washed her face with cold water, then tried to begin writing to her parents again.

Not knowing what to say, she finally abandoned her letter and curled up on the sofa, still listening to the Billy Joel album, and reading one of the scripts she had brought home with her. When the phone rang again she went over to answer it, apprehensively. Maybe it was Jamie calling to apologize. Maybe it was David—he hadn't called yet that day. Maybe it was her parents—having mental telepathy about the dilemma she was in, sensing how she needed to talk to them.

"I miss you. Come home." It was David.

"I can't."

"I love you, Ericka. But I can only take this for so long."

"Then stop calling every day. I need time. Why

456

can't you understand that? If I were one of your patients you'd understand."

"You ought to be delighted that I can't be that objective. And frankly, after going through all this, I think I'd advise my patients differently than I might have before."

"David, please—"

"Give me a chance. I made a lot of mistakes with you—with us. But obviously you're more important to me than anything else or I wouldn't be pleading with you to come back to me. I love you."

Ericka picked up her glass of wine again and sighed heavily. She needed desperately to be left alone. She was not going to submit to this kind of pressure. From either of them.

"I'll change. Just give me a chance."

"David, I believe you will try to change. But that's beside the point. I just have to do what I'm doing. *I'm sorry.*"

"Let's get pregnant," he said. "I think one of the problems is that we don't have any children. You'd feel differently if you had a family. And if you felt more of a commitment from me. I give you my word—"

"You're not listening to me."

"Is it Jamie?" His voice was so full of pain that it reached over into Ericka.

"No. It's me."

"Did he call?"

"Yes. Tonight."

"I knew it—"

"And I told him exactly what I've been telling you.

457

That I have no idea what I want. Other than that I want more."

"I want to give you more."

"That I need *time*," she continued, frustrated.

"What did he say?"

"He wasn't very nice about it. But I don't care. I really don't."

"I love you, Ericka. I'm sorry we're going through this." David hung up after that and Ericka, bursting with conflict, went back to her letter again.

After an hour of intense writing, in which she'd poured out her heart and tried to analyze it, she decided not to send the letter.

Chapter Twenty-Four

KELLY FELT EXHILARATED AS RON PULLED HIS PORSCHE INTO the private driveway of Touch. Even from the outside the swank private club looked glamorous. After submitting their names and the name of the party they were to meet to a bouncer-type character who approached their car at the entrance, they were given a cordial nod and allowed to proceed.

Walking into the foyer of the club, they were asked to sign the guest register. Kelly looped her arm through Ron's and smiled at him, wishing he would comment on how she looked. She always felt slightly intimidated whenever they went out with Clayton. His dates dressed to the nines and Kelly never felt chic enough, even though she might have when she'd left her house. Tonight her gabardine suit had seemed too tailored, her suede dress not good for dancing, and she'd been afraid she'd be cold during dinner in her bare wool crepe. Finally she had decided on her long black sequined cardigan over an ivory satin cowled blouse and a short, straight black velvet skirt.

"Kelly! Ron!" Clayton Smith greeted them both with a bear hug. Clayton had been a linebacker in college. He was tall and still solidly built. He had a mop of tousled auburn hair and devilish green eyes like Kelly's. They could have been brother and sister.

"Meet Julie," Clayton said, introducing his attractive date.

Kelly sized her up with some relief: pretty but not dazzling.

They all slid into the U-shaped booth, Kelly next to Julie, between the two men.

"This is fabulous," Kelly said, looking around the restaurant, taking in the sleek Art Deco decor. The designer must have spent a fortune, she thought, noting the artistically etched bas-relief glass panels and doors, then the sweeping brass, lacquer, marble, and chrome fixtures.

"Wait until you see the disco. That's really something," Clayton said.

"So I've heard."

Then Clayton and Ron proceeded to dive into conversation, leaving Kelly, as usual, to get to know Clayton's date, whom she would probably never even see again.

Julie, it turned out, was twenty-six years old, an entertainment attorney in a high-powered Century City law firm, and as she chatted on about herself,

Kelly began to feel dated and unaccomplished. When Julie made a condescending reference to Kelly's prior role solely as a "home engineer," Kelly tried to glorify her photography career, but it failed to elicit anything other than sympathy from Julie. She distinctly viewed Kelly as a housewife now turned "hyphenated" career woman. Julie said how lucky *she* had been. Just six years' difference in age had placed them in different generations. Julie was quick to let Kelly know that since she was thirteen she had wanted to be a lawyer. All of her friends had planned on having solid careers too. Some were doctors. Some were lawyers. Some were in the film business. All of them were ambitious.

Now, why does that sound so great and glamorous? Kelly asked herself. Ron's a lawyer and she certainly had never looked upon his career with any envy. But then again, Julie was only twenty-six, had short stylish brown hair and great big brown eyes, and *looked* glamorous.

As Ron and Clayton joined their conversation, Ron and Julie discovered that they had gone to the same high school—Pacific Palisades High—and that they knew a great many people in common.

"Alexis Jamison. How do you know her?" Julie's eyes were bright as she and Ron began batting names back and forth. Kelly turned to Ron, curious to hear how he would phrase his explanation. Alexis Jamison was a name she'd been hearing for ages. One of Ron's first sexual conquests.

"I dated her."

"You're kidding!"

Ron looked at Kelly and smiled as though to say, what a small world. "You're friends with Alexis?" he asked Julie. "How's she doing?"

"Great! She looks terrific."

"*She* was going to law school, last I heard. Did she?"

"Yes! She's in a big downtown firm."

"Really? I can't believe it—Alexis?"

"I know. She was always such a sexpot. I used to go out with her younger brother. That's how we became friends. Nobody realized how smart she was."

Alexis, like Julie, had also been lucky. Even though Alexis was closer in age to Kelly, she, too, seemed to have done things right. She had slept around, enjoying a certain status as a sexpot. Then she had gone off to become a lawyer, unencumbered by a husband and children. Kelly tried to keep a lid on her frustration as she sat there listening enviously. Everybody, it appeared, had lived right except her. Julie. Alexis. Ron. Even Brandon with his big box of old flames.

"Jennifer Lee Sondheim!" Julie was exclaiming. "Now, how do you know her? She's only a couple of years older than me."

Kelly looked at Ron. "He dated her too," she explained. *Before* she became Jennifer Lee Sondheim the actress, Kelly added. Jennifer was a frequent face in movies of the week. A TV star who made Kelly cringe every time she appeared on the screen. Ron never lost a chance to tell her that Jennifer had the best body of any girl he'd ever known. Even Clayton's ears picked up at the mention of her name.

462

"You're kidding!" Julie looked surprised. "Jennifer's now a client of mine. How'd you meet?"

"I was her chaperon on a teen tour to South America," Ron said.

"Her chaperon! I'm surprised you're not still trying to do that," Julie teased.

Kelly gave Ron an artificial smile. Not only did Ron have a glowing résumé of old girl friends, he also had a glowing résumé of travel experiences. When Kelly had first met Ron she had been so impressed with how well traveled he was. But evidently he had gotten all that travel curiosity out of his system before he married her. With his parents no longer subsidizing his trips, he was content to go skiing in Mammoth, to sun in San Diego, and to take the kids to see national parks. Only Kelly was left longing for exotic trips. Perhaps *she* should become a chaperon.

Over a lavish dinner, Ron and Julie continued their discussion about Palisades High, talking about a string of old teachers they had had in common, and the food in the cafeteria. Then they shifted to law and Julie mentioned a friend of hers who was a judge.

"She wears nothing under her black robe but a string of pearls," she said. "Isn't that wild?"

After dinner, Clayton suggested that they move into the disco for some drinks and dancing.

Kelly's mood improved as soon as she walked into the discotheque. The room was beautiful and made her feel as though she were in Monte Carlo or the South of France. The dance floor was curved and made of marble, lit up by tiny lights on a smoked-

463

glass dome ceiling. The lights were reflected in strips of mirror. Adding to the romance of the scene were tall, slightly arched palm trees and a lush green landscape set in an atrium.

She sank into a small cushy sofa close beside Ron, taking his hand and trying to get him to pay attention to her. She agreed to the Midori daiquiris Clayton was ordering for everybody. The pale melon-colored drinks, all frothy and served in enormous glasses, reminded her of Brandon. This had been the special concoction he had ordered for them at the Bel-Air Hotel—his initial lure. Thinking about him suddenly made her melancholy. Well—she hadn't missed out on *everything*. She was just late. And typically things had been out of order for her. At this particular moment, however, she couldn't have felt more justified. She looked over at Clayton, who had his hands all over Julie.

A Donna Summer song pounded out of the expensive sound equipment, spreading rhythm and the desire for movement throughout Kelly.

"May I have this dance?" Clayton bowed in front of the ebullient Julie, taking her hand and drawing her onto the marble dance floor. Kelly watched, wishing Ron would ask her to dance but knowing he would not.

Clowning, she got up in front of him, as Clayton had done with Julie. 'May I have this dance?" she asked.

Ron was watching the couples on the dance floor, bobbing his head to the beat. "It's nice to watch. I enjoy watching."

"C'mon, Ron. You know I love to dance. It wouldn't kill you to dance with me."

"I'm too full."

Kelly settled back against the cushions, frustrated. Ron put his hand on her leg.

"What do you think of her?" he asked.

"I don't know," she said. "She's nice-looking. But a little young. What do you think?"

"Okay. Young."

After a few dances, Clayton and Julie returned to the table out of breath, but glowing from the exercise.

"Why aren't you two getting out there?" Clayton asked.

"Ron doesn't like to dance."

"C'mon." Clayton led Kelly onto the dance floor. Julie sat down beside Ron.

In a few moments, Kelly noticed Ron and Julie dancing beside them. She felt hot with anger.

"I thought you didn't like to dance, old man," Clayton said, smiling broadly at Ron.

Ron laughed awkwardly.

"I don't know why he doesn't like to dance!" Julie shouted over the music to Kelly. "He's a wonderful dancer!"

"She asked me to dance," Ron explained to Kelly, apologizing to her as he handed his parking ticket to the attendant. "I'm sorry, honey. I really am—but what could I do?"

"You could have said no like you said no to me. You could have said you were too full!" She didn't bother to mask her hurt. She desperately wanted him to understand.

"You're making too big a deal over this."

Ron's Porsche was pulled up alongside them and they got in, Kelly fuming, Ron looking impatient.

"I'm sorry, Kelly. But there's nothing more I can say. Let's just forget about it."

Suddenly Kelly turned to Ron, her eyes blazing. "I can't just keep forgetting about these things. I don't forget about them. They collect inside me, growing into larger and larger resentments, becoming less and less manageable. You make light of *everything* that's important to me, if it doesn't suit you. I'm sick of it! I can't live with it anymore. I've really had it with your unresponsiveness and your damned insensitivity to my needs—"

"Hold on a second," Ron said, stopping short at a red light and automatically putting his hand out to protect Kelly.

"No!" she shouted, moving away his hand. "You brush me off like lint, irritating dust particles that attach themselves to your clothes. In that pompous voice of yours you tell me, 'That's not real life, Kelly. You live in a fantasy world!' "

"You do."

"Why, because I need for you to get off your ass every now and then and try and act like you love me? Because I love to dance—and I'm angry because you wouldn't dance with me?"

"I danced with you—"

"Once. Because I was ready to burst into tears after you'd danced three times with her. How do you

466

think that makes me feel? You're so *worried* about a stranger's feelings. Why don't you worry about mine? It wouldn't have killed you to get up and dance with me."

"So next time I will."

"You know, it's just not that difficult to make me happy. If you'd only try a little you'd see remarkable results. . . ." Kelly said unsteadily, her eyes filled with tears.

"I'm not a romantic person!"

"So go out of your way a little and try to be. Pretend you're in love with me and you're trying to woo me. How would you be if you were single and dating?"

"I shouldn't have to try that hard with my wife. That's bullshit. You want bullshit?"

"I guess I do, then." She closed her eyes, her hands forming tight fists. How could she ever get through to him? This was just too important to her to let go. It was humiliating the way he made so light of all of her needs, brushing them off the way he did, not wanting to be in the least bit inconvenienced. It was so easy for him to make fun of her. To demean her needs as superficial, or silly. But in her heart she knew he was wrong. He was just too damn selfish. Too damn lazy. And she wondered how much he really loved her. She thought about Brandon and how special she had felt with him. Maybe it wasn't real. Maybe it wasn't long-lasting. But he had made her feel marvelous. Desirable. Happy. And though only temporarily, in love. But that wasn't what she wanted. She didn't *want* to fill in what she wasn't getting from Ron with someone else. She didn't want to be looking.

They were both silent the rest of the way home. Kelly felt as though there was a volcano erupting inside her. Before, there had been rumblings. Now it was an out-and-out explosion—a burning outpouring of emotional conflicts, surging and flowing fast from out of her core.

In this high-voltage silence they proceeded into the house. Ron went into the kitchen to get something to drink while Kelly went upstairs to check on the kids. They met again in the bedroom, where Kelly was sitting on the edge of the bed overwhelmed by her thoughts. She watched Ron as he began to get undressed, stiffly taking off his tie and then removing his shoes. She was thinking about Brandon and the way they'd undressed each other. She was visualizing him so clearly. Hoping there wouldn't be others.

With her voice full of fear, quivering, she began telling Ron how lonely he made her feel. How hollow. And how she was afraid of what those feelings could inevitably lead to.

"What are you saying, Kelly?" Ron demanded angrily.

"I'm saying," she responded, trying to compose herself, "that your lack of responsiveness could push me to find it in someone else." What she couldn't say was that it already had.

They stood for a moment staring at one another, the meaning of Kelly's words sinking into him. She could tell by the stunned look in his eyes, by the way his lips were parted, that she had at last struck a chord in him. He looked at her for a moment, then pulled her up from the bed and closed her into his arms. He pressed his cheek hard against hers and whispered huskily how he loved her. How he was sorry. He was holding on to her tightly, as though saying through this embrace that he never ever wanted to lose her. She tried to push away, to look into his eyes, but he wouldn't let her go. For the first time she knew he was worried, as though intuitively he understood that he *could* lose her. Then there were tears wet on her cheeks and she didn't know if they also belonged to him. She tried to look but he wouldn't let her. "I love you," he said again, swallowing heavily. "And I'll try." She tightened her arms around him, then put her hand soothingly on his head, feeling somehow that he would try. And that was really all she wanted.

Chapter Twenty-Five

"WE'RE RUNNING HARD AND FAST.

"Now concentrate on your breathing.

"And stretch.

"Reach out with your stamina.

"Extend your energy.

"Imagine that we're running through Manhattan now. Down Second Avenue. Flying on superhuman limbs. Feel that break with your consciousness—feel that high that soars your senses beyond pain into freedom.

"The streets are blocked off. The crowds are cheering us on—they're holding placards: *Hurrah for the New York Marathon.*

"We're euphoric as we carve the avenues in evenly paced flight.

471

"Now we're tearing through the South Bronx . . . then Harlem . . . gliding through the urban jungle . . . see the curious faces lining the streets and staring out at you. They flock to their front porches and watch as you fly fearlessly down the block. No gangs, no fights, just the wonderful movement of limbs.

"Then fresh lush greenery replacing weathered concrete as we move invincibly through Central Park.

"Exotic. Hot and sexy. Feel the power.

"Feel the high.

"And extend."

Kelly moved her own limbs, mesmerized by the fantasy being called out by the health club's new exercise instructor, who was trying to pull the tired class through their twenty minutes of aerobics. His seductive Brazilian accent was penetrating, commanding. Kelly matched his movements with inspired grace, feeling little creases of sweat forming under her breasts that were now molded by her hot and clinging T-shirt.

She had formed the images of the marathon so clearly, and the thought of such an adventure, running through ordinarily forbidden areas like Harlem or Spanish Harlem, had her spellbound. Ron, of course, would never go. He would think that she was crazy even to contemplate it.

But it obviously appealed to this swarthy-looking man bouncing through his aerobics on the little platform in front of her with NEW YORK MARATHON printed in slick white letters across the deep green T-shirt that was cut just flimsily enough to show off his marvelously formed chest. The thin material was stretched tightly against the midriff, which was hard and flat, with rolling swells of muscle. His olive skin was glistening from under it—smooth and hairless. The headband he was wearing emphasized his celery-colored eyes and foreign-looking bone structure.

"Okay, class, take your pulse," the instructor was saying, shaking out one glorious thigh, then the other. Aerobics were over, and after taking their pulse rates it would be time to move into stretching.

Kelly placed two fingers on her jugular vein and counted, walking around the room with the rest of the class. With so much adrenaline released into her system, she felt slightly high.

"Crossing the finish line is outrageous. It's like a climax."

Kelly looked up startled to see the instructor breathing heavily in front of her. He was mopping his forehead with a terry towel.

"I noticed the way you move, so effortlessly. You'd probably love it," he continued. "Have you ever run a marathon?" His accent was beautiful.

Kelly shook her head no, then looked over, embarrassed, to Kirstin and Ericka, who were standing next to her.

"You should consider it," he said, gently pulling her shoulders back and flattening his palm against her stomach. Then, walking back over to his platform and putting on another album, he began leading a series of stretching exercises. Kelly felt him staring at her as she bent down to touch the ground. Warmed up and limber from all the aerobics, she was able to fold her body forward flat against her

473

thighs and practically touch the carpet with the tip of her nose.

The exercise instructor's gaze was still on her as she unfolded herself and stretched up to touch the sky.

Not a chance, she told him in a smooth glance. Not only had she already been through that, but she had been through it with the best.

At least now she had a more seasoned perspective on it all, she thought, dipping into a deep knee bend along with the rest of the class, and looking over at her reflection in the mirror. She thought about Ron and the changes she'd seen in him in the last couple of weeks. They weren't dramatic changes, but they were important ones to her. Mostly he'd been more sensitive—not rushing to turn on the TV set; slower, more interested lovemaking; awkward compliments on the way she looked.

Ericka watched Kelly bending in more perfect form than anyone else in the class. She'd been aware of the instructor's interest in Kelly and she wondered what her friend was thinking. A short while back, Kelly would have said no to any advances the instructor might have made, *but* she would have fantasized wildly about him afterward, telling both Ericka and Kirstin how luscious she thought he was. Now Ericka guessed that, at least temporarily, Kelly's fantasies wouldn't be so vivid. Perhaps in private Kelly might fill him in to heighten her sexual satisfaction, but she wouldn't fantasize about him in any grand outrageous way as she might have before—actually wanting to live out the fantasy.

"Onto the floor for leg work."

Ericka stretched out on her side according to the instructor's directions, lifting her left leg slowly into the air for a series of stretches, then bending it down and out. Amazing, she thought, how in such a short time all of their lives had been so changed. And all as a result of Kelly's fantasies untamed and threatening their own. It had seemed like such innocent fun. But now, looking back, Ericka was surprised that none of them had taken their problems more seriously. The fantasies were just outgrowths of their submerged predicaments. While her own life was the most radically changed, Kirstin, she felt, had been hit with the brunt of it. And really, Ericka thought, all three of them should be grateful.

Pointing and flexing, Kirstin swung her long, slender leg back and then forward, stretching and tightening. She felt terrifically relaxed—renewed. She was thinking about her anniversary that was coming up shortly—how she wanted to do something special for Leonard. She was eager to celebrate their triumph of being together, with Kirstin no longer haunted by ghosts, Leonard no longer haunted by suspicion. The trauma that had shaken them nearly out of their nest had in the end, Kirstin thought, brought them much closer together than ever before. They had discovered that they couldn't bear to lose each other. That what they had together was sacred, to be cherished and protected with everything they had.

What could she do that would be a tribute to this new passage in their marriage? Something that would symbolize great growth; their deeper bond. Kirstin switched over onto her other side to begin working on her right leg. She wanted to plan something intimate. Something that would truly make Leonard happy. Maybe she was better off just asking him, she decided, smiling at the simplicity of her solution. Beginning a series of buttock tucks, Kirstin glanced over at her two friends. Kelly was moving easily, Ericka was puffing with effort. They both caught her looking their way and they exchanged meaningful smiles. This was another bond that had been strengthened in Kirstin's life—her friendship with these two women, which surpassed any other female relationship she had ever had. In such a short time, all of their lives had been radically altered, and they felt connected through their experiences.

After class the three of them sat down at the juice bar and ordered a round of Sunshine Slammers, the health club's eye opener, a thick blend of fresh orange juice, strawberries, banana, and yogurt.

Sipping her drink through a straw, Kirstin turned to Ericka. "So has David still been calling?"

"Yes, every day," Ericka responded. "Sometimes three or four times a day."

"Do you think you'll go back to him?" Kelly asked.

"Well, can a leopard change its spots?"

"No, I don't think it's possible," Kirstin said.

Kelly wondered. Her leopard appeared to be changing his spots, but then again she was changing too.

"Neither do I." Ericka swirled her straw pensively around the tall glass.

"So what does that mean—will you go back with him anyway?" Kirstin asked.

"I still don't know. If David really *were* to change, maybe."

"And what about Jamie—have you heard from him?"

"Nothing," Ericka said. "Not a word."

"So he's honoring your request, for the time being," Kirstin suggested.

Ericka shrugged, smiled, and sighed, all three actions blended together into one gesture. "The truth is—for now I'd like to toast my independence. I have no idea what's going to happen to me. But it feels good."

Kelly touched her glass first to Kirstin's, then to Ericka's.

"A toast to our futures," Kirstin said. "Now that we've resolved our fling." She looked at Kelly and smiled. "God, what a weight has been lifted off me because of this."

"Actually, I think what you did was heroic. To be frank, I was impressed," Kelly said. "Besides, would you do things that differently if you were twenty years old again, and in the same predicament?"

"I don't know," Kirstin said reflectively. "But listen, Kelly. You're thinking of my life like a book. I'm just glad that it's all out in the open now and behind me."

"What happened to the blackmailer? Are you pressing charges?" Ericka asked.

Kirstin shrugged. *"We're* not. But I'm sure the agency is going to do something." She took another sip of her drink and looked at Kelly. "And what about you? That gorgeous new instructor today was testing you—were you tempted? Or are you cured for now?"

"Cured for now," Kelly said honestly.

"You know, I think *you're* probably also trying harder with Ron now," Kirstin pointed out, and Kelly agreed, feeling grateful for the changes in their relationship. With Ron finally understanding how she felt and legitimately trying to make amends, her anger had dissolved.

"I think we should cancel everything today and go over to the Bistro Garden for a long celebratory lunch," Ericka said, standing and stretching, and looking happy. She finished off the rest of her drink, then led the way toward the locker room.

ON LEAVING CHARLESTON
ALEXANDRA RIPLEY

Live this magnificent family saga —from the civilized, ante-bellum South through the wreckless, razzle-dazzle Jazz Age

Southern heiress Garden Tradd sheds the traditions of her native Charleston to marry the rich, restless Yankee, Sky Harris. Deeply in love, the happy young couple crisscross the globe to hobnob with society in Paris, London, and New York. They live a fast-paced, fairy-tale existence, until the lovely Garden discovers that her innocence and wealth are no insulation against the magnitude of unexpected betrayal. In desperation the gentle woman seeks refuge in the city she had once abandoned, her own, her native land—Charleston.

$3.95   16610-1-17

Catch SPRING FEVER with Dell

As advertised on TV